I SEE YOU

I SEE YOU

Patricia MacDonald

This first world edition published 2014
in Great Britain and in the USA by
SEVERN HOUSE PUBLISHERS LTD of
19 Cedar Road, Sutton, Surrey, England, SM2 5DA.
Trade paperback edition first published
in Great Britain and the USA 2014 by
SEVERN HOUSE PUBLISHERS LTD.

British Library Cataloguing in Publication Data

MacDonald, Patricia J.
I see you.
1. Family secrets–Fiction. 2. West Philadelphia
(Philadelphia, Pa.)–Fiction. 3. Suspense fiction.
I. Title
813.6-dc23

ISBN-13: 978-0-7278-8405-3 (cased)
ISBN-13: 978-1-84751-521-6 (trade paper)

Typeset by Palimpsest Book Production Ltd.,
Falkirk, Stirlingshire, Scotland.

*To Lorene Cary, with love and thanks for all
those soul-expanding walks.
Long may we ramble together!*

ONE

Restoration House, West Philadelphia

The pale gray twilight filtered through the grimy windows of Restoration House and formed watery patterns on the worn linoleum. A group of grim-faced men sat in a circle of folding chairs and listened intently as a burly black man named Titus described his descent into suicidal depression. 'The doctor at the VA said I had PTSD. All I know is I didn't want to live.' He squeezed his hands together into one large fist while tears ran down the creases of his face.

'And now?'

Hannah Wickes watched from her seat at the outer edge as the group leader stared gravely at the bent head and tattooed neck of the suffering ex-serviceman.

'Still not sure,' he said, heaving a sigh.

'But you're still here. Talking to us.'

The vet nodded and met his gaze.

The group leader smiled. His face, pock marked and scarred from burns, still managed to look gentle. 'We have to keep talking. We all have to keep talking. And we'll meet again next week. I want to see you here, Titus.'

'I'll be here,' said Titus.

'Good,' said the leader. 'Meanwhile, Anna here has some information for all of you that she's put together.' He nodded at Hannah.

Hannah took a deep breath. She found herself shaken by the depth of the vet's emotion. She understood his pain all too well. She pulled herself together and tried to speak in an official tone. 'A lot of our servicemen and women here at Restoration House have complained about the difficulty of getting the benefits they are entitled to. This Saturday morning at ten, we are having a workshop. Bring your paperwork. There will be people here to try and help untangle some of these problems. We've got some volunteers from the university whose computer skills are dazzling. They can help with those government websites. You should all be receiving the benefits that have been promised to you by your government.'

The men in the group murmured agreement.

'OK, listen up,' said the group leader, whose name was Frank Petrusa. 'If you're interested in this workshop, there's more information in this pile on the desk. We meet next time on Wednesday, 'cause I have to be at a meeting in Washington on Friday.'

Amid high-fives and exhortations to have a good week, the group broke up and the men filed out of the room, a few of them stopping to pick up the printed material which Hannah had made available.

Frank spoke quietly to Titus, his prosthetic hand resting gently on the ex-serviceman's shoulder. Watching them, Hannah felt, as she often did, that it was good for her to be working here. It kept her problems in perspective. In the course of the last year, it had sometimes been difficult not to sink into despair. She had applied for work at Restoration House, a non-profit in West Philadelphia, which focused on veterans and their families. She was interviewed by Father Luke, a veteran and defrocked priest, who still used his honorific. When Father Luke asked for her references she asked if she could speak in confidence. Father Luke assured her that she could. Then she told him that her very existence here in West Philadelphia was off the grid. He had asked few questions and hired her anyway, and Hannah had become a part of the compassionate family at Restoration House.

'Hey, Anna, wait up,' said a gruff voice.

Hannah turned in the doorway and saw Frank heading toward her. He was dressed in a sweatshirt, fatigue pants and combat boots and was itching his left wrist with the fingers of his right hand. His left hand had been blown off by an IED in Iraq, and he wore a prosthesis, which seemed to give him no end of discomfort. Hannah waited until he reached her. She often marveled at the fact that he emanated good will, despite the lingering effects of his terrible injuries.

'You're amazing,' Hannah said as he approached. 'You really know how to reach these guys.'

'I've been there,' he said simply. 'I understand what they're feeling. Hey, I just want to make sure you are going to Father Luke's birthday party tonight.'

'Yes,' said Hannah. 'We are looking forward to it. Where is that restaurant again? I got a flyer in my mailbox but . . .'

'Ebony's Beans and Greens, at 56th and Walnut.'

The party, in celebration of Father Luke's sixtieth birthday, was being given by his life partner – the man for whom he had given up the priesthood. Spencer White was a middle-aged, overweight accountant from the neighborhood. Spencer and Father Luke had quietly become a couple years ago. Both men were devoted to the work at Restoration House, Father Luke as an employee and Spencer as a volunteer. The birthday party was going to be a simple affair but it promised to be special for Hannah and Adam, who rarely ever went out. 'I'm bringing my husband, Alan,' she said. 'I want everyone to get to know him a little bit.'

'I look forward to meeting him,' said Frank. 'I was beginning to wonder if he actually existed.'

'He exists, I promise you,' said Hannah, smiling.

'Where does he work?' Frank asked.

'Well, he's kind of a roving troubleshooter. He works for a group called the Geek Squad. They go out on calls to help people with computer problems,' she said. She did not say that it was a difficult way for a man to make a living after being in charge of IT at a local phone company. Considering their situation, Adam felt lucky to have steady work.

'Wow, maybe he can help me,' said Frank, 'I can't do squat-all on that old computer of mine.'

'He probably could,' she said.

'OK, well, I'll see you there,' said Frank. He waved his prosthetic hand as he headed off toward the kitchen in the back of the house. Hannah went in the direction of the nursery.

The nursery was the most cheerful room in the rundown, nearly crumbling West Philly mansion. The grateful families of vets who had once found respite there had donated cots, books and toys. Two of the young women from Penn who volunteered on weekends had enlisted art students to paint a colorful mural on the wall.

Hannah stood in the doorway and looked in. Sydney was busily engaged with two other children in a game of go-fish on a toddler-sized table. The teacher, a lovely, brown-skinned young woman named Kiyanna Brooks, who wore steel-rimmed glasses and long, elaborate cornrows, gave Hannah a signal to stay quiet till the game was over. Hannah smiled and nodded, gazing in at Sydney.

For all of the past year, Hannah had watched Sydney obsessively, like a doctor watching a transplant patient, for signs that she was rejecting this new life they had grafted on to her old world. Sydney's new friends knew her as Cindy, and she had adjusted pretty quickly to that. Hannah, Sydney and Adam lived in walking distance from Restoration House in a Victorian brownstone owned by an elderly black woman named Mamie Revere. Mamie lived on the first two floors and the Wickes, now known as the Whitmans, lived on the third floor in an apartment which was fairly light, if a bit cramped, and almost devoid of modern conveniences. Hannah often caught herself starting to bemoan the lack of air-conditioning and a dishwasher. It wasn't as if there was any remedy for that situation. The apartment would simply not accommodate some of the appliances Hannah wistfully craved. Neither would their finances, which had been strained ever since they left Tennessee. It was just another thing to get used to.

If Sydney disliked it in the city, her new home, she never made it known to Hannah and Adam. She went to a daycare in the next block each morning, and afterwards Hannah collected her and brought her to the nursery at Restoration House, while Hannah helped out with counseling programs for veterans and their families.

'Go Fish!' Sydney cried, and the game soon came to an end as a little boy at the table threw down his oversized cards and declared victory.

'No fair,' Sydney insisted.

Hannah stepped in before a fight broke out. 'Come on, Cindy,' she said, taking the child by the hands. 'Time to go see Mamie. Did you know you're staying at Mamie's till we get home tonight?'

'Where are you going?' Sydney demanded.

'To a party for Father Luke,' said Hannah.

Sydney looked stricken. 'I want to go to a party,' she insisted.

'You and Mamie will have your own party,' Hannah assured her.

Indeed, two hours later, as Hannah came down the two flights of stairs from their apartment and stuck her head into Mamie's living room, she could smell something suspiciously like the scent of a cake baking wafting out into the hallway. Mamie's house was often redolent of chicken cooking, and lavender potpourri, covering up a certain mustiness from well-worn furniture and a long-overdue refresher of the paint job, but tonight, even with the front windows open to let in the autumn air, it smelled decidedly of caramel and sugar.

'Mamie,' Hannah cried. 'We're here.' She turned to Sydney, whose hand she was holding. 'I want you to be good for Mamie. Do everything she says.'

'I will,' said Sydney. 'I'm always good.'

'Yes, you are,' said Hannah, bending to kiss Sydney's cheek and ruffle her soft fair hair.

Mamie came bustling out from the depths of the house, and immediately ordered Sydney to take off her shoes and come join her in the kitchen.

'I smell cake,' Sydney announced.

'Yes, you do,' said the elderly woman. 'And after our supper we're going to have us a piece. Right now, it needs to cool.'

'I can't thank you enough for this, Mamie,' said Hannah. 'This is where we're going to be. Ebony's Greens and Beans. And you have my cellphone number if you need me.'

'Oh, the food is fine there,' Mamie assured her. 'Their hush puppies are as light as air.'

'We're looking forward to it,' said Hannah. 'We won't be late.' She called out to Sydney to say goodbye, but Sydney had already scampered along and was making herself at home in the kitchen.

'Don't worry about a thing,' said Mamie.

Hannah smiled and nodded, although worry was just a normal part of her every waking moment. She went out into the hallway, and called up the stairwell for Adam. 'Come on, honey,' she said. 'We need to go.'

She heard the keys jingling as Adam locked the door, and then he was descending the stairs. 'Where's Syd— Cindy?' he asked.

'She's discovered a cake in Mamie's kitchen.'

Adam smiled. 'Good,' he said. 'She'll be OK.'

Hannah took a deep breath and nodded. They walked through the foyer lined with Mamie's family photos. The largest photo was of her eldest son, Isaiah, who was a longtime member of the Philadelphia City Council. Mamie was understandably proud of him, but Hannah sometimes wished the councilman would devote a little time to helping his aged mother. The house had been in decline for years, and Councilman Revere never seemed to notice. Adam spent a lot of free time doing chores around the property.

Hannah went to the front door, opened it, and stepped outside into the crisp autumn evening. She inhaled the complex scent of the city. When they'd first moved here, she'd found the cacophony of smells and sounds to be overwhelming, but she had gotten to the point where she sometimes liked it. After a year, she'd felt like they might be safe here, and that helped.

'Beautiful night,' said Adam. He had adapted more easily. He traveled all over Philadelphia to his assignments. He saw the tapestry of city life as a much larger picture than Hannah did. And, even though it had been her idea originally, he accepted more easily than she that they had done what they had to do. No looking back.

'Feels weird to be wearing a tie again,' he said.

'I'm sure Father Luke will appreciate it,' Hannah said. Adam's job had no dress code. In fact, being the oldest person on the staff, he did his best to always look casual, so that he wouldn't appear out of place. The Geek Squad had hesitated to hire him at first, because of his age, but they handed him a messed-up laptop as a test, and Adam was able to clear its viruses and have it running smoothly in record time. After that, he was hired, with no questions asked about his past. That was the beauty of young people, he told Hannah. They weren't interested in your resume. They lived in the present. Adam's supervisor was twenty-five and had magenta-colored hair, but Adam had adjusted to that too.

They went down the steps.

'Which way?' Adam asked.

'56th Street,' said Hannah, pointing uptown. 'Not too far. We can walk.'

A scruffy-looking young woman wearing camouflage pants and a filthy canvas jacket was seated on a low wall in front of Mamie's house, drinking out of a bottle in a brown-paper bag. Her black hair was cut short in a buzz cut, and there were dark circles around her eyes. Adam looked askance at the rheumy-eyed young woman, but Hannah smiled at her. 'Hey, Dominga,' she said.

The girl ran a hand over her buzz cut. 'Hey, Miz Anna,' she said shyly.

As they continued down the block, Adam looked at his wife with raised eyebrows. 'Friend of yours?' he asked.

'She's a vet. Suffers from PTSD. She comes to the group at Restoration House sometimes.'

'Looks like she suffers from too much alcohol,' Adam observed.

'She self-medicates,' said Hannah thoughtfully. 'They have a lot that they're trying to forget.'

'I think I'll self-medicate a little bit myself tonight,' said Adam. 'It's been a long week.'

Hannah squeezed his hand. As long as she had Adam and Sydney, her world still made sense to her, no matter what the conditions of their life might be. 'Why not?' she said. 'This is it.'

They had arrived at the modest storefront of Ebony's Beans and Greens. The smell of slow-cooking soul-food greeted them. There were party lights strung out over the striped awning, and they could hear laughter from inside.

'Hey, you made it!'

Hannah looked up and smiled at the sight of Frank Petrusa, walking down the block toward them, arm in arm with Kiyanna Brooks. Hannah tried to cover her surprise. She hadn't realized that the group leader and the head of the nursery were a couple, though clearly they were. They had certainly kept their relationship under the radar. Of course, Hannah generally avoided asking people personal questions, for fear that she might be called upon to answer such questions in return.

'Frank! Kiyanna. I want you both to meet . . . Alan, my husband.'

Kiyanna smiled her broad, beautiful smile, and extended a graceful hand. 'Nice to meet you. We were beginning to wonder if we ever would.'

Adam shook her hand warmly. 'The pleasure's mine. You run the nursery, right?'

'I do. I'm very fond of Cindy. She's a very bright little girl.'

'She . . . Thank you,' said Adam.

'And this is Frank,' said Kiyanna.

'Frank Petrusa,' said the group leader, extending his good hand.

'Frank runs the PTSD group,' said Hannah.

'My wife speaks very highly of you,' said Adam pleasantly.

'She speaks very highly of you too,' said Frank in his gruff voice.

Adam looked at Hannah fondly. 'Nice to know,' he said.

Kiyanna laughed. 'Let's get in there and have a drink on it,' she said.

Hannah felt something she hadn't felt in such a long time. A festive evening unfolding. Friendships being forged. It was almost like being home. 'Yes, let's,' she said.

Mamie had made them a supper of macaroni and cheese with some applesauce. Sydney had eaten heartily but still eagerly attacked the piece of cake when Mamie put it in front of her on a little plate.

'Aren't you gonna have cake?' the child asked Mamie.

Mamie grimaced and rubbed her chest. 'Not right yet,' she said. 'I'm feeling a little . . . something . . . indigestion.'

Sydney finished her cake and carefully carried her plate across the room. She had to stand on tiptoes to put it on the counter next to the sink. Then she turned to look at Mamie. 'Can I watch TV now?' she asked.

'You sure can.' Mamie struggled to her feet, and glanced at the sink. 'I'm gonna leave them dishes till later,' she said apologetically.

Sydney had already scampered out into the living room and was pushing buttons on the remote.

'Now just stop that,' said Mamie. 'Let me do that.' She took the remote from the child and aimed it at the TV.

'Come on, now. Oh, what's wrong with this thing?' Mamie shook the remote, frowning at it.

'I can do it,' said Sydney.

Mamie shook her head. 'You probably could. Better than I could.' Mamie peered at the remote, and then suddenly, she squeezed her eyes shut. She let the remote fall from her hand. It clattered on the worn wood floor beyond the Oriental rug.

Sydney rushed to pick it up. 'You dropped this, Miss Mamie.' She held it up to the old woman, and then took a frightened step back. There was a terrible look on Miss Mamie's face, and she was clutching her chest. Her warm brown skin had taken on a grayish cast.

'Oh, Lord,' Mamie whispered. 'Something is wrong.' And then she collapsed on the floor.

Sydney began to whimper. She cautiously approached the woman lying on the floor. 'Miss Mamie,' she whispered.

The old woman did not answer.

'Miss Mamie, wake up,' Sydney pleaded, pushing her shoulder with her pudgy fingers. But the old woman did not stir.

'Miss Mamie,' she cried, and then, when there was still no answer, Sydney began to wail.

TWO

Dominga was nodding off. The empty pint bottle of Night Train had slid off her lap and landed, still in the brown-paper bag, on the dry grass beside the wall. Every so often Dominga started, and had to right herself on the low wall where she was sitting, but then the haze would return. She had the dream that she often dreamed. She was back in the desert camp, dry and dusty. The men around her were strangers, not the buddies she knew. Everywhere she looked guys were maimed and bleeding. Dominga knew it was her responsibility to go after the enemy, but her arms and legs would not move. It was like she was paralyzed. The sergeant was yelling but Dominga couldn't figure out what he was saying.

Someone in the camp began to cry. It sounded like a child crying, and Dominga knew she had to find the child, to help. But where? She jerked awake. The wailing did not end with the dream. She heard it still. The frantic cries were coming from the window of the house behind her. Dominga blinked a few times, and forced her eyes to stay open. The child's cries were piercing, jangling her nerves. Dominga stood up unsteadily.

As she gathered her wits, she realized that it was the voice of a little girl, a little girl calling for help.

Unlike in the dream, all her training, so long ignored and forgotten, seemed to return to her in a torrent of protocols which she needed to remember. She struggled to pull herself together. Weaving slightly, she made her way to the break in the wall, and up the walkway to the front stoop of the old house. Carefully, she climbed the steps, and hesitated. The cries came again. She leaned over and peered into the bay window, her eyes blinking to adjust to the light within. Then she saw where the cries were coming from. A little blonde-haired girl was huddled on the floor, next to the body of an old black woman with gray hair. The child was crying out at the old woman, 'Miss Mamie, Miss Mamie!'

Dominga felt a rush of pity for the child. She knew how it felt to be left alone like that. She had felt that way for much of her young life. She did not want to frighten the child any further. 'Hey, little one. It's OK,' she called out as kindly as she could. 'It's OK. I'll help you.'

The child looked up, perplexed by the voice coming through the window.

For a moment, her sobbing stopped.

'Listen to me,' Dominga said. 'Do you know how to unlock the front door?'

The child's eyes were wide and filled with abject terror. 'Nooooo . . .' She began to sob again.

Dominga thought about it. The child was pretty small. She probably wouldn't be able to reach the lock and turn it. The woman on the floor was lying still. She might be dead. If she had a phone, she'd use it, but Dominga was using tracphones that she bought at the bodega, and the last one she had just ran out of minutes. Dominga had to make a quick decision. In a way it felt good. The adrenaline was pumping through her, and her head felt clear. She hesitated, and then she decided.

Years of living in the neighborhood had taught her to keep a weapon handy when she was on the street. A switchblade rested in the zippered pocket of her nylon jacket. She pulled the switchblade out, snapped it open, and cut a large slice in the screen of the living-room window. Using her hands, she pulled the screen apart, wide enough so that she could force her sturdy body through the opening.

'I'm coming in now, chica,' she cried out. 'Don't be afraid.'

She climbed over the window sill and fell to the floor beneath the window. There was a telephone sitting on the end table beside the sofa. She grabbed up the receiver and dialed 911.

'What is your emergency?' asked the operator.

Dominga explained that there was a woman lying on the floor. The operator told her to check for a pulse, but Dominga had already crawled over to the prostrate woman and was holding her free finger and thumb on her wrist. 'It's faint,' she reported, 'but she's alive.'

The operator recited the address, and asked if it were correct. For a moment, Dominga was flummoxed. 'I don't know,' she said. 'I just heard a child crying and came in. It's near the corner of 50th and Chestnut.'

The operator assured her that there was help on the way. 'In the meantime . . .'

'I know what to do in the meantime. I'm a soldier. I was in Iraq,' Dominga said abruptly. 'Just tell them to hurry.'

'Miss Mamie,' the child wailed.

'Don't be afraid,' Dominga said, as she positioned the old woman's head so that her throat was open, cleared her mouth out and began to compress her chest. 'Miss Mamie's going to be OK.'

Oblivious to the drama unfolding at Mamie's house, Hannah and Adam ate heartily from the soul-food buffet which had been laid out in Father Luke's honor. They each had a couple of drinks, and even danced a few times. When, after their last dance, they returned hand in hand to the table they were sharing with Frank and Kiyanna, Kiyanna smiled complicity at Hannah.

'You two are cute as can be,' she said.

'Thanks,' said Hannah.

'How long have you been married?'

Hannah waved the question away. 'A looong time,' she said.

'And Cindy is your only child?'

Hannah moved the straw in her drink around and took it between her lips as if this were an operation requiring great concentration. 'Yes,' she said.

Kiyanna nodded thoughtfully, not wanting to pry but clearly curious.

'We'd just about given up hope when she came along,' Hannah explained.

'She's really a sweet little girl.'

'Thanks,' said Hannah. She didn't want to talk about this subject but she didn't want to be rude to Kiyanna, who had been nothing but kind to Sydney ever since Hannah had been bringing her to Restoration House.

'What about you?' Hannah said. She glanced over at Frank, who was picking out a piece of pie from the dessert buffet. 'Are you two . . . together?'

Kiyanna sighed, and gazed at Frank. 'Yeah. Yeah. We are.'

'At work you're very . . .'

'Businesslike,' said Kiyanna. 'Yeah, we try to be cool about it.'

'Is it serious?'

Kiyanna smiled bashfully. 'Yeah, I think it is.'

Hannah nodded. 'You make a nice couple.'

Kiyanna frowned. 'Frank was married when he went to Iraq. When he came home, she'd found somebody else. He's still got some trust issues.'

'Well, trust is essential,' Hannah admitted.

'I'm trying to convince him to go with it,' said Kiyanna, stirring her drink.

'I've seen him work with those vets. He has such a good heart,' said Hannah. She glanced over at her husband, who was deep in conversation with the thin, anemic-looking Father Luke, and his large brown-skinned partner, the party's host, Spencer White. 'Alan and I have been through a lot together,' she said. 'A lot.'

Not long after that, Adam suggested they should think about getting home. They had Sydney to think about. Hannah agreed, and they said their goodbyes to the festive group.

The streets were quiet at that hour, except for the occasional boom box passing by, or motorcycles or arguments in doorways as they passed. The city. Hannah had never expected to enjoy life in the city but there was something about it that appealed to her, even though they had chosen it mainly for anonymity's sake.

'Did you have a good time?' she said to Adam.

Adam nodded. 'I did,' he said. 'I like the people you work with. They seem like nice people.'

'They are,' said Hannah. 'I like them too.'

'I like being out with you, again,' he said.

Hannah smiled at him ruefully. 'I know what you mean. I felt almost guilty having fun.'

'Maybe our life is going to get some semblance of normalcy at last,' he said.

'You think they'll have a party at Geek Squad headquarters?'

Adam shook his head. 'They really aren't into real people. They like to party with their avatars. No need to get cleaned up.'

Hannah laughed and squeezed his hand as they turned the corner onto 50th Street. And then she gasped. 'Adam. Look.'

He had already seen it. An ambulance. And the blazing lights of police cars.

'That looks like our house,' Hannah said.

'Not necessarily,' said Adam.

But Hannah had already broken into a run. The closer she got, the more convinced she was that the emergency vehicles were parked outside Mamie's house. 'Please, God,' she said. 'Let Sydney be all right. Oh, we should never have left her, should never have gone out.'

She was breathless by the time she arrived at the house. She could hear Adam's footsteps pounding on the pavement behind her. She ran up to the crowd of police, and saw at once the open bay on the ambulance. She grabbed the arm of the nearest officer. She could hardly form the words.

'My daughter? What happened? Where is she?'

The officer turned to her with a serious look on his face. 'Are you the little girl's mother?'

'Yes. Where is she?' Tears rose to Hannah's eyes. 'Is she all right? What happened?'

'She's all right. She's right over here in this squad car. Hey, Mickey,' the officer called out. 'The kid's mother is here.'

Hannah sagged against the nearest vehicle. She felt Adam behind her, gasping for breath. She reached around and grabbed his hand. 'She's all right,' Hannah whispered.

Suddenly, the milling crowd of officers parted, and a policewoman was standing just a few yards from Hannah, holding Sydney by the hand.

Hannah caught the child's eye and fell down to her knees, her arms open.

'Mom, Mom,' Sydney cried, rushing to her.

Hannah thought she had never smelled anything as sweet as the child's hair, or felt anything so welcome as those little arms wrapped around her. 'You OK?' she asked, squeezing her.

Sydney nodded. 'Miss Mamie fell down. She got sick and fell down,' the child said gravely.

'Oh my God,' said Hannah. 'How . . .? What happened?'

Adam prodded Hannah in the back. 'Get up,' he whispered. 'We need to go.'

Hannah looked up at him, perplexed by his urgent tone, and then heard a voice booming beside her.

'Mrs Whitman. Mr Whitman.' Isaiah Revere, Mamie's eldest son, approached them. They had met several times over the course of the last ten months, when he came to pay a visit to his mother. He was a bald man in his late fifties, wearing a nicely cut overcoat in a muted brown. He also wore a tie and gleaming cordovan shoes.

Hannah rose to her feet and shook his outstretched hand. 'Hello, Mr Revere. How is Mamie? Is she going to be all right? What happened?' she asked.

Just then, the bay doors slammed shut and the sirens on the ambulance began to wail.

Isaiah's forehead was furrowed. 'They think she had a stroke. They still have to do a lot of tests. I'm headed over to the hospital in my own car. I just wanted to commend your little angel here, Cindy. She was very brave. Weren't you, dear?'

Sydney, huddled in Hannah's arms, nonetheless looked directly at the city councilman. 'Miss Mamie fell down. She's sick.'

Isaiah Revere smiled. 'She is. But she's going to be all right. The doctors are going to take care of her.'

Hannah shook her head. 'What happened? Who found her?' she asked, looking at the collection of police vehicles, the ambulance gearing up to roar away. 'Cindy's too young to call for help.'

'Well, in fact, we have this lady to thank,' said Isaiah. With that he turned and gestured to a mannish-looking young woman standing nearby, speaking with another officer. Hannah immediately recognized the vet whom they had passed as they left for the birthday party.

'Can you come over here, soldier?' Isaiah asked. 'These are the child's parents.'

'Dominga?' Hannah said.

Dominga, looking somewhat shy, nodded. 'Hi, Anna,' she said.

Isaiah Revere looked surprised. 'You two know each other?'

'Yes. Well, I work at Restoration House. It's a non-profit for vets.'

'Apparently Ms Flores here heard your daughter screaming and went to the window. She saw my mother lying on the floor, so she made a quick decision and went in through the window.'

Hannah could feel Adam tugging on her arm. 'Hannah, let's go in,' he whispered. 'Cindy needs to get inside.'

Hannah felt annoyed at her husband for his abruptness. She too wanted to commend Dominga for her quick thinking. 'Dominga, I don't know how to thank you.'

Dominga tried to shake off the praise. 'Just did what needed doin',' she said.

A bright light suddenly shone into Hannah's face. 'Councilman Revere. We got your call. We're here from *Channel Ten News*. We heard your mother was ill. What's going on?'

Sydney lifted a pudgy hand to cover her eyes. Hannah froze, realizing, too late, why Adam had wanted them to slip away.

'Thank you for coming. I'll tell you what's going on,' said Isaiah Revere, addressing the microphone. 'I am on my way to the hospital to attend to my mother who was taken ill in her house tonight. But before I go, I want to point out that she would undoubtedly be dead but for the quick thinking of this young woman, Dominga Flores, who broke in and called 911. My mother was alone with this small child whom she was caring for.' The cameraman turned his apparatus onto Hannah, who had Sydney in her arms.

Heart pounding, Hannah averted her face as best she could.

'Ms Flores is an Iraq war vet, who has suffered greatly after her participation in that conflict,' said Isaiah. 'It's not been an easy road for Dominga, as I understand it. She is without work, and without a place to live. But when my mother was in desperate trouble, and Ms Flores was facing an emergency, all her skills as a soldier came into play, and she performed heroically.'

Hannah heard Adam groan softly behind her. She felt paralyzed, trapped in the camera's glare, exposed.

By this time several other news networks had showed up on the scene, answering the call from the councilman's office. Anyone else would be on their way to the hospital or in the ambulance with their mother. Hannah realized, too late, that for Isaiah Revere, this was a political opportunity. He would never let a chance go by to collect a few votes. She felt as if she wanted to throw up, or faint. But she was holding Sydney, and they were talking about a young woman who had rescued her child. She couldn't just turn her back and walk away.

'I just wanted to point out, before I leave for the hospital, that Ms Flores's actions should serve as a reminder to us of how we have failed our veterans in this country, even though they have never failed us. They respond on our behalf, no matter what, every time they are called.'

Dominga looked embarrassed but also proud. Hannah's stomach was churning but she tried to smile. Maybe no one will see it, she told herself. It's a local news item. It will come and go in a day. What are the chances that anyone a thousand miles away would see it?

'How do you feel, ma'am?' asked the reporter.

Hannah nodded. 'Grateful. Very grateful,' she whispered, although, in truth, she felt sick to her stomach, her heart was hammering, and she wished that the ground would open up and swallow her, and Adam and Sydney, so that they vanished completely, and no one could ever find them again.

THREE

Eighteen months earlier

Hannah Wickes stuck her trowel into the soil and gently waggled it until she had a shovel full of dirt. 'Now,' she said to the toddler who crouched beside her, 'have you got your flower?'

Sydney nodded gravely and lifted the little cup-shaped mound of dirt with one blooming red impatiens in the middle of it. She handed it to her grandmother.

'No, you do it,' said Hannah, smiling. She wiped her forehead with the back of her hand as Sydney carefully placed the seedling into the hole Hannah had dug.

'Now we pat,' said Hannah.

Sydney obediently pushed soil into the hole around the seedling, and patted dirt down on it with her tiny palms.

'Good,' said Hannah. 'And a little drink . . .' She gave the toddler the plastic watering can, and Sydney poured out a stream of water on the seedling.

'Hold up,' said Hannah, laughing, and tilting the spout of the watering can up into the air. 'Not too much.'

Sydney nodded gravely, then rose from her crouch and looked up at the deck which ran along the back of the house. 'Mama!' she cried. 'Look what I did. I planted a patient.'

'Impatiens,' said Hannah, smiling, and kissing the top of the child's head.

Hannah's daughter, Lisa, was seated at the table on the deck, her pale skin shielded by the umbrella anchored in the center of the table. Her dark hair, a mass of unruly curls, was tied back with a shoelace. Her laptop was open in front of her, and she was making notes on a pad beside it. Lisa lifted her head and gazed at her daughter through her narrow black-rimmed glasses. 'That's wonderful, Sydney,' she said.

'Come and look,' Sydney insisted.

'I will. Just give me a minute,' said Lisa.

Hannah spoke softly to the child. 'Mommy's got a lot of work to do. You have to study a lot if you want to be a doctor.'

Lisa continued to peer at the computer screen and jot down notes. 'It's all right, Mother,' she said with a sigh. 'I'll come and look. I just need to finish this chapter.'

'It's all right, honey. You finish your chapter.'

'It's not a problem,' said Lisa. She got up from the chair, slipped her feet back into her rubber thongs and walked down to the little flower garden. She crouched down beside Sydney and said, 'Let's see.'

Sydney pointed to the newly planted flower with a pudgy finger. 'Look. I did that.'

Lisa nodded approvingly. 'You're doing just great,' she said. 'Mommy loves you.'

Sydney beamed. 'You can plant one,' she said.

Lisa frowned. 'Not right now, darlin',' she said. 'Can't take the time.' Sydney's dark eyes lost their gleam. Hannah was tempted to urge her daughter to take a break and plant a flower. But she knew better than to interfere. Lisa was nothing if not focused on her work. It wasn't as if she wasted a lot of time on herself. She wore no makeup and was indifferently dressed, as usual, in a baggy shirt and cut-off jeans, which did nothing to enhance her slender frame. When they had offered to get her contact lenses, Lisa said she didn't have time to go for appointments and make the necessary adjustments. Glasses were fine.

Climbing back up the steps to the deck, Lisa turned and blew Sydney a kiss. Sydney hesitated, and then blew her a kiss back. Cheerfully the child crouched down again and renewed her attack on the dirt while Lisa resumed her place at the table beneath the umbrella. Hannah looked from one to the other, thinking that, as a child, Lisa would never have been appeased as easily as Sydney was.

Lisa had always been headstrong, and daring to the point of recklessness. At the age of eighteen she announced that she was pregnant. She refused to give up the baby, or name the father. Hannah feared that someone older at college had taken advantage of her daughter, who, thanks to her intellect, was always attending school with people much older than herself. Lisa was somewhat plain, and she had had very little experience with boys. But Lisa insisted that she had not been assaulted, and that she wanted to keep her baby. Adam said that if Lisa insisted on being careless she was going to have to take care of Sydney on her own. Hannah had reminded him gently that she had become pregnant with Lisa when she was only eighteen; Adam fumed that it was different for them. They were ready, even at that young age, to accept responsibility.

But Hannah knew that Adam was really more disappointed than angry. He had had boundless hopes for his only child. At the age of four, Lisa could multiply and divide, and her IQ tested off the charts. With her pregnancy, Adam saw all Lisa's prospects vanishing into a fog of single motherhood. He needn't have worried. In fact, despite her pregnancy, and the birth of Sydney, Lisa barely skipped a beat. She, who had finished high school at sixteen, was able to get through a pre-med program in college in three years, despite her pregnancy, and was accepted to medical school at Vanderbilt, near their home in Nashville. She had grants and scholarships but her hours were long and erratic and she still needed help from her parents. Hannah put Sydney in daycare several hours a day while she worked part time at social services, but she spent the rest of her time looking after her granddaughter.

'I need another patient,' said Sydney, tugging at Hannah's work shirt.

'Well, let me get one,' said Hannah, clambering to her feet. She turned abruptly toward the backyard picnic table where she had placed the flat of seedlings. As she did she saw her neighbor, Rayanne Dollard, gazing at them across the low hedge which separated their yards. Hannah waved and walked over to the hedge to speak to her.

They had been friends and neighbors for years. When Lisa and Rayanne's son, Jamie, were small, he and Lisa had worn a path through the hedge, crossing to one another's houses. Lisa was a tomboy with enormous energy. Jamie, though older than Lisa, was always shy, and glad to follow her lead. Their friendship lasted until high school when Jamie became interested in NASCAR while Lisa loved drawing in the style of Japanese anime and reading essays in German. The rift between them, though sad, seemed inevitable. Throughout high school they said hello across the hedge, but never visited. Jamie now worked for a logging company out in Oregon. He'd recently announced to his parents that he'd met the right girl, and a wedding might be on the horizon.

'How are you?' Hannah asked.

Rayanne frowned. 'Oh, I'm fine.'

'You don't look fine. You look worried.'

'I am. It's Chet,' she said, referring to her husband. 'He just doesn't seem himself these days. He's very tired.'

'Has he had a checkup?' Hannah asked.

Rayanne rolled her eyes. 'You know men and doctors.'

'I do,' said Hannah.

'How's your doctor holding up?' Rayanne asked, nodding toward Lisa.

'It's been tough,' Hannah admitted. 'Medical school is hard enough. But losing Troy has really hit her hard.' Lisa's first real boyfriend, Troy Petty, was a licensed practical nurse at the hospital. He had lived in a rented bungalow out by J. Percy Priest Lake. When he first came around, calling on Lisa, Hannah and Adam had to stifle their desire to object. At twenty-six, he was nice-looking, if not handsome, and five years older than their daughter, whose life experience was in no way equal to her academic accomplishments and her status as a second-year med student. But they knew from long experience that any objection would have been met with stubborn insistence from Lisa. Luckily, though he was of average intelligence and far from prosperous, Troy was certainly a gentleman, and even Sydney seemed to like him. Adam and Hannah liked him themselves. Then, two weeks ago, he was alone in his bungalow when a gas leak from a propane heater caused an explosion which leveled the little fishing camp. Troy was killed in the blast. Adam and Hannah just thanked their lucky stars that Lisa and Sydney weren't visiting him at the time.

'Such a shame,' said Rayanne, shaking her head. 'A young man like that. He really seemed like a nice guy. I'm sure you were hoping it might turn into something serious.'

'Well, we want to see her happy, of course. And they did seem happy together. But we never thought it would be something permanent. She's only twenty-one, and we're not all that eager for Lisa to leave us. We'd miss her and Sydney so much.'

'Oh, I know you'd miss that little one like the very devil.'

Hannah followed Rayanne's gaze to Sydney. 'It's true,' she said. 'I can hardly imagine life without Sydney anymore.'

'I don't know how Lisa even found the time to date anybody,' Rayanne marveled.

'She does have a punishing schedule. I imagine it will take her a while to get over this loss. She keeps it to herself but I think she's been very upset. Still, she's young. She has plenty of time to find someone.'

'I'm sure she will,' Rayanne agreed.

Hannah heard a familiar voice from inside the house.

'Hey, where is everybody?'

'Oh, Adam's back. Listen, honey, I hope Chet gets to feeling better.' Hannah reached over the hedge and squeezed her friend's hand. Then she started back toward her house. 'We're out back,' she called.

Adam came out the patio doors onto the back porch, still wearing a dress shirt with the sleeves rolled up, and his loosened tie. 'How are my girls?'

'Hi, Daddy,' said Lisa, hopping up from her chair to give her father a hug.

'Pop-pop,' Sydney exclaimed. 'I planted patience!'

'Did you now?' Adam asked. 'Look at that.' He gazed in admiration at the lopsided red flowers planted in the new dirt then came down the steps and hugged his wife, as Lisa settled herself back down to her computer and her notes. 'You two have been busy, I see.'

Hannah smiled and gazed down at Sydney. 'She's quite the little gardener.'

'Sydney, you are doing a fine job.' He crouched down to the toddler's level. 'Any chance you got a hug in there for your old grandpa?'

Sydney threw her arms enthusiastically around his neck, her muddy hands leaving pudgy palm prints on his Tattersall shirt. Hannah looked fondly at the pair of them. Despite his grandparent status, Adam was still youthful looking. His hair was sprinkled with gray, and he wore his glasses a lot more these days. But in many ways he still looked like the sturdy football linebacker she had met on her first day of college. He could still make her heart flip when he kissed the back of her neck.

Adam straightened up.

'How was your trip?' Hannah asked. Adam was a supervisor in the IT department of the phone company. His job required continuous updating on innovations, which required that he be on the road a part of every month, meeting designers and programmers.

'Good. Good,' he said. 'It's still cold in Chicago.' He shivered playfully.

Hannah hugged him with one arm. 'Glad you're home.'

'I see you were talking to Rayanne.'

Hannah nodded. 'Chet's under the weather,' she said. 'She seems worried about him.'

'You know, when I saw him the other day I thought he looked like he was dragging a little,' said Adam. 'I hope he's OK.'

'I hope so too. Rayanne's trying to make him get a checkup.'

Adam nodded. Then he cocked his head toward the porch. 'How's our girl doing?'

Hannah glanced at Lisa. 'A little bit better, I think. She has been getting some rest, which doesn't hurt, with her schedule.'

'Good. She needs that. Hey, I think I'll have a beer to celebrate being back home. Can I get you one?'

'No thanks. After I get cleaned up,' said Hannah.

'I'll have one,' said Lisa, not lifting her gaze from the computer screen but obviously hearing every word they said.

Hannah could tell that Adam was about to protest. She gave him a meaningful look of reproval. Lisa had only recently turned twenty-one but she was a medical student and a mother and there was no rational reason to deny her a beer. The problem was, Hannah thought, that Adam still saw her as his little girl. Hannah's warning glance said, without words, that it was high time he began to treat Lisa as the woman she had become.

'Two beers coming up. I'll be right back,' Adam said, climbing the steps up to the deck and letting himself into the kitchen. Hannah sank down on the picnic table bench in the shade of a tall evergreen. The late afternoon shadows were beginning to stretch across the yard. Sydney had resumed her digging, and seemed to be covered in dirt almost from head to toe. Hannah figured she would put her casserole in the oven and then pop Sydney in the bathtub before dinner. She did not have the heart to ask Lisa to bathe her. Lisa seemed so overwhelmed lately between work and the loss of Troy. Hannah suspected that she was barely holding herself together.

'Almost time for you to go in and get washed up for supper, pumpkin,' said Hannah to her granddaughter.

Sydney shook her head. 'No. More patients!'

Just then the back door opened and Adam stepped out onto the porch. He was not carrying any beers. Behind him there was a man in a suit and a uniformed police officer following him.

Hannah frowned and stood up. 'What's going on?' she asked.

Adam studied his daughter for a moment. Lisa seemed to feel the weight of his gaze. She looked up, her expression inscrutable behind her black-rimmed glasses.

'These men want to talk to you,' Adam said. 'They're from the police department.'

Lisa closed the laptop and rested her hands on it. 'To me? About what?'

'About Troy,' her father said.

Lisa shook her head. She looked genuinely perplexed. 'What about Troy?'

The man in the suit stepped forward. He had a bushy mustache and a sheen of perspiration on his forehead. 'Ms Wickes? I'm Detective Hammond. Perhaps you remember me. We spoke when I questioned everyone at the hospital after the explosion.'

Lisa shook her head impatiently and then seemed to reconsider. 'Oh sure,' she said.

'You were the last person to see Mr Petty alive?'

'Well, I guess I was,' said Lisa. 'I was just lucky I didn't stay over that night. I had a really early class so I left. Otherwise, I wouldn't be talking to you here today.'

'So you claim that you were with Mr Petty on the night of the explosion but that you left his house before it occurred.'

'Well, obviously,' said Lisa. 'I'd be dead if I were there when it occurred.'

'You two parted on good terms?' asked the detective.

'Yes, why?' asked Lisa.

'No argument between you. No harsh words.'

Lisa's eyes narrowed. 'Why are you asking me this?'

'Did you have an argument?' Detective Hammond persisted.

Lisa shook her head. 'I don't know. We might have had some . . . words. So what?'

'Words about what?' asked the detective.

Lisa lifted her chin. 'I don't remember. Anyway, what difference does it make?'

'We have received all our lab results back now. It seems that the explosion in Mr Petty's house may not have been accidental after all.'

Lisa stood up and came around the table. 'What? You think he blew himself up on purpose? That's ridiculous. Why would anyone do that?'

'No, we don't think that.'

'Well, then, I don't understand,' said Lisa, frowning.

Hammond looked at her impassively. 'The coroner's report indicates that Mr Petty may have been unconscious at the time his house blew up.'

'Well, he was certainly conscious when I left him!' Lisa exclaimed.

'We thought you might know something about it.'

Lisa regarded the detective with narrowed eyes, her arms crossed over her baggy shirt. 'How would I know anything about it?'

'Now, wait just a minute,' said Adam. 'That's ridiculous. How can you even say such a thing? My daughter had nothing to do with that explosion.'

Detective Hammond continued staring at Lisa. 'That last paycheck the hospital sent Troy Petty – he was able to cash that check. Sign it and cash it. Just hours after his cabin blew up. That's quite a trick, for a dead man.'

Lisa stared back at him. 'That would be,' she said.

'We have security-camera footage from the store where it was cashed. Care to take a guess who really cashed it?'

Lisa lifted her chin defiantly and did not reply.

Leaving Sydney digging in the flowerbed, Hannah mounted the porch steps, looking from the cold-eyed detective to her daughter in frantic confusion. 'Wait a minute. What are you talking about? This has nothing to do with Lisa.'

'Lisa Wickes,' said Detective Hammond, nodding to the uniformed officer, who pulled a pair of handcuffs from his belt. 'We're here to arrest you on charges of larceny and suspicion of murder in the death of Troy Petty. I must caution you that you have the right to remain silent . . .'

'Wait! What?' Hannah cried. She turned to her husband. 'Adam, stop them. Tell them they can't do this!'

Hearing the alarm in her grandmother's voice, Sydney, still seated in the grass, began to cry. Hannah looked helplessly from her daughter to her granddaughter. 'It's all right baby,' she crooned, although the panic in her voice betrayed her. Sydney started to wail.

Lisa stared at the police officers contemptuously. 'You're making a mistake,' she said. 'And you're scaring my daughter.'

'Can't be helped,' said Hammond. 'I have to explain your rights. You have a right to an attorney. If you cannot afford one . . .'

'This is ridiculous. You are making a big mistake. My daughter is a brilliant student. Lisa,' Adam barked, 'don't say a word. I'm going to call a lawyer.'

Detective Hammond looked at Adam with a gaze that was almost sympathetic. Then he shook his head, and followed behind the patrolman who had cuffed Lisa's narrow wrists and was leading her off the deck and down to the waiting squad car in the driveway.

FOUR

A dam made one call after another until they were able to reach Marjorie Fox, a top-flight defense attorney from a big Nashville firm. Ms Fox told them to meet her at the courthouse. In a daze, as if she were moving through a bad dream, Hannah called Rayanne to ask for help.

Rayanne immediately agreed to come over and watch Sydney while they went downtown. Hannah and Adam sat numbly in court while Lisa and Marjorie stood before the judge. An indifferent clerk read out the charges of larceny and first-degree murder. Hannah gasped but Marjorie frowned at her, and indicated that she should keep silent. When asked, Lisa proclaimed herself 'not guilty.' The district attorney asked that bail be denied but the judge agreed with Marjorie that Lisa be granted bail. Bail was set and Marjorie advised them of a bail bondsman to contact. Feeling stunned, and cornered by circumstance, Adam and Hannah agreed to put up their house for collateral. Then they returned home.

Sydney was fed and in her pajamas. Hannah scooped up her granddaughter and sat shaking, leeching warmth from the toddler on her lap. Rayanne wanted to know everything but Hannah shook her head. 'Ray, I can't, right now,' she said. 'I just can't.'

Rayanne nodded. 'I understand,' she said. She quietly let herself out, leaving them, in a delayed state of shock, to wait for their daughter's return. Hannah felt as if the world had suddenly spun off its axis. She thought that for as long as she lived, she would never be able to forget the sight of Lisa – her brilliant, determined daughter – being led away in handcuffs by the police. She had another indelible image in her mind of a defiant Lisa, standing in the dock wearing the skirt and sweater her mother had brought to the courthouse for her.

The phone rang and Adam went to answer it. Then he came back into the kitchen. 'That was Marjorie Fox. The bail has been paid and they are heading home.'

'Adam, I just . . . I don't believe this is happening,' said Hannah. 'Me neither,' he said. 'Hey, little one, isn't it past your bedtime?'

'I wanna see Mommy,' said Sydney.

Hannah shook her head in a warning. 'She'll be here soon,' she reassured the child.

Adam sighed and nodded, realizing that they had to allow Sydney to stay up long enough to see her mother. After all, she too had watched Lisa being removed in handcuffs. She needed to see her mother walk back in the door. He grabbed the remote and put a cartoon network on the television and beckoned for Hannah to follow him. Reluctantly, Hannah slid her granddaughter off her lap, and propped her up among the pillows on the sofa. Then she went and joined her husband in the kitchen.

'Did Marjorie say anything else?' Hannah whispered.

Adam's face was drawn. 'Just that she's bringing her home.'

'I don't understand any of this. It makes no sense.'

'Well, apparently she did cash his paycheck, Hannah.'

Hannah sighed. 'I know. But why? There must be some explanation . . .'

'And, apparently, they have evidence that the explosion was not an accident, according to Ms Fox.'

'It doesn't matter. You know Lisa isn't capable of doing this.'

'I know that. But the police don't. They just know that she was there right before it happened. And that she cashed his check.'

'Adam, I don't believe my ears. You make it sound as if you believe this might have happened the way they said.'

'I don't,' he said stubbornly, 'but you know what Lisa is like. Sometimes she doesn't think before she acts . . .'

Of course Hannah knew what he meant. Lisa had always been moody, and volatile and a magnet for mischief. But she was also a hard worker who had distinguished herself with her grades and her honors. She shook her head in disbelief. 'You mean, like, borrowing a kid's bike, or somebody's earrings, and forgetting to return them? Or skipping school? Those are normal things. Kid things . . .'

'Having a baby, and not even telling us who the father is.'

'Having a baby is not a crime, Adam,' Hannah reminded him coldly.

'I sometimes think we made excuses for her,' he insisted.

Hannah felt her knees wobble. 'What are you talking about? She was an extraordinary child. No one knows that better than you. She was always the youngest in her class. And the smartest. And, let's face it – nobody ever likes the smartest kid in the class. I think she felt left out so much of the time.'

'Even extraordinary children have to play by the rules,' he said.

'We taught her that,' Hannah cried. 'You know we did. Just because she was . . . a little bit unusual, you can't possibly think she could have . . .'

'I don't think that,' he protested. 'I don't.'

'I would hope not,' said Hannah.

'I'm just so . . . frustrated. How could this have happened? How could the police have made a mistake like that?'

Hannah looked at her husband tenderly. Tears stood in his eyes. He had devoted his life to their family. The most illegal thing he had probably ever done was to get a parking ticket. He was completely lost in this maze of crime and legalities. 'I know,' said Hannah. She slipped her hand through his arm. 'I feel the same way.'

Adam nodded and sighed, wiping his eyes.

'There's some explanation,' said Hannah. 'There has to be.'

There was a sound of the front door opening and suddenly they heard Sydney yell out, 'Mommy.' They hurried back into the living room to see Lisa on her knees, holding the toddler close. Marjorie Fox stood behind them, her hands clasped over one another on the handle of her briefcase.

'Lisa,' Hannah cried, and rushed to her child.

Lisa shook her head, as if in warning. She looked down at Sydney. 'Must be past your bedtime,' she said calmly. Then she straightened up. 'I think I'll take Sydney up to bed,' she said. 'Marjorie, can you fill them in?'

'I will,' said Marjorie.

Sydney offered each of her grandparents a kiss, and then climbed cheerfully into her mother's embrace. Lisa carried her off.

Hannah indicated a chair and the attorney sat down. 'Can I get you anything?' Hannah asked.

Marjorie shook her head. She was a striking brunette, about forty, with a strong jaw and penetrating brown eyes. 'I'm fine,' she said.

Adam turned off the TV with a remote and sat down in the other chair. Hannah sat on the sofa. 'Okay. What's the bottom line?' he asked.

'Well, as you know, they're charging her with murder in the first degree. Second degree larceny.'

'Oh my God.' Hannah doubled over, devastated anew at the gravity of the charges.

Marjorie shook her head. 'Don't despair. The fact is, these outrageous charges are actually going to work in our favor. I don't know how much you follow local politics but we have a district attorney who is embattled. He's new and somewhat inexperienced and he has lost several of his biggest cases in this town. He's hoping to hit one out of the park and redeem himself with this case but he's seriously overreaching and he's made a very poor decision in my opinion. He is never going to be able to prove first degree,' said Marjorie calmly.

Hannah looked up at her, skeptical but hopeful. 'Are you sure?'

'Well, this is my job. I'm pretty confident. No guarantees, of course.'

'We understand,' said Adam grimly.

'Everything went smoothly with the bail bondsman,' said Marjorie. 'There are certain conditions, which I explained to Lisa. She can continue to go to school and do her rounds. Otherwise, she has to stick pretty close to home. No alcohol. No drugs. Not so much as a traffic violation. She has to report for every court appearance. The normal stuff . . .'

'She will,' said Adam firmly.

'I don't understand this,' said Hannah. 'Why would they blame Lisa for this horrible thing?'

Marjorie said, 'Well, I haven't looked at the evidence yet. I'll have the results of discovery in the next few days. I'll be able to tell you a little more then. I had a brief consult with the prosecutor. They've got her dead to rights on this check-cashing charge. Security camera footage that shows her doing it. So we have to explain why she did it. Show that there was no criminal intent.'

Hannah's face flamed. The thought that her daughter would do such a thing filled her with shame. 'What did she say about that?' Hannah asked grimly.

'You'll have to ask her that yourself. Everything she tells me is privileged.'

'Even though we're paying the bill,' Adam observed angrily.
Ms Fox did not blink. 'Regardless,' she said.

'And the . . .' Hannah could not bring herself to say it. 'Troy's death.'

'Well, the prosecution maintains that the explosion was not an accident. And that apparently, Troy had been knocked unconscious before it occurred.'

'That doesn't mean that Lisa had anything to do with it,' Hannah protested.

'No, it doesn't,' said Marjorie.

'And beyond that?' Adam asked.

'I'll know more tomorrow. I will have my investigators on this right away. We have to find out if Troy had enemies. I don't know yet if he had a record. But there has to be someone else who would be more likely to blow up his house than his medical-student girlfriend.'

'Right,' said Hannah. 'Of course.'

'From what I know so far, this case sounds very circumstantial,' said Marjorie reassuringly. 'I feel fairly confident that we can beat them on this.'

Lisa returned to the living room. She had changed into her jeans. Her curly hair looked matted and lifeless, and she had twisted it up into a lopsided bun. She wore no makeup, and her gray eyes looked faded behind her glasses.

'Is she OK?' Hannah asked.

Lisa nodded and sat down at the other end of the sofa.

'I've been explaining to your parents what will happen next. You know the rules about bail.' Marjorie pointed an index finger at her client. 'Don't mess it up.'

'No way,' said Lisa with a shudder. 'I had enough of that jail this evening.'

'Good.' Marjorie stood up. 'I better run. I'll talk to you tomorrow.'

Adam and Hannah thanked her, shaking her hand, and Adam walked her to the door. Hannah sat down again beside her daughter. She wanted to reach out and pull her into her arms, but Lisa had always resisted physical affection. It made her uneasy. Hannah settled for patting her hand.

'Are you OK?' she asked.

Lisa shrugged. 'Not really, Mom. I still can't believe any of this.'

'Ms Fox seems to think that their case isn't very strong.'

Lisa shook her head. 'Whatever. They seem to have something to prove, and for some reason they are focused on me.'

Adam closed the front door and came back into the room. He sat down in a chair opposite Lisa and rubbed his hands together.

Lisa sighed. 'Go ahead, Dad. Say whatever's on your mind.'

'All right, I will,' said Adam. 'Why in the world did you cash Troy's paycheck?'

Lisa laughed. 'Really? Is that all you want to know? I expected you to start accusing me of murder.'

'Lisa, don't even say that word. We would never think that. And your father is moving heaven and earth to try to help you,' said Hannah sharply.

Lisa nodded. 'Sorry.'

'The paycheck?' Adam demanded.

'He owed me money. It was that simple. He signed the check and handed it to me before I left. I went to the store near the hospital where they cashed our paychecks. I wanted to get the money before he changed his mind.'

'You don't have any money to lend,' said Adam. 'You can barely make ends meet as it is.'

Lisa sighed and closed her eyes.

'Can you answer me?' Adam said impatiently.

'Look, I gave it to him because he seemed desperate for the money. I think I wasn't the only one he owed money to. But I wanted to be paid back. I took the check and I cashed it. Like you said, I can't afford to lend people money. I got angry, OK, and I insisted on getting what was owed me.'

'And that was it?'

'That was it.'

'Did you tell the police that?'

'I did,' said Lisa. 'They didn't seem to care.'

'And you have no idea how the explosion happened?'

'Are you kidding?' Lisa cried. 'How would I know? Thanks a lot, Dad.'

'I want to believe you, Lisa. More than you know. But the police don't just arrest people for no reason.'

'Well, in this case they did. OK, Dad?' Lisa shook her head in disgust. 'I should have known you wouldn't believe me. I hear you going around bragging about me being in medical school. When you're talking about that, I'm your precious little girl. But let one thing go wrong, and you turn on me . . .'

'One thing go wrong?' Adam cried. 'This is a little more than one thing going wrong.'

'Sorry I didn't say what you wanted me to,' Lisa yelled at him. 'This is exactly what I would have expected from you.'

Hannah shook her head. The peace between Adam and Lisa was always tenuous. Since she had become a teenager, Lisa had resisted her father's every effort at discipline. There was some struggle between them that just could not be resolved.

'Mommy . . .' Even though the sound was muffled, Hannah could hear Sydney's cries coming from her bedroom down the hall. Lisa heard them too.

'I'll go,' she said more quietly. 'I'm exhausted anyway. I think I'll go to bed.'

Adam took a deep breath, and when he spoke his voice was shaky. In fact, his whole body seemed to shake. Hannah felt immediately protective of him. It was true that he held Lisa to a high standard but no higher than he expected from himself. 'Look, Lisa, I'm sorry. I'm upset. Maybe I'm not being fair.'

'You're not being fair,' said Lisa. 'Nothing unusual there. But I don't have to defend myself to you. Goodnight, Mom.'

'Goodnight, darling. Try to get some sleep,' said Hannah, reaching up to her.

Lisa bent down and placed an awkward kiss in the vicinity of Hannah's eyebrow. 'I'll see you in the morning,' said Lisa, avoiding her father's gaze.

After she was gone, Hannah turned to her husband. 'Adam, what are you doing? We have to be on her side. She needs us now. We have to support her through this. You know that, don't you?'

'Yes, of course. I know it.'

'So why are you acting this way?'

Adam held his head in his hands. 'I don't know.'

'Can't you do that? Can't you be on her side?'

'I'm scared, Hannah,' he groaned. 'I'm just so scared. Our daughter arrested? Charged with murder?'

Hannah shook her head. 'It's a mistake. It's all going to be resolved. Meanwhile, we have to be strong. For Lisa and for Sydney.'

'You're right,' he said. 'And I will. I'll do my best. I promise.'

Hannah looked over at him, the man she had fallen in love with at eighteen. He was good through and through. He always tried to do his best for them. Lisa knew how to push his buttons but all he had ever wanted for her was the sun and the moon and the stars. Hannah got up from the sofa and went over to where he sat. She was frightened herself but, right at that moment, Adam needed consolation more than she did. She perched on the arm of the chair and rubbed his back. 'I know you will,' she said reassuringly. 'You always do.'

FIVE

A fragile peace held in the house as they edged closer to the date of Lisa's trial. Lisa went to class and did her rounds and pretended not to hear the whispers in the hospital. She had frequent meetings with Marjorie Fox, though she reported very little about their conversations to her parents. The news coverage was continuous. Every day some article appeared with a photo of Lisa glowering and looking stressed, and an inset photo of Troy, his soft blond hair falling across his forehead, his biceps bulging under his nurse's scrubs. The deceased. New information was scant but there was no shortage of photos. Photographers trailed in Lisa's wake.

Adam sat up late going over their accounts, to see where they could borrow enough money to pay the high-powered attorney. After three nights in a row of watching him struggle, Hannah sat down beside him. 'Tomorrow,' she said, 'I'm going to take Sydney and go visit my mother.'

Adam shook his head. 'No,' he said. 'I know what you're thinking but I don't want you to do it. We'll manage somehow.'

'I've made up my mind,' said Hannah. 'She can help us. You know she can.'

'That's not the point,' said Adam. 'I know how you hate to ask anything of her. I don't want you to have to do that.'

'It's for Lisa,' said Hannah. 'I'll go there and beg if I have to.'

'You'll have to,' Adam predicted. 'I wish we didn't have to involve her in this.'

Hannah shook her head. 'It's no sacrifice on her part. She'll never miss it. Besides,' she said with a grim smile, 'she loves to see me grovel.'

Adam sighed. 'I hope Lisa appreciates this.'

'She's my only child,' said Hannah matter-of-factly. 'What wouldn't I do for her?'

Hannah's mother, Pamela, wasn't overly fond of children but she expected to see Sydney occasionally. And Hannah told herself that Sydney's presence would ensure her mother's impatience, and thus, a short visit.

Hannah explained to Sydney that they were going to see Gram Pam as she dressed her in a pull-up diaper and a sundress. There was a walled terrace outside of her mother's garden apartment in the assisted living facility where she could play in the sun. Hannah brought along a little basket of toys for her to play with. They set out after breakfast, and made the twenty-minute drive to the Verandah, which was the name of the shady, beautifully kept complex.

The staff, in their cheerful flowered scrubs, all cooed over Sydney as Hannah carried the toddler past the gracious, light-filled common rooms to her mother's unit. At seventy, with her deteriorating muscular condition, Pamela could no longer live on her own, and she wouldn't consider living with Hannah and Adam. Pamela had had four husbands, the third of whom was Hannah's father. That marriage, like her first two, ended in divorce. Pamela had left each of her marriages considerably more prosperous than she had been going in. From her fourth husband, whom she outlived, Pamela inherited a sizable estate, which, in addition to her investment portfolio, afforded her a generous income in her old age.

Hannah was glad that her mother was financially secure although she had never felt comfortable about her mother's turbulent love life. She often thought that her own, early marriage was hastened by her desire to escape from the chaos in Pamela's shadow. Pamela was alone now but Hannah noticed that she often spoke about one of the widowers on the premises who belonged to her bridge group. Hannah recognized the signs. Husband number five was in the wings.

Still carrying Sydney, Hannah knocked on the door to Pamela's apartment and opened it. 'Mother. We're here.'

Pamela, whose pale blonde hair was stiffly coiffed, was dressed in a perfectly crisp mint-green linen pantsuit. She paid a laundress to keep her clothes looking perfect. Although she had always loved high heels, she was now forced to wear sensible white sandals on her pedicured feet.

Pamela rolled up to them in her smartchair, and accepted a kiss on her still-soft cheek from Hannah. Hannah steeled herself against her mother's customary scent of light floral perfume and medicinal breath. Sydney squirmed away from her great-grandmother's kiss and ran to the French doors which led out to the patio. The last time they visited Sydney had witnessed a noisy standoff between a bluebird and a squirrel. No doubt she was hoping for a repeat performance. Hannah walked over and opened the door for her, setting down the basket of toys on the pavers.

'Stay out of the flowerpots,' Pamela commanded.

Sydney made herself at home on the terrace while Hannah placed a box of pralines on the counter. 'I brought your favorites,' she said.

'I can't eat those anymore,' Pamela said dismissively.

Hannah sat down in a chair near the open door so she could keep an eye on Sydney. 'You can offer them to the bridge group.'

'Oh, they won't eat them. Everybody has dietary restrictions. Except for Christina Shelton. Her husband was Jock Shelton, the senator. Did I tell you that?'

'Yes, you mentioned it,' said Hannah. She knew that her mother was most pleased to be living in the same complex as the widow of a senator. Even more pleased that she belonged to the same group of ladies who regularly played bridge together. 'Well, give them to Christina, then.'

'Oh, she's off in the rehab. Since she broke her ankle. I don't know what's taking so long.'

Hannah didn't know, and didn't care. 'So, how are you, Mother?'

'Well, to be honest with you, a little beleaguered lately. Everywhere I go, the TV is blaring, and I have to answer the same question. "Isn't that your granddaughter accused of killing that man?"' She shook her head. 'That Troy Petty was a nice enough young man but he was entirely unsuitable. As I told her when she first started seeing him, if you dive into the trough, there's no point in complaining about the muck. Of course, you're the ones who gave your approval to this unsavory situation. How could you have even allowed her to get tangled up with a low-class fellow like that?'

Despite her many marriages, Pamela still saw herself as the arbiter of correct social behavior.

Hannah sighed. 'She's an adult, Mother. She lives her own life. She makes her own choices.'

'Oh for heaven's sakes, Hannah. She's the definition of a child. She still lives under your roof, like a schoolgirl. Why shouldn't you have a say in what she does and whom she sees?'

Hannah counted to ten. 'She needed our help to go to medical school, OK? Between her studies and the baby, she wasn't capable of handling it all herself. Of course we agreed to help her.'

'Well, you didn't do her any favors. And in my opinion, you should have let her stand on her own two feet a long time ago, when she went and got pregnant. That would have taught her a lesson.'

'I thought you might give her the benefit of the doubt, Mother.'

'Oh, don't misunderstand me. Lisa is a brilliant girl. She'll land on her feet when this trial is over. You'll see.'

Hannah took a deep breath. 'Well, yes, but until she does she's going to need a bit more help. We are trying to work it out but this attorney is very expensive.'

Pamela tilted her head back. 'Ah, so now we come to the heart of the matter. I was wondering to what I owed the pleasure of this visit.'

'Mother, that's not fair,' said Hannah. 'You act as if I only come when I want something. That is just not true.'

'Splitting hairs,' Pamela declared.

Hannah knew better than to argue. She had often withered under her mother's contemptuous gaze. In fact, she wished she could just get up and walk out right now, but the memory of Adam's worried eyes as he went over their finances cemented her to her seat.

'How much this time?' Pamela demanded wearily, as if she had been constantly besieged by Hannah in search of money. There was no use in reminding her that they had only asked her twice before for any money in the course of their marriage, and both times, they had paid her back.

Hannah did not want to discuss it. She got up, pulled the bill for Marjorie Fox's retainer from her purse and put it on her mother's white French-style writing desk. Pamela set her chair in motion and whirred over to the desk.

'You don't have to give it to me now,' said Hannah.

'Let's get it over with,' said Pamela grimly.

'We'll pay you back as soon as we possibly can.'

Pamela sniffed, and proceeded to write the check. She waved it at Hannah, who was forced to reach for it and lift it from her fingers.

Hannah looked at the tidy sum which her mother proffered. 'Thank you, Mother,' she said. She folded up the check and slipped it into her wallet.

Just then, there was a wail from the patio, and Hannah looked out. Sydney had toddled after a squirrel on her pudgy legs and tumbled down, scraping her knees. Hannah ran out and scooped her up, holding her close.

'Don't cry. Oh, I'm so sorry. It's all right. Mom-mom will fix it.' She carried the child into the doors and through the apartment toward her mother's pristine bathroom.

'What's the matter?' Pamela asked, whirring up to the wide bathroom entrance.

'She fell and skinned her knee,' said Hannah. 'Do you have Band-Aids?'

'On the shelf beside the sink.'

Hannah propped the toddler up on the edge of the sink, and began to dab at Sydney's bleeding knee with a wet, snow-white washcloth.

'You'll ruin that washrag,' Pamela predicted.

'I'll bring you some new ones,' Hannah said evenly.

'You're babying her too much,' Pamela observed.

For a moment Hannah closed her eyes, and counted to ten. Then she gently applied the Band-Aid to Sydney's skinned knee. 'That's what you do with babies, Mother. You baby them.'

SIX

On Thursdays, Hannah always worked late. Hannah didn't mind it on those evenings when Adam was away on business, as he was tonight. Someone had to be in the office for the working mothers who couldn't make it during business hours.

Dr Fleischer, the psychologist who did assessments on the families whose cases Hannah handled, leaned into her office. 'Hey, Hannah? How are you holding up?'

Hannah sighed. There was no use in pretending that she didn't know what the psychologist was referring to. 'Just putting one foot in front of the other,' she said. 'The trial starts in two weeks.'

Jackie Fleischer, a thin, attractive woman in her late fifties, was new to the office. Lately arrived in Nashville after years in New Jersey, she was somewhat of an exotic creature to the other staff members. She often dressed in mandarin jackets and trousers with an Asian flair, and Hannah looked forward to getting to know her better. Maybe they would even be friends, given the opportunity.

'And your daughter? How's she doing?'

'It's pretty difficult for her,' Hannah admitted. 'She hears the snide remarks. The whispers. She ignores them, and goes about her business. Medical school takes all your concentration. She's in her second year,' she pointed out with a defensive hint of pride.

Dr Fleischer shuddered. 'Oh, I know it. Even though it was a hundred years ago, I remember the pressure when I was doing my clinical work for my doctorate.'

'She doesn't want to be derailed by this trial. Especially since she isn't guilty.'

'Of course not,' said Dr Fleischer. 'How's her little girl?'

Hannah hesitated, glancing at the photo of her granddaughter on her desk. 'She's doing all right. It's tough. She doesn't know what's going on but she's aware of the tension.'

'She a lot like her mother?' Dr Fleischer asked off-handedly.

Hannah was about to say 'yes' when she stopped herself. Was Sydney like her mother? Hannah knew that she felt differently around Sydney than she had around Lisa at the same age. Sydney was a calm, quiet child, cherubic in a way that Lisa never was. Sydney seemed to be unfurling like a flower bud, where Lisa had been fiery, easily frustrated, forever in motion. At least Hannah had been young in those days, and could keep up with her daughter. If her granddaughter had been like Lisa, Hannah did not know if she could have managed. 'My granddaughter is a lot more . . . serene than her mother was at that age.'

'Funny, isn't it,' said Dr Fleischer, 'how kids can be so different than their parents.'

'I guess you would know,' Hannah observed.

'Keeps me in business,' said Dr Fleischer wryly.

The phone on Hannah's desk rang and she picked it up, as Jackie waggled her fingers in a goodbye wave.

'Your client is here,' drawled the receptionist.

Through the phone, Hannah could hear a woman's shrill commands from the reception area, and the noisy, obstinate retorts of a little boy. 'Send her in,' said Hannah.

Sometimes, with all the upset in her own life, it was hard for Hannah to concentrate on the problems of the families – mostly women and children – on her schedule but, as often happened, she found herself pulled, once she got to work, into the shattered lives which presented themselves to her. This evening, she found herself trying to explain how the school was going to handle an attention deficit-disorder diagnosis to a young woman who looked on hopelessly as her son jiggled and jumped around, letting out little shrieks, compelled to touch everything in Hannah's office. The young woman had dark circles under her eyes, and was visibly missing several teeth. Meth addict, Hannah thought, although she tried to avoid jumping to conclusions about people. But after twenty years of working for family services, there were patterns that could not be denied. Even when she jumped to conclusions, she tried not to judge her clients too harshly. Life was tough for a single mother, especially when her child had special needs.

'Marcus,' cried the scrawny mother, really only a girl, 'if you don't sit down this minute I'm gonna grab you and wail on you.'

Hannah frowned. 'Wailing on him is not really the answer, Shelby Rose. He can't really control it.'

The girl looked at Hannah with wide, frightened eyes. 'Well, I can't stand it much more. He never shuts up.'

The phone buzzed, and she excused herself and picked it up. 'Hannah Wickes,' she said.

'Miz Wickes,' whispered Deverise, the receptionist. 'I know you have a client with you but this caller says they need to speak with you right away.'

'Who is it?' Hannah asked.

'A Ms Granger for you.'

'OK,' said Hannah, her heart thudding at the realization that it was Sydney's daycare provider. 'Thanks.' She turned calmly to Shelby Rose. 'I'm going to have to take this,' she said.

Shelby Rose looked at Hannah helplessly. 'Is that it?'

'You have to contact the school about handling Marcus's medication. And come back in two weeks and let me know how he's doing. You may see a great improvement.'

Hannah could tell from the look on the girl's face that she didn't want to leave the safety of the office. Out in the world, Marcus was a never-ending juggernaut of nervous energy, and the potential for disaster was everywhere. Hannah pointed to the phone. 'I'm sorry but I have to speak to this person.'

Shelby Rose grabbed Marcus roughly by the arm. 'Come on, we're goin',' she said, and practically dragged the protesting child out of the office. For a moment, Hannah felt guilty, but then, she couldn't find it within her to care as much about her clients as she did about her daughter. She pressed the blinking white button and drew in a breath.

'Hannah Wickes.'

'Mrs Wickes? This is Tiffany Granger.'

Tiffany ran the daycare where Hannah dropped Sydney off in the morning, on her way to work. It was a small group of kids and Tiffany had them in her home, which was outfitted to accommodate their every need.

Hannah was galvanized by the sound of concern in that soft Southern accent. 'What is it? Is Sydney OK?'

'Well, yes, she's OK. But her mom was supposed to come pick her up about an hour ago, and she's still not here. She's not answering her phone.'

Hannah felt her face flood with color. She glanced at the clock. 'I'm so sorry.'

'I wouldn't bother you but my first-grader has a play at school tonight, and I don't want to miss it. I called Mr Wickes's cell but he said he's in St Louis on business.'

'Yes, he is. I'm so sorry about this. Look. I will come right away. But it's going to take me half an hour to get there. If you need to drop her off I can arrange . . .'

'No,' said Tiffany calmly. 'I can wait. We'll see you when you get here.'

Hannah returned her phone to her pocket, grabbed her light jacket, and headed out the door.

'Mom-mom,' Sydney cried, and rushed to embrace her grandmother.

Hannah picked up the toddler and held her close.

'Here's her backpack,' said Tiffany.

'I'm really sorry about this,' Hannah said.

'It happens,' said Tiffany, a short, compact young woman who wore her hair skinned back in a tight ponytail, so that her round white face looked like a moon. 'Signals get crossed.'

'Sydney's mother hasn't called?' Hannah asked worriedly.

Tiffany avoided Hannah's gaze, and began to clear up the living room, putting toys into a plastic laundry basket beside the taupe-colored recliner that faced the large flat-screen TV. 'No, ma'am,' she said. 'Haven't heard from her.'

Hannah gazed at the young woman tidying up the room, her clothes neat, her ponytail smooth. Tiffany had two children herself though she couldn't be more than twenty-five. She radiated competence and calm.

'I've tried to call her,' said Hannah. 'There must have been an emergency at the hospital.'

Tiffany was placing a series of hollow plastic boxes, one inside of the other.

'Maybe so,' she said carefully. 'It happens now and then.'

Hannah nodded. 'Guess that's why they call it an emergency room.'

'Well, I know her work at the hospital keeps her very busy. And I'm sorry I pulled you away from work but I didn't know what else to do. There was no one else I could call to come get her. What with that fellow, Troy, dying in that . . . explosion . . .'

Hannah frowned at her. 'Troy? What about him?'

Tiffany's white complexion turned vaguely pink. 'Now, Mrs Wickes, I know we have never discussed this but I just want you to know for the record that I don't believe for one minute that Lisa had anything to do with that poor man's death.'

'Thank you,' said Hannah stiffly. 'I appreciate that.'

'It's like I told my husband. You don't entrust your child to just anyone. You don't give someone that kind of responsibility for your precious child unless you think they are pretty great.'

For a second Hannah was confused. And then she realized what Tiffany was suggesting. 'What do you mean?' Hannah asked. 'What responsibility?'

Tiffany nodded, her eyes wide. 'Oh, I was sure you knew. Lisa told me it was OK to let Sydney go with him.'

A chill ran through Hannah. She knew that Sydney had been out to Troy's home by the lake a few times. Sydney had loved the lake, and Troy had showed her how to fish. Hannah had simply assumed that it was Lisa who picked her up and brought her out there.

Tiffany pressed her lips together. 'At first I thought he might be her father. He certainly seemed to love that little girl.'

'No,' said Hannah, flustered. 'He is not Sydney's father.'

Tiffany persisted. 'It seemed like he was. He always had time to look at the pictures she drew and such. I'm sorry, Mrs Wickes. You seem surprised.'

Hannah's face was hot. 'Well, Lisa never mentioned that . . . I mean, it's not as if Troy had any . . . He's not related to Sydney, is all I'm saying.

Tiffany pursed her lips and avoided Hannah's intent gaze. 'Yes, I prefer to have someone related come and get the child. But Lisa herself told me it was OK. I have to bide by the mother's wishes.'

Hannah tried to imagine what had possessed Lisa to give Troy the responsibility for picking up her child. It had to have been an extreme circumstance. Sydney hardly knew Troy. 'Well, I suppose, in an emergency, as you say . . .'

'Lisa does have lots of emergencies,' said Tiffany with a hint of disapproval in her tone. 'But I have to admit, he was always reliable. Whenever I'd have to call him to come get Sydney he was always willing, always cheerful . . .'

'You called Troy?' Hannah asked incredulous.

Tiffany looked at her blankly. 'Any number of times. Lisa told me to.'

'Momma, momma, momma,' called out a little barefoot girl who scampered into the living room, her hair up in pigtails.

'Momma's talking to Sydney's nana right now,' Tiffany reproved her daughter mildly.

'I need you,' the child insisted. 'Come see what I made.'

'I've got to be going,' said Hannah. She felt the implications of Tiffany's words like a slap. She avoided the caregiver's gaze.

Hannah walked Sydney out to the driveway. Sydney was leaping in giant steps down the driveway, explaining how big she was and how she could cross over the ocean in three steps.

Sydney let herself be lifted up and placed in her car seat. Hannah buckled her in and gave her a kiss on the top of her head. Somehow she managed to drive home, though her mind was racing. When they got to the house, she opened the back door to retrieve her granddaughter.

'You hungry?' she asked.

Sydney nodded and looked out the window.
'We'll get you some supper.'
Sydney nodded again. She did not ask about her mother.

SEVEN

Hannah heard Lisa's voice outside. She glanced at the clock on the mantle, and then went to the front door to peer into the darkness. Lisa, who had just gotten out of her car, was talking to Rayanne's husband, Chet, who was out taking his fluffy little black-and-white dog for a walk. The lively Havanese was on a leash and straining to get going. Hannah could not hear what Chet and Lisa were saying but she watched them wave at one another, and then Lisa came up the steps to the house. Hannah moved away from the door and let her enter.

'Yikes. You startled me,' said Lisa accusingly. 'What are you doing hovering by the door like that?'

'Come down to the kitchen,' said Hannah. Without waiting for a reply she turned and went down to the kitchen at the end of the hallway. She had a feeling that this discussion could get intense, and she didn't want to wake up Sydney, asleep in her bedroom at the other end of the house. Lisa, still wearing a lab coat over her untucked shirt and jeans, came into the kitchen, casually opened the refrigerator, and pulled out a bottle of iced tea. Before Hannah had a chance to state her grievance, or demand an accounting, Lisa went on the offensive.

'Mother, what in the world happened tonight with Tiffany?' she asked.

For a moment, Hannah was dumbstruck. Then she stared back at her. 'What happened? Tiffany called me to come get Sydney when you didn't show up. That's what happened. I had to leave work and run over there. You were nowhere to be found.'

'I was at the hospital. I couldn't get away. When I got to Tiffany's, there was nobody home. I didn't know what had happened to Sydney. I called Tiffany's cellphone and there was no answer.'

'You were an hour late,' Hannah said accusingly. 'It was just lucky Tiffany was able to reach me. I went and got Sydney.'

Lisa collapsed onto a stool, rested her elbow on the counter and pushed her glasses up, rubbing her eyes. 'You could have texted me.'

'I could have,' Hannah admitted. 'But you didn't do me or Tiffany the courtesy of letting us know what was going on.'

'You know,' said Lisa coldly, 'this is not like working at McDonald's. A doctor can't always predict how things are going to go. Sometimes situations arise.'

'Have you forgotten how to use a phone?' Hannah cried. 'There was nobody there to pick up your child. Especially with Troy out of the picture.'

Lisa looked at her with narrowed eyes. 'Why do you say that?'

'She told me. Tiffany told me. You had your boyfriend come and pick Sydney up at daycare. You told her to call him,' Hannah cried.

'He's a nurse,' said Lisa evenly. Then she corrected herself. 'He was a nurse. He was very responsible.'

'Why was he picking her up at all? You hardly knew this man. How could you?' Hannah demanded.

'Don't be ridiculous. Of course I knew him. We dated for months. Sydney liked him. I brought her out to the fishing camp a number of times. Tiffany wanted an extra contact number, just in case. So I gave her Troy's number.'

'You should have had her call me.'

'Mother, you do enough for me and Sydney as it is. I couldn't bear to ask for any more favors.'

'And tonight? Why didn't you call Tiffany to tell her you'd be late?'

'I didn't have time to call anyone,' said Lisa as if explaining bedtime to a stubborn child. 'We had an emergency and they were assessing our responses.'

'So that's it. You just leave her.'

'What is it you don't understand about the term emergency?' said Lisa, peering at her mother as if she were simple-minded.

Hannah shook her head. 'You need to watch that attitude of yours.'

'Mother, I am tired,' Lisa said. 'I'm under a lot of pressure. In case you've forgotten.' She raked her fingers absently through her dark, uncombed curls.

'Yes, I know. So am I,' said Hannah. 'Believe me. Life has been very tiring lately.'

'Oh, because of me,' said Lisa. 'Because I obviously deserve to be standing trial for killing Troy Petty.'

'I didn't say that. I didn't mean that,' said Hannah. 'And you know it.'

'I'm not so sure,' said Lisa.

Hannah took a deep breath. 'Look. No one could believe in you more than me. But no matter what is happening in your life, that's no excuse for neglecting Sydney. You have a child who depends on you. Your child has to come first. Always.'

Lisa sat silently on the stool. Hannah could not tell if she was fuming, or just reconsidering. Finally she said, 'You're right. You're absolutely right.'

Hannah sighed, her anger spent. She sat down opposite Lisa, her indignation derailed by the sight of her daughter's haggard face. It pained her to see Lisa looking so embattled. She worked so hard at her studies, and Hannah couldn't even imagine how draining that had to be, especially with a child at home and this trial to worry about, the press following her every move. Her mother's instincts rose to the fore. 'Lisa, I know you're tired. I know how much this is taking out of you. And being a parent isn't easy. But there are no days off from that responsibility.'

'I hate it when you talk about responsibility,' said Lisa, rolling her eyes.

Hannah smiled. 'I know you do.'

Suddenly, Lisa frowned and lifted her head. 'What's that?' she said.

'What?' Hannah asked.

Lisa shook her head. 'I thought . . . Yes, I hear it again. Do you hear something?'

A weak reedy voice was crying out plaintively, though it was barely audible.

'Who is that?' said Lisa. Sliding off the kitchen stool, Lisa walked out of the room and back toward the front door.

Hannah hesitated then followed behind her daughter.

The street was quiet, except for the sound of rustling leaves. Clouds scudded across the moonlit sky.

'There. Now,' said Lisa.

Hannah didn't hear anything, and was about to say so, when Lisa held up a finger in warning. 'There,' she said.

Suddenly Hannah heard it. It was a low, keening sound,

intertwined with the sound of the wind. They walked out into the yard, looking to either side. Lisa peered through the garage windows while Hannah went to the sidewalk and scanned up and down the street.

'Lisa. Look.'

In the yard two doors down a man's bent legs were half hidden by a wide, blooming crape myrtle. Lisa sprinted to the man's side. Hannah followed close behind her, and gasped when she recognized him: Chet, pale and sweaty. His dog was lying beside him, making piteous noises.

'Oh my God,' said Hannah.

Lisa fell to her knees, lifting Chet's wrist to take his pulse and asking him questions. Chet's voice was barely audible in reply.

'Take it easy,' Lisa said. Without looking up at Hannah, she issued commands in a calm voice. 'Mom, go and get my bag. It's in the front hall. Hurry. And call for an ambulance.'

Hannah rushed to do what she was told, dialing 911 as she ran. 'I'll get Rayanne,' she called back.

Lisa nodded dismissively, intent on what she was doing. She had begun to compress Chet's chest with her clasped hands.

Hannah grabbed up the medical bag, than ran to the Dollards' house, and roused Rayanne, who was nodding off over a crossword puzzle.

'I knew it!' Rayanne cried. 'I knew he wasn't feeling well.'

They could hear the sirens already. As they rushed back to where Chet lay, they saw Lisa working feverishly over him. She was competent, professional and completely focused on saving the life of their old family friend. Hannah felt her heart swell with pride. She was suddenly furious at the preposterousness of the charges against her daughter. Lisa was young, and she had her lapses of behavior, like anyone young. But this was someone whose mission in life was to save lives. Not to take them. 'It's all right,' Hannah said to Rayanne. 'Lisa's got this.'

'I know,' Rayanne whispered. 'Thank God she's here.'

The ambulance arrived quickly and Chet was loaded inside while Lisa talked to the EMTs, explaining how she had found him, and what she had done to treat him.

Rayanne wanted to climb into the back of the ambulance with her husband but the EMTs were firm. There was not enough room. Chet was in a dangerous condition and they needed to work on him.

'I'll drive you,' said Hannah. 'Come on.'

As they hurried across the lawn back to the driveway, Hannah stopped to speak to Lisa, who was headed back inside the house. 'I'm going to take Rayanne to the hospital. She's too upset to drive.'
'OK. Sure,' said Lisa.
'If you're hungry, there's some leftovers in the fridge . . .'
'Go. I'll be fine,' said Lisa. 'All I want to do is sleep.'

It was four a.m. by the time Hannah returned home with Rayanne in tow.

Chet had spent hours in the emergency room, and in X-ray. It was hours more before he was resting comfortably in CCU and Rayanne was able to see the doctor. She kept urging Hannah to leave her there, that she would get a taxi home. But Hannah couldn't bring herself to do it. There was so much lonely downtime at the hospital. She just wanted to keep her friend company in these most stressful hours. Rayanne finally saw a doctor at around three o'clock, only to learn that Chet's condition was stable now, but was going to require surgery. Rayanne was advised to go home and get some rest. The two women walked out into the starry night, crossed the parking lot and got into Hannah's car.

'I can't thank you enough,' said Rayanne.

'Don't be silly,' said Hannah. 'You've always been such a help to me.'

Once in the driveway, Hannah made sure that Rayanne was safely in her house and the lights were on before she went into her own quiet home. She only turned on a few lights, not wanting to wake Lisa and Sydney, who were, most likely, fast asleep. She wished, more than anything, that Adam were home, and she could crawl into bed beside him, and rest up against his strong, warm body. But he would be gone for another day. Despite her own exhaustion, she was keyed up, and not quite ready to get into bed. She took a shower, got into her pajamas and a robe, and made herself a cup of cocoa. She still did not feel sleepy. She didn't want to turn on the TV. The noise might disturb the sleeping girls.

Finally she went into the living room, sat down in the corner of the sofa and picked up her iPad. She wanted to flip through screens looking at recipes or movie-star news or anything that would require no thought or energy.

The headlines on her home page were not very intriguing. Luckily, not a lot seemed to have transpired in the world since she had last looked. She noticed that she had a few new emails. The advertisers never slept, she thought. They never quit. She opened her email account, and saw that, as she suspected, she had breathless offers from the usual companies. She deleted them one by one, and then she noticed that she had an email from Taryn Bledsoe, the mother of Alicia, one of Lisa's high-school friends with whom Lisa still hung out occasionally.

The email had no title but for a series of exclamation points, and it did have an attachment. Hannah frowned at it curiously. She and Taryn, who worked as a legal secretary, had been friendly when Alicia and Lisa first went to high school together, but their relationship had been strained when the girls were suspended for a prank they pulled together. In recent years, though the girls remained friends, Hannah had hardly seen Taryn. Hannah opened the email and looked at it. It was only one line. 'This is called asking for trouble.'

Hannah's heart started to pound. Trembling, she opened the attachment. It was a photograph of Lisa. With the superb technology of current phones, the photograph was crystal clear despite the fact that it was taken in a dark bar. Lisa was wearing a blouse which was unbuttoned to reveal a black push-up bra. She was hoisting a bottle of Jack Daniel's to her lips, her eyes merry. Hannah's scalp prickled and her stomach churned as she stared at it. The photo was dated and timed that evening. The time when Hannah was picking up Sydney. The time when Lisa was unreachable, 'delayed' at the hospital by an emergency.

EIGHT

Hannah thought about waiting for morning. She knew how tired her daughter was. How badly she needed her sleep. But right at this moment she didn't care. She went into Lisa's room and shook her.

Lisa's eyes shot open but they looked merely puzzled at the sight of her mother. 'What?'

'Get up,' she said. 'Come with me.'

Lisa was too groggy to argue. She pulled on her robe and followed her mother down the hall to Hannah's room. 'What's going on?' she mumbled.

Hannah closed the door behind them and turned on Lisa. She held up the iPad with the photo on it. 'Do you want to explain this?'

Lisa squinted at the image. 'Is that my iPad?'

Hannah stared at her. 'No, it's ours. And I want an explanation.'

Lisa shrugged. 'What is there to explain?'

'You told me that you were held up by an emergency at the hospital. Instead, it appears that you went out drinking when you were supposed to be picking up your child.'

Lisa frowned. 'What are you talking about?'

'Don't deny it, Lisa. This photo has a date. And time.'

Lisa yawned. 'All right. Yes. I went out. I figured that you would get Sydney. I needed to relax. I had a drink. Couldn't this have waited till morning?' she asked, rubbing her eyes.

'Are you kidding me?'

'Sorry. You're right. Sorry,' said Lisa.

'Sorry? That's all you have to say? Besides the fact that you neglected your child and lied to me about where you were,' Hannah cried, 'you were in a public place! Under the terms of your bail, alcohol is forbidden.'

Lisa rolled her eyes. 'The alcohol police.'

'They can revoke your bail if you get caught.'

'I'm not going to get caught,' said Lisa with a sigh.

'Oh, really? This picture might be on the front page tomorrow,' Hannah said, shaking the iPad at Lisa.

'How did you get that, anyway?' asked Lisa, squinting at the photo.

'Taryn Bledsoe emailed it to me. To warn me.'

'She's always been a tight ass.'

Hannah was furious. 'She wanted me to know that you are in danger of losing your freedom. If the court gets wind of this . . .'

'I was with some friends. Nobody's going to rat me out. Just chill, Mom.'

Hannah glared at her daughter. 'Don't you tell me to chill. We put our house on the line for you. For your bail. If your father knew that you went out drinking . . .'

'I'm sure you'll tell him,' Lisa observed drily.

Hannah shook her head, incredulous. 'Do you realize how serious this could be? For all of us?'

'And you'll remind me a million times. Look, I didn't ask you to put your house on the line.'

'Did you think we were going to let you sit in jail?'

'You could have,' said Lisa.

'No, we couldn't. Of course we couldn't. We love you. We'd do anything for you. I don't understand how you could be so careless!'

'I'm still young, all right?' said Lisa ruefully. 'Sometimes I just need to . . . blow off some steam.'

Hannah looked at her daughter, shaking her head. 'Believe it or not, I do understand that,' she said. 'But people are looking for any excuse to blame you. To look at you and say, "See! Of course she killed that guy. She's wild, she's out of control."'

'I'm not out of control.'

Hannah felt her temper rising again. 'What do you call this?' she asked, shaking the small screen at her daughter.

Lisa did not reply but her face was an expressionless mask, as if their conversation was turning her to stone. There was a silence in the room and, once again, Hannah was grateful that Adam would not be home until tomorrow.

'Well?' Hannah demanded.

'Fun,' said Lisa bitterly. 'I call it fun.'

Hannah closed her eyes and balled her hands into fists.

'Are we done?' said Lisa.

'Go back to bed,' said Hannah.

'Look, Mom, I didn't do it to upset you. I just . . .' Lisa shrugged. 'Sometimes I feel like I have to . . . forget everything.'

'Good night, Lisa,' said Hannah.

Lisa opened her mouth to speak again, and then thought better of it. She left the room, pulling the door shut behind her. Hannah went and sat in the rocker by the front window. Years ago, she had sat in that same rocker, in their first apartment, holding Lisa, her baby, rocking and daydreaming. Imagining her daughter's life. College and marriage. Fame and children. In all her wildest dreams, she had never once imagined a murder charge with her daughter accused. Rocking that baby, it was impossible to imagine such a thing. Now, all these years later . . . Hannah sighed and gazed out at their leafy front yard, their quiet street. It was impossible still.

The next day Hannah nearly knocked over Jackie Fleischer as she arrived late to work, and barreled through the front door of social services.

'Oh, sorry,' Hannah said. 'I'm so sorry. Am I too late for the meeting?'

'You didn't miss much,' said the psychologist. 'I'll fill you in.'

Hannah sighed. 'Thanks. I owe you.'

'Did you have your coffee yet?' Jackie asked.

Hannah shook her head. 'I was up late, and I forgot to set my alarm. So I ran out of the house. I haven't had anything.'

'I've got that espresso machine in my office. Come on.'

Hannah didn't really like espresso but she was grateful, and seriously in need of some caffeine. She followed Dr Fleischer into her office.

The walls were covered with framed photos of waterfalls and forest canopies, along with occasional close-ups of unusual birds or exotic flowers. The effect was both colorful and soothing. Dr Fleischer and her husband, empty-nesters, often went on adventurous trips to observe and photograph the wonders of nature.

Hannah took the cup that Dr Fleischer proffered, and sat down. She added a packet of sugar and took a sip. It seemed less bitter than the occasional espressos she had had in fancy restaurants. In fact, it was pretty good. She sipped it carefully.

'I'm a wreck,' she said.

Dr Fleischer sat down in the corner of the loveseat in her office. She cocked her head and looked at Hannah. 'So what's going on with you?'

Hannah sighed. 'Well, you know my daughter is out on bail, waiting for this . . . trial to begin. She's . . . chafing, shall we say, with the restrictions. Letting certain things slide. Acting up a little bit when she should be keeping her nose clean. She's never been good with . . . limits.' Hannah was aware, even as she said it, that she was soft-pedaling Lisa's offenses, that she desperately wanted this psychologist to agree to how normal Lisa's behavior really was.

'How are *you* feeling?' asked Dr Fleischer. 'This is obviously taking a toll.'

'I just want to help her get through this,' said Hannah. 'Once this horrible trial is over, we can get our lives back.'

'You seem pretty confident that it will turn out well.'

Hannah shook her head. 'Oh, don't kid yourself. I'm sick with worry. I mean, it's a trial. With a jury, anything can happen. We just have to rely on Lisa's attorney to get at the truth.'

'Which is?'

'Well, either it was an accident, or somebody else is responsible for Troy Petty's death. I don't expect the attorney to produce the guilty person. That's not her job. Although she certainly charges enough. But I do expect her to show the jury that Lisa had nothing to do with it.'

'Do you and your husband talk to Lisa about the case? Is she able to shed any light on why she got blamed for this? Besides that thing with the paycheck, of course . . .'

Hannah blushed and shook her head. She shouldn't have been surprised. Every detail had been in the papers. 'She meets with the attorney all the time. She doesn't really want to dwell on it. We get our information from the internet or the paper, just like everybody else.'

'But she must tell you what the attorney said.'

'Honestly,' said Hannah, 'she doesn't really talk about it.'

Dr Fleischer shook her head. 'I'd have to insist on knowing if I were you.'

'I want to. But I try not to lean on her too much.' Hannah frowned, thinking of their arguments from the night before. 'I mean, sometimes I forget because she has such a demanding profession, and a child, and she's still just a young girl.'

'You seem to have the weight of the world on you,' Dr Fleischer observed.

'Well, she's my daughter. I can't even bear the thought that somehow, by some judicial error, she might be . . .' Hannah couldn't even bring herself to say the word 'convicted'.

'No, of course not.' Dr Fleischer tapped her chin with her slender fingers. 'It's got to be weighing Lisa down too.'

Of course, Hannah started to say. And then, for a split second Hannah thought of the photo on the iPad. Lisa's unbuttoned shirt, and that wink as she slugged the Jack Daniel's. Hannah's stomach seemed to shrivel inside of her, and she felt the coffee sloshing acidly in her gut. Then she shook her head, as if to shake the image out of her mind and shake off its effects. 'Of course,' she said. 'Of course it is. She's only human.'

The phone rang in Hannah's pocket and she fished it out. She looked at the name on the caller ID, and then she looked at the psychologist.

'I have to take this,' she said, setting down her coffee cup. 'Will you excuse me?'

The psychologist nodded, and Hannah gathered up her things and answered the phone at the same time, stepping out into the hallway.

'Yes?' Hannah expected to hear a voice telling her to wait for Ms Fox, but instead it was the defense attorney herself.

Marjorie Fox skipped the pleasantries. 'You need to get down here to the courthouse right now. Lisa's already here with me.'

'Why?' Hannah asked, with a sickening feeling in her stomach.

'There's a problem. A photograph on the internet. Meet us there in twenty minutes.'

Oh God, no, Hannah thought. 'I will,' she said.

NINE

Hannah was able to reach Adam on the phone when his plane landed. He grabbed a cab and slid into the seat beside her in the courtroom as Judge Endicott, seated on the bench, came straight to the point. 'Young lady, you were told at the time that bail was granted that there were conditions to your remaining free on bond, were you not?'

Lisa, who stood beside her attorney, looked almost like a child playing doctor. She was still wearing her white lab coat that she wore on rounds. Never much of a clothes horse, that coat seemed to be Lisa's favorite item of clothing. Hannah suspected that her daughter enjoyed the status that it conferred.

Lisa looked gravely at the judge. 'Yessir, I was.' Marjorie whispered something in her client's ear and Lisa nodded. 'Your honor, I meant to say.'

'Did you think I was joking about those conditions?' he asked.

'Nossir. No, your honor. Of course not.' Lisa sounded sincere. Contrite.

Hannah could feel Adam's fingers gripping hers. Having her hand in his was soothing, as ever. They sat quietly, following every word. The judge's expression was cool.

'What do you have to say for yourself?' the judge asked.

Lisa fidgeted and looked pained. 'Well, I realize I should never have been out in that bar. I certainly should not have let someone take my picture like that. I should have known better. My friend just took me by surprise.'

The judge's eyes narrowed. He gazed unsympathetically from the photo to Lisa, who stood, hands demurely clasped, in front of him. 'Some friend,' he said.

'I didn't realize it until it was too late,' Lisa admitted.

'If you hadn't had your picture taken, you wouldn't be here, would you?'

'Well, probably not,' said Lisa. 'In all honesty.'

'Your evening out at a bar would have gone undetected,' he observed.

Adam grimaced and raised a hand as if to stop Lisa from speaking, but Lisa had decided to try being coy. She gave an embarrassed shrug and pushed her glasses up onto the bridge of her nose. 'I really wasn't there that long. Honest. It's not as if I closed the place down,' she said.

'Is that a joke?' the judge asked.

Lisa looked annoyed. 'Well, maybe not a funny one,' she said.

The judge shook his head. 'Perhaps you think these conditions of bail are unreasonable.'

Lisa straightened up at his tone. Coyness was not going to work. She resumed her cool demeanor. 'Not so much unreasonable,' she retorted, 'as disproportionate.'

'To the crime?' the judge asked, raising his eyebrows.

'To the situation,' Lisa corrected him. 'Your honor, despite my youth, I am involved in a very demanding course of study. I'm able to do work that is normally done by a much older person. All my colleagues are much older than me. When it's time to relax, they don't go out for an ice-cream soda.'

'Indeed,' said the judge, his face betraying no expression.

'And let's not forget that my work is about helping people. About saving lives,' Lisa reminded him piously.

Marjorie Fox sighed but Lisa looked quite satisfied with her own response.

'Right,' said the judge. 'One could argue that you shouldn't even be subjected to the same sort of restrictions that ordinary defendants are subject to.'

Hannah grimaced. She could hear the sarcasm in the judge's voice. Belatedly, Lisa seemed to notice the disapproval in his tone. Even though Marjorie put a warning hand on her arm, Lisa shook her head and spoke up.

'Don't misunderstand me, Judge Endicott. I know that I have to comply with whatever conditions you set. I am accustomed to adapting to difficult situations. I was just exhausted from a very draining day, and I had a lapse of judgment. It won't happen again, I promise you.'

She spoke respectfully, and sounded reasonable. But Hannah knew exactly how Lisa's unrepentant attitude, her self-exculpatory words were falling on the judge's ear.

'You know, I hear you speaking to me, and it's as if you regret having missed a bus, or not finishing your laundry. Do you understand the gravity of this situation, Ms Wickes?' the judge asked.

'Dr Wickes,' said Lisa.

'It's my understanding that you are still a student,' said the judge in a withering tone.

'That's sort of a technicality,' said Lisa. 'I am seeing patients.'

'When you've earned the title, I will use it. And not until. Now about this situation . . .'

'You mean, the drinking?' Lisa asked

'I'm talking about the charges you are facing in your upcoming trial,' he said sternly. 'Do you understand their gravity?'

Lisa nodded. 'Yes. Oh yes, I do. Of course.'

'Hasn't your attorney explained these charges to you? You are charged with murder in the first degree. And larceny in the second degree.'

Lisa nodded again. 'I know, sir, I do.'

Judge Endicott studied the woman standing in front of him. Then he shook his head. 'I don't think you do, Ms Wickes. I don't see, from your manner and your responses here, that you understand the seriousness of this situation at all. The very fact that you were even granted bail is highly irregular. I was making allowances for you in light of your youth and your unblemished record, not to mention the fact that you are a mother. But those conditions of your release on bail were not suggestions. They were orders. Surely someone with your level of intelligence understands the difference. There are no "do-overs" in Superior Court,' he continued.

Lisa opened her mouth to speak. Frowning, Marjorie Fox whispered urgently in her ear.

'No, no, Ms Fox. I'd like to hear what your client has to say,' said the judge.

'I do understand what you are saying, and I can assure you that, going forward, there will be no other lapses of this kind,' said Lisa. 'Your honor.'

Judge Endicott studied her pensively. 'You should heed the advice of your attorney. Do you realize what harm you have done to yourself by your own behavior and your responses here today?'

Lisa looked puzzled and somewhat irritated. 'I believe I've tried to address you as one intelligent person to another.'

'Your honor,' Marjorie Fox interrupted, 'my client is young and immature, despite the high level of study she is engaged in. As you can plainly see, she's a young woman who's never been in serious trouble, and it would be, in my opinion, an unnecessary cruelty to take her away from her child and her medical studies, deprive her of her freedom and send her into the prison population.'

The judge peered at Lisa. 'Do you share custody of your daughter with her father?'

'Her father's not involved,' said Lisa.

'So, where was your child when you were out . . . relaxing with your colleagues?'

'She was with my mother. My mother loves taking care of her.'

'How fortunate for you,' said the judge.

'I can't be in two places at once,' said Lisa.

Marjorie frowned and gave Lisa a warning look.

The judge studied Lisa for a few moments, lost in thought, and Hannah squeezed Adam's hand, praying that the judge would be lenient.

Then, the judge shook his head. 'Ms Wickes, many of the defendants who appear here before me are uneducated and socially backward. Many of them can barely understand these proceedings. You, on the other hand, are a young woman blessed with many advantages. But these advantages don't excuse you from the rule of law. You disregarded the terms of your bail as if they didn't apply to you. You seem more annoyed than regretful to be brought before this court. The world may treat you as gifted, and therefore exempt from certain requirements. But not in my courtroom, you're not.'

Lisa stared at him, openmouthed, as if, belatedly, she understood that her bail was actually in jeopardy. 'Your honor, please be reasonable.'

Marjorie Fox exhaled and shook her head.

The judge glared at Lisa. 'It is my job to be reasonable, young lady. The defendant's bail is revoked. Bailiff, escort the defendant to the county jail. She will remain there until the time of her trial.'

Hannah's knees gave way and Adam was able to catch her and hold her up before she collapsed to the ground.

For a moment, Lisa looked stunned. Then she turned and whispered to Marjorie Fox, 'What a prick!'

'I told you what to say to the judge, Lisa,' said the attorney evenly. 'I warned you. And you ignored me.'

'I told the truth. Isn't that what you're supposed to do in court?'

'You acted as if this were a conversation between equals. Now you have to suffer the consequences. From now on, do as I tell you.'

'Come along,' said the bailiff, snapping the handcuffs on Lisa and prodding her toward the door.

Lisa looked back at her parents and shook her head. 'Do you believe this? Tell Sydney there's no justice,' she said.

'Not "Tell Sydney I love her",' said Adam through clenched teeth.

'Don't,' Hannah said.

Hannah and Adam were silent on the ride home. They stopped to pick up Sydney at Tiffany's house, avoiding all conversation with the curious babysitter, and then retreated into their own house. Sydney wanted to play outside but Hannah convinced her to stay in and play with her dolls in her room. Adam went into his office and closed the door. Hannah sat curled up in the corner of the sofa for a while, thinking about all that had happened. Lisa had been rash and had spoken inappropriately to the judge. Hannah didn't actually blame the judge for being angry. He didn't realize that Lisa's social skills didn't match up to her level of education. Thanks to her extreme intelligence, Lisa had skipped grades and been out of sync with people her own age for most of her life. She had missed out on the socialization that happened naturally to most kids. It made Hannah's heart ache to think of her child, her wonderful, brilliant medical student, locked up in the county jail, wearing some kind of jumpsuit, eating from a chow line with a bunch of drug addicts and prostitutes. A headache formed over her eye at that image.

When she couldn't stand it any longer, Hannah got up and

shuffled into the kitchen, knowing she needed to put something together for supper. She looked out the kitchen window at the Dollards' house, and felt guilty for not having called Rayanne about Chet. She didn't want to call because she didn't want to talk about what had happened to Lisa. But, she reminded herself, when there was an illness in the family, nobody cared all that much about the problems of others. She decided to give Rayanne a quick call before she could learn about Lisa's revoked bail on the six o'clock news.

As she had suspected, she had no need to explain anything about Lisa.

Rayanne launched into a description of Chet's condition, and everything the doctor had said about the surgery it was going to require, and every detail of how Chet was feeling. She never even asked about Lisa, and that was simply a relief to Hannah. She murmured encouragement to her friend, and hung up feeling better for at least having checked on her neighbors. She opened her freezer door and wondered what she could thaw out for dinner. It suddenly all seemed too daunting. Maybe we can get pizza delivered, she thought. As she was staring hopelessly into her freezer, she heard a knock at the door.

Go away. She shrank from the sound, and thought about not answering it at all. The knock on the door came again. There was no use in hiding, she thought. Soon enough, the trial would be on, and they would be forced to face the press, the public, the world. With a sigh, she closed the freezer, went to the front door, and opened it.

Alicia Bledsoe looked uneasy, and waggled her fingers at Hannah. 'Hi, Mrs Wickes,' she said. 'Is Lisa here? She hasn't been answering my texts.'

The girl at the door was overweight, with an ivory complexion, shiny brown hair and large, wary brown eyes. She and Lisa had been friends in high school. Alicia had taken an instant liking to Lisa, and although Lisa was a few years younger, an awkward adolescent, and often isolated, Alicia was the follower in the friendship, and would get involved in whatever scheme she dreamed up. Hannah had been secretly grateful to her for befriending Lisa. She stepped aside and Alicia came into the living room.

These days Alicia lived at home, worked at a fast-food restaurant and was attending community college part time, whereas Lisa had raced through college, had a baby and went on to medical school.

Somehow their old high-school friendship still seemed to hold. However, Hannah suspected that it was Alicia who was responsible for the photo of Lisa which had led to this difficult moment. She wanted to be sure that Alicia was aware of her responsibility in all this. There were consequences to that kind of sophomoric stupidity.

'I'm afraid we got some bad news today,' said Hannah grimly.

Alicia immediately looked stricken. 'Oh no. What?'

'Lisa's bail was revoked. She has to stay in the county jail until the trial.'

Alicia's big eyes welled with tears. 'Oh you're kidding. Why?'

'Because of that photograph of Lisa drinking Jack Daniel's, Alicia. That was taken on your phone, wasn't it?'

Alicia nodded, her face twisted with guilt.

'Apparently it got on the internet and it got back to someone in the police department, and from there to the superior court. She was called in from the hospital today and the judge revoked her bail.'

'That's so mean,' Alicia protested.

'Staying away from bars and alcohol was one of the bail conditions,' Hannah said.

Alicia shook her head. 'My mother told me she was going to send it to you. I was so mad at her.'

'I'm glad she sent it. Your mother was right to warn me. Where else has it gone? To Facebook? To Twitter? For all the world to see?' Hannah demanded.

Alicia was grimacing, still stricken by the news of her friend's incarceration.

'I know you didn't mean any harm by it,' said Hannah. 'Lisa should never have been out drinking in the first place, and you don't have to tell me that it was her idea, because it probably was. I know my daughter.'

Alicia wiped a tear off her round cheek. 'Oh, Mrs Wickes. I'm so sorry.'

Hannah sighed. 'Well, it's too late for sorry. It was a big mistake to put that photo on the internet. Now Lisa has to pay the price.'

Alicia shook her head. 'I told her not to.'

Hannah frowned and hesitated. 'Not to what?'

'Well, not to take a selfie in the first place.'

Hannah blanched. 'A selfie? Lisa took the picture?'

'I tried to warn her. I did. But she grabbed my phone and held it out and took it. And then she just loved it so much that she posted it right away to Twitter. And now this happens. I'm so sorry, Mrs Whitman.'

Hannah stared at the girl in her living room. 'She did it herself?'

'She didn't mean anything by it,' Alicia protested. 'I wonder who ratted her out. How did the judge find out about it?'

Alicia was already busy looking for someone to shift the blame to, away from Lisa. Hannah, on the other hand, was looking at Alicia, but her mind was racing as she thought about her daughter.

The life of a typical teenager had been denied to Lisa because of her prodigious intellectual gifts. Often, when Lisa acted up, Hannah looked the other way, because, fundamentally, she saw Lisa's extreme intelligence as both a blessing and a curse.

But this time Lisa's thoughtlessness had caused her to lose her bail. And she had tried to shift the blame to somebody else. Well, Hannah thought angrily, if that was how she wanted to live her life, so be it. But she had acted as if Sydney didn't even matter.

She didn't intend for this to happen, Hannah reminded herself, trying to calm herself down. Lisa just wasn't thinking like a mother. But then again, thought Hannah, if she admitted the truth to herself, Lisa rarely did.

'I should never have given her the phone,' said Alicia. 'This is all my fault.'

Hannah looked at Lisa's friend helplessly. 'I wish that were true,' she said.

TEN

Although it was mid-September, the first day of the trial was sultry and Hannah dressed accordingly. She wore a silky T-shirt over a calf-length skirt and sandals but she carried along a sweater. Marjorie had warned them that the courtroom would be kept chilly, in deference to the judge's robes, and the fact that the jury needed to be alert through all the testimony.

As she checked herself in the mirror before leaving the house, she noticed that her hair looked limp, and there were dark circles under her eyes. These few weeks had been a form of torture. Visiting

Lisa at the county jail had forced all of them to face up to the unthinkable – what the future might hold. Before Lisa's bail was revoked, and she was still waking up every morning in her childhood bed, it was easier to discount the possibility that this trial might lead to the end of life as they knew it. Of course, they knew that it was possible that Lisa could be convicted. But arriving for a visit at the jail and seeing her emerge in an orange jumpsuit brought that fact home with dreadful clarity.

'*No*,' Hannah said sternly to the mirror. 'She is innocent, and she is going to be acquitted.'

Adam stuck his head into the room. 'Are you about ready? We need to drop off Sydney before we go.'

'Just about,' said Hannah. Hannah and Adam had taken Sydney to see her mother twice. Sydney had clung to Hannah during the visits, and the last time Hannah suggested they go, Sydney had pitched a fit and refused. Rather than bring a screaming child into that mausoleum where every sound reverberated, Hannah went with Adam or by herself.

At least the trial could begin now. Waiting for it to begin had been terrible.

And there was a hopeful part of Hannah which believed that this prosecution was spurious, that they had nothing substantial against Lisa, beyond that unfortunate check-cashing. It could all be over in no time. 'Please,' she thought, closing her eyes and speaking in a whisper. 'Let it be over quickly. Let my baby come home.'

Chanel Ali Jackson jiggled impatiently as an intern from make-up dabbed at her forehead with a sponge. Chanel smoothed the front of her form fitting dress.

The intern stepped back and scrutinized the reporter's hairline. Then she nodded. 'You look fine.'

Chanel flashed her dimpled smile as another technician handed her a microphone and the cameraman directed her to move five feet to her left. Chanel did as she was directed. The assistant director looked at his stopwatch and then pointed at Chanel. She raised her mike and began her smooth delivery.

'Adrian,' she said, addressing the host back in the studio, 'I'm here at the Lisa Wickes murder trial. Wickes is the young medical student with the genius IQ who is accused of the murder of her former boyfriend, hospital nurse Troy Petty.

'Petty died in an explosion several months ago in his rented bungalow out near J. Percy Priest Lake. In opening arguments this morning the prosecution said they will prove that the defendant, Lisa Wickes, killed Petty in an argument over money. They stated that they will present videotaped evidence that Lisa Wickes cashed her old boyfriend's paycheck on the night that he died. The prosecution contends that Wickes knocked Petty unconscious and then used candles and a propane stove to cause an explosion.

'The defense claims that Lisa Wickes had no part in causing the explosion which killed Troy Petty. They insist that Troy Petty signed over his check to her, and Lisa Wickes cashed it because her boyfriend owed her money. What really happened to Troy Petty? That question will be up to the jury.'

As she was smoothly outlining the schedule of trial testimony, Chanel suddenly spotted a familiar vehicle. As the car turned the corner, she ordered to the cameraman to follow her because she was about to make a move. As she rounded the corner, she saw a couple getting out of the car on the other side of the street.

Chanel bolted across the street without looking, the cameraman immediately in her wake.

'Excuse me, excuse me. Mr and Mrs Wickes,' she called out, thrusting her microphone, her whole body, in fact, in the path of the couple who were trying to hurry into the side door of the courthouse. 'I'm Chanel Ali Jackson, from *Channel Six News*, Nashville. Can I talk to you for a moment?'

Hannah looked startled. Adam wore a pained expression.

Chanel was not about to let them elude her. She focused her laserlike, sympathetic gaze on Hannah. 'Mrs Wickes, you heard the opening arguments this morning. Does the prosecution have a strong case, or does it seem to you that their case against your daughter, Lisa, is purely circumstantial?'

'My daughter is innocent of this crime,' said Hannah, although the expression in her fine, gray eyes was anything but sanguine. 'This trial is going to show that.'

'We have no further comment,' said Adam stiffly.

Chanel ignored him, concentrating on the defendant's mother. 'This has got to be the hardest thing in the world, to watch your child subjected to all these terrible accusations,' she suggested.

Hannah nodded. 'It's very difficult,' she said. 'But I believe that justice will prevail.'

'How do you keep going?' Chanel asked. 'I don't know if I could do it.'

'Our granddaughter needs us,' said Hannah simply. 'We have to be strong for her.'

'How is Lisa's daughter holding up?' Chanel asked gently.

'She's a child. She doesn't understand too much about what is happening. But she misses her mother.'

Adam Wickes raised his hand, palm up. 'All right. That's enough questions.' He put a hand under his wife's elbow and began to guide her past Chanel and into the courthouse.

Hannah nodded and pressed her lips together as Adam steered her away.

Chanel turned back to the camera. 'There is a lot more of this trial still to go. We'll be here, keeping you apprised of every development. This is Chanel Ali Jackson, reporting from the courthouse in Nashville, as the prosecution in the murder trial of Lisa Wickes get ready to call their first witness.'

'God, I just hate this,' Adam said.

'I know. I feel like a sideshow attraction in the circus. Let's get in our seats,' Hannah said.

Other reporters called out to them as they made their way through the security checkpoint and into the courtroom, but Hannah held tight to Adam's hand and did not look around. They took their seats behind the empty defense table, and waited as the room filled up with court personnel, journalists and onlookers. The door to the right of the judge's bench opened, and two burly court officers came through, flanking Lisa, towering over her. Lisa's curly hair was clean and shiny and she wore it loose so that it formed a dark halo around her pale, bespectacled face. She was wearing the modest navy and white dress which Marjorie Fox had suggested Hannah buy for her, low-heeled pumps and handcuffs on her wrists and ankles. Hannah was struck anew by the sight of her daughter here in the court, dressed as if ready for Easter, and in chains. It was almost more than Hannah could stand. She let out a little cry, and Adam put his arm around her and squeezed her, as if to give her strength.

Lisa nodded at them as she was led to her seat at the defense table, and gave them a thumbs up with her shackled hands. Hannah smiled back at her hopefully. Adam nodded gravely at his daughter. Marjorie Fox, who had already arrived, stood up to greet her client. Across the aisle, the prosecution team was conferring.

'All rise,' said the bailiff.

Everyone stood as the judge entered and sat down. 'Bring the jury back in,' he instructed the bailiff. The courtroom was respectfully quiet, if a little restive, as they waited for the jury to appear. The door beside the bench finally opened again, and the twelve jurors came in and took their seats. Judge Endicott, a gray-haired, balding man with half-glasses, waited until they were all seated, welcomed them back and reminded them to listen carefully, take notes and not discuss the case until it was time to deliberate.

'Very well. Let's proceed. Mr Castor, will you call your first witness.'

The D.A. called the first officer at the grisly scene at Troy Petty's bungalow after the explosion. 'Part of the front of the house and the roof blew off. The victim's body was mangled and charred.'

'How did the explosion occur?'

'As far as we can tell, gas was escaping from the propane stove, and there were lit candles in the house. When the flame from the candles ignited the gas, it caused an explosion like a bomb going off.'

The spectators in the courtroom murmured.

'No one else was in the house at the time?'

'We did not find any other victims,' said the officer.

Marjorie rose to question the witness. 'Could someone have left the gas on accidentally so that it filled the room?'

'Sure you could,' said the officer. 'The pilot light can go out. It could happen. But the only way you wouldn't notice the smell was if you were not in the house at the time. Or unconscious. Otherwise you would have smelled it.'

Next, D.A. Castor called the coroner, Dr James Evans, to the stand. He was an old man, a no-nonsense type with wire-rimmed glasses, and a well-tailored but ancient suit. The coroner took his oath, recited his credentials and proceeded to describe, in sickening, clinical detail, the corpse of Troy Petty which he had examined.

'In your opinion,' asked the D.A., 'what was the cause of death?'

'The deceased died of injuries sustained in an explosion.'

'Were there any injuries on the body not related to the explosion?' asked the D.A.

'The victim had a head wound which he may have incurred before the explosion. He appeared to have been struck on the back of his head by a blunt object. He was, most likely, unconscious at the time of the explosion.'

'Was there a weapon found in the house?'

'Yes,' said the coroner. 'A brass desk lamp with a heavy base was found near the body. There was blood and tissue on the base, which belonged to the deceased.'

Hannah's shoulders hunched; she closed her eyes and shook her head slightly at the vivid image created by the plainspoken coroner. The testimony was damning. At the same time, it did not prove that Lisa had done anything. How could anyone think that Lisa could ever have hit a man as burly as Troy Petty with that much force? Adam gripped her chilly fingers with his own.

Castor turned to the defense table. 'Your witness.'

Marjorie Fox arose and approached the witness in the box. 'You referred to that lamp as a weapon and you said that Mr Petty was unconscious when the explosion occurred. Could he not have sustained that head wound, and been knocked unconscious by debris falling on him?'

'Possible. But unlikely. The head injury was caused by a direct blow to the skull.'

'Could the lamp have been pulled out of the socket by the force of the blast? Could it have flown up and whacked Mr Petty in the head?'

'He could have been hit by debris, but a direct hit like that would be highly unlikely.'

'But it's not impossible that his head injury was incurred during the blast.'

'Not likely. But not impossible,' Evans conceded.

'Dr Evans, what if Mr Petty had been outside, doing some nighttime fishing on his dock? What if he had walked back into the house at the moment of combustion?'

'He would have been blown back out the door,' said the coroner.

'And if he came in, smelled the gas, and approached the propane stove to turn it off? Would his body have remained in the house during the blast?'

'It might have,' the coroner conceded.

'Did you do a toxicology test on Mr Petty's remains?' Marjorie asked.

The coroner nodded. 'I did.'

Marjorie looked at him innocently. 'Did you find any traces of alcohol in his system?'

The coroner nodded. 'Yes, I did find traces.'

'Enough to determine if he was intoxicated?'

'I determined that his blood alcohol was at the legal limit.'

Marjorie pounced. 'In fact, could intoxication have accounted for Mr Petty's inability to recognize the danger he was in as the gas filled the house?'

'It might have slowed his reaction time. However . . .'

'No further questions,' said Marjorie.

'Objection,' said the D.A. 'The witness should be allowed to answer.'

'Sustained. Finish your answer,' said the judge.

'The victim would have had to be unconscious not to notice the smell.'

'Or just severely inebriated,' said Marjorie tartly.

'The defense attorney is testifying,' the D.A. objected.

'Withdrawn,' said Marjorie politely. 'No further questions.'

ELEVEN

The coroner's testimony and Marjorie's cross-examination were the last exchanges of the day. Hannah and Adam left the courtroom feeling slightly hopeful. It seemed as if Marjorie had turned the prosecution's witness, the coroner, against the people's case, because of the opportunity his testimony gave the jury to see other possibilities for Troy's death. 'Reasonable doubt,' said Adam into the darkness, as he held Hannah in his arms that night. His words soothed her, and she fell asleep more easily than she had in weeks.

They were the first spectators to arrive in the courtroom the next morning. But they were not there before Marjorie Fox and Lisa, who were already seated at the defense table. Marjorie was making notes on papers and frowning. Lisa saw her parents and her eyes lit up behind her glasses. Hannah and Adam slipped into the two chairs directly behind her. Hannah ran her index finger gently down the side of Lisa's face. Lisa smiled at her.

'How are you holding up?' Hannah asked.

Lisa shrugged. 'Not too bad. I read. I try not to listen to the other prisoners, who are howling most of the time. I tell myself that it's almost over.'

'Let's hope so,' said Adam.

'I thought we did really well yesterday,' Lisa enthused. 'The coroner seemed to waffle.'

'Yes,' said Hannah. 'By the way, Sydney sends kisses.'

Lisa nodded and then frowned as Marjorie leaned over and told her to turn around. Lisa did so just as the 'all rise' was announced, and the judge entered the courtroom. Although she did not turn back around to look at her parents, Lisa lifted two crisscrossed fingers to show them. It was a symbol, Hannah realized uneasily, which could have two very different meanings. One indicated 'Hoping with all my might'. The other meant, 'I am not telling the truth.'

The first witness of the day whom the prosecutor called to the stand was a middle-aged woman who lived on the same dirt road as Troy Petty. Vera Naughton had hair like a haystack from being bleached mercilessly and she held it off her face with a black elastic headband. She was clearly in her fifties, was overweight and wore a wildly patterned turquoise and black stretchy top, black stretch pants and black patent-leather thonged sandals.

She took the stand in an almost dainty manner and when asked where she lived by the D.A., she launched into the story of her life which had led her to that house near J. Percy Priest Lake.

'My husband, Beaufort, bought that land so we could build out there and he could go out in his boat whenever he wanted to. Of course, he was an air-traffic controller at the Nashville Airport but he got asthma and then he hurt his back and he had to take early retirement which meant . . .'

'Mrs Naughton,' the D.A. interrupted. 'Just tell us, briefly, where you live in relation to the house Troy Petty was renting.'

Like a chastened but obedient schoolgirl, Vera pointed at the map which stood on display next to the other prosecution exhibits. 'I live right there. Two doors away.'

'Right where?' asked the D.A. 'Can you point your home out to the jury?'

Vera frowned and craned her neck. Then she started to rise from the witness box. 'May I?' she asked coyly.

The D.A. nodded, and Vera descended from the box and approached the map which sat on an easel. She leaned forward, and squinted at it.

'It's little bitty on this map,' she said, but then she placed a pudgy index finger on a spot over which it had been hovering. 'Right there.'

The D.A. gallantly swept an arm toward the witness box and Vera resumed her seat, wiggling herself into a comfortable position.

'Now on the night in question, the eighth of March, did you hear the explosion at that house?'

'Oh my, yes,' said Vera. 'You couldn't miss it. It shook my whole house. I ran down there. The front of Mr Petty's house was blown apart. The rest of it was on fire. I called nine-one-one.'

'Did you see anyone else in the vicinity?'

'No, I did not,' said Vera. 'But I saw her leaving just before I heard the blast.'

'Who did you see?' asked the D.A.

'I saw the defendant. I was putting the cover on my cockatiel's cage and I glanced out the window and saw her. She was driving fast away from his house.'

'And you're sure it was the defendant?'

'It was her. I know her car, and I recognize her. She's been down our road many times before.'

Hannah sighed with anxiety as Marjorie rose, pulled down on the peplum of her suit jacket and smiled at the witness. She walked toward the witness box.

'So, Mrs Naughton, did you see any other cars on your road that night?'

'No.'

'Do you normally sit and look out the window all evening?'

'No, of course not,' she scoffed.

'So any number of cars could have come and gone, and you just didn't see them.'

'It's possible, I suppose,' Vera admitted. 'I just know that I saw her. I'd seen her come to visit Troy. Sometimes with her little girl.'

'Now, the explosion occurred at eight o'clock, according to the police reports. At what time did you see Lisa go by in her car?'

'It must have been about seven,' said Vera. 'But I could see her clearly. It wasn't dark yet. In the spring it's still light at that hour.'

'Well, actually,' said Marjorie, 'on the eighth of March it *was* dark at seven. Daylight Savings didn't begin until the tenth of March.'

Vera looked chastened. 'I'm pretty sure . . .'

'So it must have been closer to six o'clock,' said Marjorie. 'A full two hours before the explosion.'

Vera frowned. 'Well, maybe. I'm sure it was still light,' she admitted sheepishly. 'Otherwise I wouldn't have been covering the bird's cage. They need darkness to sleep.'

'No further questions,' said Marjorie.

Hannah and Adam glanced at one another and Hannah nodded slightly. Marjorie Fox had made the woman sound as if she had not really thought about the time until she was on the stand.

'This case is falling apart,' said Adam in her ear.

'God, I hope so,' Hannah whispered.

The next witness, Dr Joan Ferris, was from the forensics team who examined the crime scene. The pretty, young explosives expert wore a dark suit and her hair in a no-nonsense knot which bespoke confidence and seriousness. She testified that the explosion occurred because someone had turned on the gas in an old-fashioned propane heater, and had failed to light the heater. There were illuminated candles in the room and, when the room filled up with gas, it was ignited by the candles. The heater was recovered, the knob still turned to the 'on' position.

'Could this heater have been turned on by accident?' the D.A. asked.

'No, that wouldn't be possible,' said Dr Ferris.

When Marjorie had a chance to cross-examine, she asked the forensics expert if there were fingerprints on the on/off knob.

'Impossible to lift after the explosion and all the water damage in the house from the fire being extinguished,' said Dr Ferris.

'Now, Dr Ferris, you testified that this heater could not have been turned on by accident.'

'That's correct,' said the young scientist. 'You have to push down on the knob and turn it.'

'But it would be possible for someone to turn on that gas and then become distracted, and fail to light it, letting the gas escape from the heater unnoticed.'

'Certainly it would be possible,' said the forensics expert equably. 'That's the main reason why more up-to-date propane heaters light automatically. To prevent that from happening.'

Marjorie thanked her for her time and returned to the defense table.

Hannah and Adam knew that the forensics expert had done them no harm. In fact, she seemed to be quite open to an accident scenario.

The succeeding testimony, however, was an undeniable blow.

A detective from the Nashville police showed the surveillance tape which had been made on the night of the explosion at a convenience store near the hospital. There, quite clearly, was Lisa, handing across a check and, after a brief discussion in the course of which she produced a card and showed it to the clerk, receiving cash in return.

'How did you come to be in possession of this tape?' asked the D.A.

Detective Hammond said that the clerk, who was also the owner of the store, a Mr Bahir Zamani, heard about Troy Petty's disappearance on the news and came forward with the tape.

Mr Zamani was called as the next witness.

'Mr Zamani,' asked Castor, 'is it your policy to cash the paychecks of employees at the hospital?'

'We sometimes do that, if we know the person,' replied the brown-skinned, mustachioed witness calmly.

'Did you know Troy Petty?' asked the D.A.

'Yes, I did. He had come into my store for several years.'

'So, on the evening of the eighth of March, when the defendant appeared asking to cash Mr Petty's paycheck, didn't you find that a bit unusual? Clearly she is not Troy Petty.'

Zamani nodded. 'She told me that she was Mr Petty's fiancée and that he had asked her to bring it in. Indeed, I had seen her in the store with him from time to time. And the check was signed by Mr Petty.'

'Did you recognize his signature?'

Zamani squirmed on the stand. 'Well, I assumed. I don't memorize the signatures of all my customers.'

'So, a young woman brings in someone else's signed paycheck and you don't even check to be sure that the endorsement is valid?'

Mr Zamani smiled sheepishly. 'I should have checked. I admit that. But I allowed myself to be careless because I did recognize her. She is a very attractive woman.'

Hannah glanced at her plain-featured, bespectacled daughter, and, realizing how meaningless it was, still felt pleased for her. To be described as very attractive.

'If you don't mind my saying so, that's not a very professional way to do business, Mr Zamani,' said D.A. Castor.

Zamani looked down at his hands. 'I am aware of that, sir, and I am exceedingly sorry.'

'Detective Hammond testified that you brought this tape to the attention of the police.'

Zamani nodded enthusiastically. 'When I saw the news reports about the explosion at Mr Petty's house, I decided to bring the tape to them. I was concerned that it might be significant.'

'Thank you, Mr Zamani. Your witness.'

Marjorie approached the baleful-looking shopkeeper with eyes flashing. 'Was this tape made by a hidden camera, Mr Zamani?'

The shopkeeper shook his head. 'No, there's a sign in my store which states quite clearly that there is a surveillance camera at work. You can see the screens above the counter.'

'So, if Lisa were trying to do something wrong or illegal, it wouldn't make sense to go, undisguised, to a place where she was known, and allow the transaction to be filmed.'

'I wouldn't think so. No,' said Mr Zamani. 'That was my very thought when I cashed the check.'

'No further questions,' said Marjorie.

Mr Zamani got up from the witness box and walked back past the defense table. For a moment he glanced over at Lisa, almost apologetically, but Lisa looked away, as if she had no further use for such a man. Zamani sighed and lowered his head, as if he were the one accused.

Hannah felt exhausted when she returned home. She wished she could just lie down in a dark room and sleep, but there was still Sydney to care for.

As she and Adam got out of the car and freed Sydney from the car seat, Rayanne came over and greeted them.

Hannah set Sydney down in the grass and turned to her friend. 'How is Chet doing?'

'Scheduled for surgery the day after tomorrow,' said Rayanne. 'Jamie's flying in tonight.'

'It will help Chet to have him here,' said Adam.

'I know,' said Rayanne. 'And his new girlfriend is coming with him.'

'Oh, nice,' said Hannah. 'This must be serious.'

Rayanne nodded. 'I think maybe it is.'

'Good. You'll have lots of support. I wish I could do more . . .'

'Don't be silly,' said Rayanne. 'You have your hands full. How's it going? I saw a little bit on the news but they don't really tell you anything.'

'I don't know,' said Hannah. 'I'm afraid to be too hopeful. But the more it goes on, the more the case against Lisa seems flimsy.'

'Soon we'll all be celebrating,' said Rayanne encouragingly.

The two women nodded and clasped hands, each one wondering if the other would, indeed, have something to celebrate.

TWELVE

The first witness the next day was one who, Hannah thought, was bound to make problems for Lisa. Hannah knew without even hearing the testimony what was about to occur. This witness was going to present a painfully personal and admirable version of Troy Petty. Hannah dreaded to hear whatever else she might have to say.

'Call Nadine Melton to the stand, please.'

A pretty, fresh-scrubbed young woman with a soft blonde haircut came up and took the oath.

'What is your relationship to the deceased, Ms Melton?'

The young woman choked back a sob and apologized. 'Troy was my older brother.'

'Did you have a close relationship with your brother?'

'We were very close. He raised me and my younger brother, Ronnie, after our mother died. I spoke to him every week. He often came and stayed with us.

'Troy was like a parent to me. He was very responsible when it came to me and Ronnie. We were his family and he treated us like his own children.'

'Would you say that your brother was a careless person? A person who, for example, might not notice a house filling up with gas?'

Hannah was a little surprised by the vagueness of the question, and the fact that Marjorie did not object to it. She whispered this to Adam. 'The sister is very sympathetic. Probably doesn't want to harass her.'

Nadine was already shaking her head. 'Not at all. My brother was very conscientious. He was a nurse. He kept everything in order. He paid attention to details.'

'So, did it surprise you to learn that he had left candles burning in a house that was filling up with gas?'

'He wouldn't do that,' said Nadine bluntly.

'Do you know the defendant, Ms Melton?'

Nadine shook her head.

The judge leaned over and counseled her. 'You need to speak your answers aloud.'

'Sorry,' she whispered.

'Do you?' the D.A. repeated. 'Know the defendant?'

'I never met her. Troy told me about her. He could hardly believe that a smart girl like that, who was going to be a doctor, would be interested in him at all. Never mind pursue him, which she did do. That was typical of him. He never gave himself enough credit.'

'So, he was happy in the relationship.'

Nadine squirmed. 'At first. He couldn't stop bragging about her. And he loved her little girl. He always had a way with children. All people, really. I mean, he was a nurse. He was kind.'

'At first. And then what changed?' asked the D.A.

'He didn't say too much but I could tell he was unhappy. I asked him why but he wouldn't say. In fact, he said that he couldn't tell me. His exact words were, "I can't tell you."'

'Were you surprised when you learned that the defendant had cashed your brother's paycheck the night of the explosion?'

Nadine's eyes turned steely. 'That's an understatement.'

'The defense claims that your brother gave her his paycheck to cash because he owed her money. Did that sound right to you? Was Troy ordinarily careless about money?'

'No. Never. He was very careful.'

'Did he have a lot of debts?'

'No. No debts. He paid his rent on time. His truck was paid for. He never went shopping for himself. He had no fancy tastes. He didn't gamble. No.'

'Did he ever ask to borrow money from you?'

Nadine snorted. 'From me? Never. He deprived himself 'cause he liked to help out me and my brother. I told you. He was like a parent to us.'

'Thank you, Ms Melton. Your witness.'

Hannah watched as Marjorie rifled through her papers for a few seconds and then stood up. She walked over to the witness box and leaned against it in a friendly manner.

'Ms Melton. How old were you and your brothers when your mother died?'

'I was five. Ronnie was three. Troy was twelve.'

'Obviously your brother wasn't old enough to take care of you at that point.'

'No. We went to live with our father, who didn't want us, and then our grandparents. And finally, Troy was old enough, he just took over. He became our parent.'

'That was a big responsibility for a young man.'

'Yes, it was.'

'So, clearly this is a great loss for you,' said Marjorie.

Nadine nodded. 'Yes. A great loss.'

'You seemed to have turned out very well after so much upheaval in your childhood.'

Nadine lifted her chin. 'I like to think so.'

'And your younger brother?'

'What about him?'

Marjorie glanced around the courtroom. 'I don't see him here,' she said mildly.

'He couldn't come. Ronnie was . . . he had to go to a home for a while.'

'What kind of a home? You mean a foster home?'

'No. A halfway house,' Nadine mumbled.

Marjorie regarded her with raised eyebrows. 'Why a halfway house?'

'He has . . . problems.'

'With?'

'Prescription drugs. He has a bit of a problem with self-medicating. His life was the worst of the three of us. As the youngest.'

'I'm sure that's true,' said Marjorie sympathetically. 'So your brother Ronnie was recently released from a drug rehab, was he not?'

Nadine shrugged.

'Ms Melton, could you answer?'

'Yes.'

'What about now? Is he clean now?'

'Objection, your honor. Relevance?' demanded the D.A.

Marjorie looked at Judge Endicott. 'The witness has testified that her older brother liked to help out his younger siblings. I submit that helping someone support a drug habit can be very expensive. It might account for his borrowing money from the defendant.'

'Overruled,' said the judge. 'Witness will answer.'

Nadine lowered her head. 'He's . . . trying to stay straight. It's not easy.'

'Did Ronnie ever get into debt with any drug dealers? Any debt that perhaps he couldn't repay? Any debt where he might have turned to his brother, Troy, for help? When you learned that Troy was missing, didn't you accuse your younger brother of just that?'

'I don't remember,' Nadine demurred.

'Do you know a drug and alcohol counselor from the Sunrise Halfway House named William Trumbull?'

Nadine shifted uneasily in her chair. 'Yes. What about him?'

Marjorie turned to the bench. 'Your honor, I wish to read into evidence a part of this deposition from Mr William Trumbull, defense exhibit 5-B. The witness cannot appear in person because he is now working at a halfway house in Talkeetna, Alaska.'

'So noted,' said the judge.

The prosecutor jumped up and insisted on having a look. After perusing the paperwork, he resumed his seat.

Marjorie turned back to Nadine. 'Ms Melton, in his deposition, Mr Trumbull testifies that you and your brother Ronnie argued about this very subject. Mr Trumbull asserts that he heard you suggest to Ronnie that it might have been his, and I quote, "lowlife druggie friends" who had harmed your brother Troy in some way?'

Hannah gripped her husband's arm. 'How does Marjorie know that?' she whispered.

Adam shook his head. 'She's got investigators. She's good.'

Nadine blanched and looked incredulous, as if she too was wondering how Marjorie Fox knew this piece of information. 'That was a private conversation,' she insisted.

'So you did say that to your brother Ronnie?'

'That was before I knew about Lisa forging his name and cashing his check,' Nadine protested stubbornly.

'You did say that.'

'Yes,' Nadine admitted.

'No further questions,' said Marjorie, returning to the defense table.

Hannah grabbed Adam's forearm. 'That's it,' she said. 'If it wasn't an accident, then that's what happened. I'll bet you anything.'
Adam nodded. 'It has to be.'

When they got home that night they felt almost happy, for the first time in what seemed like ages. The D.A. had called several witnesses whose testimony did nothing to change the impact of Nadine's admission about her brother's drug use. The possibility that Troy had, indeed, had to deal with dangerous drug dealers on his brother's behalf was the reasonable doubt that they had been seeking to show all along. It certainly explained why Troy might have borrowed money from Lisa, and why he might have owed her his entire paycheck.

That evening, as they settled into the safety of home, Adam drank a beer while Sydney played beside him, and Hannah made dinner. They talked about the day's testimony, each one reminding the other of how a hostile witness, Troy's sister, had inadvertently given evidence which was helpful to Lisa.

When they sat down to eat, they had a glass of wine and toasted Marjorie Fox. 'Whatever this costs,' says Hannah, 'she will be worth it. She is terrific. I mean, she has seen right through this thing. She knows that Lisa is innocent, and she can prove it.'

'Don't say innocent,' Adam insisted. 'I wish she had never taken that check . . .'

'You heard the sister. The younger brother was in trouble. Everything that Marjorie brought out today made perfect sense. Troy must have needed the money, and Lisa lent it to him. Even though she couldn't afford it. You know how impulsive she can be.'

'I know,' he said.

'I know,' Sydney crowed, poking her forefinger into her mound of mashed potatoes.

'You are making quite a mess,' said Hannah cheerfully.

'Wait till she gets to the chocolate pudding,' said Adam.

'Pudding!' Sydney exclaimed, waving her spoon in the air.

After Hannah got up to fetch the pudding, and Adam wiped Sydney's chin, they resumed their conversation where they left off. 'It's the only explanation that makes sense,' said Hannah. 'Maybe Troy was worried about his brother that night, and had too much to drink. He must have gotten a little high and fell asleep, and didn't realize what was happening with the gas . . .'

'It makes perfect sense. No jury could convict her after today,' said Adam confidently.

'No,' said Hannah, as if she were sure. 'They couldn't, could they?'

'All gone,' cried Sydney, whose lips were surrounded by a ring of chocolate.

Adam lifted Sydney from her booster seat. 'I think this little lady needs a bath, don't you?'

'I do,' said Hannah, smiling. 'I'll clean up the dishes.'

Adam carried his giggling granddaughter to the bathroom, while Hannah carried the dishes to the sink. Out of the kitchen window she could see a light on at Chet and Rayanne's next door. But the cars were gone. She assumed that Jamie had made it home from Portland, though she had not yet set eyes on him. Chet's surgery was to take place in the morning. They were probably at the hospital, spending those last anxious hours with him.

Please, God, she thought. Be good to Chet and Rayanne too. The way you were to us today.

Then she plunged her hands into the foamy dishwater and began to scrub the pots, almost tempted to whistle. Lisa would be home soon. Justice would be done. She sighed, and closed her eyes for a moment, enjoying the relief she hadn't felt in ages. From the bathroom, she could hear Adam making motorboat sounds and Sydney in the tub, squealing with delight.

THIRTEEN

'I hate going to the hospital,' Adam said the next morning as they drove in the direction of Vanderbilt. 'Even to visit.'

'I know, but we have to,' said Hannah. 'There's a parking spot.'

Adam pulled the car into the spot. 'I know we do. I'm just being grumpy. I want to support Rayanne. I'm sure she is at her wits' end.'

'Thank goodness she has Jamie with her. I hope Chet will be all right.'

Adam parked near the visitors' entrance and they went inside and rode the elevator up to the fourth floor. Rayanne had told Hannah that they were waiting for news, in a lounge down the hall from Chet's regular room. Hannah glanced at the clock above the nurses' station as they got off at the fourth floor. Chet's surgery had been due to start at seven. It was now nine. That meant that it should be half over. They walked down to the lounge and looked into the open door.

Rayanne was sitting with two other people in a corner of the lounge. She looked up and saw them, and her sad eyes lit up. Hannah hurried over to her friend and enveloped her in a hug.

'Thank you for coming,' said Rayanne. 'I know you have so much on your own plate. But it helps to see you here.'

'Court doesn't start till ten today. We wanted to stop in before we went. Any news?' asked Hannah.

Rayanne shook her head. 'A nurse came out and told us that there were some delays but not to worry.'

'Right,' said Hannah. 'I'm sure you're not worrying a bit.'

The young man sitting opposite Rayanne stood up and extended a hand to Adam. 'Hey, Mr Wickes.'

Adam brushed the proffered hand aside and gave the young man a bear hug.

'Jamie! Good to see you.'

Jamie turned to Hannah with a big smile. She could hardly believe it was the same scrawny kid who used to play with Lisa. He had filled out and grown a few inches. Hannah embraced him too. 'Hi, Jamie. How are you doing?'

Jamie shrugged. 'Hanging in there. This is my girlfriend, Greta,' he said proudly. Hannah shook hands with the fresh-faced blonde girl beside him. Greta beamed back. She had perfect teeth and a ring in one nostril.

'It's good you both could be here for this,' said Hannah.

'Oh, of course we're here. Wouldn't let my mom go through this alone.'

Hannah smiled at the newly confident young man. You never know, when kids are little, she thought, which ones are going to emerge as winners. Jamie had always seemed the most unlikely of successes, but clearly he had become someone with lots of possibilities, and had a girlfriend who, judging from her admiring gaze, saw him as a catch. 'You always were a good kid.'

Jamie blushed but did not object. Rayanne grabbed his hand. 'I don't know what I would have done without him. And we're so grateful to Lisa, of course. I swear she saved Chet's life when he collapsed.'

'Yeah, Mom told me about that,' said Jamie. 'Thank God she was there.'

'Thanks. I'll tell her you said that,' said Hannah, beaming. It was wonderful to hear praise heaped on Lisa. Not exactly what she had been experiencing the last few days. 'Your mom's been bragging about your new job,' she said. 'Sounds like you've landed a really great position.'

'I've been lucky,' he said modestly.

'You like it out there in the north-west?'

'It's God's country,' Jamie said firmly. 'We love it.'

'Well, we'd rather have seen you under different circumstances,' said Adam, 'but all the same it's good to set eyes on you again.'

'Same here,' said Jamie.

'I wish we could stay longer but we have to go to court.'

'I understand,' said Rayanne. 'Nothing could be more important than that.'

Hannah turned to Jamie. 'I'm sure you've heard about the trial.'

Jamie looked uneasy. 'I did. I couldn't believe it.' He turned to Greta. 'These are our next-door neighbors that I told you about.'

Greta nodded solemnly.

'The prosecution is due to wrap up this morning. Lisa's lawyer is very good. So far, she has really poked holes into their case. As far as I can see, their case is circumstantial, but circumstantial or not, the whole thing is a nightmare,' said Adam frankly. 'We're just hoping it will soon be over and we can get Lisa home.'

'Her lawyer said that Lisa will take the stand today, to testify,' said Hannah.

'Lawyers don't usually let a defendant do that unless they're sure you're innocent,' Greta piped up.

'Greta's in her first year of law school,' Jamie explained proudly.

Hannah nodded, not mentioning what Marjorie had told them – that she had advised Lisa against testifying. 'You saw what happened at the bail hearing,' Marjorie said. 'She's a loose cannon.' But Lisa had insisted on her right to defend herself and would not be dissuaded. Marjorie told them that she planned to prep Lisa extensively for her testimony and keep her on a short leash.

'Tell her I was asking for her,' said Jamie.

'I will,' said Adam.

'Um, can I get you guys some coffee from the cafeteria?'

'Oh, you don't have to do that,' said Hannah.

'These two might want to stretch their legs,' said Adam, realizing before Hannah did that Jamie and his girlfriend might want to escape from the gloomy waiting room for a little while, now that someone was there to sit with Rayanne for a little bit. 'Bring me back a small coffee, regular.'

Hannah shook her head. 'Nothing for me. Thanks, dear.'

'No problem,' said Jamie. He and Greta headed for the door, arms around one another's waist, as if they had been longing for the opportunity to entwine themselves again. Young love, Hannah thought with an indulgent sigh.

'She's a very nice girl,' said Rayanne.

'I can see that,' said Hannah, as Adam sat down and glanced at the baseball game on TV. 'He deserves a nice girl.'

The morning session in court was brief. The prosecution presented an expert on combustion, who asserted that the gas valve could have been left open up to two hours, given the lack of airtightness in Troy's rented fishing camp, and the gas would still have exploded when it came in contact with the candle flames. That meant that even if their eyewitness had been an hour off in the time she saw Lisa drive by, Lisa could still have been the one responsible.

They also presented a video deposition from Claude Dupree, one of Troy's old buddies from nursing school, who lived and worked at a hospital in Hawaii. Claude said that on the night in question, before Lisa arrived, they Skyped and Troy told him that he was planning to break up with her. 'I asked him why,' said Claude. 'I thought he really liked her. Troy told me that this woman, Lisa, was bad for him, and he couldn't continue with it. "She's on her way over," Troy said. "I'm going to put an end to it."' With the deposition of this last witness the prosecution rested.

The judge announced that there would be a break for lunch, after which the defense could call its first witness. Jurors were cautioned not to discuss the case, and everyone left the courtroom.

Hannah and Adam went outside to get some air. They sat on a bench in a park across from the courthouse. 'What did you think about that last witness?' Hannah asked.

Adam shrugged. 'It's just talk,' he insisted. 'It doesn't necessarily mean anything. Two guys bullshitting.'

Hannah nodded thoughtfully, worried.

As they returned for the afternoon session, Hannah heard someone calling her name. This was nothing unusual in the vicinity of the courthouse, and normally she did not acknowledge it or turn around. Almost always, it was someone from the press. But this time she heard a familiar note in the voice and turned to look. Jackie Fleischer was crossing the street, and motioned for Hannah to wait. Hannah waved back and stood in place.

'What are you doing here?' Hannah asked.

'I wanted to come to court this afternoon. Just to offer some moral support,' said the psychologist.

Hannah was touched. 'I really appreciate that. Thank you.'

'I was hoping you wouldn't think I was intruding.'

'Intruding? Are you kidding? How would it be possible to intrude on us? Every moment of our lives is reported on television. I'm just glad to see a friendly face. The defense begins its case this afternoon.'

'Yes, I heard that on the car radio,' said Jackie. 'It sounds like the prosecution's case is pretty feeble.'

'Let's hope the jury thinks so. Come along. You can sit with us,' said Hannah.

Jackie nodded as she joined Hannah and Adam, who began to edge forward, making slow progress through the courthouse doors.

After Judge Endicott reminded the jury of their responsibility not to make up their minds before all the testimony was in, the defense was asked to call its first witness.

'The defense calls Lisa Wickes to take the stand, please,' said Marjorie.

Lisa stood up and walked purposefully to the witness stand. She was wearing a dark suit with a skirt, and her hair was pulled back from her face with a headband. She looked even younger than her twenty-one years, serious and studious. She took the stand and promised gravely to tell the truth.

'She looks so young,' said Jackie. 'Just a kid.'

'She is just a kid. But this is aging her by the day, I think,' said Hannah. 'Her and her parents.

'Oh, here we go,' said Jackie seriously, as Marjorie Fox was given the nod by the judge.

'Lisa,' Marjorie began in a casual tone, 'tell this court how and when you met the deceased, Troy Petty.'

'We met last October. I'm a second-year student at the medical school at Vanderbilt, and Troy was an LPN at the Vanderbilt Hospital. I'm often at the hospital for my studies, and one day we kind of saw one another and we were both . . . interested. He's – he was – a good-looking guy. I don't usually attract guys like Troy,' she said with a little self-deprecating smile.

Seated halfway back in the courtroom, Troy's sister, Nadine, shook her head in disgust, but there was a little titter of indulgent laughter from the other spectators.

'And how would you characterize your relationship with Mr Petty?'

'Well, we were certainly close. We saw each other, exclusively, for several months.'

'We heard testimony that you sometimes brought your two-year-old daughter with you when you went to Mr Petty's fishing camp by J. Percy Priest Lake. Were you concerned that your daughter might form an attachment to Mr Petty which was not warranted by a casual relationship?'

Lisa shook her head. 'No. I was not worried. Not at that time. Not about that. She liked going out there. It was pretty out by the lake, and Troy was good to her.'

'Almost like he was auditioning as a stepdad,' Marjorie offered.

'Objection,' said the D.A. wearily. 'Calls for speculation.'

'Sustained.'

'Withdrawn. We heard testimony from Claude Dupree's deposition that Troy Petty was planning on breaking up with you on the evening of the explosion. Did you know this when you went to Mr Petty's house on that evening?'

'We had already discussed it on the phone,' said Lisa, and there was a little gasp of surprise in the court.

'So, you knew about this?' Marjorie asked.

'Yes, I knew,' said Lisa.

'Were you upset about this development?'

Lisa shook her head. 'No. In fact, I was the one who insisted on it. I think he just said that it was his idea to his Skyping buddy to save face.'

'If you were so determined to break up with him, why didn't you just do it on the phone?'

'He owed me money, and I went out there because I wanted it back.'

'He had borrowed money from you.'

'Yes.'

'Do you know why he needed it?'

'He said it was important, so I lent it to him. I didn't press him for the reason.'

'Were you in the habit of lending money to friends?'

'No. But I believed him when he said that he needed it.'

'So, this meeting at his home was your idea?' asked Marjorie.

'Yes. But I think he had hopes of making me change my mind. He had already opened a bottle of wine and started drinking. He had every candle in the place lit. Looked more like he was anticipating a seduction than a break-up.'

'Would you say he was drunk when you were there?'

'No . . .' said Lisa slowly. 'At that time he'd only had a glass or two. I don't know how much he drank after I left.'

'Were you tempted, in the course of your conversation, to change your mind about breaking up with Mr Petty?'

'No,' said Lisa firmly. 'Never. There was never any chance of our . . . resolving things.'

'So at this last meeting between you, he willingly gave you his paycheck? Is that correct?'

'Not willingly. But he knew that he owed me money. He threw the check at me and told me to get out. So I took it and I left.'

'Did you turn on the gas line to the propane heater before you left Troy Petty's house?'

'No. I did not.' Lisa shook her head emphatically.

'Were you, in fact, angry, and eager to get revenge on Mr Petty for breaking up with you?'

'No. I told you. I broke it off with him. I just wanted to get away from him.'

'Thank you,' said Marjorie. She turned to the D.A. 'Your witness.'

The D.A. almost seemed pleased, as if Marjorie had given him a gift. He walked up to the witness box, a look of consternation on his face. 'Ms Wickes, we seem to have a case here of "He said, she said". You watched Mr Dupree's deposition, where he said that Mr Petty was planning to break up with you. Now, when Mr Petty is not here to dispute your version, you make it sound as if it were all your idea.'

'It was my idea,' said Lisa coolly. The expression in her gray eyes was impassive.

'Ms Wickes, as I understand it, you are a single mother who lives with your daughter at your parents' house. Weren't you, in fact, hoping to make Mr Petty the stepfather of your child? Weren't you hoping to be moving out of your parents' home and in with Mr Petty?'

'No,' said Lisa.

'I submit that you were hoping exactly that. Why else would you bring your child along on dates?'

'I wanted to spend my free time with her. And Mr Petty lived right by a lake. It was pretty there. He showed her how to fish.'

D.A. Castor pursued it. 'An unwed mother, still in school, saddled with a mountain of debt. Living at home with her parents. Finding a man willing to take that burden on must have seemed almost impossible.'

'Well, if you put it that way,' said Lisa coolly, 'perhaps I'm not that great a catch, so to speak.'

The spectators tittered, relieved to have a light moment in the testimony.

'They say that "hell hath no fury like a woman scorned",' said D.A. Castor. 'Didn't you, in fact, feel completely betrayed by Mr Petty when he broke off your relationship? Didn't you pick up something heavy – the brass desk lamp perhaps – and whack him over the head with it? Didn't you turn on the gas and leave with his paycheck? All to get back at him for dumping you?'

'No, I did not,' said Lisa. 'I wanted to get away from him. He was dangerous.'

'I see. Now that he can't speak for himself, you are claiming that Troy Petty struck you? Did you ever call the police, seek treatment for your injuries?'

'I didn't have injuries. He didn't strike me. But he *was* dangerous. He had certain . . . proclivities that I didn't know about . . . that were disgusting.'

'Sexual proclivities?'

'That's right,' said Lisa.

The D.A. rolled his eyes. 'Come, come, Ms Wickes. You're a medical student. I'm assuming you're not naive. Surely you could have simply said no.'

Lisa lowered her head and took a deep breath. 'He didn't ask me.'

D.A. Castor raised his eyebrows. On the one hand, the D.A. was clearly excited that Lisa seemed to have revealed a motive, beyond greed, for her alleged actions. On the other hand, he wasn't exactly sure what was developing here. He hesitated, clearly considering the possibility of no more questions. And then he changed his mind and decided to go for it. 'He didn't ask you? Are you saying he forced himself on you? Is that why you decided to kill the man?'

Lisa looked him in the eye but her voice was calm. 'I didn't kill him. But if I had, no one would have blamed me. I caught him behaving indecently with my two-year-old daughter.'

FOURTEEN

'**Y**ou lying bitch!' Nadine Melton cried out from her seat in the courtroom.

Lisa looked at her blankly as the courtroom erupted around them. Hannah felt woozy. She looked at Adam, who was equally stunned. They could not believe what they had heard. Suddenly it all made sense. Now Hannah understood why Lisa had not seemed very upset when she learned of Troy's death. Cashing his paycheck almost seemed frivolous, compared to this hideous allegation. She herself felt a sudden, murderous fury at Troy Petty.

'Order in the court,' the judge shouted, slamming down his gavel.

Nadine would not be silenced. 'You horrible monster! How dare you say such a thing about my brother? He was a saint. He would never, never . . .'

'Bailiff,' the judge instructed angrily, 'have that woman removed.'

The bailiff lumbered over to Nadine and virtually lifted her, flailing her arms and protesting, from her seat. He had to half-push, half-drag her from the courtroom.

'Wow,' said Jackie, still gripping Hannah's hand. 'She never told you or Adam about that?'

'Adam would have killed that young man with his bare hands,' Hannah said. Suddenly, a terrible thought crossed her mind. She turned to Adam. 'She never . . . You didn't know?'

'Are you kidding?' he said. 'I would have broken his neck.'

His unfeigned fury was all the reassurance she needed.

The D.A. hurriedly tried to turn this unsavory image of the victim to his advantage by going on the attack.

When the courtroom simmered down, the D.A. took a deep breath and approached the witness stand again. Lisa regarded him coolly.

'Ms Wickes, are you claiming that Mr Petty raped your daughter?'

'No. I'm saying that he was undressed, and behaving in an indecent manner around her. I think he was preparing to actually assault her.'

'So your story,' he said scornfully, 'is that nothing actually happened. Because if he'd actually assaulted your daughter, there would be forensic evidence of that assault. Conveniently, there is no evidence to be found, is there? Because it never happened.'

'No, it didn't happen,' said Lisa. 'I made sure of that.'

'By killing him?' asked Castor.

'No, by getting myself and my daughter away from him,' said Lisa calmly.

'Aren't you, in fact, attacking the character of the deceased in an effort to excuse your own actions? You can say anything you want about Mr Petty, now that he cannot defend himself. Didn't you just fabricate this alleged indecent behavior to try to draw attention away from your own crimes?'

'No,' said Lisa calmly. 'That's what he intended. He intended to harm my daughter. Naturally, I was not going to see him ever again. I just wanted to get my money back first.'

The D.A. walked slowly to the prosecution's table, his eyes narrowed, as if he were lost in thought.

'Mr Castor?' asked the judge.

The D.A. turned back to stare at Lisa. 'If this outlandish charge of yours is true, wouldn't that, in fact, give you even more reason to want to kill him? I mean, what parent wouldn't be outraged? Was that what made you so angry that you knocked him out and then turned on the gas, causing the explosion which resulted in his death? After, that is, you made sure to take his paycheck and forged his signature.'

Lisa sat up straight in the box, silent and aggrieved. 'No,' she said. 'I didn't kill him. It's not up to me to rid the world of sexual perverts. I just had to protect my daughter from this one pedophile.'

The D.A. was red in the face. 'Tell the truth, Ms Wickes. Isn't this just a desperate effort on your part to smear an innocent man who cannot defend himself?'

'It's the truth, whether you like it or not.'

Castor looked disgusted. 'I have no further questions of this witness,' he said in a sarcastic tone.

As soon as Lisa was excused, Marjorie called a man named Carl Halloran to the stand.

Carl Halloran, fit-looking, middle-aged and wearing a polo shirt, took the oath and sat down.

'Mr Halloran,' said Marjorie, 'could you tell us what you do for a living, please?'

'Yes, ma'am. I own the Sunflower Acres sleepaway camp out on Rider Lake.'

'Tell us a little bit about your camp.'

'Well, it's a charitable organization. Fully funded by contributions. I founded it when my wife and I lost our . . . our son, Gregory, when he was seven years old.' The courtroom fell silent as the witness, who looked stricken for a moment, composed himself and continued. 'It's a place where kids who are sick, with very serious illnesses, can come to have a few weeks of recreation with other kids who are just like them. We have lots of equipment adapted for children with handicaps. We have nurses on our staff, and doctors always available.

'Did Troy Petty ever work at your camp?'

'Yes, ma'am. He did. About ten years ago.'

'Was he a good employee?' Marjorie asked.

'I thought so. At first. He seemed to be very caring when it came to the children. He told me that being at the camp inspired him to become a nurse.'

'But you fired him, correct?'

Halloran nodded, and then said, 'Correct.'

'So why was he dismissed from your employ?'

Carl Halloran frowned. 'There were allegations made against him. By a camper. A seven year old girl.'

'What sort of allegations?' Marjorie asked.

'She claimed that Mr Petty had sexually molested her.'

'Objection!' D.A. Castor exploded. 'This is an irrelevant, blatant attempt to smear the character of the victim. Mr Petty was never in his life charged with a sexual assault.'

'Your honor,' said Marjorie calmly, 'the District Attorney has suggested that my client perjured herself with regards to Mr Petty's intentions. Mr Halloran is here to supply relevant evidence which will reinforce my client's account of Mr Petty's character.'

'Mr Petty is the victim, your honor,' the D.A. insisted. 'He is not on trial here.'

'Nonetheless,' Marjorie insisted, 'the jury's decision about my client's fate rests, in part, on whether or not they see her as a truthful witness. Mr Halloran's testimony supports her account.'

The D.A. shook his head emphatically. 'There were never any charges of sexual molestation brought against Troy Petty. Ms Fox's goal is simply to cast aspersions on the character of the victim. She hasn't even been able to produce the so-called victim in question,' the D.A. asserted.

'Your honor, we cannot produce the camper who made this complaint because she died not long after the alleged incident,' said Marjorie solemnly.

There was a murmur of horror and dismay in the courtroom.

'Attorneys, approach the bench,' the judge commanded.

Marjorie Fox and the D.A. stood before the judge, and a heated discussion ensued among them in urgent, quiet voices.

Hannah shook her head in disbelief. 'Oh my God. Troy was a monster. Think what might have happened to Sydney,' she whispered.

'The D.A. would love to ask more about it but now he doesn't dare,' said Jackie. 'The answer might only make it worse. See that guy at the prosecution's table frantically working the iPad? The D.A.'s got his assistant trying to google the information right now. The D.A. walked right into this trap. He really has only himself to blame. All he can hope for now is damage control. He needs to have the witness dismissed.'

'How do you know that?' Hannah asked. 'You sound like a lawyer.'

'I testify a lot in custody hearings. This is not my first time in court. One of the accepted rules among attorneys is that you try never to ask a witness a question unless you already know the answer they are going to give. This D.A. clearly didn't investigate the testimony that this camp owner was going to give. Really. This is bad for the D.A. Good for Lisa, though.'

'Step back,' said the judge. The two attorneys did as they were bidden. The judge turned to the jury. 'Ladies and gentlemen of the jury, the testimony of this witness will be stricken from the record. You will disregard his testimony . . .'

'Your honor,' Marjorie protested.

The judge glared at Castor. Then he turned to Carl Halloran. 'Mr Halloran, you are excused.'

Hannah turned to Jackie. 'What just happened?'

Jackie spoke in a whisper. 'The D.A. won the battle and lost the war.'

'Meaning?'

'The judge ruled that the witness can't testify. The jury is forbidden to consider his testimony in their deliberations. But do you think anyone in this courtroom will be able to shake that image of a mortally ill child being molested by our so-called victim?'

'I know I couldn't,' said Hannah.

'Neither can anybody else.'

Carl Halloran stepped down and left the courtroom.

Hannah looked at Adam. 'To think I was actually glad that Lisa had such a nice boyfriend.'

Adam shook his head, disgust in his eyes. 'Bastard.'

With the dismissal of the camp owner, the day in court ended. Hannah could see exactly what had happened. This had turned the tide. Troy Petty may not have faced charges but in this courtroom he looked guilty. The judge announced that they would reconvene the next morning. After he left the bench, the murmurs in the courtroom rose around them. Hannah turned to Jackie.

'What do you think?'

'Quite a turn of events,' said Jackie.

'You picked a good day to come,' said Adam grimly.

'So it seems.'

'Come with me,' said Hannah. 'I'll introduce you.'

Lisa and Marjorie had their heads together at the defense table. They looked up as Hannah touched Lisa on the shoulder.

'You did a wonderful job today,' said Hannah sincerely. 'Lisa, this is my friend, Jackie, from work. I've told you about her.'

Lisa's smile was satisfied. 'Did you enjoy the show?' she asked.

Hannah frowned at her daughter's choice of words. 'It was terrible,' she said. 'I couldn't believe it.'

'She was perfect on the stand, wasn't she?' Marjorie said, beaming at her client.

'Lisa, you did very well. But why didn't you tell us what Troy was like?' Hannah asked.

'Mother, I didn't know what he was like until I caught him with Sydney. Well, it doesn't matter now. This has changed everything. Wouldn't you say?' She looked at her attorney for confirmation.

'We're not out of the woods yet.'

Adam came up and rubbed Lisa's shoulder. 'You should have told me what he was up to.' He shook his head. 'When I think about it, I just want to . . .'

'That's why I didn't tell you,' Lisa said drily. 'I was worried what you might do to him. Not that he didn't deserve it.'

'Don't say that. Even as a joke,' said Hannah.

The guards from the county jail came over to the defense table. It was time for Lisa to go. She gave her parents a smile and a thumbs-up as she was led away. Hannah blew her a kiss. Then Hannah, Jackie and Adam headed for the exit.

'I can't wait till this nightmare is over and we can take her home,' said Hannah.

'I don't think it will be long now,' said Adam.

As they walked through the busy foyer, they were accosted by Troy Petty's sister.

'Your daughter is a liar,' Nadine Melton said. There were tears standing in her eyes. 'She's trying to destroy my brother's good name to save herself.'

Adam's normally calm temperament suddenly flared. 'Listen, lady, your brother was a pervert. You heard that witness in court today.'

'It's not true,' said Nadine, tears streaking down her face.

'Did you know about that incident at the camp?' Adam demanded.

'I knew about the kid's accusation but it turned out to be false. She made it up so that she could go home from that camp . . .'

'Tell yourself that,' Adam said bitterly.

Hannah took his arm. 'Honey, don't. Don't get into this. We need to leave our fight in the courtroom. Please, Mrs Melton. We have no quarrel with you. I'm sure you didn't know about Troy. I always liked your brother. I would never have guessed this either.'

'Because it isn't true. He was kind and good. He would never hurt a child.'

'Excuse me,' Adam cried. 'But you say you *did* know about the camp incident?'

'Troy was never charged. And never arrested!' Nadine exclaimed. 'Never.'

'The fact that there were no charges doesn't mean it didn't happen. It just means that they couldn't prove it.'

'Adam, come on,' Hannah pleaded. 'Let's not make this any worse.'

'How could it be any worse?' Nadine cried. 'Troy is dead and now your lying, scheming daughter has destroyed his reputation forever. She'd say anything to save herself. Every word out of her mouth is a lie.'

'You know, I have put up with about enough . . .' said Adam.

A reporter who was standing with a knot of other journalists spotted them arguing and began to move in their direction, followed by his colleagues.

'We need to leave,' said Hannah. 'Come on.' She reached for Adam's arm but he resisted, wanting to pursue the argument with Nadine. Jackie, who had hung back to this point, listening, now helped Hannah to corral her husband and lead him through the busy foyer and to the sidewalk. 'Don't rise to it,' Hannah insisted. 'She just can't deal with the truth.'

The afternoon was steamy, and sweat trickled down them as they rushed down the steps and moved rapidly out of reach of the reporters. At their cars, Hannah turned to the psychologist. 'Thank you for coming today,' she said. 'It really helped to have you there.'

'I was glad to be there.'

Adam thanked her too and got into the driver's seat of their car. Hannah went to open the passenger door. Jackie was still standing by her own car, turning her keys over thoughtfully.

'What is it?' Hannah asked.

'I'm just wondering something,' said Jackie.

Hannah looked at her curiously.

'You just have to wonder. Maybe Sydney said something.'

Hannah frowned. 'What do you mean?'

'Well,' said Jackie, 'if Troy was a pedophile, he may have already assaulted Sydney – maybe more than once – before Lisa found out about his . . . tastes. Although I can't imagine that he spent much time alone with Sydney.'

Hannah's face flamed, as she instantly remembered Tiffany saying that Troy would occasionally pick up Sydney at Lisa's behest. That he took Sydney fishing while Lisa studied. 'Oh my God,' she said.

Jackie frowned at her. 'Did he?'

Hannah slumped against the side of the car. The hot metal of the fender seemed to burn through her silky skirt, and her sweat began to streak down her face. 'How do we find out?' she asked.

'You mean, if he assaulted her?'

Hannah nodded, and stared at her friend, her eyes wide with alarm.

Jackie sighed. 'I could talk to her. I have some experience with this stuff.'

'Would you?' Hannah asked. 'Oh, I can't believe this. I didn't even think about that . . .'

'Informally,' said Jackie. 'I could come over.'

'Tonight?' Hannah exclaimed.

'I'll call you.'

They clasped hands for a moment. 'Try not to worry,' said Jackie. Then she turned and got into her car. Hannah opened the passenger door and slipped into the car beside Adam.

All Hannah could think of as she buckled herself into the seat was Lisa giving them a thumbs up as she left the courtroom. Had it never occurred to her to wonder? When she realized what a twisted mind Troy had, why didn't she call the police? Why, instead, was she focused on going out to his house to get the money he owed her? That should have been the last thing on her mind.

'Hannah?' Adam asked.

She looked over at him. 'Jackie just brought up something terrible. Something we have to think about.'

Adam faced out over the steering wheel, shaking his head. 'I don't even want to ask,' he said. Then he turned to her, steeling himself. 'OK,' he said. 'Tell me.'

FIFTEEN

Cars were coming and going from the Dollards' house next door, and Hannah wondered absently how long Chet would be in the hospital. She watched the activity in the driveway from the same chair she had been sitting in since they walked into the house. She had done nothing about dinner. Once they had collected Sydney and come home, Hannah had cradled her on her lap, unwilling to let her go. The toddler was weary after a day at daycare and seemed content to just rest against her grandmother, toying absently with a stuffed animal.

Hannah's cellphone rang but it was on the dining-room table and she was unable to force herself out of the chair. Adam came in and answered it.

He turned to Hannah. 'It's Jackie,' he said.

Hannah reached out with one hand. 'I haven't done a thing about dinner,' she said to him apologetically.

Adam shook his head as he handed her the phone. 'I'll pick up dinner for us. You just rest there with Sydney.'

'Thanks, darling,' she said, and put the phone to her ear. 'Jackie?'

'Hi, Hannah.'

'Are you coming over to talk to Sydney?'

'I don't think so,' Jackie said slowly. 'I thought about it some more and I'm not sure it's a good idea.'

'But you said you would help,' Hannah protested.

'I don't want to do some kind of half-baked intervention. Children as young as Sydney have to be handled differently than older kids and it's just not my area of expertise. I got you the name of someone, a child psychiatrist, who specializes in very young children.'

'Are you sure you can't do it? I'd like to just keep it quiet, between us,' said Hannah.

'I'm not comfortable,' said Jackie. 'I certainly don't want to do more harm than good. But take this number. Please.'

'OK,' said Hannah. She shifted Sydney on her lap, and wrote down the name and number which Jackie offered. But as soon as she hung up, she put the information aside. There were so many questions in her mind. She didn't know if she even had the right to take Sydney to a child psychiatrist. After all, Sydney was Lisa's child, and Lisa might object. But part of her knew that it was more than that. How could Hannah ever explain why Lisa had left her child alone in the care of a strange man whom she knew so little about? Of course it was careless of her, but what if a psychiatrist regarded that as child neglect? Would the shrink feel compelled to report Lisa's actions to the authorities? What if they tried to take Sydney away from her? That was the last thing any of them needed to have happen in the course of this trial.

Hannah was pondering how to proceed, and Sydney was getting

restless to get down from her lap, when the phone rang again. Hannah answered it.

'Hannah,' a voice demanded imperiously.

'Hi, Mother,' said Hannah. She could picture her mother, seated in her hover-round chair, *Fox News* blaring on her TV. 'How are you?'

'I need you to come over here,' said Pamela in a tone that brooked no protest.

Hannah protested anyway. 'Mother, I'm exhausted. Can it wait? We've been at the court house all day. I'm just waiting for Adam to bring home some take out for dinner. Then I have to put Sydney to bed. I'm just so tired from all this . . .'

'No, it cannot wait,' said Pamela. 'It's about your daughter.'

'What about her? Just tell me, Mother.'

'There is someone you need to meet. ASAP.' Pamela hung up.

Hannah was tempted to ignore the imperial summons. She just did not need the aggravation. But it was about Lisa. And she could not remember the last time her mother had been so insistent. Not in her usual way.

'Want to take a ride to see Nana?' Hannah asked Sydney, who was absorbed with her fabric dollhouse.

'No,' said Sydney.

'Me neither,' said Hannah, with a sigh.

Adam brought home shrimp and grits from a place downtown, and promised to get Sydney ready for bed so that Hannah could go and see her mother.

'I'd go tomorrow,' said Hannah apologetically, 'but I think the defense might be wrapping this up quickly. I have to be in the courtroom.'

'Your mother's timing . . . Well, just go,' said Adam. 'We'll be fine. But drink some coffee so you don't fall asleep on your way out there.'

'I'll buy some on the way,' she promised.

Good as her word, Hannah stopped at a drive-up window and got a cup of coffee to go. Then she drove the twenty minutes to the Veranda and parked in a space outside of Pamela's building. The night was clear and warm, the crickets chirping, and the man-made pond centered in front of the main building glistened silver in the moonlight. For a moment, Hannah remembered summer nights at the lake, and wished she were just a girl again, carefree and moonstruck. But that life seemed to belong to a past she could barely remember. She trudged up the walkway and made her way to her mother's door.

Pamela answered on the first ring. 'You took your time,' she said. 'I'm here now,' said Hannah. She started to enter the apartment but Pamela shook her head and gestured that she should go back out into the hallway. Pamela, dressed in sky blue linen, her hair a platinum cloud on her scalp, rolled out of the apartment and into the hallway. 'Where are we going?' said Hannah.

'Down to Christina Shelton's apartment,' her mother said.

Hannah stifled a sigh. Christina Shelton was a living exemplar to Pamela of women properly revered. The widow of gentleman farmer and longtime state senator Jock Shelton, Christina was frail and infirm but, according to Pamela, her über-attentive children catered to her every heart's desire, the minute she desired it. 'Fine. Whatever you say.'

Pamela glared back at Hannah over her shoulder. 'You'll understand in just a few minutes. Follow me.' Hannah trailed behind her mother's motorized chair as they negotiated the hallways to the part of the building which had two- and three-bedroom apartments. They arrived at a door at the end and Pamela knocked.

'She might be asleep,' said Hannah anxiously.

'She will be asleep,' said Pamela.

Hannah frowned but waited obediently. The door opened and an aide in cheerful pink scrubs opened the door. The aide put a finger to her lips. 'She's sleeping,' said the woman, who was thirtyish and overweight with a bleached-blonde pixie cut.

'I know that,' said Pamela impatiently. 'It's you we came to see. This is my daughter. Lisa's mother.'

The woman looked startled and then smiled at Hannah, extending her hand. 'Hi. I'm Wynonna Clemons.'

'Nice to meet you,' said Hannah.

'Hannah needs to hear what you have to say, Wynonna.'

Wynonna grimaced. 'I really shouldn't leave her.'

'She can page you if she needs you. Check in on her,' said Pamela. 'Then meet us in the lounge across the hall.'

'OK,' said Wynonna. 'Give me five minutes.' She disappeared back into the apartment, closing the door quietly.

'Three bedrooms,' Pamela observed, shaking her head. 'That's the number of bedrooms a person should have.' Then she abruptly turned her chair around and directed it toward the spacious, well-appointed lounge across the hall. Hannah followed her. Pamela pointed to a Duncan Phyfe-style sofa covered in crewel-work embroidery. Hannah sat down and Pamela glided across the butterscotch gleam of the hardwood floors, past wing chairs and mahogany end tables and parked her chair beside the sofa.

'Mother, tell me again. Why, on this night when I am completely exhausted, do I want to talk to Mrs Shelton's aide?'

'Wynonna Clemons used to work at Vanderbilt Hospital as an LPN, but she was let go because she came to work several times smelling like a brewery.'

Hannah looked at her mother with raised eyebrows.

'Oh, don't bother looking shocked,' said Pamela. 'Christina told me that herself. But Christina's children felt that their mother needed a full-time aide, and Wynonna was in need of work. Her husband is disabled and they've got two kids. So Christina's children interviewed her several times and decided she might work out. As it happens, she and Christina get on very well.'

Good for Christina's sainted children, Hannah thought, gritting her teeth. She glanced at the ormolu clock on the mantle. She just wanted to go home, kiss Sydney and climb into bed with Adam. Tomorrow promised to be trying. 'Well,' said Hannah, 'I'm sure she's a very nice woman.'

'Oh, for heaven's sakes, Hannah. Stop talking as if I'm simple. I didn't call you out here to lob compliments at a nurse's aide.'

Hannah stifled a sigh. 'Did we have to do this tonight? In the middle of the trial? You see these people every day. Why tonight?'

'As a matter of fact, I haven't seen them in a while, because Christina had a bad fall and spent the last several months in the nursing home wing. Don't you remember I told you that? Wynonna took care of her there.'

'Oh, yes, I remember you saying that she fell and broke her arm and her hip,' said Hannah. 'Where was the vaunted Wynonna when that happened?'

'It was Wynonna's day off, as a matter of fact,' said Pamela. 'And I'll ask you to mind your tone.'

'Sorry,' said Hannah.

'These days, Christina spends a lot of time in her room. But I ran into them today in the dining room, and Wynonna was anxious to talk.'

'Here she comes,' said Hannah in a warning tone.

Wynonna hurried across the room, and stood in front of the sofa. 'May I?' she asked Hannah.

'Of course. Sit down,' said Hannah.

Wynonna perched on the edge of the sofa cushion. 'Your mother is a great lady,' she confided to Hannah.

'Thank you,' said Hannah, smiling thinly.

'I was just telling my daughter that you used to work at Vanderbilt.'

'That's right,' said Wynonna, nodding. 'I worked there for seven years. And then I was replaced by another nurse. That man your daughter . . . knew.'

Suddenly, Hannah understood why she had been summoned. 'Troy Petty.'

'Exactly right,' said Wynonna. 'I heard about the trial, like everybody else. But I never put it together with Mrs Hardcastle's granddaughter until Mrs Shelton told me.'

Hannah sighed. 'So you knew Troy Petty.'

Wynonna looked surprised. 'No! I didn't know him. They blind-sided me at the hospital. Fired me one day, and already had him on deck.'

'I'm sure that was very difficult,' said Hannah sympathetically. At the same time, she had to wonder if her mother's faculties were failing. Hannah had been summoned in the night to meet a woman who lost her job to Troy Petty. Apparently with good reason, because of her own alcohol problem.

'A pedophile. They replaced me with a pedophile. It's disgusting. Don't you think, Mrs H?'

Pamela nodded sagely and gazed at Hannah.

Hannah nodded. 'Ah, I see. You . . . heard about the testimony today.'

Wynonna agreed eagerly. 'Yes, everyone was talking about it. About the sick child at the camp. I already knew about it.'

Hannah looked at Wynonna with narrowed eyes. 'You knew about that?'

'Oh, yes,' said Wynonna triumphantly. 'Dolores told me all about it.'

Hannah shook her head. 'I'm confused. Who's Dolores?'

'Dolores is a nurse I used to work with. Back in the fall when I lost my job to this Petty character, she called and told me that years ago she used to work at that Sunflower camp for sick kids. She said that Troy Petty was fired for molesting one of the little campers. I told my husband, Hank, to check it out on the computer. He's a whiz on that thing. I wish he could get some computer work. He's disabled, so he's home all the time with nothing to do. In fact, your mother said that your husband works for Verizon . . .'

'This is not the time, Wynonna,' said Pamela imperiously.

Wynonna shrugged. 'Well, anyway, Hank looked into it. There was an accusation made but no charges, so they couldn't use his name.'

'Perhaps you should have brought it to the hospital's attention, Wynonna,' drawled Pamela.

Wynonna looked away, somewhat sheepishly, rubbing her hands on her thighs. 'I tried to. I tried to tell my old supervisor. She didn't want to hear it. She said they didn't fire me because of him. They said I lost my job for . . . other reasons.'

Hannah could feel her anger building. Obviously, her mother was delighted to have discovered this connection between Christina Shelton's aide and Lisa's trial. She had been called here to bear witness to Pamela's cleverness in putting the two together. She felt overwhelmed by exhaustion and out of patience with her mother. This was not some kind of parlor game called 'Make the Connection'. Then, suddenly, she thought of a way to aggravate her mother, and couldn't resist using it. 'Well, his job's open now. You might be able to get your old job back.'

Wynonna shook her head. 'No, as it happens, I'm very happy taking care of Mrs Shelton. She's so good to me. So, in a way, maybe it was just as well. Nobody at that hospital wanted to know about it. I even told your daughter about it.'

Hannah's heart skipped a sickening beat. 'My daughter?'

'Yes. When she was here one day visiting her grandmother. Mrs Hardcastle brought her over to the hospital to meet Mrs Shelton.' Wynonna smiled shyly at Pamela. 'You was so proud of her, being a child genius and all, and going to medical school at Vandy. Who wouldn't be? Anyway, when I heard from Mrs Hardcastle that your daughter worked at Vandy, I told her all about it. Lisa, right? I told Lisa all about Troy Petty. I figured she would want to know about this guy, in case she ran into him, you know?'

'You told Lisa,' Hannah said slowly. 'When was this?'

Wynonna frowned and looked skyward, waggling the fingers on one hand. 'Last winter. At your birthday,' she said, smiling at Pamela.

'She came to bring Mrs Hardcastle her birthday present. You remember that?'

Pamela nodded.

'That was nine months ago,' said Hannah. 'You're saying that Lisa has known about this for nine months?' She glanced at her mother. Pamela was watching her with a certain cold satisfaction.

Wynonna nodded. 'I never will understand why she started dating that guy. I mean, young girls do like a bad boy. I know that. I was young once too. And maybe he just charmed her. I don't know. All I can figure is that she didn't believe me, and had to find out for herself. And I guess she *did* find out. After all, she ended up killing him, didn't she?'

'*No*. She did not,' snapped Hannah.

Wynonna suddenly adopted a more reserved tone. 'I shouldn't have said that. I'm truly sorry. It's innocent till proven guilty. This is America, after all.'

Hannah could see her own hand shaking on the arm of the sofa. 'That's right. And I'll thank you not to say that again.'

Wynonna turned to Pamela apologetically. 'I'm so sorry. I misspoke.'

'That's all right, Wynonna,' said Pamela. 'You're just the messenger.'

For some reason she could not explain, Hannah was simply furious with her mother. She refused to accompany her back to her apartment. She abruptly asked a passing aide to do the honors and slipped out into the night.

All the way home, her heart was pounding. Lisa knew about Troy Petty all along? She knew, and yet she let Sydney spend time alone with him? She couldn't get her mind around it. It had to be a mistake. But there was no room for that in Wynonna's account. Hannah knew that she had to tell Adam but she could not bear the thought of his face, the look in his eyes when he heard this.

She went inside, trudging as if on the road to Calvary. When she opened the back door, she found Adam was on the phone.

'OK. That's great,' he said. 'Give Chet our very best. Tell him we'll come by and see him soon.'

He hung up the phone and turned to Hannah with a smile. She tried to force a smile onto her own face.

'That was Rayanne,' he said. 'Chet's out of the woods.'

'That's great,' said Hannah.

Adam frowned at her. 'What happened?'

'Where is Sydney?'

'Already in bed. Tell me. You're white as a ghost.'

Hannah shook her head and sat down.

'Do you want something? Tea? Something a bit stiffer?'

'Whiskey,' Hannah said. 'Just pour me a shot.'

Adam frowned but did as she asked. He handed it to her. Hannah took a sip of the searing liquid and grimaced.

'That's my girl,' Adam said, smiling briefly. 'Now tell me. What did my dear mother-in-law say that got you so upset?'

Hannah shook her head, and then angrily wiped her eyes.

'Come on. You're scaring me,' Adam said.

'Oh, God, Adam. She knew. Wynonna said that Lisa knew.'

'Back up. Who is Wynonna? What did Lisa know?'

Hannah took a deep breath and then started to explain. When she was done, Adam sat very still.

'So, if this woman is to be believed, Lisa knew that Troy was an accused child molester around the time when she started dating him.'

'Yes,' said Hannah. 'Wynonna has no reason to lie about this. Adam, Lisa told Tiffany at the daycare that Troy had her permission to pick up Sydney. How is this possible, knowing what he was accused of? Oh, God.'

Adam held up a hand. 'Now wait. Wait. Let's not jump to conclusions. First of all, we have to assume that Lisa would never have done that. We have to assume that there's some explanation. We have to start from that assumption.'

Hannah was about to protest and then she stopped. She looked gratefully at her husband. 'You're right. We do have to start from there.' All their married life, when a problem confounded her, she looked to him for help. He was logical. A clear thinker. He was calm. He never descended into hysterics. She looked to him now, willing him to arrive at some justification for Lisa's actions that would make it possible for her to breathe again.

Adam frowned, pondering the problem. 'Look, you know what Lisa's like. She's always been an outsider herself. Maybe she felt sorry for him. After all, he was accused but never charged.'

Hannah nodded but was not comforted. 'Why would she even get involved with him in the first place? Why would she take up with a guy accused of sexual assault on a child?'

'Oh, honey, I don't know,' said Adam wearily. 'Why does Lisa do half the things she does? All I can think is that he won her over with that underdog argument.'

'That's true,' Hannah admitted.

'Though it was a dumbass, reckless thing to do,' he fumed. 'Which would be just like Lisa.'

Hannah felt queasy. 'Adam, we have to know for sure.'

'We can't call Lisa at this hour,' he said. 'They won't let her talk on the phone. Let me call her attorney. She must know.'

'Yes, do,' said Hannah. But even as Adam was dialing the number, and leaving Marjorie an urgent message to call him back, Hannah tried to calm herself down. Of course, Adam was right. Lisa must have researched Troy Petty and found out that no charges were filed against him. 'She must have felt sorry for him.'

Adam embraced her tightly. 'Nothing else makes sense,' he said, as if he were reading her mind.

They both jumped when, suddenly, Adam's phone rang. Hannah held her breath while he quickly explained his question to Marjorie.

'I see,' he said. He listened for a while. 'OK. Yes. OK. Good.' He ended the call.

'What did she say?' Hannah asked, almost afraid to find out.

Adam looked gravely at his wife. 'The child who accused Troy Petty passed away from her illness some years ago. But Marjorie located her mother. She asked if the parents had ever thought of pursuing a prosecution, even though the child couldn't testify. The mother didn't want to talk about it at first. But finally she admitted that she was reluctant to go forth because she wasn't sure. At the time it happened, the child wanted so badly to leave the camp and come home. They kept urging her to stay and then, the next thing they knew . . . they got a frantic phone call to come and get her.'

'Oh my God,' said Hannah. 'Her own parents didn't believe it?'

'They . . . didn't know what to think. The child said some things that caused them to doubt it.'

'So Troy was never officially accused, but never officially exonerated either.'

'That's what it amounts to.'

'Is the mother going to testify?'

'No way. She told Marjorie that she wouldn't disgrace her daughter's memory by testifying.'

'What about Troy's memory?' Hannah protested.

'Well, frankly, I'm not too concerned about Troy's reputation,' said Adam brusquely. 'Are you? After all, Lisa did catch him with Sydney.'

'So he was a child molester.'

'Apparently. But he must have kept his secret well hidden.'

They looked at one another gravely. Lisa must have just felt sorry for Troy. Maybe she confronted him and he told her that he was unfairly accused, by a sick child, no less. Worthy of sympathy, and no threat to her daughter – until she found out differently. Hannah didn't know whether to laugh or cry. She settled for resting against her husband's chest, able, for the moment, to breathe again.

'Marjorie said that the prosecutor's office will be working all night trying to track this information down. But even if they find the child's mother, she will not go to court. She will not testify. Lisa has won the jury's sympathy. The defense is going to rest tomorrow,' said Adam. 'Then the case will go to the jury.'

Hannah's heart pounded and her mouth was dry. 'So soon?' she asked.

'It would seem.'

'Is that fair? Not to tell the truth about this child and her accusations?'

'Fair?' Adam exclaimed. 'You're worried about fair? Obviously this guy was getting ready to assault our granddaughter. Marjorie said their case is flimsy, and these revelations about Troy have given momentum to the defense. Before it dissipates she wants to make her move.'

Hannah closed her eyes and nodded. Tomorrow, Lisa's fate would be in the hands of those twelve strangers. Her daughter would either walk free or be a prisoner for many years to come. She nestled against her husband and clung to him, as if she would freefall into limitless outer space if ever he were to let her go.

SIXTEEN

The next day the courtroom was virtually buzzing. People seemed to be asking themselves what kind of man Troy Petty had actually been. It was as if a wave of garbage had floated in on the tide of testimony, and stubbornly clung to the image of Troy Petty. Nurse, camp counselor, pervert.

Marjorie called Lisa's advisor at Vanderbilt, a high-profile doctor, who testified that Lisa had not seemed at all distracted or in any way obsessed in the course of her studies. He had no idea that she was even seeing a nurse at the hospital. Alicia Bledsoe was called to the stand and swore that Lisa was not in love with Troy Petty. It was a fling to pass the time between two people who worked together. Next, Marjorie called Hannah to the stand.

Hannah was ready when her turn came. She had been prepped on her testimony by Marjorie, and warned about subjects she should not raise. She wore a sky-blue silk shirtdress that seemed to radiate serenity. Still, she felt anything but serene as she swore on the Bible and sat down in the chair in the witness stand. She looked out at the spectators, and caught Adam's eye. He gave her a thumbs up.

'Mrs Wickes, what is your relationship to my client?'

'I'm her mother. Lisa and her daughter, my granddaughter, live with me and my husband.'

'Were you aware that Lisa was dating Troy Petty?'

'Oh yes,' said Hannah. Marjorie had instructed her to only answer the questions. Not to volunteer any information.

'Did your daughter talk to you about this relationship?'

Hannah hesitated. 'When they first met, she told me that he worked at the hospital.'

'She never said that she was madly in love with him, or anything to that effect?'

'No,' said Hannah. 'Nothing like that. She seemed to enjoy going out with Troy. But, with her daughter and her studies, she doesn't have a lot of free time.'

'Did he come to your home? Did you meet Troy Petty?'

'Yes,' said Hannah. 'He came to pick her up once in a while. He seemed . . .'

'What, Mrs Wickes?'

Hannah took a deep breath. 'He seemed like a nice young man.'

'But Lisa never spoke of him as a potential husband, or father for Sydney?'

Hannah shook her head emphatically. 'No. Never.'

'Did you know she was lending him money?'

Hannah hesitated. 'No,' she said truthfully. 'I wasn't aware of that.'

'Would you have approved, if she had mentioned it?'

'No,' said Hannah firmly. 'Lisa must have known I wouldn't

approve. It was a financial struggle as it was, with expenses for medical school, and caring for Sydney. That's probably why she never mentioned it.'

'Are you surprised to learn that she lent him money?'

'No,' Hannah admitted. 'Lisa always had a soft spot for anybody in need. Or in trouble.' She grimaced inwardly. That wasn't precisely true. Lisa often chose to associate with people whom Hannah and Adam thought were questionable, and she would get angry if they criticized her choices. It wasn't the same thing exactly. But it stemmed from the same impulse, she thought loyally.

'Thank you, Mrs Wickes.' Marjorie turned Hannah over to D.A. Castor.

The D.A. peered at her, and approached the witness box. 'So, it's your testimony that if your daughter had been madly in love with Troy Petty, she would have told you so.'

Hannah hesitated. 'Probably. Yes. Ever since she was little, when she was enthusiastic about something, she would kind of bubble over with it. At least initially.'

'What about when she was angry?' he asked. 'Would she tell you that?'

Hannah took a deep breath. Marjorie had prepared her for this line of questioning. The D.A. was trying to trap her. She was ready.

'No. She pretty much kept her anger and her disappointments to herself.'

Hannah could see the irritation in Castor's eyes. He thought he had cornered her, but she had evaded him. 'Did Lisa ever mention to you that she caught Mr Petty preparing to assault your granddaughter?'

'No. Of course not.'

'Isn't that the sort of thing you might blurt out to the people you lived with? Your parents? Your child's grandparents?'

'I'm sure she was terribly ashamed for having brought him into her daughter's life. She just went ahead and broke up with him. That's what I would have expected her to do.'

'You wouldn't have recommended that she call the police? Report Mr Petty as a predator?'

'I might have,' Hannah admitted. 'But I didn't know about it.'

'Your granddaughter is not the only child out there, Mrs Wickes. If this man was the predator that Lisa made him out to be, he needed to be stopped.'

'I agree. But I'm sure that Lisa's first thought was to get her own child away from him. And she did.'

'So she just let it go. Never reported him.'

'She may have intended to. We'll never know. He died before she could.'

'Maybe that was your daughter's way of stopping him. Making sure he could never hurt any other child.'

Hannah remained calm. 'No matter how many reasons you come up with, Mr Castor, the fact remains that my daughter would never have killed Troy Petty. She's studying to be a doctor. She intends to be a healer. Not a killer.'

Castor pursed his lips. 'No further questions for this witness.'

'I think we'll break for lunch right here,' said the judge.

Hannah was excused, and she left the courtroom.

'How did I do?' she asked when Adam met her outside.

'You did great,' he said sincerely.

'Marjorie warned me he would ask about that.'

'You were ready for him. Marjorie knows her stuff,' said Adam, shaking his head admiringly.

After lunch, Marjorie called the parole officer for Troy's brother, who claimed that Troy was paying off one drug dealer after another because of his brother's habit. With that, the defense rested.

After another break, D.A. Castor was invited to give his summation to the jury. He stood up wearily, dark circles under his eyes. Then, the young D.A. squared his shoulders and went to work, trying to salvage his decimated case. As Castor outlined it, Lisa had multiple motives to kill Troy Petty. There was the check for $450 which Lisa cashed. D.A. Castor pounded on this fact, saying that the convenience-store tape was positive proof of Lisa's guilt. But then, as if trying to shore up his argument against the lack of hard evidence in the explosion, and unable to discount the testimony given by Carl Halloran, he insisted vaguely that this was also a crime of passion. According to Castor's summation, Lisa had arranged for the fishing camp to explode because she believed Troy was trying to assault her daughter. And then, on top of that, Troy Petty had the temerity to try to break up with her. Perhaps she was even jealous, Castor said. She sits before you coolly now but who knows what was really in her heart. He did his best to dismiss the lack of forensic evidence as unimportant. He insisted that it could not have been an accident, and that there was no one else, according to Castor, who would have any reason to want Troy dead. Even to a layman like Hannah, his summation seemed to be without substance and all over the map. But then again, she thought, that was the way she needed to see it.

When Castor was done, Marjorie Fox was allowed to give her summation. Marjorie glanced at Lisa, who was watching her with large, hopeful gray eyes.

Marjorie stood up, smoothed down her skirt and walked purposefully over to the jury box.

'In a homicide,' she began, 'the police are trained to look for three things. Means, motive and opportunity. In the death of Troy Petty, the only means and opportunity which tie Lisa Wickes to this crime are purely circumstantial. She had been at his house but left the premises several hours before his faulty propane heater leaked enough gas to combust with some burned-down candles and blow the place sky high. Troy Petty may have been knocked unconscious before the explosion, or he may have had so much to drink that he didn't notice the gas build-up, and he was battered in the head, and everywhere else, *by* the explosion.

'In other words, it may have been simple carelessness, an accident. But the District Attorney insists on blaming Lisa Wickes, because she cashed Troy Petty's check. We do know that Lisa left with Mr Petty's paycheck in her possession several hours before the explosion occurred. But did she steal it, or did he owe it to her? What we know from Lisa's testimony is that Troy Petty had run out of credit with her. She had found him in a situation with her baby daughter which was so reprehensible that she immediately wanted out of the relationship. Was she upset about that? Sure. Was she distraught about losing Troy? I don't think so. The fact was that all she wanted from Troy Petty was the money which she loaned him. Hence, she left his house with the check.

'No, when you really look at it, this case boils down to one question – motive. The state would have you believe that my client, Lisa Wickes, a young woman with a near-genius IQ, a young woman doing brilliantly in medical school, decided to attack and murder Troy Petty because she wanted to get her hands on his four hundred and fifty dollars. Or, if you can't quite buy into that scenario, perhaps it was because he was going to break up with her,' said Marjorie sarcastically.

'All right. Take a good look at this woman. We all understand how difficult it is to become a doctor. The years of study and dedication which it requires. Lisa is committed to seeing it through. A career stretches before her – long, lucrative and respected. Why in the world would she toss that all away?

'A crime of passion, perhaps? Ladies and gentlemen, we have all heard about crimes of passion. They defy logic. A person becomes so obsessed, so consumed by the object of their desire, that they will commit unspeakable crimes in the name of that so-called "love".

'Yet you heard Lisa's supervisor maintain that Lisa was not distracted from her studies or her work. Her best friend, Alicia Bledsoe, testified that Lisa was just not that enamored of Troy Petty. And who would know better than her best friend? Her mother, who lives with her, saw no evidence of obsessive love. Quite the contrary. We have only the most perfunctory of emails between Troy and Lisa, and no testimony that even suggests they were "crazy in love".

'Could the passion have been anger? Fury at finding him attempting to assault her child? Well, anyone would be furious about that. Of course. But take a good look at Lisa Wickes. Her recollections are calm, a little sad, and, most of all, disgusted. She seems to regard her relationship with the . . . deceased from the kind of objective distance which one expects from a doctor. The doctor she is in the process of becoming. Fury, anger, despair – do you see any of that in Lisa Wickes?

'So, if it wasn't a crime of passion then – that's right, she did it for the $450. This is a young woman on track to make hundreds of thousands of dollars, possibly millions over the course of her chosen career. Does it seem likely to you that she would throw it all away for $450?

'We know for a fact that Lisa had Troy's check. And that she cashed it. But what seems more likely? That Lisa would steal this check and cash it in plain view of security cameras? Or is it more likely that Troy Petty did, indeed, owe this money to Lisa because he was paying off his brother's drug debts? He owed it to her. Maybe she had been sympathetic to his plight, but then, when she'd found him trying to assault her child, she'd lost every ounce of sympathy. She'd become disgusted by him and never wanted to see him again. She just wanted her money back.

'Ladies and gentleman, this case, in the end, comes down to common sense. We all know that there is a balance of power in every relationship. Who had more power in this one? Lisa – young, talented and embarking on her brilliant, respected career? Or Troy Petty, with his shady history of preying on children and the burdensome debts in his family.

'People don't kill for vague reasons. In my experience, they kill for very specific reasons, or because they are in the grip of powerful emotions. Killing another human being is a reprehensible act. The polar opposite of the physician's credo – first, do no harm. Killing another human being is also a really great way to derail your own life. Even the most mild-mannered people can get angry and lash out – I grant you that.

'But absent a compelling motive, you are left with that all-important issue of reasonable doubt. Ask yourself why would she do it, and you will soon arrive at the decision that I have. Lisa Wickes had no compelling reason to kill Troy Petty. Her life did not revolve around the attentions of this young man. Especially after she caught him interfering with her two-year-old daughter. This relationship was over, way before Troy Petty's house blew up with him in it. Lisa Wickes had already moved on.

'I ask you to consider all you have heard about this case, and acquit Lisa Wickes now. Send her back to her studies and her young daughter. Send her back to become a healer, to spend her life productively, doing good. Because Lisa Wickes will do good in a way that most of us can never hope to emulate. Consign this case to the dustbin where it belongs, and send Lisa Wickes back to her purposeful life.'

As Marjorie Fox brought her closing argument to an end, Hannah could feel the sentiment in the courtroom shining like sunlight on Lisa. She looked at Adam, who seemed lost in thought. 'I think she has convinced them.'

Adam frowned, and nodded. 'Let's hope so.'

'She was worth every penny.'

Adam understood what she was saying. 'It certainly seems that way. She made the state's case look . . . feeble.'

The judge thanked the attorneys for their summations. Then he glanced at the clock. 'In view of the hour,' he said, 'I am going to wait until tomorrow morning to charge the jury. I will ask the jury management team to have our jury assembled in the courtroom tomorrow morning at nine o'clock sharp at which time they will be charged, after which they will retire to commence their deliberations. Court is dismissed.'

Hannah and Adam filed out of the courtroom with the other spectators, and waded through the clamorous crowd of reporters. They avoided looking left or right as they were pelted with questions. They made their way to their car, and locked themselves inside.

'The next time we go back in there will be for the verdict,' Hannah observed.

'The last time we ever see the inside of a courtroom, I hope,' he said fervently.

'Amen,' she said.

'Let's pick up Sydney and go home.'

SEVENTEEN

The three of them spent a quiet night at home, going outside only long enough to have dinner on the deck. It was a lovely evening, the late sunset spilling orange and lavender across the sky. Sydney spotted a bunny in the far end of the yard and banged her spoon on her Peter Rabbit decorated plate, as if in appreciation. They were too tired for conversation. Adam seemed quiet and distracted during dinner and Hannah could understand it. Their ordeal was almost over, and it had depleted each of them. Tonight she seemed to have more energy than he did, so she volunteered to clear the table and get Sydney ready for bed while he retreated into his home office. He gratefully took her up on her offer.

She watched an old movie on TV for an hour after Sydney was in bed, and then she went down to his office and stuck her head in. 'I think I'm going to go to bed early. I am beat,' she said.

'I'll be right behind you,' he said.

She kissed him on the top of his head and made her way down to their room. As she set out her clothes for the next day, showered and washed her hair, she was overcome with weariness. She brushed her teeth automatically, yawning like a sleepy child. Then she went down the hall to Sydney's room, and looked in on her granddaughter. She knelt down beside the low trundle bed, and brushed Sydney's hair gently off her flushed, softly rounded face. 'It's almost over, baby doll,' she whispered. 'Mommy will be coming home soon.'

Sydney stirred but did not awaken. Hannah watched her grand-daughter tenderly as she shifted in her bed, still clutching her teddy bear under her arm. The question about Troy swam back into her mind. Did he hurt you? she wondered. Did that monster touch you? Hannah felt almost physically sick at the thought, and a part of her could not deny that she was glad Troy Petty was dead. She wondered, briefly, if Troy had indeed been guilty of interfering with that termin-ally ill child at the summer camp. Perhaps there was nothing that Troy wouldn't do to gratify himself.

He's dead now, Hannah reminded herself. He's dead and he could never hurt Sydney, or any other child, again. She leaned over and kissed the toddler's warm cheek. They would have to get to the bottom of it one of these days but the immediate danger was over. Once Lisa was home again they would call Jackie's referral and take Sydney for a professional evaluation. And they would provide whatever treat-ment was necessary – if it was necessary. Oh, my sweetie, I hope it's not, Hannah thought. I just hope and pray he didn't get to you.

By the time Hannah got back to their room, Adam was sitting up in bed, reading. She climbed in beside him and snuggled against him. She tried to stay awake but it was no use. 'Love you,' she murmured, and almost as soon as she rolled away from him, she was fast asleep.

She wasn't sure what woke her. Probably a bad dream. She had had lots of those lately. But whatever it was, she came awake with a start. She lay on her side, her heart pounding, and hoped she had not cried out in her sleep. She didn't want to awaken Adam. He desperately needed some rest.

She closed her eyes again, hoping that the panicky feeling would subside, and she could drift back to sleep, but in a few moments she realized that it was out of the question. Eyes closed or not, she was wide awake.

Hannah rolled over carefully, checking for Adam's quiet, steady breathing. But she heard nothing and, as her eyes adjusted to the darkness, she saw that his covers were thrown back, his side of the bed empty. She glanced over at their bathroom door. There was no bar of light beneath it. In fact, the door was ajar, the bathroom dark.

He probably can't sleep either, she thought. How could either one of them be expected to rest, knowing that Lisa's fate was now in the hands of the jury? Hannah lay there, thinking about her daughter. Hannah had actually been happy when Lisa became involved with Troy. Obviously, Lisa was no virgin, but her relationships had been short-lived and seemingly loveless. Troy actually seemed to care for her. Hannah worried that she would never be able to trust anyone after Troy's betrayal.

Hannah put a hand on Adam's still warm pillow. She had always tried to impress on Lisa that the one you married needed to be special. A clear choice. No second thoughts. That didn't mean he had to be the perfect man. Just the perfect man for you. Someone you could trust with your life. Someone who would always put his family first. Someone whose love was the rock in your life. Obviously not someone like Troy Petty.

Hannah frowned, wondering where Adam was. Had he gone down to the kitchen to eat something? He always hated himself when he did that. Adam was a disciplined person, faithful in his exercise, cautious with his drinking. It always kind of amused her when he got up in the middle of the night and ate snacks. Proof that he was human, just like everybody else.

Maybe I'll join him, she thought. We may as well spend this sleepless night together. Hannah sat up, pulled on her wrapper and slid her feet into her slippers. Then she went out into the dark house in search of him.

As soon as she walked out into the hallway, she saw that he was not in the kitchen. It was pitch black at that end of the house. And he wasn't in his office either. The light was on, however, in Lisa's room, a glowing bar visible beneath the closed door.

Hannah frowned, and walked over to it. Why would he be in there? She reached for the doorknob and turned it slowly. The door opened in. At the desk by the window he sat, working on Lisa's laptop.

'Adam?' she said.

He jumped and turned around, a guilty look on his face.

'What are you doing in here?' she asked.

Adam turned back to the laptop and stared at it, pushing a couple of keys. The screen changed with each tap of his fingers. 'Looking for something,' he said.

'On Lisa's computer? I don't even know Lisa's password,' Hannah said.

'It's Sydney's birthday,' he said.

Hannah smiled, pleased at this notion. 'Well, of course it is,' she said. 'After all, I use hers.'

Adam's eyes did not leave the screen. 'She knows that, doesn't she?'

Hannah frowned at him. 'Yes, of course.' She came in and sat down on the end of Lisa's bed, from where she could look over his shoulder at the screen.

'What are you looking for?' she asked.

'I'm tracking her history,' he said.

'You mean her search history?'

'It's a bit more complicated than that,' he said. He did not bother to explain. He knew that Hannah's familiarity with the workings of computers was rudimentary.

'What are you looking for?'

Adam pressed some more buttons, the cool light of the screen reflecting, sickly silver, on his face. 'Something that isn't here,' he said.

'Is that a riddle?' she asked with a trace of impatience. 'I'm awfully tired for riddles.'

'No,' he said.

'Then what is it?' Hannah demanded, feeling suddenly annoyed at him. She would never get back to sleep now.

'Something that should be here, but it's not,' he said, still tapping at the keyboard.

Hannah frowned at him. 'Stop talking nonsense. What do you mean?'

Adam swiveled the seat of the desk chair around and looked at Hannah directly. 'I went back to last winter. I looked up your mother's birthday. That was the date when Lisa spoke to Wynonna about Troy, and then I went forward from there. It was three weeks after that that she first went out with Troy Petty.'

'We talked about this,' said Hannah defensively. 'You and I agreed that she probably felt sorry for him. The underdog, unfairly accused. That's just like Lisa.'

Adam shook his head. 'She didn't search it.'

Hannah frowned. 'Didn't search what?'

'Her accusations. Lisa started to date him but she didn't research Wynonna's accusations.'

Hannah shook her head and peered at him as if he was losing his mind. 'Oh, Adam, what are you doing? That doesn't mean anything.'

'Really?' he asked. 'This Wynonna person tells her that a guy she works with is an accused pedophile. And the next thing you know, she starts dating him. And she didn't even do a search on the incident at the camp? Lisa's the mother of a small child. She's told that this guy is a pedophile and she goes out with him anyway, without even doing the most basic search? Who would do that? You wouldn't do that. You'd do a search on him first thing.'

Hannah felt suddenly indignant. 'Maybe she asked him about those charges, and he explained it to her. Did you ever think of that? Or maybe she looked it up at work.'

Adam looked at her stubbornly. 'She hasn't got time to make that kind of search at the hospital. And I don't believe for one moment that she asked him. Look, I don't care if she risks her own safety, but to risk Sydney's?'

Hannah slid off the end of the bed and stood over him, her hands on her hips. She felt tears pricking her eyes but she did not wipe them away. 'Why are you doing this? She's your daughter. You're supposed to defend her, not trump up reasons to vilify her. You're worse than the prosecutor. We're about to get her home. We're about to get our lives back, and all you can think to do is invade her privacy and try to make her out to be . . .'

'Reckless,' he said, pushing the desk chair back and standing up. He pointed his index finger at Hannah. 'Don't deny it. She's reckless and you know it.'

Hannah shook her head angrily. 'I'm not listening to this. There's something wrong with you. That's all there is to it. You insist on thinking the worst of her.'

'She deliberately risked her daughter's safety. And we still don't know if the worst happened to Sydney, thanks to all that alone time with Troy Petty. That little surprise lies ahead when we get her to a competent shrink. Lisa put Sydney in harm's way and went on about her business. That's the plain truth of the matter. How can you say that's OK?'

'I'm not saying that's OK,' Hannah protested. 'But you're just borrowing trouble. She could have searched that anywhere. There's a computer on her phone, for heaven's sakes. Of course she looked into it. She looked into it and found out that he was never charged.'

'But of all the men in the world, this was the man she chose to date. To leave her child with,' he said flatly.

'Oh, excuse me,' said Hannah sarcastically. 'Now it's about the fact that he was suspected of a crime. A crime for which he was never charged. I thought this was about the fact that Lisa didn't research him.'

'It's about her deliberate carelessness,' he countered.

'You're just fishing for some reason to blame her. How do you know she didn't look it up on another computer? Or call someone? You're just being . . . completely unfair,' Hannah cried.

'I don't think so,' he said.

'Maybe she's defiant because you don't trust her,' Hannah insisted. 'Maybe you're angry because we had to pay for a lawyer.'

'You're damn right I'm angry,' he said. 'She's partly to blame for this. You insist on pretending that none of this is her fault.'

Hannah drew herself up, insulted. 'I'm her mother. I'm aware of her shortcomings. Maybe more than you are. I'm the one who has gone to school when she got in trouble, or to see the guidance counselors while you were at work. I have talked to her till I'm blue in the face. I am not blind to the fact that she can be reckless and careless and she can act without thinking. But don't tell me that she doesn't love Sydney. That she wouldn't protect her from harm, because that is just not true.'

'I wish I could be sure of that,' said Adam, shaking his head.

'You're talking about our child.'

'She's not a child any longer,' he said stubbornly.

Hannah knew Lisa's faults as well as Adam did. Better, maybe. Over the years she and Lisa had had more than their share of arguments. But Adam just seemed to be piling on blame. Now, when they were almost out of the woods. It wasn't fair. 'If you feel that way, maybe you shouldn't be here when Lisa comes home,' she hissed.

Adam jerked back as if she had slapped him, and glared at her. Hannah could see that he was making an effort not to reply. For her part, she felt horrible having said that to him, but she was in no mood to apologize.

'I'm not going anywhere,' he said. 'Someone has to look out for Sydney.'

'Like I don't?' Hannah demanded.

'If the shoe fits . . .' he said.

You bastard. How dare you, she thought, but she didn't say it. She couldn't. They'd had their fights over the years but she had never called him names.

'I'm sorry,' he said immediately. 'That wasn't fair. I know you'd do anything to protect Sydney. Or Lisa. Come on. Look, we shouldn't be arguing about this. We need to stick together. Let's go back to bed.'

Hannah shook her head, avoiding his gaze. 'You go ahead.'

Adam put the desk chair back under the desk, and tried to cajole her. 'Come on, babe. I didn't mean to hurt your feelings. I'm . . . We're just worn out.'

Hannah shook her head again. 'Go on.'

He hesitated, peering at her worriedly, and then left the room. Hannah let him go. She sank back down onto the side of her daughter's bed, limp with despair. After a few minutes, she pulled the covers back and slid under the sheets. She hugged one of Lisa's pillows to her chest, thinking that she would never sleep now. She was shaking from the unfamiliar sensation of having bitter words with Adam. Why is he doing this? she thought. Here we are. Almost OK, and now he does this. Why? She fell asleep with the question descending, like a cloud of paralyzing fog, around her brain.

EIGHTEEN

The two of them seemed bruised, and were quiet at breakfast, politely passing the butter and jam. 'Did you get some sleep?' he asked her finally.

'I slept,' she said. 'Not well. But I slept.'

'I missed you,' he said.

'I didn't mean to sleep in Lisa's room. I just passed out,' she said.

'I'm sorry about that whole business last night,' said Adam. 'I was feeling . . . I don't know. At my wits' end.'

Hannah leaned over and wiped some cereal off of Sydney's chin. The toddler was subdued as well. 'Never mind,' she said. 'I understand.'

'What are you going to do today?' he asked.

'Besides wait for the phone to ring?'

'Of course,' he said.

Hannah shook her head. 'Well, I'm behind at work but I'm too stressed out to concentrate on anything. I think I'll just keep Sydney here and spend some time with her.'

'I have to keep my mind busy somehow. I think I'll go into the office,' Adam said. 'I have so much piled up.'

'What if the verdict comes in?' Hannah asked, looking up at him, startled.

'The minute they call,' he said. 'Get me on speed dial. I'm there.'

'Marjorie might call you first,' said Hannah.

'Either way,' he said.

Hannah sighed.

'If you want me to stay here with you . . .' he said quickly.

'No,' said Hannah. 'We'll be fine.' She leaned toward Sydney and shook her head, smiling. 'We'll be fine, won't we?'

Sydney began to giggle and tried to feed cereal to her grandmother. Hannah gently declined.

'We'll have a walk in the park,' she said to Sydney.

'Hopefully,' said Adam, 'we won't have long to wait.'

Hannah looked up at him and their worried eyes met. 'I don't know what to hope for.'

'Marjorie said that they won't take long if they're going to acquit,' Adam said.

'Then I'll hope for quick,' Hannah said.

'Me too,' he said, gathering up his laptop case and kissing Sydney on the top of her head. 'Love you.' He smiled warily at Hannah.

She smiled back. 'Love you too.'

She was almost afraid to leave the house but Sydney was eager to go out into the sunny day, and Hannah knew it was the best thing. A picnic, she thought. A day of grace. She made them sandwiches and drinks, and packed the thermal lunch bag in the back of Sydney's stroller. She checked twice to make sure her cellphone was charged before she slipped it into her pocket and followed Sydney out into the driveway. Sydney was big enough to walk, and once they got to the park Hannah planned to get her out of the stroller, but right now she felt the need to hurry, so as to avoid having to answer a million questions from people on their street. She settled the toddler comfortably in the stroller and began to push her down the driveway and along the neat sidewalks to the park at the end of the block. In the park there were wide, winding pathways, which flanked a meandering stream. The clear stream burbled over rocks under a leafy canopy of low-hanging branches. Once they reached the pathways, Hannah lifted Sydney out of her stroller, and let her explore the periphery of the paths, collecting little stones to toss into the water.

So intent were they on their mission that they didn't notice the rolling wheelchair until it had almost reached them. Hannah glanced up and then her face broke into a smile. 'Chet! Rayanne!' She straightened up and hugged both her neighbors, leaning down to embrace Chet in the wheelchair. Chet's skin was still a pale, grayish color, and there were deep circles under his eyes, but he smiled broadly and his eyes lit up. 'You are a sight for sore eyes,' Hannah said sincerely to Chet.

'I'm a mess,' he said. 'But I'm getting there. Good to see you two.'

In truth, Rayanne didn't look much healthier than her husband, but she, too, seemed delighted to see Hannah and Sydney.

They both admired Sydney's collection of pebbles, and Chet expressed encouragement at Sydney's pitching arm as the toddler tossed them into the stream.

'It's so good to see you out and about,' said Hannah sincerely. 'I wish I could have been a better friend to you through all this.'

Rayanne squeezed Hannah's hand. 'Don't be silly. You've had your own problems. Where do things stand? I admit I haven't been paying attention to the news.'

'The case has gone to the jury,' said Hannah. 'This morning.'

Rayanne looked sympathetically at Hannah. 'I'll pray for you.'

'You better,' said Hannah.

'Did Jamie go back?' Hannah asked.

'Not yet. It's been great having him here. He's been such a help to me.'

'I'll bet.'

'His girlfriend has to go back tomorrow. Jamie's here for a few more days.'

'I'm sure you're glad of that. Keep him here as long as you can,' said Hannah.

Rayanne nodded. 'Listen, if you get the call from the courthouse, you just drop that little one off with us.'

'Oh, Ray, I couldn't,' said Hannah. 'You've got enough to worry about.'

'I insist,' said Rayanne. 'She feels at home at our house. I don't want that child suffering any more upheaval than she's already had. I mean it, Hannah. You just leave her with me.'

Hannah sighed. 'I am so grateful to you. That would really be a load off my mind. Of course, this jury could take a week to decide.'

'Whenever it comes,' said Rayanne. 'Day or night. You hear me?'

'Thank you,' said Hannah.

Chet looked up from the game he was playing with Sydney. 'That's what friends are for,' he said.

Chet and Rayanne continued on their perambulation through the park while Hannah and Sydney loitered by the stream. Sydney wanted to take her flip-flops off and step into the water, so Hannah took off her own sandals and joined her at the edge of the shallow, rocky brook. The water which ran over her feet was icy cold, and felt wonderful. The autumn leaves were golden and they fell in spirals from the rustling branches and landed on the surface of the sun-dappled water. The shining gray stones formed a timeless pattern in the bed of the stream as the water tumbled over and past them. Hannah felt somehow relieved of her constant burdens, just standing there, letting Sydney splash around as they enjoyed the early autumn day. She remembered bringing Lisa here when she was a toddler. Nothing had ever been peaceful with her. Still, Hannah was grateful then for this oasis from the heat and the noise of life, and she was grateful now.

Finally, Sydney tired of her explorations and said she was hungry. They sat at a little picnic table under a tree, and had their lunch. Then Sydney chased a few birds, trying unsuccessfully to wrap them in her pudgy arms. Finally weary, she raised her arms to Hannah, indicating that she wanted to be picked up. Hannah bent down and lifted the slight child up. The feel of Sydney's damp hair, her warm, rosy skin and her beating heart was balm to Hannah's soul. She was almost happy for the first time in ages. The jury had the case, and they were going to acquit Lisa. There was no way they couldn't, she told herself. She remembered last night, and Adam's search on Lisa's computer. It was like a cloud over the sun but Hannah was determined to put it out of her mind. This whole nightmare was soon going to be over, and Lisa would be reunited with her parents and her child. Hannah felt it so strongly, she was almost able to convince herself that it was going to happen.

She settled Sydney back into her stroller, put on her own sandals, and, after looking at her phone to be sure that she had not somehow missed a call, walked back toward the house. Sydney fell asleep in the stroller, and Hannah did not want to wake her. She parked the stroller under a shady tree, and pulled up a chair beside it. Before she knew it, Hannah too was asleep.

She was awakened by her phone. Her heart leapt, and she blinked at the display, trying to see who was calling.

Marjorie Fox. Still groggy, she fumbled to answer.

'The jury is coming back in. They have a verdict,' said Marjorie.

'Oh my God,' said Hannah.

'Get down to the courthouse.'

'I will,' said Hannah. 'Right away.'

She speed-dialed Adam, who answered on the first ring. 'They have a verdict,' she said.

'I'm on my way. What about Sydney?'

'Rayanne already told me to leave her with them.'

'OK,' he said. 'I'll see you in ten minutes.'

Hannah took the sleepy, protesting toddler into the house, and gathered up some food, drinks and toys to take to Rayanne's. Then she quickly changed her own clothes. She could hear Adam's car in the driveway as she fixed her hair.

She walked out of their bedroom and met him coming in the door. They looked at one another, fear and hope and anxiety mingled in their eyes. They embraced briefly.

'I'm going to wash my face,' he said.

'I'll take Sydney next door and meet you at the car,' she said.

Sydney wanted to walk over but Hannah scooped her up, protesting that there was no time. 'We're going to see if we can bring Mommy home,' Hannah explained as she shifted the bag of supplies, whispered in Sydney's ear and knocked at Rayanne's back door.

The door was opened by Jamie, who seemed startled by the sight of them. 'Hi, Mrs Wickes,' he said.

'Jamie, we just got a call from the lawyer. There's a verdict. We're on our way to the courthouse. Is your mom here? Or your dad?'

'Dad's sleeping. Mom went to the store.'

'Oh,' said Hannah. 'Well, your mom said that she would watch Sydney when we had to go to the courthouse.'

'That's no problem. Greta and I can keep an eye on her. Come on in, Sydney.' He reached for the bag. 'My mom will be back in a few minutes.'

'I don't know how to thank you,' said Hannah. 'I'm sure you and Greta have better things to do.'

'Not a bit,' said Jamie magnanimously. Just then Greta came into the kitchen.

Jamie turned to her. 'I told Mrs Wickes we'd watch Sydney till Mom got back.'

Greta immediately brightened. 'Oh, 'course.' She put out a hand to Sydney, who looked up at her, fascinated. 'Come with me, you little minx,' she said.

Hannah smiled, feeling lucky for their support, and tears of exhaustion pricked her eyelids. 'Thanks so much.'

'Good luck,' said Greta.

'Right,' said Jamie. 'Good luck.'

Hannah thanked them both again and stepped out onto the back porch step.

Jamie hesitated, and then followed her outside closing the door behind him.

'Mrs Wickes,' he said. 'Do you have a minute . . .'

Hannah turned to look at him and saw consternation in his eyes. Just barely, she thought. It must be about his parents. She reminded herself to be patient. 'What, Jamie?' she asked.

'I've been following the trial,' he said. 'I read all of the testimony. There was something I wanted to talk to you about . . .'

Hannah frowned. 'About the trial? Can it wait? This isn't really a good time.'

Jamie nodded. 'Sure. Of course this isn't the time. It's just that . . .'

The door of the Wickes house opened and Adam emerged, waving to the two of them as he brandished the car keys. 'Hannah, let's go,' he called out.

Jamie pressed his lips together. 'Never mind,' he said.

'We really do have to go,' said Hannah.

'You go ahead,' said Jamie. He nodded his head sharply, as if he had made a decision. 'And don't worry about Sydney. We'll take good care of her.'

'Are you sure?' Hannah asked uncertainly.

'Absolutely. You take your time. And give Lisa my best.'

Hannah gave a sigh of relief and rushed to the car where her husband waited.

The courtroom was crowded with spectators, TV cameramen, reporters and officers of the court. Hannah and Adam were worried about where to sit but Marjorie gestured to them to come up to the front. When they got there, Marjorie dismissed two of her support staff who were saving seats behind the defense table and immediately ceded them to Hannah and Adam.

'She thinks of everything,' said Adam admiringly.

Lisa turned around and looked at them wide-eyed. 'This is it,' she said.

'Don't be afraid, darling,' said Hannah, trying to grab her hand.

'I'm not afraid,' said Lisa.

Hannah looked at her daughter, and knew that it was true. Somehow, she wasn't afraid. She was as calm and detached as if this were all happening to someone else.

The bailiff ordered them all to rise, and everyone in the courtroom stood up dutifully as the judge took his seat on the bench. 'Bring in the jury,' said Judge Endicott.

Hannah clutched Adam's hand as the jury filed in and took their seats across the courtroom from Lisa. Hannah studied their faces, trying to read their expressions. You hold my daughter's fate in your hands, she thought. Please, please, don't take her away from us. Or from her child. Please.

The judge turned and faced the jury. He asked the foreman to stand, and then asked if they had reached their verdict. The foreman announced that they had.

Hannah felt as if her heart were being squeezed in her chest. She glanced at Adam and saw his strong features, rigid with anxiety. With excruciating slowness, the judge explained the charges again, and finally turned to the foreman.

'On the first count, murder in the first degree, how do you find?' asked the judge.

The foreman hesitated and glanced over at Lisa.

'Not guilty,' said the foreman.

A loud gasp and cries erupted in the courtroom, and the judge slammed down his gavel. The crowd lapsed into quiet. Lisa turned and looked at her parents, her eyebrows raised, her face wreathed in a smile. Hannah felt as if she could rise from her seat on wings of happiness. She looked into Adam's eyes through grateful tears. He was squeezing her in his arms.

'She's free,' Hannah whispered. 'Oh my God. It's over.'

'Order in the court,' the judge intoned, banging the gavel. The spectators quieted down to a hopeful murmur.

'On the second count, larceny in the second degree,' said the judge.

The jury foreman did not hesitate. 'Guilty,' he said.

The spectators were quiet. Hannah looked in bewilderment at Adam. 'What does this mean?'

'I'm not sure,' said Adam, his gaze trained on Lisa. 'I don't understand. I guess they think she stole the check from Troy.'

The judge offered to poll the jury individually but Marjorie graciously declined.

'In that case,' said the judge, 'I'm ready to pass sentence on the defendant.'

Lisa obediently lowered her head.

'Lisa Wickes,' said the judge. 'You have been convicted of the crime of larceny in the second degree. I hereby sentence you to two months in the county jail in addition to time served.'

Lisa nodded humbly.

'Bailiff will take the defendant back into custody.'

As the bailiff came toward Lisa, she turned and looked at her parents. Hannah reached for her daughter and managed to encircle her in an awkward embrace. 'It's all over, darling,' she said. 'You'll be home in no time.'

'It's so unfair,' said Lisa. 'I didn't steal the stupid check.'

The bailiff gruffly told Lisa to raise her hands to be cuffed. Hannah let her go reluctantly. Adam was shaking hands with Marjorie, thanking her profusely. He turned to Lisa, who looked pleadingly at her father. 'Two more months?' she cried.

Adam, who had put a consoling hand on her arm, pulled it away. 'It will be over before you know it,' he said. 'We were lucky.'

'Why?' Lisa complained. 'I didn't do anything.'

'Lisa, quiet,' Marjorie hissed. 'The judge is speaking.'

The judge thanked the jury for their service and dismissed them. He asked the two attorneys to his chambers for a conference, and then court was dismissed.

Lisa looked back at her parents, both relief and resentment in her gaze, as she was led away. Adam shook his head. 'Doesn't she realize how lucky she is?'

'I guess it's hard to feel lucky when you're going back to jail,' said Hannah.

Buoyed along the crowd, Hannah and Adam clung to one another, and made their way out of the courtroom. Reporters besieged them for comments, and they responded to everyone in the same way.

'We're very relieved,' said Hannah. 'Thank goodness the jury understood that my daughter was innocent.'

'Not exactly innocent,' said a bearded young reporter for the *Tennessean*. 'She was convicted of larceny.'

Adam turned and looked at him. Hannah could see that he was forcing himself to respond calmly. 'We believe that it was a misunderstanding about the check but we accept the jury's verdict. The important thing is that they realized our daughter did not kill Mr Petty, and that she will be coming home in a few weeks. We are very grateful.'

Hannah clung to Adam's hand, almost blissfully unaware of the cameras, the flashing lights, the shouted questions. Thank you, Lord, she thought.

'How are you feeling, Mrs Wickes?' asked Chanel Ali Jackson, putting a microphone in front of Hannah's face.

'Happy,' said Hannah. 'Relieved. This nightmare is finally over.'

No sooner were the words out of her mouth than her gaze fell on Troy Petty's sister, Nadine Melton. She was standing, largely ignored by the press, with an assistant prosecutor, and she was gazing at Hannah and Adam, wiping away angry tears that would not stop flowing. As Hannah met her gaze Nadine shook her head, almost as if in warning. In spite of her relief, Hannah felt an unwelcome stab of anxiety. No, she thought. It is over, and she forced herself to look away.

NINETEEN

Rayanne and Chet were waiting for them with a bottle of champagne. Hannah and Adam exchanged hugs with their friends, and with Jamie and Greta.

Sydney was giddy with excitement, even though she didn't really understand what was going on. They all toasted the verdict, and Hannah felt as if the bubbles were going directly to her head.

'So when will she be home?' asked Rayanne.

'Two months,' said Hannah, embarrassed in spite of herself. 'I don't believe she stole that check but we weren't going to argue. Not after that verdict.'

'Of course not,' said Rayanne.

Adam, who had scooped up Sydney and was holding her on his lap, shook his head as he sipped the champagne. 'Lisa was upset that they had convicted her of taking the check. I don't think she understood how close she came to spending the rest of her life in prison.'

'For something she didn't do,' Hannah reminded him loyally.

'I am completely wrung out,' said Adam. 'That was exhausting.'

'I'm sure you are,' said Chet solemnly.

'In a couple of weeks, when we've both got our legs back under us, let's go out and play nine holes,' said Adam.

'You're on,' said Chet.

Rayanne and Hannah exchanged a fond glance. You never realized, Hannah thought, how precious your everyday routine was, until you were in danger of losing it. Both of their families had skated close to the edge. But they were all going to be OK.

'Well, I don't know about anybody else,' said Adam, 'but I'm going to make it an early night.'

There were murmurs of agreement all around.

'Rayanne said you're leaving tomorrow, Greta?' Hannah asked.

Greta nodded, and Jamie tightened his grip around her waist and tilted his head to smile into her eyes.

'Well, I wish you could stay longer,' said Hannah. 'We didn't get to spend enough time with you.'

'Next time,' said Greta.

Next time. It had such a positive, optimistic sound to it. Greta was already planning to return to Jamie's home town. Hannah thought to herself what a nice girl Jamie had found. 'Jamie, this one's a keeper.'

Jamie beamed at the compliment. 'I think so!'

Hannah felt a little pang at the sight of him, obviously happy and deliriously in love. Jamie and Lisa had been devoted chums as children. Hannah had always secretly hoped that it would turn into something more. But once they were teenagers, the differences between them became more pronounced. Jamie avoided books and his grades were average. He much preferred playing sports to studying. Lisa, with her glasses and her unruly hair, was young for her class and a brain, as kids said so condescendingly.

As if being a brain should be viewed as a handicap, Hannah thought. Now, all the judgments of school days were behind them. Jamie had grown into a fine young man with a steady, if unexciting profession. Lisa, now that this trial was over, had a future of unlimited possibilities in medicine. The last shall be first, she thought.

'Well, Adam's right. We need to get home and get this little one into bed. Thank you all for standing by us.'

They all took their leave with repeated thanks and congratulations and kisses. Adam and Hannah crossed the short distance to their house, Hannah carrying Sydney, and they went inside and closed the door. Their world felt safe and sensible again. Everyone went to bed early, and peace reigned in the two houses.

Hannah was awakened from a restless sleep the next morning by the sound of a car pulling out of Chet and Rayanne's driveway. Jamie, she thought, taking Greta to the airport. She glanced out the window. It was too early to tell if the day had not fully dawned or if it was going to be overcast. She thought about getting up, even though there was still no sound from Sydney. And then, even as she considered arising, she fell back to sleep.

She awoke again to Adam nuzzling her neck, and she rolled into his arms and into lovemaking in their delicious, familiar way. Before long, they were asleep again, and only awoke when Sydney toddled into the room and climbed up into the bed with them.

'What time is it?' Hannah asked, as she absently wrapped one of Sydney's soft blonde curls around her finger.

'It's after nine,' said Adam.

'We really slept,' Hannah observed.

'We needed it.'

'Let's go out to breakfast,' said Hannah. 'Somewhere where nobody knows us.'

'You're on,' said Adam. 'But we'll bring two cars. I want to go to work.'

'I think I'll play hooky one more day,' said Hannah. 'I'm so beat. And I want to spend the time with Sydney. And go see Lisa this afternoon.'

They murmured agreement, and Hannah thought how lovely it was to have their normal life back. Of course, things weren't normal for Lisa. She was still in the county jail, and might be facing consequences for that larceny conviction at medical school. But considering what they might have been facing, it seemed slight.

They drove out of Nashville, halfway to Shelbyville, and had breakfast at a cafe that served sausage, biscuits and eggs all day. The cafe was in a ranch-style log house, and the owner's grandchildren were playing on the porch. Sydney entered cheerfully into the game while Hannah and Adam finished their coffee and watched them right outside their window table.

Adam and Hannah kissed before getting into their separate cars and then Adam kissed the top of Sydney's head. 'Come home early,' Hannah said. 'I'll make something you like for dinner.'

'What?' he asked.

'I'll figure something out.'

'I know you will.' He smiled and got into his car, and waved as he pulled away. Hannah buckled Sydney into her car seat and headed for home.

The phone rang right after lunch, and it was Lisa. 'Do you believe that crappy jury convicted me?' she protested.

'Darling, all things considered, we were lucky,' said Hannah, pained by her daughter's attitude. 'You should be grateful.'

'That's easy for you to say,' Lisa sniffed. 'I'm stuck here for two months and God only knows what will happen to my scholarships.'

'We'll figure it out,' said Hannah soothingly. 'Don't worry. I'm sure we can reason with them about your scholarships. Right now, I'm just so relieved.'

'Mother, I don't understand what you're so happy about. Here I was, accused of some crime that was really just an accident. And now I have to spend two more months in this place!'

Hannah tried to see it from Lisa's point of view. She told herself that she too would be upset if she faced jail time for something she didn't do. But in light of what the outcome could have been, it was difficult to feel unhappy. She changed the subject. 'I was thinking of coming to see you today. Can I bring you anything?'

'A file in a cake,' said Lisa, only half joking.

'It won't be long and you'll be home.'

'Yes. But with a record. This is ruining my life. I wish I'd never gotten involved with that idiot.'

'Troy.'

'Yes, Troy. What a mistake.'

Hannah thought back to Adam scouring Lisa's hard drive. Looking for the search that wasn't there. She pictured Troy's sister, watching her almost pityingly after the trial. Then she shook her head. 'It's all over now,' said Hannah. 'Let's think positive. Sydney sends kisses.'

'Great,' said Lisa.

'See you later,' said Hannah, but before the words were out, Lisa had hung up.

For a few moments, Hannah sat, staring at the phone. Then she sighed and put it back in her pocket. She scooped up Sydney, took her outside to water the flowers and then she watched Sydney play with the water from the hose until it was time for her nap. After Sydney was settled in her bed, Hannah went back to the living room to read. The thought of the drive to the county jail was unappealing, but once Adam got home she was determined to go and see her daughter.

A knocking at the back door roused her, and she went to see who it was.

Jamie stood on the doorstep.

Hannah smiled at him, puzzled. 'Jamie. How are you?'

Jamie met her eyes briefly and looked away, 'I'm OK.'

'I heard you leaving the house this morning,' said Hannah. 'Did Greta get her flight all right?'

'Yes. Just fine,' he said. 'Thanks.'

'Your folks?' Hannah asked, frowning.

'They're fine. Can I come in, Mrs Wickes? I need to talk to you.'

'Sure,' said Hannah. 'Come on in.'

Jamie came into the kitchen. He was a slim young man, tall with broad shoulders. Today he was wearing a neat oxford-cloth shirt and jeans. There was nothing hip-hop about Jamie. His hair was a little bit spiky, in his one concession to fashion. He turned to Hannah. 'Is Mr Wickes here?' he asked.

'No, he's at work. Did you need to talk to him?'

Jamie frowned. 'It might be better if it was just you and me.'

'OK,' said Hannah, feeling a little puzzled by his troubled air. 'Come on in the living room,' she said, leading the way through the house. 'Have a seat.'

'Where's Sydney?'

'Taking a nap,' said Hannah.

'She's a nice little girl,' said Jamie, nodding. 'Greta was crazy about her.'

'You think you two will . . .' Hannah let it go, seeing the look in his eyes.

'Maybe . . . someday,' he said, frowning. 'Look, I need to just . . . say this before I lose my . . . nerve.'

Hannah pulled back from him. 'Say what? You seem so . . . worried.'

'Worried. That's a good word for it. I am worried. I didn't even tell my mother I was coming over here because I didn't want to discuss this with her. Or my dad.'

'Well,' said Hannah carefully, 'if you're concerned about something, you might as well just . . . say so.'

Jamie nodded but still he hesitated.

'Jamie?'

'Right. OK. You remember how Lisa and I used to be friends when we were . . . younger.'

'Sure,' said Hannah. 'You two were inseparable as children. And you stayed friends for a long while there.'

Jamie frowned, his gaze faraway. 'Did she ever tell you,' he asked, 'why we stopped being friends?'

Hannah shook her head. She was not going to repeat Lisa's assertions that Jamie was too stupid to be friends with. Hannah always suspected that Lisa was just covering up her hurt feelings when Jamie got involved with sports and NASCAR. She thought that maybe he had come to find it embarrassing to be known as the friend of someone younger, even if she was in the same grade. Lisa was plain and brainy and uncool in the eyes of the older boys. 'I thought you two just grew apart,' said Hannah. 'You were a little older than her. It was just one of those things,' she said.

Jamie frowned. 'No, it wasn't,' he said.

'It wasn't?' said Hannah, taken aback.

'It was something very specific,' he said.

'OK,' said Hannah. Part of her wanted to say, do we have to deconstruct this long-gone friendship right now? I am so weary from all that has happened. Is this really the time and place? But she stayed silent.

Jamie glanced at her, and then looked away. He was kneading his hands together absently, rubbing the backs of his hands with his long fingers. 'I have a very important reason for bringing this up.

I wouldn't be troubling you with it otherwise. You'll understand when I tell you.'

'OK,' Hannah said again, nodding. She was overcome with a feeling that she was going to regret listening to Jamie's explanation. She wanted to stop him but couldn't think of a good reason to do so.

Jamie took a deep breath. 'I've tried not to think much about this over the years. It was too upsetting. But I was following the trial, particularly when Lisa took the stand and talked about Troy Petty. About being disgusted, finding him . . . you know . . . with Sydney.'

Hannah watched his face, wondering what in the world he was getting at. 'Well, unfortunately there are men like that,' she said. 'Pedophiles.'

Jamie looked up at her, anguish in his eyes. 'I would never mention this to you, but there's an innocent life involved here.'

'Jamie, I don't know what you're getting at but I've got to tell you,' Hannah snapped, 'this is all becoming too weird . . .'

'All right. All right,' he said. 'Look. Something happened when my father's sister and her family came to visit. I was about . . . I had just turned seventeen that summer.'

Hannah dimly recalled the visit. Chet's sister lived in Arizona, and came only rarely to Tennessee. 'I remember that,' she said.

'My cousins, Shane and Alberta, were just toddlers. And my mother asked me to mind them so they could go and visit some great-aunt of theirs near Chattanooga. Well, she gave me my choice of minding them or going to Chattanooga, so the choice was easy I said I would do it. We had that little kiddy pool set up. And the swings. I figured, how bad could it be?'

Hannah nodded, remembering that time.

'Well, Lisa came over. You know how we always were. Back and forth through the hedge,' he said, and there was a catch in his voice. 'Even then, she was like my best friend.'

'I know,' said Hannah, and she heard the note of warning in her own voice.

Jamie heaved a sigh and looked down at his own, interlaced fingers.

'So,' Hannah prodded him.

'So, she came over, and we were playing in that little pool with them, and drinking Cokes. You know, just whiling away the afternoon. And I said I had better take them in and find them some dry clothes. Lisa said she'd help me, and she followed me into the house. I was rummaging around in their suitcases for some dry clothes while Lisa peeled off their little swimsuits.'

'She wasn't used to small children,' said Hannah.

Jamie ignored the interruption. 'I finally found a pair of shorts and a T-shirt for each of them, and I looked up, saying eureka or something like that, and Lisa had her arms around them. She was kissing them and such . . .'

'Affectionately,' said Hannah, supplying the word.

'And then I realized that she had taken off the top of her suit.'

'Jamie, look, if you're about to tell me that you and Lisa . . . I always assumed that maybe you two experimented a little bit. I don't find that shocking.'

Jamie looked at her darkly and Hannah retreated into silence. 'This is about the children. Lisa was nuzzling them and she said to me, "They're so cute." I was a little . . . surprised, but I agreed with her that they were cute. And then she said, "Take your suit off."'

Hannah said nothing. The silence in the room was deafening.

Jamie shook his head. 'I didn't get it at first. I was so shocked to see Lisa like that. Without her top. I won't lie to you. I'd often imagined it but I never really held out much hope that anything would happen between us. Anything sexual, I mean. I was a jock, but really, I was too . . . timid. Still, I knew that the kids shouldn't see her like that. I thought maybe she was trying to say to me that she wanted to, you know, mess around. Obviously I was in favor of it, but not in front of the kids. "Lisa," I said, "not right now. I mean, later, yes, when we're alone . . ."'

'She wasn't even looking at me. Her eyes were glittering and she was staring at them. They were like cherubs. I mean, the picture of innocence. And she said, "Come on, Jamie. Let's play with them. Let's take them into the bedroom. I want to watch you do it with Alberta. Wouldn't you like to do that?"'

'You just wait a minute,' said Hannah jumping up from the sofa. 'Why are you saying this? Take that back. That is just sick. That's the product of a teenage boy's sick mind.'

Jamie did not take offense. He scarcely moved. 'I could hardly believe it myself,' he said. 'But there was no mistaking what she said. Her tone of voice.'

'Tone of voice,' Hannah scoffed. 'You're making this up.'

Jamie refused to be interrupted. 'When I didn't respond, she started fondling Shane. I felt like I was frozen, watching it.'

'You are lying,' Hannah thundered. 'That is just shameful. Get out of my house. That's your own filthy mind. Get out of here.'

Jamie stood up and his chin was trembling. 'I took him away from her and told her to put on her top and get out of the house. I told her not to come over again while my cousins were visiting. She said I was a prude and a jerk and that she didn't want anything more to do with me, period. She said she would never come back. And she didn't.'

'What is the matter with you?' said Hannah. 'I can't believe you would make up this story about Lisa, after all these years. Are you crazy?'

'I heard what she said about Troy Petty when she was testifying. She claimed that he was getting ready to assault Sydney. But the things she said? Those were the very same suggestions she made about my cousins years earlier.'

'That's not true,' Hannah protested. 'Your mother would have said something to me years ago.'

'I never told her,' he said.

'Why wouldn't you tell her?' Hannah demanded.

'I was ashamed!' he cried. 'How was I going to say that to my mother? Besides, I didn't want Lisa to get in trouble. I . . . I cared about her. Despite that, I still cared about her. She stayed away from me after that but I wouldn't have done anything to hurt her. Now I wonder if I made the right decision.'

'This is vicious of you. Just vicious, Jamie. Why are you saying these things now, when the trial is over? Are you still so angry that she rebuffed you all those years ago?'

Jamie shook his head wearily. 'I didn't want to say this to you. That was the last thing I wanted to do. Believe me. But when I heard her testimony, her acting so . . . indignant, I knew she was lying. I suspect it was the other way around. She suggested it, and Troy was shocked and threw her out. I had to say something to you. Sydney can't protect herself from Lisa. You have to do it.'

'Get out of here. I don't want to hear another word!'

'I'm going. I'm so sorry. Sorry I had to tell you.'

Hannah sat back down on the sofa, her heart pounding. She refused to look at him.

'I'm only telling you this for Sydney's sake, Mrs Wickes. You have to know this about Lisa, because Sydney needs to be protected.'

She did not answer him or meet his gaze.

In a few minutes, she heard the back door open and then close behind him.

TWENTY

The house was quiet when Adam returned. He came in the back door and called out, 'Anybody home?'

Hannah sat in the living room, in the exact spot where she had been sitting when Jamie left her. She heard Adam's call but did not answer. She could hear Sydney crooning quietly in her bedroom. Her nap was long over, and she had played quietly for a while with her toys. Now she was restive and looking for some attention, but Hannah did not attend to her. Adam walked into the living room and saw her. He heard Sydney calling out from her room.

'What are you doing sitting in here in the dark?' he asked.

Hannah looked up at him. 'Will you take care of Sydney? I can't.'

'What's the matter, darling? Are you all right?'

'Will you?' she asked.

'Of course,' he said. He hesitated a moment, frowning at her, and then he went down the hall, calling out to Sydney. Hannah heard their happy cries of greeting, and then Sydney came barreling into the living room and climbed up on Hannah's lap while Adam banged around in the kitchen. He came in and offered Sydney a sippy cup. Sydney took it eagerly and began to drink.

Adam sat down beside Hannah and peered at her. 'What's going on?' he asked. 'I'm sorry if I'm late. But you still have time to get over to the county jail before visitors' hours are over.'

Hannah shook her head numbly.

'I've got an idea,' said Adam, switching on the television to a cartoon channel. Sydney was instantly absorbed. 'You watch for a while. I'm going to talk to Mom-mom in the other room.'

He guided Hannah off the couch and led her into their bedroom. He left the door ajar so that they could see Sydney, and indicated that Hannah should sit on the loveseat in the bedroom alcove. Then he sat down beside her, and slung his arm over the cushion behind her. 'OK,' he said. 'What's the matter?'

Hannah shook her head. 'I don't even want to say it.'

Adam frowned. 'Honey, what happened between our breakfast and now?'

Hannah was quiet for a minute. He waited patiently, watching her face. 'I had a visitor,' she said.

'OK.'

'Jamie.'

Adam nodded.

'He came over because he had followed the trial. He thought we should know something. Something he knew about Lisa that had to do with her testimony.'

'What would he know about Lisa or her testimony? He and Lisa aren't even in touch. We've hardly seen him in the last three years.'

Hannah looked her husband squarely in the eye. 'He said that when they were teenagers, Lisa suggested that they . . .' She couldn't continue.

'What?' Adam asked. 'You're scaring me.'

Hannah drew herself up, and looked away from him. 'He said that Lisa wanted him to molest his two-year-old cousin so she could watch.'

'He . . . what . . .?' Adam shook his head. 'No. No. That's ridiculous. What the hell is he talking about?'

'He followed the testimony. When Lisa said that she had caught Troy getting ready to molest Sydney . . . Well, Jamie came to tell me that it was Lisa who was interested in that sort of . . . activity.'

Adam stared at her.

Hannah turned and faced him. 'He meant it, Adam. He wasn't lying. He was mortified to even say such a thing to me.'

'He comes up with this now? It doesn't make sense. He never said anything before.'

'He said that the only reason he was telling me this was because he was worried for Sydney.'

Adam shook his head. 'No. That's . . . not possible.'

They both sat in silence, trying to convince themselves that it was not possible.

'Adam, I've been thinking about this obsessively ever since he left. What if it is? We both wondered why she dated a man who was accused of being a child molester. Maybe she sought Troy Petty out for exactly that reason.'

'No. Do you hear yourself? *No.*'

'I don't want to believe it!' Hannah cried.

'*No.* I'm telling you, no. Listen to me,' said Adam. 'Think about it. Where do these pedophiles make all their connections?'

'I don't know,' said Hannah miserably.

'On the internet,' he said.

Hannah nodded. 'Yes, I suppose.'

'Suppose, nothing,' he said. 'That's how they do it. That's how they find one another.'

'Yes,' she said slowly.

'So, the other night, when I went through Lisa's entire search history, there was nothing like that there. No kiddie porn,' he said, grimacing at actually speaking the words. '*Nothing* like that. If Jamie's accusations were true, if this were some kind of secret thing that Lisa was . . . doing, she would have been looking at those sites, I would have found it. I work with computers. I don't want to bore you to death with the details but, believe me, I've combed through it and I'm telling you, there is no way.'

In spite of herself, Hannah felt encouraged by his words. 'I know if anyone could find it, it would be you. It's just that you were the one who was bothered by the fact that she didn't search Troy Petty when Wynonna told her about his past . . .'

'I thought it was strange,' he admitted. 'But facts are facts. She didn't have any of that crap on her computer.'

Hannah tried to take heart, tried to nourish a fragile hope. 'You're right. If this was something . . . real, she probably would have.'

'Of course she would have . . . And besides, you work with social services. You've seen every kind of antisocial behavior. Have you ever known a woman who would do that?'

Hannah searched her memory. 'No. Not personally. But I've heard of such things. We all have. You see it on the internet. There's no end to the perversity of people.'

'I know,' he insisted stubbornly. 'But not Lisa.'

Hannah stared bleakly at her husband. 'If you could have heard him telling this story . . . It was . . . horrible.'

'Hannah, you know he always liked her. He always wanted her to be more than a friend. Maybe he just said this stuff to try to finally . . . pay her back somehow.'

'Jamie? Chet and Rayanne's Jamie?'

'People act ugly when they're hurt. They often want revenge.'

'That's a pretty sick way to pay someone back.'

'Well, we're talking about some sick things here.'

Hannah looked at him pleadingly. 'So you don't think there could be any truth to it.'

'No,' he said defiantly. 'I think he is . . . trying to punish Lisa for dropping him as a friend all those years ago.'

Hannah wanted to believe him but a little voice inside was nagging at her. That doesn't make sense. 'You have to be right,' she said, in defiance of her doubts.

'Mom-mom,' Sydney cried out from the living room. 'More juice.'

Adam managed a smile. 'We're being summoned.'

'I promised you a decent meal,' she said hopelessly.

He shook his head. 'It doesn't matter. We can have a sandwich. Are you going out to the jail?'

Hannah shook her head. 'I don't think I can do it. Not tonight. Lisa will be mad.'

'Are you kidding me? After all we've been through, I'm not too worried about Lisa being mad. You just lay low. It's all right now. Put this out of your mind,' he said.

'Mom-mom,' Sydney cried.

Hannah stood up and took a deep breath. 'Easier said than done,' she said.

Lisa called at nine o'clock and demanded to know why her parents had not come to visit. Adam took the call, and told his daughter that Hannah had a bad headache and had gone to bed early. He said that they would come to see her in a day or two, and Lisa, sensing a distance in her father's voice, immediately scaled back her imperious demands.

After he hung up the phone, he turned to Hannah. 'I think she needed a dose of reality. We have jumped through hoops for that girl. Now she can cool her heels a little bit.'

Hannah, who was lying back against a large sofa cushion, gazed anxiously at her husband. 'Were we bad parents?' she asked.

Adam shook his head. 'I never thought so. We didn't spoil her. We always loved her and paid attention to her.'

'Nothing makes sense to me right now.'

'I know. Maybe you should try to go into work tomorrow. That might help,' he said. 'Take Sydney over to Tiffany's for the day. She can run around with the other kids. It might do her good. We all need some normalcy.'

'Maybe you're right,' said Hannah. 'I don't want to be in this house. I don't want to look out the window and see Jamie and wonder why the hell he would say such a thing.'

'I don't know why Jamie would do that either,' said Adam, 'but I have to believe that he was just trying to rattle us. For some reason.'

Hannah nodded. 'You're right. I'll go to work.'

'Let's go to bed,' he said. 'It will seem better in the morning.'

The next morning, after a sleepless night, it did not seem better. Hannah took Sydney to Tiffany's and drove to work. Going into the office she felt as if she were coming down with an illness. She was shaky inside, and felt weak. Her co-workers congratulated her on Lisa's acquittal, and she tried to seem appreciative. Her list of clients was a demanding one. She didn't have a moment to think until lunchtime.

Jackie poked her head into Hannah's office and greeted her warmly. 'Want to go eat out under the trees?' she asked. 'There's a guy selling Greek food from a cart out there.'

'That sounds great,' said Hannah, thinking how much she would enjoy this simple pleasure. Lunch outside, with a friend. She wrapped up her work and met Jackie in the lobby. Together they stepped out into the warm, beautiful September day.

Once they were settled on the park lawn across from the office, napkins spread on their laps, they began eating their falafel pita pockets.

'It's so good to have you back,' said Jackie at last.

'It's good to be back,' said Hannah, picking desultorily at her sandwich.

'It was a good result,' Jackie said.

Hannah nodded. She sat in silence for a moment, thinking about Jamie and wondering if she dared to even bring it up.

'You still seem worried,' said Jackie.

Hannah sighed.

'What is it?' said Jackie.

Hannah suddenly had an idea of how to explore what she was

thinking about without actually admitting it. She looked over at her friend. 'Actually, it's work-related. I have a client who is truly bizarre. I'm not sure what to do.'

'Tell me about her. I love bizarre!'

Hannah took a deep breath. Then she plunged. 'Have you ever encountered a female pedophile? Particularly a mother who would . . . exploit her own child?'

Jackie set down her sandwich in its waxed-paper wrapper. She patted her mouth with a paper napkin, and then balled it up in the palm of her hand. 'Not personally. But of course such things do exist,' she said.

'That person would have to be completely crazy,' said Hannah.

'Or a psychopath,' suggested Jackie.

'Like I said. Completely crazy,' said Hannah.

'Well, not technically. Psychopathy is not considered a mental illness like schizophrenia or bipolar disease. For one thing there's treatment for those conditions. There are drugs that can help to control them.'

'There's no treatment for psychopaths?' Hannah asked warily.

'No. Nothing that works. On the other hand, you can be a psychopath and function just fine in the world.'

'I thought psychopaths were serial killers and things like that,' Hannah protested.

'Well, it's sort of a continuum – psychopathy. It runs the gamut from depraved criminals to corporate CEOs. What they all have in common is that they don't have the same internal limits that normal people do. Their right-and-wrong gyroscope has malfunctioned. Or just doesn't exist.'

Hannah nodded. Her food tasted like dust in her mouth.

'Does that sound like your client?' said Jackie.

'I hardly know her,' Hannah protested, frowning. 'But no. I don't think so. Not really. She seems pretty normal to me. I'm thinking it must be . . . some effort to discredit her. You know how these custody disputes can go.'

Jackie shrugged. 'Don't be too sure. Psychopaths are expert liars,' she said. 'Often they are highly intelligent people. Capable. Professional. From normal families. It's not a pathology that's known to stem from abuse. Some experts think that it's inborn. That's why it's so hard to comprehend. But psychopaths don't have a depravity meter like the rest of us. They can't be shocked or troubled by things that normal people find repulsive or reprehensible. They have a complete lack of moral restraint.'

'That's an interesting term,' Hannah murmured.

'It's quite accurate,' Jackie insisted.

'So, have you ever treated a psychopath?'

'You mean with therapy?'

'Yes.'

'I've had patients in treatment who . . . I didn't know were psychopaths. Not at first. But it became clear over time. With real psychopaths, there's no way to treat them.'

'No way? Even if they seek out help?'

Jackie shook her head. 'They don't seek out help. Not really. They don't see themselves as damaged. Of course, I've attempted to treat them. Once in a while, in a court-mandated case, you get one as a patient. And you can't tell right away if you have a psychopath in your office. It's a pathology which takes a while to recognize. But once you diagnose it, you realize that any effort to treat them is futile. They don't change. They can't.'

'Probably fairly rare,' said Hannah. She put the rest of her sandwich back into the bag. She no longer felt hungry.

'Not as rare as you might think,' said Jackie. 'They walk among us, seemingly normal. A mother who would assault her own child? Or let someone else assault them? Sure.'

The beautiful day suddenly felt threatening to Hannah. 'Well, I don't understand it,' she said abruptly.

'No one does. Would you like me to have a session with your client? Maybe I could determine . . .'

Hannah felt as if there were a giant hand, squeezing her heart. 'No,' she said. 'Never mind. As you say, what's the use?'

TWENTY-ONE

After lunch, Hannah told her supervisor that she wasn't feeling well, which was certainly true. She said that she needed to go home. Her harried overweight supervisor, a widower named Ward Higgins, had a compassion for people which never seemed to fail. He said that she probably came back to work too soon. 'You've been through an ordeal,' he said. 'You need a few days to recover.'

'Maybe,' said Hannah, collecting her things and heading for the door. She drove home, almost blindly, unaware of what was happening around her. Luckily, the route home was familiar, and she arrived back at the house without incident.

She hurried inside, avoiding even a glance at Rayanne's house. She slammed the door and locked it, leaning her back against the door and staring into the depths of the cool, dark house. When she and Adam had bought this house they were so excited to be home-owners with a yard for their little daughter to play in, and a park down the street. Immediately they set about turning their house into a happy home. And they succeeded, Hannah always thought. Years later, when Sydney arrived, unexpectedly, they welcomed their granddaughter in, and tried to make it happy for her also. Hannah felt tears rising to her eyes. Yesterday it had seemed as if their nightmare was over. Until Jamie knocked at the door. And now . . .

Hannah forced herself to concentrate. She had come home for a reason. Her conversation with Jackie had been sickening, and yet she could not avoid the implications of what her friend had said. There was no use in pretending that she hadn't heard it, hadn't understood. Everything that Jackie was saying about female psycho-paths rang an uncomfortably familiar bell. She tried to tell herself that it wasn't possible, but she had to know. She didn't know how she was going to find out but she was going to make a start.

With an effort of will, she pushed herself away from the door and walked down the dimly lit hallway to the door of Lisa's room. She turned on the overhead light and looked inside. Everything was neat and orderly, as it always was. She had tried never to intrude on her grown daughter's privacy. After all, she had told herself, it wasn't as if Lisa had been lying around the house, slothful and unambitious. She was in medical school. Any parent would be proud of that. And the fact that she was single and had a child – that was practically the norm these days. Hannah had always insisted to herself that she had no right to rummage through her daughter's sanctuary. The other night, she had been appalled to find Adam going through Lisa's computer. Lisa had not been perfect – in fact, sometimes her behavior had been disturbing and inexplicable to them. But surely she deserved her privacy.

Not any more, Hannah thought. If there was something secret

about Lisa's life, she would find it in there. Cleverly hidden, no doubt. Lisa knew that her father worked with computers at Verizon. She must have known that he could access her information if he wanted to. No, if she had a secret life, the evidence would be somewhere else.

Hannah took a deep breath, preparatory to entering the room. And if there was no secret life, if Jamie had been lying, if this ugly, lurking suspicion which was now weighing on Hannah's heart had nothing to it, then no one would ever have to know that she had searched through Lisa's things. She would tell everyone, including Adam and Lisa, that she had come home from work early, feeling ill, and lay down, and that was the end of it. She said a brief prayer that this was exactly what these next hours would bring. She would find nothing. There would be nothing. Nothing but innocence and evidence of Lisa's hard work. Nothing to make a mother anything but proud. Please God, she thought.

She stepped into the room and looked around. She would start with the desk. The desk, she figured, would not yield any obvious clues. Lisa was too smart for that. But it was the logical place to start. Hannah sat down in the desk chair, and began to search.

The afternoon sun poured through the window, and then began to fade as Hannah went through all of Lisa's belongings. She looked in every drawer, in every plastic box, on every shelf. She searched relentlessly. It didn't help that she wasn't sure what she was looking for. Some evidence of perversion. Some proof that Lisa indulged in evil, callous behavior. Instead, she found medical texts, underlined and annotated, photos of high-school friends acting crazy, and adorable photos of Sydney wearing cute hats and sundresses and Halloween costumes. After several hours, Hannah sat down on Lisa's bed and looked around the room.

She had tried to put everything back but she knew that there would inevitably be things out of place. When Lisa returned, she would complain bitterly that her mother had been in her room, and how dare she? And, Hannah thought, with a relief bordering on bliss, she would gladly admit her guilt. Say that she was looking for something. She would make something up. What did it matter? It didn't. This was not the room of a psychopath. A child molester. This room was exactly what it appeared to be – the room of a young mother, a hard-working medical student, her own, wonderful daughter.

Hannah was exhausted but felt better than she had in twenty-four hours. She had not tried to avoid the worst. She had confronted it. And found nothing. I'm sorry, Lisa, she thought. I shouldn't have doubted you.

She looked at her watch. It was four-thirty. Soon she would need to go and pick up Sydney. She could hardly wait to hold her granddaughter in her arms and cover her with happy kisses. She decided to stop at the cupcake shop which had opened on Briley Parkway before she went. She would buy each of them a cupcake to celebrate, and one for Lisa too. Perhaps she could take it to the county jail and ask them if Lisa could have a little treat.

Hannah closed the door of Lisa's room, went down the hall to the bathroom and splashed her face with cold water. She misted her hair with the hair product Lisa used, and then she crushed bunches of her hair with her hands, crunching waves into the chin-length haircut. She gave herself an apprehensive glance in the mirror, and then went down the hall to the kitchen where her car and house keys rested in a bowl on the counter by the door. She pulled up a jingling set, and then realized that she had grabbled Lisa's by mistake. She set them back down in the bowl, and rummaged for her own keychain. And then she stopped. With a sinking feeling, she picked up the first set that she had handled and looked at them again.

There was a car key, a house key and a key for her locker at work. They had all been here in the bowl, ever since Lisa lost her freedom on bail. But dangling them before her troubled gaze now, Hannah saw that there was another key on the chain. A new key which she had never noticed before.

Hannah pressed the unfamiliar key into her own palm and stared at it. It looked familiar, and she struggled to place it. She frowned at it, willing herself to recall where she had seen a key like this before. Stop it, she told herself. What difference does it make? It's just a key. It could be for anything. But somehow she knew better. And then she remembered. Before she moved to the Veranda, but after she was starting to lose her strength and her balance, Pamela used to have a post-office box, and Hannah would often fetch her mother's mail for her. This was the kind of key that opened her P.O. box.

The key seemed to weigh down her palm. She took a deep breath, trying to decide. She had gone this far. She might as well satisfy her

curiosity. She passed their local branch of the P.O. on her way to
the cupcake shop. She could stop in on her way, ask to see the box
and settle the matter, for once and for all. She slipped the keys into
her pocket, grabbed her own set from the bowl and let herself out.

Rayanne was out in the backyard watering the flowers. She gave
Hannah a cheery wave, and Hannah realized immediately that Jamie
had been as good as his word. He had not mentioned that story
about Lisa and his young cousins to his mother. Rayanne did not
blush or shrink from Hannah, or act any differently at all, as she
surely would have had she heard that story. He had kept it to himself,
like he said.

Hannah waved back but did not stop. She got into her car, and
pulled out of the driveway with a feeling of relief. She stopped at
the local P.O. where they had done business for the seventeen years
they had lived at the same address. Hannah waited in a short line
for a postal clerk whom she did not recognize.

Hannah showed him the key. 'This is the key to my daughter's
P.O. box. She's . . . not able to pick up her mail, so I thought I
would pick it up for her. But I've forgotten the number. Could you
just find that out for me?'

The clerk frowned at Hannah. 'Are you authorized to use the
box? Is your name on it?'

'No,' said Hannah airily. 'But I thought since I was here . . .'

'No, I'm sorry, ma'am,' he said. 'You have to be an authorized
user to access the box.'

Hannah realized that this was more complicated than it seemed.
'Is the postmaster here?' she asked.

The clerk nodded. 'I think he's in the back.'

'Could you get him for me, please,' said Hannah.

The clerk pushed an intercom button and called for Darren
Billings. Then he said politely, 'Would you mind stepping to one
side so I can serve the next customer.'

'Certainly,' said Hannah, stiffly moving over to stand by the door
which led to the inner workings of the branch. She felt embarrassed,
as if the clerk had caught her trying to do something illegal. At
least she knew that she would not be treated that way by Darren
Billings. In a few moments the door opened, and a bald, middle-
aged black man with a gray goatee and half-glasses looked out and
scanned the lobby. He smiled broadly when he saw Hannah. 'Hey,
Hannah, how are ya?'

They shook hands warmly, and Hannah hoped that the postal clerk had noticed her personal greeting from the postmaster. Busy with the next customer, he did not seem to be paying attention. 'Hi, Darren,' Hannah said. Darren had been their letter carrier when they first moved to the house in Nashville, and he and Adam had bonded over many conversations about the Tennessee Titans in the mornings when he delivered the mail. Darren had since moved up to become the postmaster of this local branch, but they had always maintained their friendly relationship. When Darren's oldest son applied for a job at Verizon, Adam introduced him at the office and gave him a recommendation.

'What can I do for you, dearie?' Darren asked.

Hannah took a deep breath and held up the key. 'I'm sure you've heard about Lisa. The trial and all . . .'

Darren grimaced. 'I do know about it,' he said kindly. 'I'm so sorry . . .'

'It's all right,' said Hannah. 'But she needs for me to collect her mail while she is . . . incarcerated. I brought this key but I don't have her box number. And, obviously, I can't just call her up whenever I please at the jail, so I thought I'd just come down and get the number from you.'

Darren took the key from Hannah, and frowned at it. 'Well, actually, if you're not an authorized user . . .'

'That's what the clerk said. But you know me, Darren . . .'

'Hannah, I'd love to help you but I couldn't even if I wanted to.'

'Oh, come on, Darren. Can't you bend the rules? We've known each other for how long?'

'It's not that. You see, this key is not for a box in this branch.'

'It's not?' said Hannah, taken aback.

Darren shook his head. 'Nope. This serial number here on the key is the code for another branch.' He lowered his voice. 'The branch by Vanderbilt, actually.'

Hannah felt her hopes sinking. 'I guess she forgot to mention that,' she said, trying to cover her embarrassment.

Darren peered at her. 'The fact is no one's going to give you the box number if you're not an authorized user. Can you ask Lisa to add you? I have a form you could bring to her to fill out.'

Hannah avoided his gaze. 'No. I'm afraid . . . Darren, I have to be honest with you. No. There are reasons why that would not be . . . likely to happen.'

'I see,' he said.

Hannah glanced at him, her face flaming, expecting to see disapprobation in his eyes. Instead, he was frowning at the key.

'The only way . . .' he said slowly.

Hannah watched him warily.

'Well, legally, we're not allowed to disclose that number. So the only way that you can get it, if you don't already have it, is, for example, if you are serving legal papers on someone, you can fill out a form at the branch, and they will give you the box number so you can mail them, and thereby serve them those legal papers. Do you understand?'

Hannah's eyes widened. He knows, she thought. He understands that I need to get into the box without asking Lisa for the number. And he is trying to help me do just that. 'I think so,' she said. 'Rather than, say, showing somebody the key . . .'

'Nobody can give you that number so that you can use the key on the box. The only way a person can get that number . . .'

Hannah nodded. 'Is if a person can demonstrate that they have something which needs to go into the box. Legal papers to serve, for example.'

'That's right,' said Darren.

'I understand,' said Hannah.

'I hope that might help.'

Hannah squeezed his forearm. 'Thank you, Darren.'

Darren put his hand over hers and patted it. 'I wish I could do more.'

Hannah nodded, and had to fight back tears. 'Give my best to your family.'

She rushed from the post office, and went back to her car. She sat behind the wheel, clutching the key, trying to decide what to do next.

TWENTY-TWO

Hannah left the post office, rushed to buy the cupcakes and picked up Sydney. They watered the garden after they arrived home and had their cupcakes in the backyard.

Hannah tried not to let the child see how distracted she was. After they came inside, Sydney, who was tired from daycare, sat quietly in the living room, playing with her stuffed animals while her grandmother started supper. Then the phone rang. Hannah rushed to answer it.

'What happened to you?' Lisa demanded when she heard her mother's voice. 'You haven't come to visit. Are you gonna leave me all alone here for the next two months?'

'I'm sorry, Lisa. I've been so . . . busy.'

'You sound . . . strange,' said Lisa accusingly.

'Do I? I'm sorry. How are things going for you there?'

'Oh, terrific, Mom. I got elected social chairman of cell-block ten.'

Hannah did not reply. She was thinking about Jamie's accusations, and the mysterious key to the post-office box.

'That was a joke, Mother.'

'I know it was, darling. Forgive me.'

'What's going on? You're as faithful as a St Bernard. How come you didn't come by? Don't say you're too busy. I don't believe you.'

A St Bernard? Hannah thought. Is that how I seem to her? We'll see about that. 'I'm too tired, all right,' said Hannah in a snappish tone. 'Just too tired.'

Lisa was quiet for a moment, and Hannah felt like she could sense her daughter calculating what to say next. Finally Lisa said ruefully, 'I thought I could always count on my mother, no matter what.'

'Have I ever let you down?' Hannah asked coldly.

Lisa was silent. Then she said, in an equally cold voice, 'I have to go. Sorry I bothered you.'

Instantly, automatically, Hannah felt guilty, felt regretful. 'I'll try to come tomorrow,' she said.

'Don't go out of your way,' said Lisa, hanging up.

After a few moments of sitting, staring at her cheerful grand-daughter, Hannah got up with a heavy heart and finished making dinner. Adam came in just as she was putting it on the table, and kissed her on her forehead. 'Smells good,' he said. 'Can't wait.'

Hannah said little during dinner, despite his questions. Afterwards, he offered to clean up while Hannah bathed Sydney and put her to bed. When she came back into the living room, he was sitting in the corner of the sofa, waiting for her. He had not turned on the television.

'What's going on?' he asked. 'Are you just tired from work?' Hannah shook her head, and sat down opposite him.

'What then?'

'I came home from work early,' she said, choosing her words carefully. 'I had lunch with my friend Jackie, and while we were talking, I had this brainstorm. Very casually, I offered her a hypothetical situation. I said that I had a female client who was accused of sexually abusing her children. I asked Jackie if she had ever heard of that. Jackie said that she had, but only when the woman in question was a psychopath.'

Adam frowned at her. 'Psychopath? You mean like a serial killer.'

'No,' Hannah insisted. 'That's just it. People think that's what it means. Actually a psychopath is someone whose internal gyroscope doesn't work when it comes to choosing right from wrong. They have – what were her exact words – a lack of moral restraint.'

Adam and Hannah stared at one another for a moment without speaking. 'And you think . . .' he said.

'It struck a chord in me . . . what Jackie said.'

Adam did not protest, or contradict her. Hannah felt, with a sickening certainty, that he too recognized these symptoms. 'So,' she said, 'I came home and I searched through all of Lisa's things.'

'What were you looking for?'

'I didn't even know. Something, anything that would give us proof, one way or the other.'

'And you found . . .?'

'In her room, I found nothing. Everything was in order. I was telling myself that I had become hysterical for no reason. I was actually full of hope. And then I found this,' said Hannah, holding up the key.

Adam frowned. 'What is it?'

Hannah turned the key over in her palm and studied it. 'It's a key to a post-office box. I finally recognized it 'cause I used one when I went to get Mother's mail for her. So, I took the key, and went down to our branch and had a talk with Darren. He said it wasn't from a box there. It's a key to a box at the Vanderbilt branch. He said that they could not open it for us unless we were authorized.'

'Of course not,' said Adam. 'This is why post-office boxes still exist in this internet age. It's privacy, guaranteed. People carry on clandestine affairs, or run illegal businesses out of them.'

'We have to know what's in that box.'

Adam stared at her, not replying.

'If she has something to hide she's too smart to leave it on her computer. She knows how computer literate you are. She wouldn't do that.'

'I suppose not,' Adam admitted. 'But what exactly do you expect to find?'

'I don't know,' Hannah admitted, feeling suddenly exhausted. 'I just know that I have to find out.'

'So how can we do that?' he asked calmly.

She gave him a grateful glance. He understood. 'I asked Darren. He said if someone had legal papers that had to be served on Lisa, they could get the box number so that the papers could be delivered.'

'Legal papers,' Adam asked. 'You mean, like, her lawyer.'

'Anyone with legal papers,' said Hannah. 'They don't have to know what the papers are.'

'I don't understand,' said Adam. 'How would that help us?'

'One of us goes in and gets the number, thanks to the legal paperwork. Then we have the box number. The other one goes in and opens the box. With this key.'

Adam looked at her, almost admiringly. 'You have a devious mind.'

'I got it from dealing with my daughter,' she said grimly.

Adam frowned. 'This sounds so . . . desperate.'

'I am desperate,' said Hannah flatly,

Adam nodded. 'I understand. I have some user agreements in my desk that look very official.'

'Thank you,' she said.

Adam shook his head. 'Don't thank me. We may regret this.'

'That's what I'm afraid of,' said Hannah.

'We'll do it in the morning,' he said.

They gazed into one another's eyes, conscious that they were both willing to go to any lengths to discover the truth. 'Tomorrow,' she said, and he nodded.

The next morning, they dropped Sydney at daycare. Then they went home to prepare. Hannah found a legal documents envelope from social services in her desk. Adam gathered up some paperwork, and they put their official-looking package together.

Adam put on a suit, and stood looking at himself in the mirror as he tied his tie. 'Do I look like an attorney?' he asked.

Hannah nodded. 'Maybe it's nothing. We can go visit her this afternoon and make it up to her for thinking badly of her.'

'Nothing would please me more,' Adam said, unsmiling, smoothing his tie down over his shirt. 'Let's get this over with.'

They didn't speak as they drove to the Vanderbilt post office. Adam picked up the envelope and got out of the car. 'Wish me luck,' he said.

Hannah nodded, and he rapped on the outside car-door frame before he walked across the street and into the post office. She sat waiting for him, watching the world go by. She had driven Lisa over here to the university when she was getting ready to apply, many times when she was an undergraduate, and then again, when she decided to apply to medical school. She remembered Lisa sitting nervously in the passenger seat, looking like a child playing dress-up in her business suit, when she went for her interviews. Hannah remembered how proud she had been of her brilliant daughter, who wasn't about to let her extreme youth, or motherhood, or anything else get in the way of her goal to be a doctor.

Please God, she whispered to herself, closing her eyes in prayer. Let it be nothing. Let this all be nothing.

The driver's door opened, and Hannah started, and opened her eyes. Adam slipped into the driver's seat. He was no longer carrying the envelope. 'Seven hundred and eighty-five,' he said.

Hannah pressed her lips together, and ran a finger over the key which she held tightly in the palm of her hand. 'Seven hundred and eighty-five. Got it,' she whispered.

It was Hannah's turn to get out of the car. She waited for the traffic to pass, her heart thudding, and then she crossed the street and walked up the steps to the post office. She went inside the busy branch. People were coming and going, doing business at the window and filling out forms at the tables scattered around the lobby. She forced herself to look calm and walk slowly. She went over to the bank of post-office boxes and scanned the numbers. She found 785 and inserted the key. The door clicked and swung open when she tugged at the key.

Inside was a handful of letter-sized envelopes. Hannah reached in and pulled them out. She was tempted to tear them open right then and there, but she knew better. She jammed the letters into her shoulder bag, and relocked the box. Then she headed back out into the morning sunshine, her heart heavy with dread.

They did not speak on the way home. Without having to discuss it aloud, they simply drove home and slipped into the house.

'Do you want coffee?' Hannah asked.

Adam shook his head.

'Me neither,' Hannah whispered. She followed her husband into the living room, and sat down beside him on the sofa. She pulled the envelopes from her bag, and put them on the coffee table. They both stared at the results of their deception.

All of the letters were for Lisa. Some were handwritten, some were addressed on a computer. The return addresses were from all parts of the country, as far away as California.

'Maybe she's into pen pals,' said Adam.

Hannah did not even smile. 'Do you want to open them, or shall I?'

In response, Adam sighed and picked one up. Its return address was Alabama, a town only a few hours away. Adam ran his finger under the flap and opened it. He pulled out a sheet of paper, and a photograph fell out and landed on the coffee table. It was an ordinary-looking man of about forty, slightly overweight, wearing a hunter's cap and camouflage, and holding a rifle.

A man sending his photo? Suddenly, Hannah wondered if all this imagined secrecy had simply been because Lisa was a little sheepish about having joined a dating service. Her heart lifted with hope.

Adam unfolded the paper and began to read. Hannah watched his face. His expression, studiously noncommittal at first, began to change. His eyes widened, and his mouth dropped open. Suddenly, he groaned. 'Oh my God,' he said, crushing the letter in his fist. 'Oh, Jesus.'

'Let me see,' she said, prying the wadded piece of paper from his fingers.

'Oh, Hannah,' he said shaking his head. There were tears in his eyes. 'Don't even look.'

Hannah ignored his warning and began to read.

'Dear Lisa,' it read, 'I received your response to my ad in the THFLG newsletter. I am so excited to meet you and your little princess, Sydney. You are a couple of beauties. I promise you that I will give her a first time that none of us will ever forget. I appreciate that you want this to be a special experience for her, and for yourself. I will be gentle and firm as I show that little angel the delights of a grown man's love. The three of us can meet at my hunting cabin, time to be determined, for a weekend to remember. I am enclosing a photo of myself, as you requested. I also have the paperwork from the lab which will prove to you that I am disease-free, and will give you a copy when we meet. In answer to your other question, I go about seven to eight inches, fully erect. I know it's a lot for a little girl to handle but with you to guide me, all will be well.

'In closing, let me say, Thank Heaven for Little Girls forever!

'Yours sincerely . . .'

Hannah let out a cry, fainted, and slid off the couch, gashing her head on the coffee table as she fell.

TWENTY-THREE

Hannah came to, cradled in her husband's arms. He was shaking her. His face loomed over hers, his gaze frantic.

'Hannah, are you all right?' he demanded. 'Talk to me.'

Hannah nodded and swallowed hard. 'Let me go,' she whispered.

He released his hold on her except his steadying grip under one of her arms. Awkwardly, she scrambled up from the floor and sat down on the sofa. She didn't dare try to stand up. She felt as if she would topple over if she did so. There was a spatter of dark red droplets across the rug beneath the corner of the table.

Adam pushed himself up and sat down beside her. He pulled a handkerchief from his pocket and dabbed at the blood which had run down Hannah's face from her scalp wound.

'Ow,' she exclaimed.

'Does that hurt?'

'A little,' Hannah admitted.

'Maybe I should take you to the ER.'

'Forget the ER. I won't go.'

'You were out cold for a few seconds.'

'From shock,' she said, probing her cut scalp gingerly with her fingers. 'Not from this.'

'Are you sure?' he asked.

'Absolutely. I was trying to obliterate everything that happened in the last hour.'

'It didn't work,' he said.

Hannah glanced at the innocuous-looking pile of letters scattered on the coffee table in front of them. 'How could it?' she said. Then she raised her hands and covered her eyes and her face.

Adam closed his eyes too, and they sat that way for a few minutes, knees touching, their breathing loud in the quiet room.

When Hannah removed her hands from her face, there were tears running down her cheeks. Some of the tears mixed with the blood and formed a spidery red pattern along her chin. She looked hopelessly at her husband.

'Do we need to open the others?' she asked.

'I already know everything I need to know,' he said.

'So do I,' said Hannah, and she let out a sob.

Adam massaged her bent spine absently with his open palm. Hannah rubbed her eyes with her fists, as if she could somehow grind away the sight she had seen. It was no use. The words were now in her brain, frozen there forever.

'Lisa cannot be allowed to be around Sydney. Never again,' he said, and his voice was shaking.

Hannah nodded. 'No. Obviously not.' Of all the heartbreaking things she had faced in recent months, this was the worst. 'I . . . I can't comprehend it.'

'Truly,' he said.

Hannah shook her head and kneaded her forehead which was beginning to throb. 'I just cannot believe this. Adam, what should we do?'

'I don't know. I feel like I don't ever want to set eyes on her again.'

'We can't tell anyone about this.'

'Why would we want to?' he cried.

'We can't, that's all.'

'Because we're ashamed?'

'Well, I am ashamed. Aren't you?' she countered.

'That's the least of my concerns.'

'But do we want this all over the papers? All over the news?'

Adam looked at her in disbelief. 'Are you worried about Lisa's reputation? Isn't it a little late for that?'

Hannah shook her head miserably. 'I can't deny that I dread

facing that. Every reporter saying that about Lisa. Even if it's true. But that's not it. I'm worried about Sydney finding out. I don't want her to ever know that her mother was willing to . . .'

'Pimp her out. A toddler,' said Adam bitterly. 'That's what it is, isn't it? It would serve Lisa right if we marched down to the police station and handed them these letters. Let them take over. I'm not sure if she's actually committed a crime but she certainly intended to.'

'I know. I know. I just . . .' said Hannah. 'I just keep wondering what is wrong with her? How could we not have known this? Could we have prevented it? Was it our fault somehow?'

'Our fault?' he demanded. 'She certainly didn't learn that depraved behavior around here. I don't know what's wrong with her. Maybe she is a mental case – a psychopath – just like your friend said.'

'I don't know,' said Hannah miserably. 'I would never have believed . . . in my wildest dreams . . . that our own daughter could ever think of such a thing. It's just . . . it's too terrible to take in.'

'Well, we have to take it in,' said Adam, 'because in less than two months she will be free and on her way home to take her daughter from us. And she'll be free to carry out her disgusting plan.'

'Can we stop her, short of calling the police?'

For a few minutes they sat in silence, each one contemplating their miserable options. Adam broke the silence.

'Hannah,' he said, 'we have to seek custody.'

For one brief, despairing moment, Hannah thought about starting the process that lay ahead of them. Wresting custody of her grand-child away from her daughter. It was not what she would have chosen. But Sydney was innocent and, as unthinkable as it was, she had to be protected from her own mother. 'I know,' she said.

'We will have to seek legal custody of Sydney. Lisa can't be allowed to visit her unsupervised. We have no choice. And we have to do it right away.'

Hannah nodded. 'Of course. You're right,' she said.

'I suppose we need to find an attorney,' he said.

'Wait, Adam, wait. Let's just talk about it. When all is said and done, it's Lisa. No matter what she's done, she's still our daughter.'

Adam looked at her impatiently. 'Meaning what? We should just pretend we don't know what she was planning?'

Hannah shook her head. 'No. I don't mean that.'

'Don't pretend that her intentions aren't as clear as day. And don't ask me to forgive her. Please, don't do that. I'm sick to my stomach as it is.'

Hannah put her hand on his, as if to stay his anger. 'I'm just thinking that we might avoid the whole public spectacle, for Sydney's sake. Maybe we can make Lisa listen to reason. Let's go and see her.'

'I don't think I can stand the sight of her,' he said disgustedly.

'Adam, listen. We have to at least talk to her first. If she finds out that we know about these letters, maybe she will be willing to just give us custody to avoid all the attorneys and the judicial circus.'

'Oh, no. Quietly is one thing but if we do this, it all has to be legal,' he said, wagging a finger at Hannah. 'Every "t" crossed, every "i" dotted. I don't want Lisa to be able to say that she changed her mind, or that she doesn't have these . . . appetites anymore,' he said, angrily brushing the letters onto the floor. 'I'll never trust her alone with that child again.'

Hannah shook her head, and her heart ached so badly that she felt as if a heart attack was imminent. 'No. Me neither,' she said.

'Oh my God, it's so sick!' he cried.

'I know,' Hannah whispered.

Again they were silent, prisoners of all they now knew.

Finally Adam spoke. 'Maybe you're right,' he said thoughtfully. 'If we lay it out for her, she'll have no choice but to capitulate. It's that, or face more charges. And we can remind her that it won't change anything that much. We've virtually had sole custody for months now.'

'That's what I'm hoping. And as hard as it is to turn my back on Lisa, we have to think of Sydney. She's all that matters now. Her safety.'

'Amen,' he said.

'So, you agree. We should try to talk to her?' Hannah asked.

'I suppose so,' he sighed.

'Should we go now?' Hannah asked him, afraid of the answer.

'It's not going to get any easier,' he said.

They were able to let Lisa know that they were coming. Because she was on work detail in the laundry, she was not allowed to come to the phone. But the operator who answered the phone promised to relay the message to her through a guard. Hannah and Adam looked at one another, and each saw anxiety and determination in the other's eyes.

'Let's go, before we lose our will,' said Adam. Hannah nodded agreement.

They were silent on the drive to the county jail, which was located in a dry, gray brown field at the edge of a commercial strip outside of the city. The drive took about forty minutes. Although Hannah looked out the window the whole way, she saw nothing. She could not have described the passing landscape if her life depended on it. In her mind's eye she was seeing her daughter. Lisa at four, on the swings. At ten, riding her bike, at fourteen, graduating from high school, a fragile child among her older classmates. She had been strange – yes. Strange because she was so much smarter than every other classmate and yet was too young to be included in their senior year privileges and hi-jinx. But when it came to a social life, Lisa was impatient with kids her own age, and found their concerns juvenile. She was often isolated. Hannah had sought out counseling for her, and she and Adam had done their level best to reassure her that she was special, gifted, lucky. A million times Hannah had allayed her own anxieties by telling herself that it would all level out for her in the end, and she would find her social niche.

Lisa's pregnancy had come as a shock, and she was five months along when Hannah noticed her expanding belly, and Lisa finally admitted to it. Hannah had always suspected that some older boy had forced himself on her, at one of the intercollegiate brainiac competitions she sometimes attended in other cities. But Lisa refused to accuse anyone, and insisted that she wanted to keep her baby, even though Hannah and Adam knew full well that she was not yet capable of being a mother. They had always agreed that they would help her. They just never realized that they would be Sydney's sole custodians a mere two years after she was born.

Adam pulled through the brick gateway topped by sharp-edged wire mesh and drove up the long driveway leading up to the prison. He turned and glanced at Hannah. 'We have arrived,' he said.

She nodded grimly. 'Let's just face it.'

Lisa was sitting with her back to the door when they arrived at the visitors' room. DCDOC, standing for Davidson County Dept. of Corrections, was emblazoned on the back of her prison jumpsuit. Hannah immediately recognized Lisa's mass of dark, unruly curls.

They walked around the table and stood there. Lisa looked up and her eyes behind her glasses lit up at the sight of them, and then, immediately, her gaze became wary. Hannah could not help herself. Despite all she knew, her heart went out to her child, who was now a prisoner in this godforsaken facility. She bent down and kissed her daughter awkwardly on the cheek. Adam remained standing, his arms crossed over his chest.

'Dad?'

'Hello, Lisa,' he said.

'Can we sit down?' Hannah asked.

Lisa waved a hand indifferently. She was studying her father's stony face. Adam pulled out a chair for Hannah then pulled out the one beside her for himself.

Lisa looked at them ruefully. 'You took your time getting here. I thought you'd never come.'

Hannah avoided her daughter's gaze. Adam stared back at Lisa steadily, unsmiling. 'This is not a social call,' he said.

For a moment Lisa looked taken aback. Her parents' support, no matter what, had been a constant in her life. She stared at them, puzzled, trying to make sense of the change in their attitudes. 'What is this? You look like you're here to scold me.'

'Not exactly,' said Hannah quietly.

'Well, what's the matter, then?' Lisa demanded. 'Is this about the trial? You were the one who was telling me how happy I should be because we won. Remember? And if this is about the check, I told you, Troy gave me that money. No matter what that jury believed, that's what happened. I thought my own parents would believe me.'

'No, Lisa,' said Hannah. 'Stop. It has nothing to do with that.'

'Just for the record,' said Adam, 'I don't believe you. Not about the check. Not about Troy.'

Hannah gave him a warning glance. 'Adam, please don't,' she said.

'Thanks a lot, Dad,' said Lisa, pushing her glasses back up on the bridge of her nose. 'I really appreciate that. So why the hell did you bother to come?'

Adam's eyes flashed angrily but he did not reply.

'We have to talk to you about something,' said Hannah.

Lisa looked from one to the other with narrowed eyes. 'What?'

Hannah folded her hands on the worn tabletop which separated her from her daughter. 'It's about Sydney.'

Lisa did not ask if there was anything amiss with her daughter. 'What about her?' she demanded.

Hannah took a deep breath and looked down at her folded hands.

Before she could speak, Adam blurted out, 'We want you to give us sole custody of her. Legally.'

Lisa's eyes widened in anger. Then she looked from her father to her mother, as if challenging Hannah to refute what Adam had just said. 'Is that true?' she asked. 'Is that why you're here?'

Hannah nodded.

'I'm in jail for two months and you want me to give up my rights to my child?' she asked mockingly.

'We are worried. We have good reason,' said Hannah, her voice trembling.

'Why would I do that?' Lisa demanded. 'That's ridiculous.'

Adam reached into the breast pocket of his jacket and pulled out the letters from the post-office box. He set them down on the table as if they were explosive.

'Because we have these,' he said.

'Adam, wait,' said Hannah, worried that he was moving too quickly with Lisa.

Lisa stared at the letters on the table. 'What are those?'

'They came from your post-office box,' said Adam calmly.

Lisa blanched. 'What? How did you . . .?'

'Does it really matter how?' he asked wearily. 'We have them. That's all that really matters. We just need you to agree to give up your rights to Sydney.'

Lisa did not pretend that she didn't know about any post-office box. She picked up one of the letters, almost curiously, and then tossed it aside. When she looked up at her father, her eyes were hard and glittering. Her face was frozen into an expression of contempt. 'Oh, I don't think so,' she said.

TWENTY-FOUR

Hannah searched her daughter's face for some sign of guilt or embarrassment. There was no shame in Lisa's eyes. No regret, or even uneasiness. Simply defiance. 'Lisa, we've read these letters. We know . . . everything,' said Hannah.

'So let me get this straight. You broke into my post-office box?' Lisa asked. 'That's a federal crime, isn't it?'

Adam's jaw sagged as if she had punched him. His hands were balled up into fists, and he was shaking. 'You have the nerve to talk to us about a crime?'

Hannah spoke sharply in a low voice to her daughter. 'Look, your father is right. We know that you have been soliciting men to have . . . I can't even say it. It's too disgusting to even say it. When I think of what you were suggesting about your own baby. Please, have the decency to be ashamed of yourself.'

Lisa turned and looked at her mother earnestly. 'Mother, I never meant for you to know about this. I knew you wouldn't understand.'

Hannah gasped. 'Understand? What is there to understand?'

'All right, look. I'm not unaware of what the world thinks about . . . unusual sexual tastes. I get it. But you need to try and expand your way of thinking a little bit. I'm not like you. I'm sure you two have done everything the same in bed for twenty years. That may be OK for you but it's not for me. Besides, I don't want to hurt Sydney. I wouldn't allow anyone to hurt her. I was very specific about that in my ad. I want her to enjoy it.'

'Oh, for Christ's sake,' Adam gasped.

'You know that what you are talking about is a crime,' said Hannah. 'A heinous crime.'

'I'm talking about pleasure,' Lisa insisted. 'Excitement.'

Hannah closed her eyes. 'Don't say another word, Lisa. This conversation cannot continue.'

Lisa looked vaguely affronted. 'You're the ones who brought it up. I'm only trying to explain. You're insisting on an explanation.'

Adam gripped one hand over his other fist, as if to prevent himself from reaching up and striking her. 'We don't need any explanations, Lisa. I don't know how you turned into this . . . this . . . abomination. It doesn't matter.'

'I'm the same person I always was,' she insisted. 'What happened to your great love for me? That's all I ever heard growing up. How much you loved me.'

Hannah stared at her daughter as if from a great distance. Lisa made it sound like it had been a burden to constantly hear that she was loved. Was she, in fact, the same as she had always been? How was it possible that they had lived with Lisa, loved her all these years, and seen no flashing lights, no warning bells of danger dead ahead? Hannah had felt only a tremor of unease now and then, and told herself it was because her daughter was smarter than other children. And therefore unpredictable, and sometimes lonely. Hannah thought of her as special. Unique. 'Believe it or not, I still love you. I still do.'

Lisa snorted. 'You've got a strange way of showing it.'

'You're our daughter, our only child, and we'll always love you.'

'Speak for yourself,' said Adam. 'I'm so disgusted, I don't think I ever want to see you again, Lisa.'

Hannah shook her head. 'Adam, don't say that. Your father and I are angry. Furious. But we are not doing this to try to hurt you. We just can't let you go near Sydney ever again. Not alone. Not ever.'

'And I'm supposed to do whatever you say? Just accept that you know what's best for Sydney?' Lisa demanded sarcastically. 'Like you did for me?'

Hannah exchanged a bewildered glance with Adam, both of them shocked by Lisa's accusation. Is this lack of a conscience in Lisa the result of our parenting? Hannah wondered. We raised her the best way we could, with all the love and attention we could muster, and now, here she sits, in jail, defending her perverted desires. 'Lisa, it's common sense,' Hannah said, almost gently. 'Common decency.'

Lisa curled her lip scornfully. 'You're right about the common part,' she said. 'You are both so . . . dull. So . . . middle of the road. Well, for your information, Sydney is my child. She doesn't have to share your values. Did it ever occur to you that she might share mine? She might actually benefit from the choices I make for her?'

Hannah looked at her daughter as if she were seeing her for the very first time. As if she were a total stranger. 'When you took up with Troy, Lisa, you knew that he'd been accused of . . . interfering with a child. You knew that when you went out with him, didn't you?'

Lisa rolled her eyes and leaned back in her chair. 'Wow, you've got a lot on your mind today.'

'Didn't you?'

'Yes, I knew. Some nurse out where Grandma lives told me about him. She told me what he had been accused of. I found that interesting. I thought he and I might have some interests in common. But it turned out that he wasn't into children after all,' said Lisa.

'In fact, he was just like you two. Very indignant about the whole idea.'

Hannah stared at her. 'You offered Sydney to Troy?'

Lisa shook her head. 'I suggested some things we all might enjoy. He went ballistic. He threatened to tell them at the medical school. He said they would kick me out if they knew. You know, you'd think, after what happened to him at that camp, that he wouldn't be so free to go around accusing people. Besides, it was ridiculous. That was between us. It was our private business.'

'You killed him, didn't you?' Adam said flatly.

Lisa looked at him defiantly. 'The gas heater exploded. I wasn't even there. Remember?'

Adam shook his head. 'I don't believe a word you say.'

'All right. That's enough,' said Hannah. 'Stop.'

'You're the ones who came over here accusing me,' Lisa protested petulantly.

'All right, look,' said Adam. 'We are going to tell you what is going to happen now and you are going to agree to it. End of story.'

Lisa turned on him. 'And what is that?'

'We are going to hire an attorney to draw up an agreement that can't be broken, giving us full and permanent custody of Sydney. And you are going to sign it. If you want visitation, you're going to have to see Sydney with one of us always present. Or a social worker. Take your pick. If you want to hire an attorney to fight this you can. But we won't pay for it this time. So, good luck with that.'

Lisa studied her father with a cold gaze. 'You've got it all figured out, don't you?'

'I don't know about that,' said Adam, pointing a finger at her. 'But I'll tell you one thing. You will do this. You can't get around us because we have these letters. It will be an easy matter to trace your communications with these perverts. If you try to fight this you, and they, are going to find yourselves all over the news and probably back in jail. Because I will not hesitate to use these disgusting letters against you in court if I have to.'

'You know,' said Lisa languidly, 'if you had been reasonable I might have been willing to consider some kind of arrangement. But instead, you barged in here and threatened me. That makes me not want to cooperate.'

'You have no choice,' he said bitterly.

A smile played around Lisa's lips, and Hannah felt a sudden fear, like a gust of cold wind, blow up in her chest. 'That's what you think,' said Lisa.

Hannah glanced at Adam, and saw the momentary hesitancy, the uncertainty in his eyes. She realized, with a sickening certainty, that he was afraid, too.

'For your information, I have done my research,' said Lisa, 'both in medicine and in psychology. And even an ignorant layman can tell you what I learned. When I first noticed these . . . interests I had, and I realized that other people didn't necessarily share them, I read about their etiology.'

'What are you talking about?' Adam asked wearily. 'I'm not here to discuss your sick sexual desires.'

'Do you know where those predilections come from, in most cases?' she asked.

Adam glared at her, and did not response.

'Most pedophiles were abused in their own childhoods. Often by their own fathers.'

Hannah gasped and blinked at Lisa, as if she were blinded by the words she had just heard.

'Now you can go ahead and try to make your case for why I should lose custody of Sydney,' Lisa continued. 'You're right. The letters will definitely work against me. But what do you think a judge will say about your petition for custody when I tell him how I was sexually abused throughout my childhood? By my father? Do you think you'll ever get custody of my daughter then?'

In that moment, Hannah thought that this nightmare, which couldn't get any worse, had suddenly become a thousand times more terrible. Adam? she thought. She wanted to die. She turned to look at her husband, afraid that he might suddenly look completely different. Like a monster. He was staring at his only child. His face was dead white and the look in his eyes was stricken, as if he were gazing upon the destruction of his very life.

Adam was looking hopelessly at Lisa. 'All your life, you've been my baby. All your life I've adored you. How can you even make up such a vile thing?' he whispered.

'In fact, I could tell them that you could actually be Sydney's father. Of course, I think that might work against you in your fight for custody, don't you?'

Adam peered at her, as if he was trying to look into her mind. 'Lisa, why say such a thing? You know it's not true. A simple test would put that lie to rest. So why even say it? Do you know what you're accusing me of? Do you realize . . .? This is evil . . .? Lisa. For God's sake.'

Lisa shrugged. 'All I know is they won't dare give her to you after I tell them that. How could they?'

Hannah sat dumbfounded, staring at her husband and her daughter, as if she had been struck by lightning.

Lisa looked at her mother ruefully. 'Anytime you want to jump in, Mother. How about taking my side in this? I'm the victim here.' Lisa looked at her mother's stunned expression in disgust. 'You are a poor excuse for a mother. Standing by and letting him have his way with me all throughout my childhood. Thanks a lot.'

'I'm not hearing this,' said Hannah dully.

'Right. You're an expert at that,' said Lisa. 'Not hearing what you don't want to hear.'

Adam pleaded with his daughter. 'Lisa, all I ever did was my best for you. Why? How could you hate me so?'

Lisa looked at him slyly. 'Why not? You're trying to take what's mine away from me. I'll shout it from the rooftops if I want,' she said.

Hannah was silent. She knew about these cases. Fathers raping their daughters. It was part of her job to deal with the fallout of such things. She had encountered horrible men who preyed on their children. Women who refused to listen to their children when they had the courage to claim they were abused. She had worked with these families. What Lisa was saying did happen in some families, and not infrequently. People liked to think that this was the rarest of abuses. They were kidding themselves. Hannah glanced at her husband. He looked like he'd been poleaxed.

'Maybe you'll stop being the adoring wifey now. Maybe you'll look at him a little differently.' Lisa's expression was satisfied. Almost . . . merry.

Hannah stared at her daughter, trying to fathom the cruelty that was behind those laughing eyes. 'Is that what you want?' she asked. 'For me to suspect the worst of your father?'

Lisa shrugged. 'You have no trouble suspecting the worst about me. Why not him?'

Hannah closed her eyes. Then she shook her head and gathered up the letters on the table, stuffing them back into her purse. 'These letters are proof. I have proof of the worst. Otherwise, I never would have believed it of you. I wouldn't have believed it was possible.'

Lisa shrugged. 'I don't care what you think. Think what you want,' she said. 'We'll see what the court says. Do you suppose they'd take a chance on giving another innocent girl into his custody?' Her eyes were maniacally bright.

'Do you think this is funny?' Hannah asked. 'Why are you smiling?'

'Because I can stop you from getting what you want,' said Lisa.

'Your father and I love our granddaughter,' said Hannah. 'We only want what's good for her. You can't be trusted to take care of her.'

'Oh, she'd be better off being the victim of this pervert?'

Hannah looked at her daughter as if from a great distance. 'You are lost, Lisa,' she said. 'God help me, I can see it now.'

Adam remained silent. Hannah wondered if he was physically all right. She looked into his pained, bewildered eyes.

'Let's go,' she said. Then, she stood up. Adam rose unsteadily to his feet as well. Hannah looked down on her daughter, still seated at the table. 'We will protect Sydney from you. I promise you that.'

Hannah started for the door and Adam followed. Lisa watched them go. Her gaze was cold and her lips were lifted in a smile.

TWENTY-FIVE

'Thank you,' he said, as he unlocked the passenger door of the car and waited for Hannah to slip into the front seat.

'Are you OK?' Hannah asked worriedly.

Adam just shook his head.

'We'll be home soon,' she said.

Neither one of them spoke on the ride home. Hannah could not wait until they were in the safety, the shelter of their house. But when they were almost to her street, she remembered Sydney. They had to pick her up.

'We have to stop and get Sydney,' she said.

Adam nodded. 'You're right. I was so distracted . . .' he said.

Hannah heaved a sigh, and Adam turned in the direction of Tiffany's house.

Sydney was waiting by the front window when they arrived. She grabbed up her little pink backpack and rushed to meet them. Hannah scooped her up, and inhaled her pure, delicious scent. She told herself that Lisa had been stopped before she could carry out her plan. Sydney was still untouched and innocent. Please, God, she thought.

She carried the toddler out to the car. Adam got out of the car and opened the back door and extended his arms for her, ready to put her in the back seat. Then he hesitated, and looked at his wife.

Hannah shook her head. 'Don't,' she said. 'Don't hesitate. Don't ever wonder.' She handed Sydney to her grandfather, who placed her tenderly in her car seat while Sydney insisted, 'Sit with me, Pop-pop.'

Adam blinked away tears but he gave her a weary grin. 'I love you, little bit.'

'Wuv you,' Sydney cried, blowing him a kiss.

Hannah put one of Sydney's favorite CDs into the dashboard so they would not need to talk. Sydney sang along cheerfully, leaving her grandparents alone with their thoughts and their recollections of the dreadful meeting with Lisa.

Hannah felt as if it had been the longest evening of her life. They couldn't really talk in front of Sydney but there was so much she wanted to say to Adam, so much information that she needed his help to process. Fortunately, Sydney seemed oblivious, banging around cheerfully among her toys, eating her dinner with gusto, taking her bath and crawling up on Adam's lap for a story before bed. Hannah took her in to her room at last, and tucked her under her covers.

'When is Mommy coming home?' Sydney asked.

'I don't know,' said Hannah.

'Tomorrow?' asked the child.

'No,' said Hannah grimly. 'Not tomorrow.'

'I'm gonna draw a picture for her when she comes home,' said Sydney.

Hannah felt like her heart was being crushed in her chest. 'Yes. That would be nice,' she said. 'We'll talk about it tomorrow.'

Sydney threw her arms around Hannah's neck. 'I love you, Mom-mom,' she said.

'I love you too,' said Hannah. 'More than you will ever know.'

Hannah left Sydney's room, pulling the door shut quietly behind her, and tiptoed down the hall back to the living room. Adam was sitting in his favorite chair from where he often watched TV, but tonight the screen was dark. He stared at it nonetheless. He looked up when Hannah came into the room.

'Did you get her off to sleep?' he asked.

Hannah nodded. 'She was tired. She asked me when her mother was coming home. She wants to draw a picture for her.'

Adam sighed. 'Poor little thing. She has no idea.'

'Thankfully,' said Hannah. 'Are you OK, darling? You look terrible.'

'I feel as if a bomb exploded inside me. It's like my chest is filled with rubble.'

'I know,' said Hannah.

Adam looked over at his wife. His face was gray and haggard. 'Hannah, I can't believe what she is doing. I mean, I heard it with my own ears but . . . I still can't believe it.'

Hannah shook her head. 'It's as if I don't know her at all.'

'How could she hate me so much? To say such a thing? Was I such a bad father, that she should hate me so much?'

She wanted to sit beside him and take his hand. She didn't want to have to see the pain in his eyes. But she remained in the chair where she had sat down when she re-entered the room. They were going to have to be strong. Realistic. This was no time to break down. 'You were a wonderful father,' said Hannah staunchly. 'From the day she was born.'

Adam looked at Hannah with narrowed eyes. He was gripping the arms of his chair so tightly that his knuckles were white. 'I'm trying to imagine how you felt when you heard that . . . accusation she made. I mean, didn't you . . . wonder if it was true? It would be only human to wonder,' he said.

Hannah started to immediately deny it, and then she hesitated. She tried never to lie to him. Certainly not when it was this important. 'All right. Sure. For a moment. Of course I did. For a minute.'

Adam winced, pierced by her words. But he had asked what she had been thinking, and Hannah knew him well enough to know that he would accept what she said stoically.

'You know, in the course of my job I've seen families where this sort of thing has happened. Children preyed on by parents and grandparents. There's no use pretending that this doesn't occur. It does,' Hannah admitted.

Adam took a deep breath and considered his wife's honest response. 'You thought it might be possible.'

'Anything's possible,' said Hannah.

'Look, Hannah,' he said. 'I'm trying to be calm about this. And fatalistic. No one could blame you for asking yourself . . .

Look, if you want me to take a lie-detector test . . . Or a paternity test . . .'

Hannah raised her hands as if to ward off a blow. 'Stop. Please. It was only the shock that rocked me for a moment. And then I came to my senses. I know you, Adam. A person's world has to have some bedrock . . . truths. If there's one thing in this world that I do know, it's that you could never do what she said.'

'Thank you,' he said humbly.

'No need,' said Hannah.

Adam grimaced. 'Listening to her, I swear, I almost thought she believed it.'

'She may have convinced herself somehow. Obviously, there is something terribly wrong with Lisa.'

'Parents are supposed to be their child's most tireless advocates. No matter what,' he said. 'I always believed that. We're supposed to support them and stay on their side.'

Hannah looked at him frankly. 'With all that we know about her now? After seeing those letters?' She shuddered as if she had tasted something bitter.

He waited for her to say more but at the same time the realization dawned in his eyes that there was nothing more she needed to say. She was saying that there was nothing he had to prove to her. He had already proved it, over the course of their long life together. That's what she was telling him. 'You don't know what that means to me,' he said.

She could feel a wave of love emanating from him, threatening to inundate her and make her weak. He wanted to come and sit beside her and pull her to him and hold her in his arms. He wanted to soak in her warmth, and share everything he felt without saying another word. Hannah shook her head in warning.

'I know exactly what it means,' she said. 'Don't think I don't.'

Adam's brief smile was like a shaft of sunlight breaking through an overcast sky. 'You're amazing. It was my lucky day when I married you,' he said.

'Mine too,' said Hannah.

Adam sighed. He understood why she was resisting that desire to find comfort in one another's arms. There was still too much that they urgently needed to say.

'I just keep seeing her face,' he said. 'I keep asking myself, why did she attack me like that?'

Hannah shook her head. 'I guess she will say anything to get what she wants. You know, what's mine is mine, and you can't have it unless I say so.'

'That's just it,' said Adam. 'Is it really Sydney that she wants? Sometimes, I don't even think she cares that much about her child. She never has any time for her. I always tried to make excuses for Lisa. Her youth. Her schoolwork.'

'So did I,' said Hannah. 'Maybe more than you. After all, I was Lisa's model as a mother. For a long time now, I've tried to tell myself that there is more than one way to be a mother. It's really stupid, isn't it? I was trying to convince myself that she was just a bit distant. More like my own mother.'

'Well, I hate to say it, darling, but your mother is nobody's idea of maternal devotion,' said Adam.

Hannah sighed. 'She tried. She was just . . .'

'Neglectful,' he said.

'Not neglectful, exactly,' Hannah protested. 'Just . . . preoccupied with herself. But that's another excuse. Inadequate as Pamela's mothering was, she never did anything to hurt me. Not like what Lisa was proposing for Sydney. Good God. Pamela would never dream of such a thing. Not on her worst day.'

'That's true,' Adam admitted.

'No, it's different with Lisa. I didn't want to see what was staring me in the face.'

'So now you think you understand her?' Adam asked.

Hannah shook her head. 'I wouldn't say that. I will never understand her. That much I know for certain. But I can see now how volatile Lisa is if she doesn't get her way. How dangerous.'

'That's why she is doing this!' Adam cried.

'She's doing it because she knows what it means. If she says these things about you, it will be impossible for us to gain custody of Sydney. Even though Lisa can't prove her claims against you, the court would never risk putting Sydney in our care. Lisa knows that. One accusation like that from her, and any chance we might have of gaining custody goes out the window.'

'Even if we can show the court what she was planning to do with Sydney?' he asked. 'We do have those letters. We don't have to admit how we got them. We have them, and we can use them. The court will see what she was planning.

Hannah gazed at him dispassionately. 'I didn't say that they would give Sydney back to her. They probably wouldn't. But they would never give her to us. Lisa's counting on that. She figures that we won't dare bring it up in court for that very reason. We would be taking a chance on losing Sydney forever.'

'If we didn't get her, what would happen to her?' he asked. 'To Sydney.'

'Custodial care,' said Hannah.

'A foster home,' said Adam.

'Maybe more than one. These cases can drag on for years. In the meantime, Sydney could end up in a series of foster homes. With no one and nothing to call her own.'

Adam put his head in his hands and groaned. 'Jesus. I can't believe Lisa would risk that. That she would put her own defense-less, innocent child in the hands of strangers, just to spite us.'

'There was a time I wouldn't have believed it,' said Hannah. 'But not anymore.'

'It's a goddam catch-22,' Adam cried. 'If we keep quiet Lisa will be able to take her daughter wherever she wants. Do whatever she wants to her. And if we protest, if we try to block her, she can make these accusations against me, and we will lose our granddaughter.'

Hannah kneaded one hand with the other. 'That's pretty much it,' she said.

They sat in silence for a few moments, contemplating the two grim scenarios.

'Maybe . . .' he said.

Hannah looked up at him. 'What?'

'Look, can we agree that the only thing that matters is Sydney?' he said.

Hannah frowned. 'Yes. That's what's important.'

'More important than us. Or our lives. She's an innocent child who deserves a chance in this world to be happy.'

'Of course,' said Hannah.

'Then hear me out,' he said. 'I can hardly stand the thought of this but, Lisa's got us in an impossible situation.'

'The thought of what?' Hannah asked, frowning. 'What are you thinking?'

Adam took a deep breath and looked at her impassively. 'Tell everyone that you believe her charges against me. Divorce me. I won't contest it. We could make it quick. That way, with me gone, and out of the house, maybe they will give custody of Sydney to you.'

Hannah stared at him.

'What?' he said. 'It's better for her to have one of us at least to keep her safe from Lisa.'

'That's crazy . . .'

'I know it sounds insane,' he cried. 'But I'm trying to think of some way . . .'

'We would never be able to see each other!' Hannah looked at him with wide, frightened eyes. 'Are you serious?'

'Dead serious. She would be safe with you,' he said.

'You would do that? You would take that . . . shame upon yourself? These lies? For Sydney's sake?'

'We have to protect Sydney,' he said. 'We are all she has. We owe it to her.'

'I know,' said Hannah. Tears rose to her eyes, and she wiped them away with a swipe of her hand. 'I'm glad that you love her that much.'

'I just don't see what else we can do,' he said.

Hannah was quiet for a moment. 'I've been thinking too,' she said.

'Thinking what?'

Hannah looked around at the comfortable room that was her home. From the mantle, photos of Lisa and Sydney smiled out at her. Parchment shades on the blue porcelain table lamps softened the light against the jewel-toned drapes, and the pile of books on the end tables beside their chairs. Sydney's toys were still scattered on the rug in front of the television. Outside, the street lights had come on, and the shadows of the tall trees in their yard dappled the street. The only sound was the whoosh of an occasional passing car and the chirping of crickets in the soft southern night.

She tore her gaze from the familiar, well-loved furnishings of her home, and looked up into her husband's worried eyes. 'We could run,' she said.

TWENTY-SIX

Present day

'Will Miss Mamie be OK?' Sydney asked.

Hannah and Sydney were lying side by side in Sydney's narrow bed. The moon threw the angular shadow of the fire escape over the bedcovers. The few toys that Sydney had were piled into a cardboard box next to a dresser they had bought for her in the thrift shop and repainted. If Sydney longed for her spacious bedroom in Tennessee, she never said as much. It was as if that old life had never existed.

'I'm sure she will be. We'll know more tomorrow,' said Hannah gently. She brushed the child's hair off of her softly rounded cheek and gazed at her. Sydney's large blue eyes were reddened from exhaustion, and the fearful tears she had shed. But her face was still as beautiful and fair as a rose in summer. Once upon a time Hannah had looked at Lisa's face just this same way. She had marveled at the sight of that wondrous creature, her daughter, her only child. And now, Hannah's life revolved around hiding Lisa's child from her. Sometimes she wondered how they could have come to such a pass, and made such a drastic choice. But then she looked into Sydney's eyes and knew that they had done the only thing they could

'I love Miss Mamie,' Sydney murmured as she settled herself in the crook of Hannah's arm. 'She lets me help her.'

'I know she does, sweet pea,' said Hannah, kissing the fragrant crown of the child's head. 'You can see her as soon as she comes home.'

Sydney yawned. 'I miss her.'

'I know,' said Hannah. After her traumatic night, the child had not been able to settle down to sleep until Hannah had sung all her favorite songs and read her half a dozen stories. By the time Sydney was sleepy, Hannah also felt herself drifting off. She could hear her granddaughter's breathing become steady and slow. She's almost asleep, Hannah thought. And then, before she knew it, Hannah too had fallen asleep with Sydney cradled beside her.

Hannah did not know how long she slept, but when she awoke her arm ached from the awkward position in which she had slept on it. She disengaged herself as gently as possible from Sydney, tiptoed out of the room and went down to the short hallway to the modest living room.

Adam was seated at the reconditioned PC, which they used for internet only. No email. No Twitter. No social networking whatsoever.

'She's finally asleep,' said Hannah.

Adam turned on the swivel chair and looked at his wife bleakly. 'We have to go,' he said.

'Go?' Hannah asked, frowning.

'We have to leave. This house. Philly. We have to move on.'

'What? Why are you saying that?'

'It's already on YouTube. It happened hours ago, and it's already had a thousand hits.'

Hannah walked over beside him, and waited as he summoned up the YouTube clip.

It was a short clip. Isaiah Revere was praising Dominga Flores for her quick thinking, and using the opportunity to make a point about how veterans were treated in this country. It was stirring in a way. And true. Even Hannah could see that. And there, at the edge of the frame was Hannah, holding Sydney. Telling the reporter that she felt grateful to Dominga. It was only a few seconds. Hannah's face flamed at the sight of herself, speaking to the reporter, giving them away.

'Maybe she won't see it, Adam,' Hannah said, trying to reassure herself as well as her husband. 'There are thousands of clips every day on the internet. On YouTube. And it's not as if she can tag us with our names. We have different names now. She'd have to watch every single clip that goes up on the internet.'

'She doesn't have to see it. What if somebody else sees it and tells her about it? Nope. This has ruined everything. We have to leave.'

'I'm sorry. What was I supposed to do?' Hannah cried. 'Turn my back on the woman who rescued my child?'

'I didn't say it was your fault,' Adam snapped. 'I'm not accusing you.'

'You might as well be,' said Hannah.

'Well, I tried to tell you that we had to leave. Why didn't you listen to me?' he cried.

Dial it back, Hannah reminded herself. She looked at her husband, and wondered how much longer he was going to be able to stand the strain of this hidden life. He had been a tower of strength from the beginning, but every so often Hannah saw signs of how this whole experience was wearing on him. Sometimes he looked as if he had had all of this runaway existence that he could stand.

'I didn't know what had happened to Sydney at that point,' Hannah said, trying to keep her tone measured. 'I couldn't walk away. I'm sorry I didn't realize why you were saying that until it was too late.'

'I saw the news van arriving,' he said.

'I didn't think they'd make anything of it,' she said. 'An old woman having a stroke. Not exactly newsworthy.'

'Her son is a politician. This was red meat to him,' said Adam.

Hannah sighed. 'Yes, I know. I know that now. I just wasn't thinking. All I was thinking about was Sydney. I thought the ambulance might be there for her. I was so relieved that she was all right.'

'I know you were.'

'I thought that distrusting everybody and being careful had become second nature. But when I saw that ambulance in front of the house I just lost it. I felt like here we'd sacrificed everything to try and keep her safe and now, we leave her side for a few hours – just a couple of hours – and all hell breaks loose . . .'

'Hannah, I understood. I do. Really. But, I'm trying to be realistic. Like it or not, once you're on the internet like this, there's no escape. Someone is bound to see it. If not Lisa, then someone else. If we stay here, she can find us. Even if Lisa doesn't see it herself, someone else might see it and mention it to her. And before you know it . . .'

'She'll bring the law down on us.'

'We did kidnap her child,' said Adam. 'We committed a crime.'

'I am aware,' said Hannah in a brittle tone.

'I'm sorry, but that's not some small thing.'

'I can't move again,' said Hannah wearily. 'Not now. I can't.'

Adam sat back in the rolling chair, his feet planted on the floor, and rubbed his hand over his face. 'We have no choice,' he said.

'It's just one little clip.'

Adam gave her a wry smile. 'So was Gangnam style.'

Hannah laughed in spite of herself. 'I don't think we're quite that fascinating.'

Adam gazed at his wife tenderly. 'Look, I know you don't want to move again. God knows, neither do I. It seems like we just got settled here. But I don't see how we can stay.'

Hannah rested her chin in her hand. 'Can't we just sit tight a little while? Maybe it will all blow over.'

'And if Lisa, or the police, turn up? We'll have to run with the clothes on our back. Wouldn't you rather have a little warning? Like we did the last time? At least we could make some arrangements.'

The last time. A little more than one year ago. Once they made up their minds, they had proceeded quickly but with extreme caution. They'd arranged their finances so that when Lisa was released from jail she would have money available. They'd arranged for their lawyer to have power of attorney over their funds. They'd taken very little with them. They'd amassed their paperwork. Sorted through their belongings. Kept only what they couldn't live without.

They'd said goodbye to no one. Not to Rayanne and Chet. Not even to Pamela.

Surprisingly, for Hannah, leaving her mother had been the hardest thing. They were not close, as mothers and daughters went, but the prospect of never seeing her again had nearly undermined Hannah's resolve. She felt responsible for her mother, even though Hannah knew that her mother would function just fine without her around. It seemed so cold and unfeeling to walk out the door without even a goodbye. That last visit had been torture. Hannah had tried to warn her without giving away their intentions. She'd wanted Pamela to be able to look back on their last conversation and understand why they had chosen this drastic course of action. Hannah had told her mother that she and Adam had begun to have doubts about Lisa's fitness as a mother. She hadn't breathed a word of what they intended to do.

Pamela had looked at her with that piercing, no-nonsense stare. 'Why?'

'Mother, I'd rather not say. Let's just say that it's . . . very disturbing, knowing what I now know about my daughter.'

'Well, then you have to do something about it,' Pamela had said.

Hannah had looked her mother directly in the eye, knowing it might be for the last time. 'That's exactly how we see it. We're going to,' she said.

They'd said no more about it, but Hannah had the definite sensation that her mother was bestowing her blessing. Or maybe she just needed to see it that way. Now she didn't even know if her mother was still alive. They had cut themselves off completely. It had had to be that way. But it had not been easy.

'What are you thinking about?' Adam asked.

'Just then, I was thinking about my mother.'

'This will be less wrenching. We've made sure not to get to know anyone too well.'

'Adam,' she pleaded. 'How can we . . .?'

'We said we'd do anything to protect Sydney. We knew this could happen.'

'But nothing has happened yet,' she protested. 'Maybe nothing will.'

'Are you willing to take that chance?'

Hannah stared back at him. 'You know I would do anything for that child. But can't we wait and see? Sydney's been through so much already. She's making a few little friends. She loves Mamie, and her daycare. Her life is beginning to make sense here. At what point are we doing more harm than good, jerking her from one place to another? Look, I agree that we need to be ready. We can start making some plans. Plan how we would leave, what we would take, where we could go. Maybe even pack a couple of bags and stow them away so we would be prepared to just walk out.'

Adam gazed out the front window at the street lights, frowning. Somewhere in the next block there was a crash, like a beer bottle breaking. Out in the street motorcycles roared by. A woman's raucous laugh was followed by a yelp of protest. It was a relatively quiet night in the neighborhood.

'Adam, listen,' Hannah went on. 'We probably have been too complacent. We should have our plans in place anyway, so that we can be ready to leave immediately. If we regard this as a warning, the next time we'll be ready to go at a moment's notice.'

Adam looked at her and shook his head. 'The next time,' he said. 'I hope we will have a moment's notice.'

TWENTY-SEVEN

Whon two weeks had passed without incident, Hannah began to breathe a little bit easier. The first few days after the clip appeared they'd been almost afraid to leave the house. Both of them had called into work claiming to have the flu. One or the other, bundled up with a hat pulled down over their eyes, would make a *blitzkrieg* run for supplies when it became absolutely necessary. Otherwise, the three of them spent long hours in their little apartment, huddling together on the bed, watching TV or reading. Hannah cooked in the tiny galley kitchen and tried to make her little family the foods they most enjoyed. Occasionally Hannah or Adam would pull back the curtain and survey the street anxiously, as if they expected to see the police, led by their daughter, marching up to the building. Every time their cellphone rang, they jumped. Sydney thought it was all a lovely game, and, thanks to the weather which had suddenly grown chilly, she was happy to stay indoors, snuggling with her worried grandparents.

As she had promised Adam, Hannah packed up several suitcases and put them back into the attic with the pull-down steps above the third-floor hallway. Packing up the bags left their closets looking forlorn, but it appeased Adam, who was still warning her that they might have to leave at any moment. Hannah knew he was right to be concerned but she could see that he also was beginning to relax, as the days passed, and there was no sign of Lisa, no word from her or from the police. Even Adam was starting to believe that they might have dodged a bullet. They might still be safe.

To Sydney's dismay, Mamie had not yet returned home. Her stroke left her paralyzed on the right side, and Isaiah had her placed in a rehab center outside the city in Blue Bell where she was guaranteed good care, and an intensive physical therapy routine. One Saturday morning, as Hannah and Sydney were venturing down the stairs to go out for a walk, they heard a key turning in the lock of the front door. Hannah froze on the staircase, and then slumped against the wall in relief as she saw Isaiah come in.

He looked up and greeted the startled-looking Hannah and Sydney, who was holding her hand.

'You look like you've seen a ghost,' he observed.

'No,' said Hannah. 'You just surprised me . . . coming in like that.'

Isaiah raised a paper shopping bag in his hand. 'I came here to go through my mother's mail.'

'How is she doing? How long till she is ready to come home?' Hannah asked.

Isaiah began to sort through Mamie's mail on the hall table. 'Come home?' he murmured, frowning at the pile of circulars which had accumulated. 'Never, if I have anything to say about it.'

'What do you mean?' Hannah asked.

'Well, I'm hoping to get her into assisted living once they spring her from the rehab. There's a perfectly nice place in Overbrook, ten minutes from where my wife and I live. There, she'd have her own apartment, everything brand new and medical staff right on the premises.'

'My mother's in a place like that,' Hannah admitted, and then wished she hadn't even brought it up. Luckily the councilman was preoccupied with his own concerns, and didn't seem to notice.

'This situation just isn't working anymore,' he said, waving a fistful of envelopes at the house around them.

'She does love this house,' said Hannah.

Councilman Revere shook his head. 'I grew up in this house. But I certainly don't want to spend time here anymore. I can't get my kids to come here for any reason. It's falling down around my mother's ears. She can't keep up with it. No, I'm looking at this as an opportunity. She'll have no choice about it.'

'Does that mean . . . What does that mean about the house? Are you going to sell it?'

'I'd be happy to unload it tomorrow but I'm trying to at least pay lip service to my mother's wishes. What? Are you worried about your apartment?' he asked.

Hannah shook her head. 'Well, we're . . . comfortable here. But we can get another apartment if we have to. We'd miss Mamie, though.'

'Did Miss Mamie get my picture?' Sydney asked the tall, well-dressed man in the hallway.

'She certainly did,' said Isaiah. 'And she wanted me to thank you. She pinned it up on the bulletin board in her room. Well, I've got to run . . .'

'Councilman, before you go, were you able to help Dominga with her situation? I haven't seen her around lately,' Hannah said.

'Dominga?' said Isaiah. 'Who's Dominga?'

Hannah felt offended that he did not recognize the name of the woman who had rescued his mother. 'Dominga Flores. The young woman, the army vet, who broke in here, the night Mamie took sick. The one who heard Cindy crying.'

'Oh, right,' said Isaiah impatiently. 'I told her to call my office. I don't know if she followed up on that. I have a lot of constituents, and I'm short staffed as it is.'

Hannah shook her head. Adam was right. Isaiah had used Dominga to create a special moment for himself in front of the TV cameras. But once that was over, he clearly hadn't given another thought to Dominga and her problems. She made a mental note to ask Frank Petrusa about her when she got back to Restoration House. Someone should demonstrate their gratitude, she thought.

Hannah and Adam finally went back to work and took Sydney back to her daycare. At Restoration House everyone was solicitous about her health, and Hannah had to make up tales about her illness. She was glad when people stopped asking her if she felt all right and began to treat her normally again. When Frank Petrusa stopped to ask after her health, she managed to change the subject by asking him about Dominga. He said that Dominga had not been in to the group in quite a while, but that Father Luke might know where she was.

One late afternoon, a week after her return, she tapped on the door of Father Luke's office. He invited her in with his usual pleasant smile. He was a man who never seemed pressed for time. 'How can I help you?' he said.

'Father Luke, I know you can't keep track of everybody,' she said, 'but I was just wondering . . .'

Father Luke pointed to a chair in front of his desk and Hannah sat down. 'About what?' he asked.

'Well, there's this vet named Dominga Flores who really saved the day, when Cindy's babysitter had that stroke.'

'Oh, sure. I saw it on the news.'

Hannah felt sick to her stomach, as she always did when anyone mentioned seeing film of that event. It must have shown on her face.

'What's the matter?' asked the priest.

Hannah shook her head. 'I just haven't seen Dominga around since that night. I wondered if she got any help. Councilman Revere said he would help her but he didn't really do anything in the end.'

'I guess once he got his soundbite he forgot about her,' said Father Luke. 'Politicians.' He sighed and then looked up at Hannah. 'I'm sorry, Anna. I'm afraid I haven't seen Dominga around here in a while. Why are you looking for her?'

'Well, I'd like to help her if I could. Obviously, she's got a problem with alcohol, and homelessness. The works. I know all the programs available. I thought if I just could talk to her . . .'

'Let me make a few calls,' said Father Luke. 'I'll let you know if I locate her.'

The next day dawned fair and breezy, a lovely November day. Hannah walked Sydney to her daycare, and then went over to Restoration House. It was so lovely that she hated to go inside. She came in and hung up her jacket. As she did, she saw Father Luke beckoning to her. She went down to his office. 'What's up?' she asked.

'I located her. Dominga Flores.'

'Oh, great. Where is she?' Hannah asked.

'Apparently, she checked into a rehab downtown.'

'That's a start,' said Hannah. 'Maybe she can get her life together.'

'I was talking with one of the counselors there. She's about to be sprung, and she has nowhere to go. No plans. I told them she could come here temporarily.'

Hannah sighed. 'I wish I could help her. I feel like I owe her.'

'Well, you may get your wish. I told her counselor that I'd send you down there with the paperwork for her to stay temporarily at Restoration House. You can go over her options with her. Encourage her to participate in Frank's groups. I think she needs that kind of group support.'

Hannah looked up at him, beaming. 'Really? I'd be glad to. That would be great. But what about work?'

'That is our work,' Father Luke said gently. 'Nothing here that can't wait. If this girl leaves rehab and ends up on the street, she's gonna crawl back into the bottle before you know it. I'm sure it would do her good to know that you cared enough about her to go out of your way. She seems to be alone in the world.'

'I'd really like to go and talk to her. Thanks, Father Luke.'

The priest waved her off, and Hannah picked up her bag and her jacket and let herself out of Restoration House. She thought about how to get to the Center City Rehab. She could take the bus. That way at least she could still see the lovely day from her seat. If she got a seat. SEPTA service was not completely reliable out in their neighborhood.

Finally, she decided on the quickest method – the subway. To Hannah, it was the most distasteful. The stations often smelled of urine, and the walls were covered with graffiti. More often than not, there were bums reeking of alcohol on the platforms, and the high-school students, who rode for free, were often rowdy. Still, it was the quickest way to go, and it would give her the most time downtown. Her mind made up, Hannah walked toward the subway station, stopping long enough to buy a paper from a newsstand on the street. If she had something to read she was less likely to be harassed, either by obstreperous kids or by drunken panhandlers. The station was still busy but the school rush was over, so that made it a bit quieter. People were coming and going up and down the steps to the subway station. Hannah joined the throng, and descended into the underground.

She had a multiple-use ticket, which she used to get through the turnstile. Once inside, she held her breath against the heavy, mal-odorous air, and made her way through the cluster of people nearest the entrance. The far end of the platform was usually the most sparsely populated. She avoided going all the way there. It was never a good idea to be too isolated. But she separated herself from the other riders and began to look down at her folded-up paper, avoiding the gaze of the other people waiting on the platform, while she kept one hand firmly clutched on her pocketbook.

She was bemused by her own precautions. A girl who grew up in semi-rural Franklin County, and thought that Nashville, Tennessee, was a giant metropolis, she had had a crash course in street smarts during this last year in Philadelphia. She had learned not to smile and say hello. She knew to avert her eyes. To keep her wits about her, to hang on like grim death to any and all bags she had with her. Unless of course, someone brandished a weapon. Then, she knew you had to let go without an argument. Your bag wasn't worth your life.

She kept her eyes lowered, ostensibly on her paper, but her gaze was distracted by movement on the tracks below. She squinted at the moving shape against the dark tracks, and realized, with a sickening thud in her stomach, that she was looking at a rat about the size of a cat, scuttling across the gravel in between the rails until he got to the metal handrails of the emergency ladder at the far end of the platform.

Hannah was repulsed by the sight. Was he coming up those rungs to the platform? Were rats able to climb a ladder? She would not put anything past those vermin who were so adaptive to the city life. Hannah was the farthest person from the entrance, and closest to the end of the platform. Suddenly, she no longer wanted to be that far from her fellow subway riders. If the rat came up that ladder and onto the platform, she did not want to be the first human he encountered. She edged her way closer to the others. At least it was not an especially unruly lot. On the contrary, there were several tired-looking women who were probably heading to work. A few noisy girls in Catholic-school uniforms were teasing one another and laughing at their own insults. A guy with a bushy beard in a black shirt with a large green, gold and red Frisbee-shaped tam covering his dreadlocks was rocking slightly on the balls of his feet. Stoned, she thought. One guy in a hoody and shades was slumped to the ground against the tiles of the wall, his chin against his chest, his hands in the pockets. The usual suspects, she thought.

From the distance she heard the train's whistle and saw the light coming closer as it approached the station. Good, she thought. Time to go. She thought about Dominga and what she was going to say to her. She had to reassure the lonely veteran that there was help, and a life worth living out there.

The roaring, shrieking train came barreling towards them. Hannah tucked her paper under her arm and renewed her grip on her bag. Along with her fellow passengers, she stepped closer to the platform edge, trying to judge where the doors would open. Suddenly, even over the deafening noise of the approaching train, she heard human voices yelping.

'Hey!'

'No!'

She started to turn to look, and then she felt it. Something powerful at her back shoved her forward and she stumbled, losing her footing. All she could see was the yellow light looming. Otherwise, despite the cacophony of the speeding train on the tracks, everything was silent. The only sound she heard, as her feet left the platform and she sailed out and over the tracks, was the frantic thudding of her heart.

She landed on all fours, on the jagged little stones between the rails. For a moment she was too stunned to move. She scrambled up to her feet but she couldn't breathe. The train, its yellow light blinding, was bearing down on her.

I'm going to die, she thought. She could hear sounds again. The roar of the train, and people screaming on the platform. Hannah stood, frozen, staring at the oncoming train. A heavyset black woman, holding a shopping bag, leaned out over the edge of the platform. She extended her hand to Hannah and shook it, as if to say, take it. Take my hand. I'll pull you up. Hannah reached up frantically but she was not even close to touching the woman's hand. Hannah saw the blur of people on the platform. Some were shouting for help, and trying to wave down the engineer, to get him to brake. One schoolgirl was sobbing.

A portly black man in a SEPTA uniform shook his head and roughly pulled the woman with the shopping bag back and away from the edge of the platform.

He's gonna let me die, Hannah thought.

Then the man looked Hannah in the eyes. Through the deafening cacophony he was speaking to her. What was he saying? It was impossible to hear his words above the din. He pointed toward the ladder at the far end of the platform. Hannah stared at him, her eyes wide with terror.

'Run,' he said.

Somehow, despite the terror, the noise and her own confusion, she heard it. Run? she thought. She must have mouthed the question. The SEPTA conductor held her gaze calmly, and nodded emphatically, pointing again, toward the end of the platform. Run? Outrun the train? That was ridiculous. Impossible.

For a second she could not move. Would not. And then, in a flash, she understood. He was telling her that this was her only chance. And he would know. There was no other chance. Somehow, it registered. She started to move. To do what he said. To run. She started slowly, and then she was running. She ran for her life, stumbling over the stones between the ties, weeping. It felt as if the whole world was shuddering with the approaching train. She thought of Adam, and Sydney. Briefly, she thought of Lisa and her heart ached for all the loss. She remembered the rat, and then, she remembered the ladder.

The train was roaring into the station, the brakes screaming. Hannah was at the ladder, grabbing the rail, pulling herself up. The train struck her.

TWENTY-EIGHT

She woke up in a dimly lit room, her head pounding. She reached up and gingerly touched her head, which was swathed in bandages. Then she tried to sit up and felt pain burst like fireworks all through her body. She was wearing a thin hospital gown, and there were bandages wrapped around her torso. Her other arm was in a cast. There was a searing pain in her leg that seemed to radiate upwards, through her body and out the top of her head.

For a second she could not remember how she got here or how she became so badly injured. Then, suddenly, it came back to her. The shrieking whistle, the yellow orb of light hurtling toward her in the dark tunnel. The shove from behind. Hannah felt tears start to trickle down her face and she gasped for breath.

Alive, she thought. I'm alive. Thank you, God. Thank you.

Her very next thought was of Adam. Did he know she was alive? Did he know she was even here?

Before the thought had actually formed clearly in her mind, the door to the room opened, and he walked in, the man she had been married to for over half her lifetime. His shoulders were rounded, his back bent, as if he were carrying a bundle of bricks on his broad back. His eyes were downcast.

'Hey,' she whispered.

He froze and looked up. His gaze met hers. It was like watching daybreak in a time-lapse photo. His frown cleared, his eyes widened, and a smile, at first tentative, and then joyous broke across his face. 'Babe!' he cried.

Hannah tried to nod. Her lips were dry as parchment. He rushed to her bedside and tried to grab her up in a hug.

'No,' she laughed. 'Don't. That hurts.'

Reluctantly he loosened his grip. He was shaking. Gently, she ran her good hand over his bent head. After a minute he raised his head and looked into her eyes. Their gaze was long and silent. I thought I lost you, each one said, without words. I was so afraid.

Hannah closed her eyes. All that she felt for him was almost too painful to endure. She felt his gentle healing kiss on her face. Then, suddenly, he moved away from her. She opened her eyes to see where he went. He pulled a chair close to her bed, and they gripped hands.

Adam shook his head. 'When they called and said that you'd been hit by a subway train . . .'

Hannah sighed. 'I know. I thought I was dead,' she said. 'I should be dead.'

Adam frowned. 'A lot of people saw it happen. Apparently, someone pushed you onto the tracks.'

'Yes. Did they catch the guy who did it?' she asked.

Adam shook his head. 'Not yet. No one seemed to get a good look.'

'I really can't remember it happening. I just remember landing on the tracks, completely stunned. The train was coming.'

Adam grimaced. 'How did you . . .?'

'There was a guy from SEPTA on the platform. Everyone else was screaming. Shrieking. The train was roaring in. The noise was deafening. But this guy . . . he just looked me in the eye and told me to run. And somehow, it registered. Somehow I heard him.'

'Run?' Adam cried. 'How can you outrun a train?'

Hannah lifted her broken arm with a wry smile. 'You can't.'

'They said it saved your life, though. The driver was trying to stop the train. The fact that you had reached the end of the platform, and grabbed onto the ladder, kept it from . . . you know.'

'Flattening me,' said Hannah. 'Killing me. I know. Honey, give me some water?'

Adam quickly found a cup of water and a straw, and put the straw in her mouth.

Hannah sipped, and felt like it was her first drink of water on earth. 'Thanks,' she said. 'I'll tell you. The man was telling me to run, and everything in me was thinking that it was the worst idea in the world, and yet, I could hear his voice in my ear, like the voice of God. I remember thinking, he's a SEPTA guy. He probably knows what to do. And then I did what he said.'

'Thank God,' Adam said.

Hannah shook her head. 'I don't remember being hit. It's just a blank.' She looked around. 'Where is Sydney?'

'With Kiyanna and Frank.'

'Oh, good,' she said.

'They've been great. They've really helped me out. She's very confused and upset. She's been having nightmares. Just awful.'

'Poor baby. Oh, poor thing. How long have I been here? What's wrong with me. I mean, these injuries . . .?'

Adam sighed. 'The accident happened three days ago. You have a mesh patch in your skull, because of the swelling from your brain. You have a broken arm. Your leg was lacerated and took fifty stitches to close.'

'Wow,' she said.

'I almost lost you.'

Hannah smiled. 'It'll never happen.'

Adam smiled, and cupped her face with his hand. 'I couldn't stand that.'

'I know. Me neither.'

They sat that way for a moment, unable to actually say all that they meant. They didn't need to. Finally, Adam said, 'There's something we need to talk about. The police want to question you.'

'Right now?'

'When they find out you're awake.'

'OK.'

'Hannah, listen,' he said quietly. 'When they question you, tell them you don't want any pictures. Say you're fearful of reprisal because they haven't caught the guy yet. We don't want your picture everywhere.'

'You're right,' she said with a slight gasp. 'That's true. Our situation is still . . .'

'Perilous,' he said.

Hannah closed her eyes. 'I won't say anything.'

'That's my girl,' he said. 'Shall I bring Sydney up to see you later?'

'Yes, please. If you don't think it would be too much for her.'

'I think it would do her good,' Adam said.

'I know it would do me good,' said Hannah, smiling.

Adam sat beside her, squeezing her hand, and occasionally kissing her fingers. Then the door opened, and a nurse came in carrying a tray with a syringe.

'You're awake!' the nurse cried.

Hannah nodded, and then looked at Adam. 'How lucky am I?' she said.

The nurse was quick to spread the word, and within an hour Hannah was visited by two doctors and a chaplain. Adam told his recovering wife that he was going to go and pick up Sydney and bring her to the hospital. Hannah allowed that this was the only reason she would let him out of her sight. They kissed tenderly before he left the room.

Hannah lay back against her pillow, exhausted. It was wonderful to know that she was going to live, but she still had a long way to go before she could even get up and out of this bed. She closed her eyes and, almost immediately, she was asleep.

A short time later, Hannah's nap was disturbed by a knock at the door. Before she was fully awake and able to reply, it was pushed open by two men in jackets and ties.

'Mrs Anna Whitman?' asked the larger man. He had a deliberate, grave air about him.

'Yes,' she said.

The man nodded to his shorter, Asian-looking companion and then they both entered the room and stood beside her bed.

'Mrs Whitman, my name is Detective O'Rourke. This is Detective Trahn. We need to talk to you about what happened in the subway.'

Hannah tried to force her fuzzy mind to focus. She was glad that Adam had reminded her of their situation. Lying in this anonymous bed, in a hospital gown, it was hard to even feel a sense of identity, never mind remember to hide the reality and stick with the story of their lives that they had created.

'Yes,' she murmured. 'OK.'

'Do you mind if we sit?' asked O'Rourke.

Hannah shook her head, and O'Rourke nodded to Trahn, who pulled two chairs up beside the bed. The detectives sat down. O'Rourke set his briefcase on the floor beside him.

'Now, tell us what happened as you remember it, Mrs Whitman.'

Hannah obediently recounted her descent into the subway, the various people on the platform, the sight of the approaching train, and then . . .

'You don't remember what happened?' asked Trahn gently.

'I really don't,' said Hannah.

'Did you see who pushed you?' asked O'Rourke.

'No, sir,' she said.

'You just . . . felt yourself being pushed.'

Hannah nodded. 'It was the strangest thing. If you'd told me this could happen, I wouldn't really have believed it. I mean, I felt this jolt at the small of my back and then, nothing . . . I didn't hear anything, I didn't see anything. It's all just a blank. How could you forget something like that?'

'Actually that's not uncommon,' O'Rourke said reassuringly. 'I've heard that from many trauma victims. The brain just shuts down for a few moments. Trying to protect you from a horrible reality, I guess.'

'I guess,' said Hannah.

'So, you didn't see who pushed you.'

Hannah shook her head.

'The next thing you remember . . .?'

'I was on the tracks. I remember a woman reached her hand out to me but I couldn't get to it. Then I heard this man from SEPTA telling me to run. And I heard it, you know what I mean? I heard it. Above all the noise and the commotion, I heard his voice. And that's what I did. I ran.'

O'Rourke nodded and consulted his notebook. 'We have varying accounts from the witnesses on the platform,' he said. 'One thing they all agree on. Apparently you were pushed by a man in a hoody. Height, weight, all of that – no consistency. But they all remembered the hoody. And the dark glasses.'

'No one stopped him? After it happened?'

O'Rourke sighed. 'That's to be expected. People were so freaked out. They were focused on you. And on that train roaring into the station.'

Hannah shuddered.

'By all accounts he ran back up the steps and out of the station. So far, we have not apprehended him.'

Hannah sighed. 'Well, I hope you do.'

'We will,' said Trahn grimly. 'It's just a matter of time. Now, while it seems most likely that this person is mentally ill, Mrs Whitman, and that you were a random victim, we have to ask you this. Is there any reason you can think of for why someone would do that to you?'

Hannah hesitated, and then she felt almost faint at the thought which swam, for the first time, into her head. Then she shook it off. 'No,' she said.

'What about your marriage,' said O'Rourke. 'Have you and your husband been having any problems? Any reason why he might see himself as better off without you?'

'*No*, Detective,' said Hannah angrily. 'Our marriage is stronger than . . . It's as strong as can be. We've had our problems, like any marriage. We've been together for over twenty years. So, obviously, we've had problems, had things go wrong. But no. The short answer is no.'

O'Rourke exhaled a deep breath and nodded. 'OK, Mrs Whitman. Now, we have here . . .' He reached down into the briefcase on the floor beside him and brought out an iPad. 'This is footage taken by a security camera in the subway. Now, you say you didn't even see your attacker . . .'

'I didn't,' Hannah insisted.

'The whole thing is on this footage. It may be very distressing for you to view it.'

Hannah felt suddenly depressed. Distressing? To see yourself attacked out of the blue. Pushed in front of a train? Yes, that was distressing.

'You look upset. Do you need us to wait on this until you've recovered a little more?'

Hannah shook her head and hesitated. Then she made up her mind. 'No. He could be on another subway platform, right this very minute. Sizing up some other unsuspecting passenger. Let me see it. I want to see it.'

'Very well,' said O'Rourke. 'I'm glad you feel that way. Trahn, can you work this damn thing for me,' he said, offering the iPad to his partner.

'Of course,' said Trahn. He set the iPad up on the arm of the rolling tray table beside the bed, and swung it over in front of Hannah so that she could have a clear view. He turned on the iPad and some numbers came up on the screen. 'Can you see it all right?'

Hannah nodded, looking at the screen in a kind of sick fascination. She began slowly to pick out some of the people she had seen on the platform. The school kids, the man in the tam, and she felt her heart jump with gratitude when she saw the woman who had reached out a hand to try to save her. She was standing on the platform, holding her shopping bag, conveying a sense of isolation that was calculated. Don't talk to me, her body language said. Don't get too close. But when the situation was desperate, that woman had offered her hand.

Then, with a jolt, Hannah saw herself coming through the turnstile, walking down the platform. Walking past that guy in the hoody slumped against the wall.

Was that him? she wondered. He looked so out of it.

She watched with a sickening fascination as she separated herself from the other passengers, and then froze as she saw something on the tracks. Now she remembered. That disgusting rat. The creature wasn't visible in the video but her reaction to him was. She began to edge back toward the center of the platform. Toward her fellow passengers.

And then, though there was no sound, she could see the reaction of the others as the train approached. Every face turned in that direction, including her own.

Every face but one.

'Now watch carefully,' said Detective O'Rourke.

Suddenly, with a movement like lightning, the person in the hoody broke free from the crowd, was behind Hannah in a few steps, reached out and pushed.

Pushed her. Off the platform and onto the tracks. Hannah broke out in a sweat at the sight of it but she tried to concentrate. This is who they were looking for This person in the hoody, who'd pushed her and turned away. As he turned, he faced the camera for a brief moment. Not long, but long enough

'I'm looking at your face, Mrs Whitman,' said O'Rourke. 'Do you see him? Is there any chance this is someone you recognize?'

Hannah was shaking her head from side to side as Trahn ran the sequence through again, and she covered her mouth with her fist to stifle a cry. This time she saw the hooded assailant get up from where he had been slumped against the wall. Rush up to her. Push her. Without hesitation. Push her onto the tracks.

'I know it's upsetting to watch. But try to think. Does he look familiar? Anything at all that you recognize about this person?' O'Rourke asked.

'Nothing. No,' said Hannah.

Yes, she thought.

TWENTY-NINE

Still holding Sydney's hand, Adam pushed open the door to Hannah's room and looked inside. There was a light on over the bed but the bed was empty. Outside the window, the bright light of day had faded to charcoal gray, and a sliver of moon rose over the trees. From the doorway Adam could see that the bathroom door was open but the room was dark. There was nobody inside . . .

'Where is Mom?' Sydney asked fretfully.

'I'm not sure. We'll ask the nurse,' he said.

Just then a young nurse in cheerful panda-bear scrubs came walking past.

'Excuse me,' he said.

'Can I help you?'

'My wife,' said Adam. 'She was in this room but she's not here. She can't really walk.'

'Oh, your wife. I'm so sorry about what happened to her,' said the nurse. 'Honestly, you never know. You have to be on your guard all the time.'

'What do you mean?' he cried.

The nurse looked startled by his reaction. 'I mean about that nut pushing her in the subway,' she said.

'Oh, right. Sure. Well, luckily, she's getting better. You all are taking good care of her here. Do you, uh, know where she is?'

'Yes. She's down in the solarium. I saw one of our aides pushing her down there in a wheelchair earlier.'

'Thank you,' said Adam, relieved. He bent over and spoke to Sydney. 'Come on. I know where to find Mom.'

Sydney was more than willing to accompany him. In fact, she wanted to skip ahead in the long corridor with its shining floors, but Adam gripped her hand tightly. They walked down the hallway toward the lounge at the end of the hall.

A lot of people passed the door to the lounge but Adam did not see anyone going in.

He hurried Sydney along, and arrived quickly at the door and looked inside.

At first, the dimly lit room, which was half-lounge, half-greenhouse, looked empty. Then, Adam made out the figure of Hannah. Wrapped in an oversized robe, she was sitting in a wheelchair near a window, partly shielded by the bank of plants which flourished in the normally sunny room. She was staring out the window, though it was really too dark to see anything but shadows.

'Babe,' he said.

Hannah did not turn around. If it had not been for the bandages wrapped around her head, Adam would have wondered if perhaps he was in the wrong place, if this woman sitting in the gloom was someone other than his wife. But Sydney did not hesitate. She cried out and rushed over to the wheelchair and tried to clamber up onto Hannah's lap.

'Sydney, no. Stop that,' Adam exhorted her. 'Mom's had a lot of stitches.'

Now that he had reached her, Adam could see that, though she said nothing, despair was written on Hannah's face. She did not cry out at the child making herself comfortable in her lap. She grimaced but wound her arms protectively around Sydney.

'How's my girl?' she whispered.

'I miss you,' said Sydney.

'I miss you too. But Pop says you're staying with Miss Kiyanna and Mr Frank. Is it fun staying there?'

The child nodded sadly.

'You like them, don't you? Kiyanna and Frank are nice, aren't they darlin'?' Adam asked the child gently.

'I want Mom,' she insisted. 'And you, Pop.'

Hannah looked up at her husband, puzzled. 'Where are you staying?'

'I've been sleeping here,' he said. 'They let me have a bed so I would be here when you woke up.'

Hannah reached out and clutched his warm, familiar hand. 'I should have known,' she said.

'Tell you what,' said Adam to Sydney. 'Why don't you come over here and sit? I brought this so you could watch a story. You want me to put Clifford on?' he asked, referring to the series of books and videos about a Big Red Dog that Sydney enjoyed. He pulled a small-screen DVD player from his pocket. 'You can watch Clifford while I talk to Mom.'

He tried to lift Sydney off of Hannah's lap but she began to kick and cry out, 'No. I won't.'

'Don't kick, sweetheart,' said Hannah. 'It hurts.'

Sydney put a pudgy hand up to Hannah's cheek. 'Sorry,' she said woefully.

'It's OK. You go look at your story. Everything's OK. I'm right here. I won't leave. Go on now.'

Reluctantly the child obeyed, and allowed herself to be stationed in the corner of a nearby sofa, the small screen clutched in her hands.

Adam came back and sat down beside Hannah.

He looked worriedly at his wife. 'What's the matter, babe? You looked better when I saw you earlier this afternoon. Did something happen?'

Hannah nodded. 'Yes. I spoke to the police,' she said.

'How did that go?'

Hannah looked back out at the darkening day. 'They had a surveillance video of the accident.'

'If you can call it an accident,' Adam observed grimly.

'Right,' she said faintly.

'Did you . . . did they ask you to look at it?'

Hannah nodded. 'I looked at it.'

'No wonder you're shook up,' he said. 'I'm sure that had to be traumatic just seeing it unfold when you're helpless to stop it.'

'That's not why,' she said.

Adam frowned. 'Why, then?'

'The person who pushed me was on the tape. They kept referring to my attacker as "the guy in the hoody". But I was able to see the face . . . Just for a second.'

'And . . .?'

Hannah turned her head and looked her husband squarely in the face. 'The police asked me if I recognized him. On the off-chance this attack might not have been random. I said that I didn't have any idea who he was.'

Adam did not reply but looked at her and felt himself dreading what she was going to say next.

'That was a lie, Adam. I only saw her face for a second, wearing dark glasses, her hair covered up. But it didn't matter. It was her.'

'Jesus,' he breathed. 'Are you sure?'

'I'd know her anywhere.' Hannah gazed at him hopelessly. 'My own daughter pushed me in front of that train.'

Adam hung his head. 'Oh, God.'

'How am I supposed to live with that?' she said.

'Oh my God. I don't know,' he said. They were silent for a minute. He clutched her hand, which lay limp and unresponsive in his. Sydney, who was lying across the lounge on a sofa, laughed out loud at something on her screen.

Adam sighed. 'This means she found us. She must have seen the YouTube clip. And figured it out from there.'

'Apparently,' said Hannah. 'She must have been watching us. Waiting.'

'Did you tell them anything? The police?'

Hannah looked at him bleakly. 'No. How could I? You and I are fugitives. Kidnappers.'

'I know,' he said.

'She must have been watching the house,' said Hannah. 'She must have followed me to the subway.'

'I suppose so,' said Adam.

'You haven't been back there, have you? To the house?'

Adam shook his head. 'As I said, I've been sleeping here. And Sydney's been at Kiyanna's.'

Hannah nodded and sat clutching the arms of her wheelchair, staring out into the night descending on the Philadelphia skyline. 'You can't go back there.'

'What do you mean?'

'To the house. You have to avoid the house.' She glanced over at Sydney, who was lying on her back, enjoying the show on her screen. For a moment her gaze softened. Then, she pressed her lips together in a determined line. 'I've been thinking, ever since I saw that surveillance tape.'

'Thinking what?' he asked warily.

'My being in the hospital. This is an opportunity.'

'An opportunity for what?' he asked.

Hannah reached over and grasped his hand. She looked at him earnestly. 'Adam, Lisa doesn't know how my recovery is going. She knows I'm here, obviously. She put me here. And it's been on the news. All she has to do is call the hospital to check on my condition. They wouldn't let her speak to me, of course, but they would tell her that I'm still here. They might tell her my condition but that's it.'

'So . . .?' he said.

'So, she knows that I am still in the hospital.'

'Well, it's not like she's worried about you.' He punched his fist into his palm. 'Honest to God, Hannah. I wish I could wring her neck.'

'But you wouldn't,' Hannah said flatly. 'You wouldn't.'

'Probably not,' he admitted. 'Though I almost wish I could. How could she do such a thing? Push you onto the subway tracks? You loved her. You were a wonderful mother to her. OK, I understand that she must hate us for taking Sydney. But she knows why we did it. She brought it on herself. We had to try to protect Sydney from her.'

'Oh, I'm sure she hates us for that,' said Hannah.

'Yes. Because she didn't think there was anything wrong with her plans to offer her toddler to the biggest pervert she could find. What kind of a monster did we raise, anyway? It makes me feel so . . . helpless, knowing how ruthless she is. Knowing that she just doesn't care. I keep asking myself, why didn't I see it? How could I not have known this about her, somewhere along the line? She lived with us all her life, and we didn't know her at all. Not anything about her. Now I can't even remember what I used to love about her.'

'I can,' said Hannah, with a sigh.

Adam wiped his eyes. 'I know,' he said. 'That's what's so crazy about it. I suppose I do too.'

'We can't think about that now,' said Hannah. 'We have to decide what to do next. I've spent the afternoon thinking about it.'

Adam reached up and laid his palm against the bandages wrapped around her head. 'Are you supposed to be thinking?' he said, smiling slightly.

'Probably not,' she said, 'but there's no stopping me.'

'OK. What have you been scheming?'

'First of all, I know you're not going to like this . . .'

Adam frowned at her.

'Just hear me out. As I said, this is our opportunity. And, in a way, nothing has changed. The only thing that really matters is Sydney. And this is our chance.'

'To do what?' he said wearily.

'You know the bags I packed? And put in the attic? Now they will come in handy. We'll ask someone to go in and get them. You can't go in there, or she might see you. And follow you. So we'll have somebody get the bags and bring them to wherever you are.'

'Wherever I am?' he asked skeptically.

'So then you'll have what you need,' she said.

'For what?'

Hannah looked at him with an unflinching gaze. 'To start over. You and Sydney have to leave.'

'Leave? What? Leave Philly?'

'Yes,' she said. 'Leave Philly.'

'You mean leave you here all alone? Oh, Hannah. Don't be stupid.'

Hannah leaned forward in her wheelchair so that her face was close to his. 'Adam, listen to me. She knows you. She knows that you would never leave me alone while I was in the hospital. That's why this is a golden opportunity. She won't be expecting it. She's probably planning her next move for when I get home, when we are all back in the West Philly apartment. So we have to seize this opportunity. You have to take Sydney and get far away from here.'

'Do you hear yourself?' he said, shaking his head. 'She's already proved that she would do anything to hurt you. You think I'm going to leave you behind?'

Hannah reached out and wrapped her cold fingers around his wrist. 'I mean it, Adam. I'm not being hysterical. I've never felt more certain of what to do. Whatever happens with Lisa, I can face it. But Sydney deserves the best protection we can give her. There's only one way to ensure that.'

'What you're proposing is suicidal,' he said grimly.

'Please try and understand,' she continued. 'At some level I don't care anymore. My child, my own flesh and blood, tried to kill me. I don't know if it's possible to feel lower than I do today. Depressed doesn't even begin to describe it.'

'I know,' he said. 'It's devastating. But you can't give up like this. We'll figure out a way to do this together.'

'Adam, this is the only way. We have this brief window of opportunity, when you two can flee from here and she won't be expecting it. She won't be looking for you. I'll still be in here for several days, and she'll expect you to stay by my side. She may not have any love or loyalty herself but she knows that you do. That's exactly why you have to leave now.'

'It's out of the question,' said Adam, shaking his head.

'Darling,' Hannah said in a low, urgent voice, 'this isn't how we planned our life. But this is the life we have. We created Lisa. We raised her, and somehow . . . she's amoral. She has no inner . . . conscience. No . . . sense of right and wrong. Nothing anybody says about psychopaths being born and not made will make me feel one bit better about this. She is out there in the world, free to harm anyone she wants to. It's hard to describe how much I feel like a failure.'

'That's not fair,' he said. 'We tried everything. We had a happy home. She never wanted for anything. We cheered her on, no matter what she wanted to do. You were the best mother in the world. Always on her side. Always thinking of ways to make her life happy. You can't blame yourself.'

'But I do,' she said. 'At the end of the day, I do feel responsible.'

'Well, so do I,' he said. 'But we can't change what's already done. In spite of all our best efforts, this is the result. And we can't do a thing to change it.'

'No, we can't. But we can be sure that Sydney doesn't pay the price. For Lisa's . . . insanity. For our blindness to it. No matter what it costs. So you have to take her far from here, now, when Lisa's not expecting you to leave.'

'And leave you at her mercy?'

'I'm ready for that,' said Hannah. 'This is my fate. I will face it.'

'Don't talk like that. It's crazy,' he insisted.

'I mean it,' she said. 'You know I do.'

He met her gaze apprehensively.

'Adam, I can't make up for what Lisa has done. I think she killed Troy Petty and then slandered him in court. And I actually approved of that. It makes me sick to think about it. I can't right that wrong, though I feel it so keenly. His poor family.' Hannah shook her head. 'I'm her mother. I have a lot to answer for.'

'She's the one who has to answer for it,' Adam insisted. 'We did what any parents would do.'

'Maybe. I'll never know. The only good thing that I can still do is to guard Sydney. Make sure she's all right. And you are the only one I trust to protect her. You have to do this. For me. Take her and go. Don't look back.'

'And what are you going to do?' he cried.

'I'll . . . recuperate,' she said. 'And when I'm ready, I'll go home.'
'Are you kidding? Home? You'll be a sitting duck. You think I'm just going to leave you there, for her to come after? To finish the job?'

'I'll figure out a way to protect myself. Or I won't. In a way, it doesn't even matter anymore. My only child tried to kill me. I don't even want to get up each day and think about that. But you have to keep Sydney away from her. No matter what. You just have to go.'

'I won't,' he said. Tears stood in his eyes. 'I won't leave you.'

'You haven't got any choice,' she said sadly. She entwined her fingers with his. 'We haven't got any choice.'

THIRTY

'Time to go back to your room,' said the nurse, releasing the brake on Hannah's wheelchair and interrupting her urgent tête-à-tête with Adam. 'They're bringing your dinner.'

Hannah looked up guiltily. 'Just give me two minutes,' she said.

The nurse frowned but nodded. 'I'll be back in exactly two minutes.'

Hannah gave her the OK sign, and the nurse went back out into the corridor.

'Two minutes?' Adam cried. 'Are you kidding? We can't. I'm not ready.'

Hannah looked over at Sydney, and her lip trembled. But she did not allow herself to weep. 'Sweetheart,' she called out, 'you have to go with Pop now. Pop will get you some dinner.' Hannah touched the bandages on her head and forced herself to smile. 'I have to stay here until I'm better. Doctor's orders. You go on now.'

Sydney rushed to Hannah and tried to embrace her. Hannah reached for her, and hugged her back as fiercely as the pain would allow.

Then she turned to Adam. She entwined her fingers with his again and gripped them with all her might. 'You are the one person in my whole life who I could always trust, no matter what. You still are.'

They stared into one another's eyes. Confusion and desperation were mingled in his intense gaze. For a moment Hannah thought he might refuse. For a moment, she wanted him to. Then he nodded. 'You can count on me,' he said.

'I never doubted it,' she said. 'Goodbye, my darling. Keep our girl safe.'

Adam hugged her as if he would crush her. Hannah held on to him for a desperate minute, and then pulled away from his embrace. She gazed at him resolutely. 'I love you both. Forever.'

He nodded, and forced himself to stand up. 'Come on, Sydney,' he said, extending his hand to his granddaughter. 'Come with Pop.'

After they left, the nurse came, and wheeled Hannah back to her room. She helped her into bed, and Hannah collapsed onto the scratchy sheets. A short time later, an orderly came in with her dinner, and put the tray on the rolling table. Hannah looked at the food, and felt her stomach contract. She shook her head.

'I can't,' she said. 'Please, take it away.'

The orderly obeyed without comment. Hannah lay back and stared at her own reflection in the dark window of her room. Was this the best thing to do? They couldn't just wait for Lisa to come and take Sydney away with her. Their choices were few. Where would they go, she wondered, thinking of Adam and Sydney, driving through the dark night? Would she ever see them again? she wondered. Or was that their last goodbye?

Tears began to trickle down her face but she wiped them away angrily.

No, she thought. This is your punishment. You deserve this. You should have realized, somewhere along the line, that your daughter lacked humanity. You should have acknowledged it and sought help, instead of making excuses for Lisa. She berated herself for a while, and then she stopped. She knew that she still had a job to do at this end. This was her plan, and she had to try her best to make it work. She reached over to the bedside table for her phone, grimacing at the pain it cost her to twist her body to one side. She groped for the phone and found it.

It took her a moment to catch her breath. Then she dialed the number of Restoration House and let it ring. Father Luke answered shortly.

'Father Luke,' she exclaimed with sincere relief. 'I'm so glad I caught you.'

'Anna, is that you?' he asked.

Hannah nodded. 'Yes. I'm . . . still in the hospital.'

'Well, I'm not surprised,' said the priest, 'given the shape you were in.'

'I'd like to talk to you,' she said. 'I was wondering if you could come by the hospital tomorrow.'

'Of course, dear,' he said. 'With pleasure.'

'And, if possible, could you bring Spencer?'

'Spencer? My . . . Mr White?'

'Yes,' said Hannah. She could hear the surprise in Father Luke's voice. Hannah had only met Spencer White, the black accountant with whom Father Luke lived, a time or two, notably at the birthday party which Spencer had hosted for his life partner. 'I have a good reason.'

'Well,' said Father Luke slowly, 'I will certainly ask him.'

'Thanks,' said Hannah. 'Please tell him it's important.'

'I'll do that,' said the priest.

'And, if you could . . .'

'What?' he asked.

'Could you get a message to Kiyanna and Frank?'

'I can call them, sure. They already left a few hours ago.'

'Tell them . . .' Hannah hesitated. 'Tell them that Syd— Cindy is fine for tonight. They shouldn't worry. Cindy won't be coming over. She and Alan are staying here at the hospital.'

'I'll tell them. Is there anything else?'

'No,' said Hannah. 'Nothing else.'

'All right, then,' said Father Luke. 'I'll see you tomorrow.'

'Tomorrow,' Hannah repeated. 'And thank you, Father.'

'Try not to worry,' he said. 'I'll pray for you.'

Hannah ended the call, and thought about what the former priest had said. She did not think much about praying, though she often thanked God for her blessings. And she had certainly asked for strength from time to time.

Maybe it would help, she thought. Nothing could feel worse than the agony she felt in her heart right now. She decided to pray for help to face her ordeal and, as she did, she fell almost instantly asleep.

Someone was shaking her awake. Hannah opened her eyes and looked around groggily. Then she suddenly remembered where she was. She remembered that Adam and Sydney were gone, and she remembered all that she was facing. Dark thoughts crowded inside her head. Outside of the windows, the day seemed to be just breaking. She turned over gingerly in her bed, wincing at the pain and stiffness after spending the night fast asleep in one position.

A nurse, pale with dark circles under her eyes, leaned over her. 'You have a visitor,' she said.

'It's not visiting hours,' Hannah protested.

'It's the Father. He comes and goes whenever,' said the nurse.

Father Luke, Hannah thought. 'Oh. Yes,' she said. 'OK. I asked him to come. Tell him to come in.'

The nurse nodded and padded out of the room. In a few minutes the door opened, and Father Luke entered, followed by Spencer White. Father Luke was a quick, wiry man with white hair and impish eyes. Spencer was large and dignified, with mocha-colored skin and close-cropped hair. He wore black horn-rimmed glasses, and a conservative brown suit with a tan shirt and a geometric patterned tie.

The two men crossed the room and stood beside her bed. Father Luke grasped her hand and smiled at her. 'Sorry to be so early. Spencer has an audit to prepare for in Media today. We thought we better stop by here early, before he has to get underway.'

'Thank you for coming,' said Hannah. 'Both of you.'

Father Luke waved off her thanks. 'I'm curious as to why you wanted to see Spencer.'

Hannah looked from Father Luke to Spencer, who was watching her cautiously, uncertain what sort of request to expect. Hannah took a deep breath. 'This has to be in the strictest confidence.'

'Of course,' said Father Luke.

Spencer nodded.

'I found out yesterday,' said Hannah, 'that what happened to me was not . . . random. My life – our lives, are in danger. I can't tell you more than that.'

'Did you tell the police?' asked Father Luke, shocked by this news.

Hannah looked at him helplessly. 'I can't. I have my reasons.'

'Anna, this situation has gotten out of hand.'

'I know that, Father. That's why I called you.'

Father Luke nodded. 'Well, what can we do? Does Alan know about this? Because if he doesn't, you should certainly confide in him.'

'Alan and Cindy have gone. They left with just the clothes on their backs.'

'They left what? The hospital?'

'The hospital. Philly. The state. They're headed west.'

'They left you here all alone?'

'I insisted,' said Hannah firmly. 'I'm not looking for sympathy. This was what I wanted. It was my idea. They are not safe here. They had to go. The thing is, we have our bags all packed and in the attic of Mamie Revere's house, where our apartment was. But the house is . . . probably being watched.'

Spencer's face wore an expression of distaste. Father Luke's was all compassion. 'Oh, Anna, this is terrible.'

Hannah felt unnerved by his concern. She did her best to remain resolute. 'That's why I need your help. I need you to get the bags for us. And to get them to Alan. When they find a place to stay, you can send them.'

'Of course. I can do that,' said Father Luke.

'Actually,' said Hannah, turning her gaze to the well-dressed black man, 'I want Spencer to do it.'

Spencer started. 'Why me?' he asked, recoiling from the suggestion.

Hannah hesitated. She did not want her idea to sound insulting. It was just a practical reality. Spencer was black and would blend in. It would appear normal for him to enter the house. Father Luke, on the other hand, might cause a blip on the radar. 'Whoever is . . . watching us, thinks that my husband and my . . . child are staying here at the hospital, with me. I don't want anyone, especially not this person in question, to know that Alan and Cindy are trying to get far away. The more time I can buy for them, the better. The thing is . . . the person watching us probably already knows about Father Luke and Restoration House. If Father Luke goes in and comes out with baggage, the person I'm worried about might be alerted. Might put two and two together. Probably would. But if Spencer went in . . . It would appear natural. Mamie's in the hospital. Someone from her family might well show up there to pick up some of her things for her and bring them to her at the nursing home.'

'Does this person know everything about your lives?' asked Father Luke incredulously.

'I don't know. But I have to think ahead. I have to assume the worst.' She looked from one man to the other. Father Luke gazed back at her openly. Spencer seemed skeptical.

'I know this all sounds weird and paranoid. I wish I could tell you more,' said Hannah.

Spencer looked at her with narrowed eyes. 'So do I.'

Father Luke looked sadly at Hannah but he spoke to Spencer. 'Hannah is in a lot of pain. She needs us to help her.'

Spencer sighed. 'You want me to go in, pick up the packed bags and bring them out. And do what? Take them home?'

'Yes, I guess so,' said Hannah. 'When things settle down I'll let you know where to ship them.'

Spencer shook his head. 'Call me dim but I have to ask. Aren't you going back to that house yourself when you've recovered? Can't you send the bags?'

'This person might follow me. Find out where I'm sending them.'

Spencer frowned at the priest. 'I don't like this,' he said.

Father Luke shrugged. 'That's up to you. If you don't want to do it, then don't. It's just a request, right?' he asked, looking at Hannah.

'Yes,' Hannah whispered, gazing down at her own hands lying limp on the covers.

'Give me the keys and we'll see what we can do,' said Father Luke.

Hannah slid open the drawer of her bedside table and reached in. She pulled out the keys and handed them to the priest. 'I wouldn't ask you if I wasn't desperate.'

Spencer was already shaking his head.

'He's very law-abiding,' said Father Luke apologetically.

'I don't need for him to break the law,' Hannah protested.

'I can hear you,' said Spencer in a frosty tone. 'Luke, can we go now? I need to get to Media.' Glancing impatiently at his watch, Spencer headed toward the door. He turned back to Hannah. 'I hope you feel better soon,' he said.

Hannah nodded and pressed her lips together in a dejected expression.

'Don't worry,' said Father Luke. 'I know him. He'll do it. He just has to get used to the idea. But, Anna, I have to say, are you really intending to go back to that house all by yourself? Knowing that the person who pushed you in the subway is still out there, hoping to . . . harm you?'

Hannah felt agitated. Spencer had already balked at her plan. She didn't want to think about what was going to transpire when she went home. She definitely didn't want to speculate aloud about it. 'I'll be here a while longer. I'm not leaving anytime soon,' she said. 'My recovery . . . you know. It will take some time.'

Father Luke's eyes were filled with worry. 'I'll let you get some rest. You need it.' He put a hand on hers. 'Would you like us to pray together?'

It won't do any good, Hannah thought hopelessly. But she nodded. 'Sure,' she said. 'I need all the help I can get.'

THIRTY-ONE

Three days later, when Hannah was about to be released, Frank Petrusa was dispatched by Father Luke to pick her up. Hannah understood immediately why he had been chosen. Based on what she had told him, Father Luke was worried that they might encounter some kind of confrontation when Hannah returned to Mamie Revere's house, and Frank, an ex-recon marine, was the best man to handle such a situation. Even with one hand missing, he had an air of indomitability. Hannah sat in the wheelchair brought to her room by the nurse, her purse on her lap, waiting for him. She gazed out at the gray day, and wondered what misery this homecoming might bring. If Lisa were still watching the house she would know instantly, the moment that Hannah arrived home in a stranger's car, that Adam and Sydney were gone. What would she do then?

Her phone rang and Hannah jumped, her heart already thumping at the thought of her daughter's implacable anger. She knew it wasn't Lisa. Only Adam had this number. Adam and Father Luke.

Adam had called several times during that week, but said they were not yet settled in a place. Hannah knew that they had headed west, toward Chicago but not which state they were in. Adam did not want to be specific. 'The less you know, the better,' he told her.

Hannah answered the phone cautiously, and was relieved to hear his voice. She explained that despite his reluctance, Spencer White had retrieved the suitcases and brought them to his house without incident. Of course, there was nowhere to send them as yet. Or was there? she asked.

Adam sighed. 'No, not yet. How are you feeling?'

'I'm . . . better,' she said.

'A lot better?' he asked.

'I'm going home today,' she said.

Adam was silent at the other end.

'Frank Petrusa is picking me up, and getting me settled in. I'll be in good hands,' she said.

'Until he leaves,' Adam said in a gloomy tone. 'Hannah, I wish I had never agreed to this.'

Hannah ignored the desperation in his voice. 'How is Sydney?'

Adam had reported that Sydney had been cooperative and quiet during the journey. 'Can a child be depressed?' he asked Hannah.

'Yes, certainly,' said Hannah.

'Then she's depressed.'

'I don't doubt it,' Hannah said.

Frank appeared at the doorway of her room and tapped on the open door. Hannah motioned for him to come in.

'Adam, I have to go,' she whispered. 'Frank is here.'

She did not give him a chance to pour out all his anxiety and his fears. She murmured her love and ended the call. She looked up expectantly at Frank.

'You ready?' he said.

Hannah nodded.

'No bags?'

'Just my purse,' she said.

'Let's hit it,' he said. He came around behind the wheelchair and put up the brake.

Hannah nodded, though her heart was pounding double time. 'Ready,' she said.

They discussed work a little bit as Frank drove her back to West Philadelphia. He told her that Dominga Flores was now out of rehab and staying at Restoration House and participating in his PTSD groups.

'Oh, I'm glad,' said Hannah. 'I was on my way to see her when . . .'

'Your accident,' said Frank.

Hannah nodded. 'Seems like years ago. Well, it's good we got her back at the House. She needs that kind of support.'

'She does indeed,' said Frank. 'When you get back to work you'll probably have a chance to help her sort things out.'

'If I get back to work,' said Hannah.

Frank frowned. 'Father Luke told me that your husband is gone. With Cindy. He said that was the way you wanted it. What happened there, Anna?'

Hannah shook her head. 'Nothing,' she said.

'It doesn't sound like nothing. It sounds like you might be in danger. Why did Alan agree to leave you here all alone? I'm really surprised by that.'

'The most important thing is Cindy's safety,' she said.

'Why is Cindy in danger?' Frank asked.

Suddenly she felt too tired to try to explain. She shook her head and looked out the car window at the city streets, thinking about all the plans that she and Adam had made when they decided to move here. They would take Sydney to the theater, the zoo and the Please Touch museum. They had done all of those things and more, although they had always found it difficult to relax and enjoy these outings in the city. Some part of them was always looking around. Always wondering. They dreamed of a day when their lives would truly feel like their own again. Now, Hannah doubted if there would ever be such a day. In a strange way, she was almost relieved that Lisa had found her. No more running away. She knew that the next time she encountered Lisa was going to be soon. It was only a matter of how soon.

'OK,' said Frank. 'I'm not gonna pry.' Frank drove expertly through the maze of streets, and pulled up against the curb in front of Mamie Revere's house. Hannah looked out the window, and then did a double take to see the For Sale sign planted in the patch of brown grass in front.

'He's selling the house,' she said. 'I can't believe it.'

'Who?' Frank asked.

'Isaiah Revere,' said Hannah.

'The councilman?'

'Yes. He grew up in this house. His mother, Mamie, owns it. But Mamie would never leave this place voluntarily. She loves it. It's her home.'

Frank shrugged. 'You can get too old to be on your own.'

'I suppose,' said Hannah with a sigh. For a brief moment, painful memories of Pamela crossed her mind. She forced herself not to think about her mother, spending her life in that assisted care facility, her family vanished. She reminded herself that right now, she couldn't be worrying about her mother. Hannah herself felt too fragile to be on her own. But it would pass, she thought. She just had to put one foot in front of the other. Daunting as it seemed, she reached for the handle of the car door. 'Frank, I can't thank you enough for bringing me home. And you and Kiyanna, for taking care of . . . Cindy while I was in the hospital.'

'Kiyanna enjoyed it,' he said. 'I did too. Cindy's a sweet kid.'

'Can I speak like your big sister?' Hannah said, feigning severity. 'You should marry that girl. Kiyanna is a gem. Not that it's any of my business . . .'

'That's all right,' he said. 'I think so too.'

Hannah smiled and pressed down the door handle.

'Anna, hold it a minute,' said Frank.

Hannah turned to look at him, as he groped under the driver's seat with his good hand, and rummaged around. He found what he was seeking and pulled it out, placing it on the seat. Hannah looked down at the scuffed wooden box between them.

'I have something for you,' he said.

'What is that?' she said.

Frank looked around in all directions. The street was quiet, and the bright autumn day had faded to gray. He made sure there was no one near the car, and then he undid the latch and opened the box. Hannah frowned, and then gasped, as he raised the lid.

Resting in the case was a black semiautomatic handgun. 'Do you know anything about guns?' he asked.

Hannah shook her head.

Frank sighed. 'This one is really very simple to use. And I think it would be a good idea for you to be armed. We'll take it in the house and I can show you.'

'Why did you bring that?' she demanded.

Frank shrugged. 'Call it a gut feeling.'

'Is that your gun?'

'One of them,' he said. He peered at her. 'Don't worry. I keep them locked up at home. Cindy never even got near one of these, I promise you.'

'Put it away, Frank. I appreciate the thought but . . .'

'Look, I know this is all unfamiliar territory. But you need to be . . .

ready. For anything. Just a short lesson, and you would at least be able to fire it in an emergency.'

Hannah shook her head. 'I don't think so.'

'Anna,' said Frank patiently, 'if you're right about this, we're dealing with someone who pushed you in front of a subway train. From what Father Luke told me, you are still afraid for your life. You need to have this. You might have to use it.'

Hannah tried to think coherently about what he was saying, although the sight of the gun unnerved her. She shook her head again. 'I couldn't,' she said. 'There's no point. I really couldn't.'

'You'd be surprised,' Frank said. 'You'd be surprised what you can do when you're facing your own death.'

Hannah raised her gaze from the gun and stared through the windshield of Frank's old jeep. 'I'm sure you're right,' she said. 'But I could never shoot her.'

Frank raised his eyebrows. 'Her? It's a woman?'

'Yes,' Hannah whispered.

Frank stared at her. 'Well, you might surprise yourself. If she's threatening your life, you might be able to use it on a woman. Take it, just in case.'

Hannah turned and looked at him. His eyes seemed to gleam in the dim light which bathed the front seat through the windshield. 'You'll have to take my word for it, Frank. I couldn't shoot it at her. No matter what.'

Frank peered at her. 'It's someone you know, isn't it?'

'Yes. Someone who . . . believes I have betrayed her.'

'Have you?'

Hannah sat silent for a moment. 'I tried not to. But . . . yes. I suppose I did.'

Frank slowly closed the lid on the box.

Hannah pushed open the car door. She turned and looked at him. 'Thank you for thinking of it, though. I know you're only trying to protect me. You, Kiyanna and Father Luke. You've all been so kind to me. But this is as far as it can go. I have to face the next part by myself.'

'Anna,' he said, 'if someone you know is stalking you, you need to tell the police. They can protect you. There's no reason to just be . . . a human target.'

Hannah shook her head. 'It's not that simple. Listen, the only other person who knows about this is Father Luke. I need to keep it that way. Will you do that for me? Keep it to yourself?'

Frank sighed. 'Do you even have a plan?'

Hannah hesitated. 'I've thought a lot about it.'

He waited for her to say more but she was done with explaining.

'I'm very tired,' she said. 'I'm going inside.'

'Let me walk you in,' he said, opening his door.

'I'd appreciate that,' said Hannah.

Once they had made their way up the dark path and into the unlit house, Frank ordered Hannah to sit down while he looked through the house.

'This is Mamie's part of the house,' Hannah protested. 'She has the first two floors. We live upstairs, on the third floor.'

'I'm sure she won't mind you sitting here while you wait,' said Frank. 'It looks as if nobody's been here in quite a while.'

'No,' said Hannah, sitting down with a sigh. 'It's a lonely house now.'

In fact, Hannah was relieved to sit down. She was utterly exhausted from the ordeal of leaving the hospital. She huddled in the corner of Mamie's overstuffed, pillow-laden sofa and looked sadly around at the lifeless room that had once been part of a bustling home. Every photo, every memento seemed to be waiting for Mamie's return. But that would likely never happen – the house would be sold. Life would move on. Hannah could hear Frank's heavy tread going up the staircase, through the house and back down. She could hear doors slamming and windows being raised and lowered again. As she heard him start down from the third floor, Hannah called out to warn him about the rickety banister. If he heard her, he didn't slacken his pace.

He came into Mamie's living room. 'All clear up there,' he said.

'Thanks, Frank,' said Hannah, getting up. 'You may as well get home. It's gonna take me a while to climb these stairs.'

'I wish you'd reconsider,' he said. 'You could stay with Kiyanna and me. We wouldn't mind.'

Hannah did not want to discuss it any further. She knew that his offer was genuine, but also that she wouldn't accept it. She had come back here to face whatever lay ahead. There was nothing to discuss. 'You better get home to her,' she said. 'I can't thank you enough.'

Frank started to protest, but then he shook his head. 'Call me if you need me.'

'I will,' said Hannah, though she knew she wouldn't. She had already involved him too far in these problems of her own making. From now on, she was determined to face them alone. Afraid but determined.

She wanted to tell herself that she had nothing to fear from Lisa. But every painful step reminded her that this was simply not true. She locked the door behind Frank then walked to the foot of the staircase, turned on the light above it and looked up. It seemed like an impossible climb. She put her foot on the first step.

THIRTY-TWO

Slowly, Hannah made her way up the stairs to the empty apartment. She walked in, set her purse down on a chair and looked around. Despite everything, she thought, they had had happy moments here. They endured the hardships willingly, knowing that they had done the only thing they could. Now, all that was gone. Everything gone. Hannah exhaled a deep sigh. She opened the refrigerator, needing something to drink and dreading what she would find. Indeed, due to the suddenness of all their departures, everything on the shelves was either shriveled, sour or furry. You should clean this out, she thought.

She took a bottle of water and closed the door again. Tomorrow, she thought. I might feel up to it tomorrow. Right now, it simply filled her with despair to look inside. Painfully, she made her way over to the freestanding wooden cabinet which served as their pantry. There were cans and jars inside. I won't starve tonight, she thought.

She went into the dimly lit living room and sat down. The house was quiet as a tomb with Mamie gone, and Adam and Sydney on their way to whatever place they were going to settle. She was all alone in the house, sitting in her chair, alert to every sound that filtered through, steeled against the possibility that the fragile quiet would be shattered at any time by the angriest of intruders. It was not a question of if Lisa would arrive. Only when. Hannah turned on the TV but its noise only made it impossible for her to hear if there was a breach into the creaky old house. She turned the TV off and picked up a book. Maybe she would take it into her room, and crawl into bed. She was exhausted from the day.

She brought her phone into the bedroom and placed it on Adam's nightstand. The sight of the bed they had shared seemed unbearably forlorn. Hannah sat down on the edge, partly so that she would not have to look at it any more.

She set out the pills that she needed to take and crawled under the covers. She picked up her book but it fell from her hands almost at once. Before she even had a chance to turn the bedside lamp off, she fell into a fitful, troubled sleep which felt, nonetheless, as if she had been sedated. Every noise woke her, and she would lie there unable to move, groggy and frightened, her heart pounding. And then sleep would tackle and subdue her again. But the feeling of fear and anxiety never left, not even in her dreams. When dawn's light crept through the windows she opened her eyes, as tired as if she had been doing battle all night. Her limbs were leaden under the covers. She had made it through the first night, although the night had seemed like a thousand hours.

This is not going to work, she thought, as she blinked her eyes against the day. This is not possible. If she tried to keep this up she would become like a sleep-deprived rat in an experiment. She was afraid to go out of the house and afraid to stay there. Hell, she was afraid to get out of the bed. She could feel depression weighing on her chest, and a combination of fear and futility that was like a cocktail guaranteed to induce paralysis.

More than anything, she wished that she could talk to Adam. But she had to face the consequences herself. If she called him, and told him how she felt, he would turn around and come running back. And that was not possible. He and Sydney needed to keep going. They needed to get far enough away. And she needed to find a way to deal with her situation.

For a while, she lay there, thinking, turning over her terrible options in her mind. She knew that sooner or later she was going to have to face Lisa's wrath and accusations and, most likely, her dangerous intentions. After all, Lisa had already tried to kill her once. Sitting here waiting for the next attempt was unbearable. If it was going to happen, why not just face it? Bring it about and take the consequences. Anything would be better than this hellish uncertainty, this constant fear and trepidation. Hannah crawled out of bed and put on her bathrobe and a warm pair of socks. She picked up her phone from the nightstand, and sat down on the edge of the bed.

She scrolled through the saved numbers on her phone, and stopped at Lisa's. Did she have the same number now? Probably not.

Hannah had canceled the service when they left Tennessee, knowing that they would have to exist with tracphones, so they could not be traced. She decided to try it anyway.

What will I say? she wondered. She didn't know. She only knew that she could not stand living in fear in this limbo any longer. It was better to deal with what was going to come. She pressed Lisa's old number and held the phone to her ear, her heart hammering. After a few moments, a voice came on the line. 'The number you have reached has been changed.'

Hannah let out a sigh of despair. It had taken all her nerve to dial, and now she had no idea how to find her daughter's number. She sat for a few minutes, holding the phone, and then, suddenly, she realized how she could get it. And resolve a heartbreaking problem as well. She was about to reveal herself to Lisa. Invite her to this confrontation. There was no reason to hide anymore.

She punched in an old, familiar number. It began to ring, and she held her breath. Pick it up, she thought. Please.

In the next moment, she heard a quavering voice say, 'Hello.'

'Mother?' she said.

There was a gasp at the other end.

'It's me, Hannah,' she said.

'I know who it is,' said Pamela.

'Mother, I know you're very angry at me. But I need to talk to you. I need your help.'

Pamela was silent at her end.

'How are you, Mother? Are you OK?'

'I'm perfectly fine,' said Pamela, whose voice was growing more assertive by the moment. 'No thanks to you.'

Hannah stifled a sigh. 'Look, Mother, I don't blame you for being furious. But I had my reasons for leaving like I did. I don't expect you to understand . . .'

Pamela sniffed. 'I do understand,' she said. 'I may be old but I'm not simple. You as much as told me what you planned to do. I don't have to be hit over the head with it. I know you left because of Lisa. Although, to hear Lisa tell it, she is blameless in this whole mess.'

Hannah heard it loud and clear. The veiled challenge which demanded that she rise to the bait. Sorry, Mom, she thought. I can't do it. 'That's what I called about, Mom. Are you in touch with Lisa?'

'Why are you asking me that? Where are you? I have no idea where you even are. Where is Sydney? Is she all right? What about Adam?'

'We're all fine,' said Hannah, smiling in spite of herself. 'We're living in Philadelphia at the moment.'

'And why couldn't you tell me that a year ago? I would have appreciated a call to let me know you were alive.'

'I'll be honest with you, Mother,' said Hannah. 'I thought you would be better off not knowing. That way, Lisa could not force anything out of you.'

Pamela was silent again.

'Did Lisa stay in touch with you when she got out of jail?'

'Yes, for a while,' said Pamela in a frosty tone. 'She came to see me several times. But when she realized I didn't know anything of your whereabouts, communication dropped off sharply.'

'I'm sorry, Mother,' said Hannah. 'For so many things.'

There was another silence at Pamela's end, and Hannah girded herself to be berated again. 'Hannah, I have to say,' said Pamela, 'I don't think you were wrong to leave. There's something that's not right about that girl.'

Hannah felt her mother's words of approval almost like an embrace. 'Why do you say that? She didn't hurt you, did she?'

'She threatened me,' said Pamela flatly. 'She said that if I didn't cooperate with her, I should fear for my life. I told her to get out. I actually had to call security. After that she would call me up just to bait me. It got so I couldn't stand to speak to her. She is a very . . . unbalanced person. I always suspected it.'

Hannah was almost guilty about the relief she felt. 'So, now you understand. That's why we had to leave, Mother. We had to do it for Sydney's sake,' she explained.

'Well, I'm sure you had your reasons.'

'I didn't want to leave you like that,' Hannah whispered, 'but I couldn't tell you. I couldn't tell anyone.'

'And now?'

'She's found me.'

'Oh,' said Pamela, startled.

'She is stalking me. It's . . . nerve-wracking.' Hannah decided on the spot not to tell her about the subway attack. There was no use in it. Pamela would only be terrified for her and there was nothing she could do about it. 'I've decided to call her and arrange a meeting. But her old number doesn't work since I cancelled the service. I wondered if you had her current one.'

'Arrange a meeting? Why would you want to meet with her?'

'As it is, I feel like I am constantly looking behind me, constantly fearful of the . . . unexpected. I just want to get this over with.'

'Do you have any idea how much she hates you now?'

Hannah remembered the push that landed her on the subway tracks. 'Yes, I think I do.'

'You be careful, Hannah. She is a dangerous person.'

'I know that. And I appreciate your concern. I will be careful. Do you have that number, Mom?'

'Yes, I have it here,' said Pamela, and Hannah could picture her mother, searching for the white-leather address book embossed with orchids that she continued to use. Pamela cleared her throat, and read the number.

'Thank you.'

'Be very cautious around her,' Pamela warned. 'She is not . . . like other people.'

'I know that. Probably something I did . . .'

'Oh, for heaven's sakes,' said Pamela impatiently. 'Not everything is a mother's doing. Look at you. You're much nicer than me.'

Hannah smiled. 'I don't know about that,' she demurred. 'I just feel that I should have seen it. I should have been more . . . alert. Called her on her behavior. I always made excuses for her because she was so smart. I used that to explain away things that I knew were wrong. I shouldn't have.'

'It wouldn't have mattered,' Pamela proclaimed. 'She was born that way, if you ask me. You two were good parents. There was no reason for her to become so . . . pitiless.'

Pitiless, Hannah thought. That's a good description. 'Thank you, Mother,' she said humbly.

'Are you coming back home?'

'I don't know what I'm doing. But I'll let you know, all right?'

'Be careful,' said Pamela. 'I mean it.'

I know, Hannah thought. She said goodbye and told her mother that she loved her. Pamela was too taken aback to reply and only muttered again that Hannah should take care. Hannah ended the call feeling better than she had in a long time. She had spoken to her mother. Whatever happened, she had talked to Pamela and told her that she loved her. It helped somehow. It helped.

Hannah looked at the number and thought about dialing her daughter. But she felt somehow too vulnerable in her bathrobe and socks. She went to the closet and began the painful process of dressing. Once she was in yoga pants and a bulky sweater she felt better, as if she still had some measure of control. She went into the kitchen and got herself something to drink, thinking, as she closed the refrigerator door, that she needed to work on that task immediately. Then she sat down at the little kitchen table, and picked up the phone. Her hand trembled as she held it. She took a deep breath, and dialed.

Her heart thudded and her hands were shaking so badly as she listened to it ring that she actually dropped the phone on the tabletop. She scooped it up quickly and held it to her ear. It was still ringing. Then she heard a click.

There was a rustling sound and then a familiar voice said, 'Leave a message.'

Hannah hesitated, disappointed to get the prerecorded message. She was about to hang up then changed her mind. 'Lisa, this is . . . your mother. I am calling because I want to see you. I need to speak with you. I know that it was you . . . in the subway station. I've seen the surveillance tapes. I don't understand how you could . . . well, never mind. Obviously, you are very angry with me. Look, I want to talk to you. I am at the apartment and I'm sure that you know where that is. Let's not play games. I want to see you. No matter what, I still care about you. Please call me back. We need to talk.' She left her number and ended the call. Then she sat, staring straight ahead, trying to calm the furious pounding of her heart.

THIRTY-THREE

Hannah made herself a cup of black coffee and forced herself to eat some dry cereal. For a long while she had sat at the kitchen table, unable to move, waiting for the phone to ring, or for Lisa to show up at the door. She could not believe that Lisa would ignore that direct summons, especially since Hannah had told her that she knew Lisa was the one who pushed her in front of the train. Hannah had challenged her to show herself, and Lisa never liked to shrink from a challenge. It had always been one of her qualities that Hannah most admired. Hannah glanced over at the front door of the apartment. Just show up, she thought. Let's get to it.

But the phone remained silent, and there was no sign of Lisa. More than anything, Hannah wished that she could just go back to bed and hide under the covers. Can't do that, she thought. You have to try and accomplish something. Wearily, she got to her feet, pulled a large black trash bag from the box under the sink and went over to the refrigerator. Worst job first, she thought. She opened up the trash bag, and then swung open the refrigerator door. Looking inside made her feel slightly nauseated and hopeless, but she knew what to do about hopelessness. Start attacking the problem

She began throwing things away. She examined every item as she took it out of the refrigerator. Most things went directly into the trash. The few items that had not reached their expiration date she placed on the counter as she dispatched all the others. Finally, when there was almost nothing left besides ketchup, mustard, mayo and relish, she began to scrub down the shelves.

She was working on the last shelf when the doorbell rang. It reverberated through her body as if she were a tuning fork. She straightened up, holding on to the refrigerator door for support.

Lisa, she thought.

Her feelings were warring inside of her. It was Lisa's perverted plans for her own child, and her lies about Adam, which had sent them fleeing from their home, from the life they knew in the first place. Hannah hated her for that. And this was the same daughter who had shadowed her, and pushed her off a subway platform into the path of an oncoming train. She hated her for that too. But this was also her Lisa. Her only child. Despite everything, the habit of worrying about her, of loving her, came naturally, unbidden.

The doorbell sounded again, impatiently. All right, she told herself. Go down and face her, and try to understand why she has done the things she has done. Hannah opened the door to the apartment and made her way painfully down the staircase. She reached the front door and put her hand on the doorknob. Would she look the same to her, now that Hannah knew her daughter was willing and able to kill? Then Hannah reminded herself that all the time they were defending her during her trial she had probably already killed Troy Petty. And they were none the wiser.

She had seemed the same. How could you not see it? Hannah wondered. That sort of corruption should be visible, like a stain. But Lisa's face, Lisa's eyes had remained as dear to her as ever. She had seen nothing.

Hannah took a deep breath, and turned the deadbolt. Then she pulled the door open. Dominga Flores stood on the welcome mat.

Hannah felt disappointed. Relieved. She tried to hide her feelings and forced herself to smile. 'Dominga,' she said. 'How are you?'

Dominga looked around uneasily. She still wore camouflage pants, and a shapeless sweatshirt; her buzz cut, which had grown out, was gelled into spikes. Her skin looked less drawn than it had been the last time Hannah saw her. And it had a little more color. The circles under her eyes had diminished somewhat. A positive effect of the rehab, Hannah thought. 'Hey, Mrs Whitman. I didn't know if you'd remember me.'

'Remember you? How could I forget? You were our hero. I was on my way to see you when . . . I had this accident.' Hannah indicated her own head, still bandaged, as well as her arm and leg.

'I heard,' said Dominga.

'So, you're at Restoration House now.'

Dominga nodded.

'Come on in. What can I do for you?'

Dominga followed Hannah into the house and Hannah closed the door behind her. Dominga shifted uneasily from one foot to the other. Uneasiness came naturally to her, as she was clearly a shy person, uncomfortable in her skin. 'Well, you know, Frank Petrusa, he sent me over.'

'Frank did?'

Dominga nodded. 'He told me you have some space available in your apartment. He thought maybe I could rent a room from you.'

Immediately, Hannah understood. Dominga was an ex-soldier. Frank had sent her here in search of a room but also as a potential bodyguard. Who better to hover over Hannah and lie in wait for her stalker? Hannah had to give it to him – it was a good solution, made up, no doubt, on the spur of the moment. She knew he was only trying to protect her, and she appreciated the fact that he cared. But it was too much to ask of Dominga. She didn't need to get into the middle of this. It could be disastrous. 'There's only a small bedroom upstairs,' Hannah said, shaking her head. 'This whole downstairs part of the house is off limits. It belongs to Mrs Revere – that's the woman you found here on the floor – and she's in a nursing home. She won't be coming back.'

'I don't need a lot of space,' Dominga insisted. 'I got nothin'. I've been living on the street.'

Hannah sighed, knowing it was true. 'But I think it's a little unfair for you to get settled in here. Did you see that the house is for sale?'

'I saw the sign.'

'So, before you know it, you might have to move out.'

Dominga looked at her, vaguely puzzled. 'I'm not planning on stayin' forever. Everything's temporary in my life.'

Hannah hesitated. 'I think Frank may have been a little misleading . . .'

'Can I see the room?'

Hannah looked at her with a level gaze. 'He told you not to pay attention if I tried to say no, didn't he?'

Dominga feigned innocence. 'I don't know what you mean.'

Hannah sighed, touched by their collusion on her behalf.

'Can I see it?'

'You go on up,' Hannah said. 'I'm still recovering from the trip downstairs. It'll take me ten minutes to get back up that staircase.

The door's open. It's the room with the single bed. It used to be my daughter's room. It's kind of a small bed really . . .'

Dominga paid no attention. She vaulted up the stairs, two at a time, and disappeared into the apartment.

Hannah leaned against the newel post and listened as Dominga's combat boots thudded from one room to the other. She didn't want a roommate in that little space, she thought. She didn't know what she and this taciturn woman would have to talk about. But despite her intention to face this all alone, the idea of Dominga, a trained soldier, living here, keeping watch, was undeniably comforting. In a matter of moments, Dominga appeared at the top of the stairs and leaned over the third-floor banister.

'This is a really nice place,' she said.

'It's small.'

'It's big enough.'

'You didn't even ask the rent,' said Hannah bemusedly.

'Frank said that my benefits would cover it.'

'I'm sure they would,' Hannah admitted. 'Since I can't give you a lease or anything, you can pay by the week. Say . . . fifty bucks?'

'OK,' said Dominga. She started to descend the staircase.

'Wait,' said Hannah. 'Before you come down . . . There's a set of keys hanging on a bulletin board by the door. Take those.'

'Oh. OK.' The soldier disappeared back into the apartment and came back jingling the keys out over the staircase. 'These?'

Hannah nodded.

Dominga tossed them up and caught them again. Then she descended the steps in a gallop. When she got to the bottom, she frowned at Hannah. 'You're really busted up, aren't you?'

'I'm lucky to be alive,' said Hannah.

'So, when should I move in?'

Hannah almost felt like smiling. The young woman asked few questions and seemed unconcerned with any detail. She was carrying out an assignment, Hannah thought. She was doing this for Frank, treating him like a commanding officer. 'Tomorrow?'

'Sooner the better,' said Dominga.

Without any other word of farewell, Dominga went out the door, stuffing the keys in her pocket. Hannah locked the door behind her. She picked up the mail and placed it on the table in the hallway for Isaiah to collect. The phone in Mamie's part of the house began to ring and she thought about answering it. But then she thought she should not involve herself. There was a machine which would pick up. Isaiah could check the messages when he came by for the mail. Hannah walked to the stairs and put her hand on the newel post. Time to make her way back up. She lifted her foot to the first step, and began to mount the steps to the third floor, resting after every couple of stairs.

She finally arrived at the door, which Dominga had left ajar, and looked ruefully back down the stairs. She probably should have brought her handbag downstairs, and walked out to do a few errands while she was already at the bottom. Too late now. The errands would keep. She had her medications, and food to eat. A book to read. It was enough.

She pushed open the door and went in. It seemed colder than when she had left. She walked over to Sydney's room and looked inside. How would Dominga like living in that child's room? Hannah thought maybe she would take down some of the posters she had put on the walls, and collect the stuffed animals off the bed. She could put them in the closet. There were a couple of framed watercolors in the hall closet she had bought at a flea market, intending to hang them in the apartment to make it more homey. She could put them up in Sydney's room for the time being, just to cover the space and make it look more welcoming. The closet was practically empty. There would be plenty of room for Dominga's clothes, which seemed to consist of camouflage pants, combat boots, T-shirts and sweatshirts. Maybe only one of each, Hannah thought. The young woman needed a place to call home. That was for sure. Maybe this would work out well for both of them.

Hannah gathered up a couple of the stuffed animals. I'll keep them on my bed, she thought. Make it a little less lonely. She walked out of the room, holding them to her chest. She went down the short hall to her bedroom and set them on the bed, up against the pillows. She stepped back to see how they looked there.

'Hello, Mother,' said a voice behind her.

Hannah cried out and whirled around. Dressed in black, Lisa sat on the chair beside the bureau, her legs crossed at the knee, her toe waggling impatiently. She stared at her mother, unsmiling.

'Lisa,' Hannah whispered.

Lisa smiled but her eyes were cold. 'You wanted to see me,' she said.

THIRTY-FOUR

'How did you get in here?' Hannah asked.

'I climbed up the fire escape and came in through the window. The lock was feeble. It gave way immediately.'

Hannah studied her daughter. Lisa looked thinner. Her curly black hair was twisted into a knot on the top of her head. Behind her glasses, her eyes were steely. In spite of everything, Hannah was strangely happy to set eyes on her. She stifled the reflex to go to her, and put her arms around her. 'Did you see Dominga?'

Lisa frowned. 'Who? Oh, you mean the dyke I saw wandering through the apartment in camouflage? I was outside the window when she came in but she didn't see me. Wasn't she the one in the video on YouTube?'

So, Hannah thought. Just as they'd feared. Lisa had seen that clip and recognized them. 'Yes.'

'Bad luck for you that her story was so heartrending. Lots of people saw that video. I wouldn't have bothered with it but somebody told me to look at it. And once I saw it, I was able to find you.' Lisa could barely contain her satisfaction. 'It was easy after that. I owe that soldier.'

'Yes, you do,' said Hannah. 'She rescued Sydney.'

'Maybe I ought to buy her a thank-you gift,' said Lisa sarcastically.

Hannah stared at Lisa, whose expression was twisted into a sneer. She could not avoid noticing the contrast between Dominga, the young soldier who had come intending to protect her, and her own daughter, who had already tried to kill her once. She shook her head. 'Why did you come through the window? Why didn't you come to the door? I invited you. You knew I was expecting you.'

Lisa's lips curved but there was no smile in her eyes. 'I thought your little invitation might be booby trapped.'

Hannah leaned over the bed and set the stuffed animals down on the pillows. 'It was no trick,' she said.

'Are those Sydney's?'

'Yes.'

'Where is she?'

Hannah stared at her. 'Let's go into the living room.'

'I asked you a question, Mother,' said Lisa.

Hannah did not reply. She walked out of the bedroom and went into the tiny living room, sitting down in an armchair by the front window. She looked outside. The trees had lost their leaves and their trunks, the branches, the sky, the street and the sidewalk all looked bleak and gray. A few people shuffled past, bundled up in coats. It was the end of autumn. Winter was warning of its arrival.

Lisa came into the living room and sat down in the corner of the sofa. It was as if it were an ordinary day. A mother and daughter, settling in for a conversation. Maybe some tea. Except that, looking at her daughter across the narrow room, Hannah felt as if she could hardly breathe.

'You can take your coat off,' said Hannah.

'No, thanks,' said Lisa. She put her hand in her pocket as if to check that there was something she needed inside. Then she glanced around the modest, shabby room. 'So how long have you been in this dump?'

'We've pretty much stayed put here since we stopped . . . running.' Hannah looked ruefully around the room. 'I admit it isn't exactly luxurious.'

'Luxurious,' Lisa scoffed. 'It's a slum.'

'We've been comfortable here, all the same. Are you still in medical school?'

Lisa shrugged and looked away, stuffing her hands in her pockets. 'I quit. They were giving me a hard time.'

'About what?'

Lisa looked at her in disbelief. 'Really? You don't know?'

'You were such a gifted student.'

'I had a hard time studying after my parents kidnapped my kid, OK?'

'I thought they might have a problem with your larceny conviction.'

Lisa looked at her mother with loathing. 'You'd like that, wouldn't you? You know, I was tempted to call the police on you when I got your message. I thought I'd tell them where they could find a kidnapper.'

Hannah gazed back at her without flinching. 'But then again, I might mention to them that I could identify you on the subway surveillance tape. As the person who pushed me off the platform.'

'So, we're even,' said Lisa calmly.

Hannah looked at her daughter in disbelief. 'Even? You think that's even? You tried to kill me, Lisa. You very nearly succeeded.'

'Not quite even,' said Lisa. 'I still want Sydney back.'

Hannah stifled the urge to start screaming at her. Instead, she forced herself to remain calm. 'Where do you live now?'

'I live in the house,' said Lisa. 'I keep it very tidy.'

'I talked to your grandmother today. She said you kept in touch with her for a while.'

'She's a horror,' muttered Lisa, disgusted. 'It was all I could do not to smack her across the face. Did she know you were hiding here? She always claimed that she knew nothing.'

'She knew nothing,' said Hannah.

'This worked out well for you, didn't it? You got away from your nightmare of a mother. And from me. You got to keep Sydney.'

Hannah shook her head. 'I never wanted to get away from you. I loved you. I loved you from before you were born. But once I learned about your vile plans for Sydney, and you threatened to blame everything on your father, we had no choice but to run.'

Lisa shook her head. 'Tell yourself that, Mother. I've never heard such pathetic rationalizing. You steal my daughter and then you make up all these excuses for yourself. You are a kidnapper. That's how the law sees it. I hope it's been worth it.'

'These have been the worst two years of my life,' said Hannah. 'But yes. It was worth it. To protect Sydney from your disgusting plans for her.'

'Enough of your excuses. Cut the crap,' said Lisa. 'And just tell me. Where is Sydney? I thought he and she were with you at the hospital.'

'He and she?' asked Hannah. 'Are you referring to your father and your daughter?'

Lisa spoke in a low tone that was almost a growl. 'Don't fuck with me,' she said. 'You know what I mean.'

Hannah clasped her hands and pressed them against her lips. She wanted to be careful what she said. She wanted to say exactly what she meant. 'Lisa, you're a supremely intelligent person. I have to ask you something because I can't come to grips with it. Were you always this way?'

'What way?' Lisa demanded.

'It's as if you don't care anything about other people. The people who love you just don't matter. Do you feel any . . . tenderness in your heart?'

'Of course I do,' said Lisa coolly. 'I care about Sydney. You thought you were entitled to take her away from me whenever you pleased. Just because you wanted her all to yourself. And Dad, on the other hand, wanted to have easy access to her. The way he did to me.'

Hannah felt her anger flare but, once again, she stifled it. 'That's not true, Lisa. Not a word of it. And you know it.'

'Were you with us every minute? You often left me alone with him. How do you know what he did?' Lisa taunted her. 'What makes you think he wasn't creeping into my room and pulling down my jammies every night?'

Hannah recoiled from the disgusting image but remained calm. 'I don't believe you, for one thing, my darling. You have told one lie after another. I don't even think you know what the truth is. And for another thing, I know your father.'

Lisa looked at her, her brow furrowed, her gaze skeptical. 'What does that prove?' she asked. 'You know him? What does that even mean?'

Hannah looked at her daughter almost sorrowfully. 'You really don't know, do you? To me, that's the saddest thing of all. You seem to have no idea what it means to know someone. To trust them.'

Lisa threw up her hands and began to pace. 'Of course I know what it means. You're saying that you know him. But what do you really know about him? You know that his name is Adam Wickes, and that you're married to him. You know where he was born, and how old he is, and all that crap. That doesn't mean you know what he'll do. Or what he's done.'

'Yes, it does,' said Hannah earnestly. 'That's exactly what it means. I know his heart. I know his character. I trust him. I believe what he says to me.'

Lisa turned and pointed a finger at her. 'Oh, I see. You believe him but you don't believe me.'

'Should I believe you?'

'I'm your child.'

'Lisa, you tried to kill me. You pushed me in front of a subway train.'

Lisa looked at her, exasperated. 'I had good reason. You took my daughter.'

'To protect her from you,' Hannah said defiantly.

'I'm not listening to this again. Where is she?' Lisa growled. 'You'd better tell me. I'm going to count to ten.'

Hannah sat back down and avoided Lisa's malevolent gaze. 'They're gone. Far away. You'll never find them.'

Lisa lifted up a wooden desk chair by its back and smashed it against the wall. It made a giant, jagged crack in the plaster. Hannah jumped and let out a cry.

'You can't do this to me,' Lisa insisted. 'She is mine. You will give her back to me.'

'I don't know where they are,' said Hannah. 'We've done it that way on purpose.'

'You bitch. I don't believe you.' Lisa reached over and grabbed Hannah by the neck. Her long fingers pressed against her mother's windpipe. 'Where's your phone?'

Hannah shook her head. She could hardly breathe. Lisa reached down and began to rummage in Hannah's pockets. 'You always carried it in your pocket. It must be . . . Ah,' she exclaimed. 'Let me have a look.' She operated the phone with one hand, keeping her grip on Hannah's throat.

Hannah's fingers clawed at Lisa's powerful hand. She tried to gulp in some air. Lisa was scrolling through the calls. 'Aha!' she cried. 'This has got to be it.' She punched in a number on the phone, simultaneously letting go of Hannah, who fell back down on the chair, gasping for breath. She rubbed her throat with her hand. Tears ran down the side of her face as she heard the call going through. Lisa held the phone at an angle from her face so that Hannah could hear the voice saying, 'Hannah? Babe? Are you there?'

'Hi, Daddy,' said Lisa in a silken tone. 'Guess what?'

There was a silence on the other end. 'Where is your mother?' he asked warily.

'She's here with me. Say something, Mother.'

Lisa held the phone out toward Hannah, who was still gasping for breath. 'Adam,' she whispered.

'Are you OK? Are you all right? What is she doing there? Has she hurt you?'

Hannah wanted to speak but only a squeak came out. 'Don't listen to anything she says.'

'Bitch,' said Lisa. She pulled the phone back and spoke into it. 'This is the way it is. Bring Sydney back and I'll let my mother live. Otherwise I'm going to finish the job I started on the subway.'

Hannah could hear Adam protesting and trying to reason with her. Lisa ended the call.

'That will bring him back,' said Lisa. 'Now we wait.'

THIRTY-FIVE

Frank Petrusa was on the phone with the VA Hospital, trying to locate Titus, who had not shown up for group. He had a bad feeling about the depressed vet, who seemed to career from hopefulness to despair without stopping at any reasonable place in between.

'Yes, I'll hold,' he said. He sighed and rubbed his good hand over his face.

People got lost in the system all the time. He would talk to a guy for an hour, and send them off to an office or an agency with detailed instructions. And that would be the last he knew of them. Sometimes it felt like herding cats.

Dominga Flores came to the door of the group meeting room. 'Sarge?' she said.

Frank lowered the receiver and looked at Dominga. 'Did you go over to the Whitmans'?' he asked.

Dominga nodded. 'Yup.'

'Did you tell her that I sent you?'

'I think she guessed,' said Dominga.

'Well, how did it go?'

'She said I could move in tomorrow.'

'Tomorrow?' Frank frowned. 'Not today?'

Dominga grimaced. She felt as if the sergeant was displeased with her. 'She said tomorrow. I didn't want to . . . you know, be too pushy.'

'Right,' said Frank. 'That's all right. I guess it will be all right.' Then he spoke into the phone. 'Yes. I'm still holding.'

'Why are you so keen on me moving in there anyway?'

'Well, you know what happened to her in the subway.'

Dominga nodded.

'After that it just seemed wise to me to have a someone living with her. Someone who could manage . . . trouble if it arose.'

'But that subway business was just kind of random, wasn't it? Life in the city and all?'

Frank hesitated. 'I'm . . . not sure,' he said. He studied the tough-looking young woman standing in the doorway. It wasn't fair to send her to Anna's, perhaps to put her in harm's way without admitting the risk. She had a right to know. A right to refuse. 'They haven't caught the person who pushed her. But Anna could probably identify them if an arrest was made. There's always the possibility that she could be targeted again, to prevent that from happening.'

'So she needs . . . like a bodyguard,' said Dominga.

'I'm hoping it won't come to that,' said Frank. 'But it could be dangerous.'

Dominga extended her hands and flexed her fingers toward her palms. 'Bring it on, baby. I'm ready. They better not mess with me. I'll tear 'em a new one.'

Frank laughed, relieved. 'Besides, you needed a place to stay. I thought it might be a good fit,' he said.

'Oh, I think it will be,' said Dominga. 'She's a good person.' Then she frowned. 'Who would want to do that? Push someone under a train?'

Frank shook his head. 'A very disturbed individual.'

Dominga dangled the keychain. 'You're not kidding. Well, it's official anyway. She gave me a key.'

Frank nodded. 'Good,' he said.

'I gotta go,' said Dominga. 'I signed up for an auto mechanics class.'

'Great,' said Frank. 'That's thinking positive!'

Dominga shrugged. 'I gotta get on with my life.'

'Yes, you do,' said Frank. The music at the other end of the phone continued to play. 'And thanks, Dominga, for doing this. I'll feel a lot better when you get moved in there.'

Dominga gave him a semi-salute and went on her way. Frank exhaled, and continued to wait for someone to answer his call. Finally a nurse who had seen Titus explained that he was currently in physical therapy.

'Good. That's a relief,' said Frank. 'Can you let him know that I called, and have him call me. You can tell him that I want him back in the group.'

The nurse assured Frank that she would relay the message. He hung up feeling somewhat better. He started to go back to his paperwork but it was difficult to concentrate. He thought again about Anna, refusing to take his gun. He wished he could have convinced her but she was adamant. There was no guarantee she would be safe, even with Dominga living in her apartment. After all, Dominga had her own life to lead. She couldn't watch over Anna twenty-four seven. Just to reassure himself, he decided to call. The phone rang and rang, and finally went to voicemail.

Frank hesitated. 'Anna, it's Frank,' he said. 'Call me back.'

Just then Kiyanna appeared in the doorway, holding her phone. 'Frank. You better take this.'

Frank set down his phone and took Kiyanna's from her elegant hand. 'Frank Petrusa.'

'Frank,' said a panicky voice. 'This is Ha—Anna's husband, Alan.'

'Hey, Alan. I just tried to call Anna but there was no answer. Where are you? Anna told Father Luke that you were headed out west.'

'She wanted me to take Cindy far away. Somewhere safe. But I didn't go. I couldn't. I couldn't leave her alone like that. She thinks we're on our way to Chicago. But we never left Philly. We've just been lying low. Listen, Frank, I just got a call. She called me.'

'Who? Anna?'

Adam hesitated. Then he spoke in a low voice. 'No. Not Anna. Our daughter.'

'Your daughter? Is there something wrong with Cindy?'

'Not Cindy.' Adam sighed and was silent for a moment. 'Frank, Cindy is not our daughter. Cindy is our granddaughter. Our daughter's name is Lisa. And she is . . . mentally ill. She's with Anna. I'm on my way there right now but I called you because you're right around the corner from our apartment. I'm terrified of what she might do. She's very . . . unstable.'

Frank hesitated a moment. 'Anna said she knew the person who pushed her in the subway. I offered her a gun for protection but she said she could never shoot this person. Is that . . .'

Adam sighed. 'Yes. I think so. Anna recognized Lisa when the police showed her the surveillance tape.'

'Oh my God.'

'Frank, I hate to even ask you this . . .'

'Hold on a second,' said Frank. He put the phone to his chest and spoke to Kiyanna. 'Go stop Dominga before she leaves the building.

We need those keys. Anna's keys. She has them. If she's already left, call her and go after her. She's on her way downtown. Hurry.'

Kiyanna nodded, turned and ran.

He picked up the phone again and held it to his ear. 'All right. Tell me everything I need to know.'

Lisa fiddled in her coat pocket.

'You might as well take your coat off,' said Hannah dully. Her voice was raspy from her bruised larynx. 'They won't be here anytime soon.'

'How long will it take them? Where are they coming from, anyway?'

'I told you, I don't know,' said Hannah. 'I don't know where they are.'

Lisa shook her head. 'Lies,' she said.

Hannah gazed at her daughter, feeling almost faint at the weight of her own failure. She was her only child and she had loved her so fiercely. 'It's not a lie. I know they were heading toward Chicago. I didn't want to know exactly where. Your father didn't tell me exactly where they are on purpose.'

'Bastard,' said Lisa.

'I have to ask you something.'

'What?'

'Did you . . . set up the explosion that killed Troy Petty?'

Lisa looked at her mother in disbelief. 'What are you doing? Working for the police? Recording me?'

Hannah shook her head. 'I just want to know. I know you were angry at him because he wasn't interested in . . . children.'

'He certainly didn't turn out to be the man I thought he was,' Lisa said tartly.

'He wasn't like those creeps you were writing to. You thought he was but he wasn't. I feel so sorry for his family. His sister. I'm so sorry that his name got dragged through the mud in court. He didn't deserve that.'

Lisa shrugged. 'Water under the bridge.'

'But why didn't you just walk away and leave him alone? He wasn't hurting you. Why did you have to . . .'

Lisa looked at her disdainfully. 'Kill him? You can say it, Mother. I had no choice about it. The fact is he was a threat. He thought that everyone at the medical school ought to know about me.'

Hannah shook her head.

'What?' Lisa demanded.

'What did I do? I just keep asking myself, what kind of a mother I was. How did you turn out this way – to be so heartless? And don't say that it was because your father molested you. We both know that's just not true.'

Lisa burst out laughing. 'Oh, Mom,' she said.

The utter normalcy of it made Hannah's heart do a sudden flip in her chest. It was as if the years had vanished and Lisa was twelve again, and amused by her mother's efforts to name her favorite singer. For a second, Hannah thought it was over. That maybe it had all been a horrible joke, meant to undermine her, to make her doubt herself as a mother. But if it was over now, that would be all right. She could live with that. 'What?' she asked hopefully.

'You look so stupid with that bandage around your head,' she said. 'How was that when you fell on the tracks? Were you scared?'

Hannah turned her head and looked out the window, wishing she could just fly away. Unhear what she just heard. Then she turned to face her child. 'I talked to a shrink about you. She said you were probably a psychopath.'

'Psycho-jargon,' said Lisa. 'She doesn't even know me. Besides, shrinks are always trying to put people in little boxes. They don't know how to cope with someone who knows what they want and won't hesitate to get it. If they want to call me a psychopath, a sociopath, who cares? What does it really mean?'

'Listen. I'll tell you what it means,' said Hannah evenly. 'It means we are not giving Sydney back to you, Lisa. Not under any circumstances. Maybe your father already called the police. Maybe they're on their way.'

'Don't be stupid, Mother,' said Lisa. 'He doesn't dare call the police. He's the criminal as far as the cops are concerned. Not me. And you are giving her back to me. She and I have adventures ahead.'

Hannah shook her head. 'We won't. Look, if you just walk away I won't tell the cops about the subway. Just leave Sydney with us.'

Lisa stood up and glared down on her mother. 'She's mine. You can't stop me. Nothing you can say will stop me.'

Hannah stared right back at her. 'I swear, Lisa, as long as I'm breathing . . .'

'Exactly,' said Lisa. She reached into her coat pocket and slowly pulled out a gun. Its dull black finish reflected the light.

Hannah cried out. 'Where did you get that?'

'Mother, I'm not fourteen. I bought it. It's all perfectly legal. I bought it and I'm going to use it on the people who kidnapped my child.'

Hannah felt as if she had been punched in the chest. She struggled to catch her breath. 'Lisa. You can't do that. You'll end up in jail.'

'For doing what I had to do to get my child back from her kidnappers?' said Lisa. She shook her head. 'I don't think people are going to see it your way.'

Hannah stood up and started to approach her daughter.

Lisa brandished the gun at her. 'Don't take another step. Do you think I'm not serious? I was going to wait until Dad got here but I could kill you right now. Why not? When he gets here I'll just show him the corpse. I'd rather do it in front of him but I'm flexible.'

Hannah looked at her only child, stunned. 'Did you always hate us this much?' she asked. 'We did our best for you. We loved you so much.'

Lisa shook her head. 'I don't hate you.'

Hannah thought her ears were deceiving her. 'You don't?'

'Well, I'm angry at you but I certainly don't hate you. You were an OK mom. And Dad. Well, all right, I'll admit – just to you – that he was . . . a decent father. The fact is you were just ordinary people who weren't really equipped to deal with someone with my gifts. It always seems so ridiculous to me to abide by your rules when neither one of you was my equal. You always were putting your heads together, comparing notes, trying to figure out how best to parent me. It was laughable, really. But none of that matters now. Whatever your mistakes, you compounded them by taking Sydney. You humiliated me by doing that. You made me look bad to the whole world. As if I were incompetent as a mother. As if the kid was better off anywhere than with me. I can't just let that go.'

'But if you don't hate us,' Hannah pleaded, 'maybe we could talk . . . Maybe there's some way . . .'

'There's no way,' said Lisa brusquely. 'This is the way it is. Don't look so offended. Now sit down.'

'I was going to get a glass of water.' She reached up and touched the bandage around her head. 'I have to take my medication.'

'You don't need your medication anymore,' said Lisa coldly. 'Sit down.'

THIRTY-SIX

F rank took the gun from the box in his car. Stuffing it under his jacket, he hurried in the direction of Mamie Revere's house. Dominga's keys jingled in his hand, and he used his prosthetic hand to hold them steady and muffle the sound. He moved quickly, lightly, like a cat. He had been a recon marine, and he knew how to traverse a landscape with hardly a sound. He also knew what could happen if he miscalculated. The lasting effects of his injuries were a reminder of that. He mounted the steps lightly, and crouched down by the front door. He turned the key in the lock as silently as he could. He heard the deadbolt click, and he slowly, carefully turned the knob and pushed the door open.

The foyer was dark. The only illumination came from the street-lamps, and some light filtering down from the top of the staircase. Frank tiptoed to the foot of the stairs and listened. He could hear the intermittent, inchoate sounds of voices. He looked up at the two flights which lay ahead of him. How could he get all the way up there without someone hearing him? What if this crazy daughter opened the door and saw him? Shot him? She could easily have a gun. I should have called the cops, he thought. Why try to be a hero? But then he thought of the despair suffusing Anna's features beneath her bandaged head, and Alan's anguished confession about his daughter. They were still trying to protect this daughter of theirs. Despite what she had done to her mother, they still wanted to shield her. And here he was, idiot that he was, going along with it.

Kiyanna had begged him to call the cops before he left Restoration House. He had made her promise not to do it. She had threatened never to speak to him again but he put his good hand up to her smooth brown face and held it there. Trust me, he said. I'll be careful. I'm coming back to you. She had turned away from him, fuming, but he knew she would honor his wishes and not make that call.

So, here we are, Frank thought. Now what? He started up the steps, trying each one before he put his weight on it, moving as slowly and carefully as possible, so as not to make the stairs creak. He reached the first landing, and felt an intense relief.

Just as he was lifting his foot to begin the second staircase, he heard a click below him. He turned abruptly, and saw the front door starting to open. Kiyanna, he thought. What did you do? Just then, a man let himself into the front door and started to cross the foyer.

Frank recognized him at once. Alan made no effort to be silent as he moved across the foyer and started up the steps. As he neared Frank, who was hiding in the shadows, Frank whispered his name.

Adam started and stifled a cry as he discerned the figure of a man in the shadows. Their eyes met. 'Frank,' he said.

At the same moment, the door to their apartment opened.

Lisa stepped out into the hallway, holding a gun. 'Who's there?'

Adam could see that Frank was gesturing for him to hide, but there was no way he was going to do that. Lisa was up there with Hannah, and a gun. No way. Adam went to the foot of the last flight of stairs, and looked up at his daughter.

'It's me,' he said.

Lisa's face lit up at the sight of him. 'Well, well. What a surprise. Did you sprout wings and fly here from Chicago?'

Adam did not answer. He started to climb the stairs.

'I asked you a question,' Lisa insisted, and her voice was razor-sharp. 'How did you get here so quickly?'

Adam ignored her and climbed to the top of the steps. 'May I come in?' he asked politely.

Lisa stepped back. 'Oh, please do. This is just what I've been waiting for.'

Hannah gasped as Adam walked in, shadowed by Lisa who was holding the gun on him. 'Adam!' she cried, and started to get up.

'Sit,' Lisa barked.

Hannah sat back down as her husband came toward her. 'How . . .?' she asked.

'Yes,' said Lisa. 'Tell us how you did that, Dad.'

'We never left the city,' he said.

'Oh, Adam!' Hannah cried.

'I couldn't,' he said. 'I couldn't go without you. I know you wanted me to but I couldn't.'

She reached out a hand to him but Lisa glared at her and swung the gun around so it was facing her. 'Don't,' she said.

'I'm sorry,' said Adam.

Hannah shook her head.

'So, the gang's all here,' said Lisa. 'Minus one. Where is Sydney?'

'In a safe place,' said Adam.

'Do you think this is a game? Where did you leave my daughter?'

Adam took a deep breath. 'Lisa, put that gun down. Let's talk about this.'

'Oh, sure. I'll do whatever you say.'

Adam shook his head. 'There's no reason for this. We can discuss it.'

Lisa grabbed Hannah by the neck of her sweater and yanked her to her feet. She put the gun to her mother's head. 'There's nothing to discuss. Sydney belongs to me. Tell me where she is.'

Adam raised his hands, as if pleading for calm. 'Stop it. I'll take you to her. Just leave your mother alone.'

'Like I believe you,' said Lisa.

'Why, Lisa?' he said sorrowfully. 'Why has it come to this?'

'How can you ask me that? After what you did? Left me in jail and absconded with my kid. I got out of jail, expecting a homecoming celebration, and found that you two had gone and taken her with you.'

'I'm sorry we had to do that,' said Adam wearily. 'But we felt that we had no choice.'

'You had a choice!' Lisa cried. 'You could have minded your own business. It was none of your business what I did with my daughter.'

'She's our granddaughter,' said Adam. 'She's a helpless, innocent baby.'

'She's not a baby,' said Lisa. 'That was always your excuse for trying to tell me what to do. Thinking you knew better than I did what was best for Sydney. What was best for me. Thinking you could control everything. Well, you can't tell me what to do. I hope that's clear to you now. I'm in charge now. I'll tell you. I'll tell you both what to do.' Lisa turned to her mother. 'Get up. Go on. Move. We're going.'

Hannah looked helplessly at Adam. She could see a warning in his eyes but she could not read what he was trying to tell her. 'Adam?'

'Don't ask him,' said Lisa. 'Stand on your own two feet for once. Move.'

Hannah felt the cold barrel of the gun against her temple. Lisa was so close to her that she could feel her breath on her neck. She wasn't sure her legs would carry her but Lisa was not giving her any choice.

'You go first,' Lisa instructed Adam. 'We're going to get Sydney. And once we've done that . . . I won't have any further use for you. For either of you. Go on. Out!'

Adam opened the door of the apartment and stepped out onto the landing. Hannah followed behind him, with Lisa holding a wad of her sweater in her hand, and the gun to her head. As they stepped out, Adam stopped.

'Go on,' Lisa insisted. 'Down the stairs.'

Suddenly Hannah saw there was a man hidden in the dark corner of the landing, holding a gun. She peered into the shadows and recognized Frank. Come to the rescue. He held her gaze and shook his head, warning her to stay quiet. To pretend he wasn't there. She should have been relieved. Grateful. But her instinct had a will of its own. A voice inside her heart was screaming that he was a soldier and he knew how to kill someone with a gun. It was an impulse – irrational, undeniable. A desire, in spite of everything, to protect her child.

'Frank, don't. Lisa!' she cried. 'Look out. He has a gun.'

'Who has a gun? Oh, please, Mother. I'm not a gullible child.'

'Listen to me. I mean it.'

'Put it down, miss,' said Frank.

Lisa looked away from her mother into the darkness just beyond where her father stood. 'Who are you?' She turned on her father. 'Did you call the cops?'

'Do what he says, Lisa,' Adam pleaded. 'Let's put an end to this.'

'I'll put an end to it!' she cried. She turned the gun sharply from Hannah's head toward Frank.

In that instant, her father saw her intention – her intention to kill Frank, this good man, who only came to help. Adam threw himself in front of Frank as, without hesitation, Lisa fired. Adam reeled backward and collapsed as the bullet entered his body.

'Adam!' Hannah cried, rushing toward her husband as he crumpled on the stairs. 'Oh my God. Adam.'

'No, stay down,' he said, clutching his shoulder.

In that instant there was another gunshot. With a cry, Hannah turned away from Adam.

Frank's gun was smoking and Lisa stood there for a moment, looking surprised.

'Lisa!' Hannah called out, as if in warning. 'No.'

Then Lisa's eyes rolled back and her limbs seemed to turn to rubber. She pitched forward, collapsing on the stairs. 'Lisa!' Hannah cried, and tried to scramble toward her daughter. She tried to grab Lisa's jacket, got her fingers on the fabric and tried to grasp it. But Lisa's body was limp, a dead weight falling. The jacket slid from Hannah's fingers. Her body tumbled down the steep staircase and came to rest on the landing.

Hannah crawled and scuttled down the stairs to her child, who was splayed out at an unnatural angle, her head against the banister, one leg on the landing and the other on a higher step. One arm was limp, bent backward.

Hannah reached her and tried to gather her daughter up into her arms.

Lisa's cloudy eyes gazed at her, as if from some other galaxy. 'Mommy,' she whispered.

'I'm here,' said Hannah. She watched the feeble spark of life fade from her daughter's eyes, along with every hope she had ever cherished. Hannah held that lost child to her heart and began to wail.

THIRTY-SEVEN

Eighteen months later

'Come, sit out on the deck,' said Hannah.

Kiyanna followed Hannah out through the sliding glass doors.

She sat down heavily on one of the chairs, her spring jacket falling open around her.

Hannah looked at her friend's slightly distended stomach, and then smiled at her. 'You've been keeping something from me,' she said.

Kiyanna smiled and shook her head. 'I figured you had enough on your mind.'

Hannah nodded. It was true, she thought. She had hardly been able to think about anything else but her own family for months. But today was different. Today, their friends had come to visit. She, Sydney and Adam had picked Kiyanna and Frank up at the Nashville airport, and then Adam had dropped them off so he could take Frank on a brief tour of Music City. Kiyanna and Hannah were left to enjoy the spring sunshine, while Sydney resumed playing in the yard with her new puppy.

'When is the baby due?' Hannah asked.

'September.'

'Boy or girl?'

Kiyanna shook her head. 'We wanted to be surprised.'

'Well, if it's a girl, I've got boxes of baby clothes I'll send you. From Sydney,' she added hastily. In fact, she still had some of Lisa's baby clothes. But anything that might have been Lisa's seemed laden with bad karma.

'I'll take them. If it is.'

'Frank must be thrilled. I can't believe you didn't tell us.'

'Just being superstitious.'

'I understand.'

'And yes. Frank is over the moon.'

'I'm happy for you two,' said Hannah. 'That baby will have a wonderful life.'

'I hope so.' Kiyanna looked down at her stomach and put a protective hand over it. 'Hannah, I hope you know that what happened . . . with your daughter, is never far from his mind.'

Hannah nodded. 'Frank came to our rescue. I never doubted that. Not for a minute. He only wanted to help us.'

'Lots of nights I wake up and find him sitting on the edge of the bed, in a cold sweat,' said Kiyanna. 'He has a lot of bad memories from combat. But sometimes it's about Lisa.'

Lisa. Hannah sighed. She still could not think of Lisa without a stabbing pain in her heart. Maybe she never would. 'I know. I go over it and over it. But it always comes down to this. She shot at Frank, point blank. She shot her father. Hell, she pushed me in front of a subway train. When I get despondent, and I do, I remember that. I remind myself of all that happened, and it numbs the pain. It makes the pain recede. Still, it's always there, lurking.'

'I'm sure it is,' said Kiyanna kindly.

Hannah and Adam had buried Lisa and moved back to their house in Nashville. Rayanne and Chet welcomed them home with a subdued happiness. Too much had happened for it to be anything other than a celebration tempered by sadness. When Pamela made her first, rare visit from the Veranda, she had treated Sydney with a tenderness that Hannah had never known as a child.

The Nashville D.A. had filed kidnapping charges against Hannah and Adam. With the aid of many witnesses, including Frank, who flew for one day to give his testimony, Marjorie Fox successfully argued to have the plea reduced to child endangerment, and Hannah had been given a suspended sentence. Adam, now recovered from his shoulder wound, had spent the minimum sentence, sixty days, in jail. In sentencing him, the judge had made a point of saying that the child was never hurt while she was in their care. Now, Adam was home at last, and Kiyanna and Frank, now married, had arrived to visit, bury the past and, hopefully, to start again.

Kiyanna looked out at Sydney, playing in the yard. 'Cindy – I mean, Sydney – seems OK.'

Hannah frowned. 'Thank God they let us keep her. Our attorney laid out the circumstances pretty clearly, and the court agreed that it was right for us to keep her. Mostly, she's OK. She has blue periods. She has nightmares.'

'How could she not? She's had more trauma in her five years than some people have in a lifetime.'

'That's for sure.'

'Does she . . . know what happened? How much is she aware of?'

'She asks questions sometimes. I've been taking her to a child psychologist, just to be sure to keep the channels open, you know.'

'I think it's a good idea,' said Kiyanna. 'Questions are going to arise.'

'I know,' said Hannah.

'Does she ever mention . . .'

'Lisa?' Hannah supplied her daughter's name. 'Once in a while. I say the usual thing. Mommy has gone to heaven.'

The two women sat in silence for a moment, each of them hoping it was true, both of them doubting it. Hannah glanced over at Kiyanna's frowning face.

'What?' she said.

'It's just so . . . baffling. Doing the work I do, I've seen plenty of children at risk. Plenty of parents with no business having children. But when Cindy was in daycare, I saw you in action. I know you two were good parents . . .'

'So, how could this have happened? Is that what you're thinking?' Hannah asked.

Sydney looked up at the two women on the deck. 'Miss Kiyanna, look what Riley can do.' Sydney then proceeded to run around the yard, and the pup followed her, barking excitedly.

'That's a cute puppy you have there,' said Kiyanna.

Sydney beamed, and planted kisses on the patient animal's head. Hannah returned to Kiyanna's unstated question. 'The answer is I don't know how it happened. I know that's not much consolation when you're thinking about the life you've created. You're bound to wonder . . .'

Kiyanna shook her head, frowning. 'I do. I can't help it. You never knew about Lisa? You never realized . . .?'

Hannah shrugged. 'There were warning signs. No doubt. But I blamed it on her extreme intelligence, on the fact that she was out of her element socially because she kept skipping grades. I made excuses to myself, even when I was uneasy. It's hard to explain. You love them so much that you tell yourself that they are normal. Within the range of normal. You can't really see them as they are sometimes.'

'How can you ever be sure . . .?' said Kiyanna.

Hannah leaned over and placed her pale hand over Kiyanna's graceful brown fingers. 'Your baby will be fine. In every way. I just know it. And you will be a wonderful mother. The two of you will be great parents. You just have to start out with all the hope in the world and believe that it will be fine. Because it will.'

Kiyanna frowned. 'I guess if you can believe that . . .'

Hannah looked out at Sydney, shrieking and smiling and rolling on the grass with her pup. Did she really believe that? That she and Adam had done their best and it wasn't their fault? Some professionals in the field of psychology had told them that it was not. That Lisa's twisted psychology was inborn. Others had looked askance and sighed when they heard her story, suggesting that indeed, they bore much responsibility. And in her heart, Hannah agreed with them. They had raised Lisa. She was a product of their genes. How could it not be their fault at some level? The minister she had talked to had preached forgiveness. Both for herself and for Lisa. Forgive, and put it behind you.

And now, she was raising another child. Her grandchild. The doubts about her own fitness to mother Sydney often surfaced in her mind. Luckily Sydney gave her little time or reason to worry. But secretly, she would always wonder. How could it be any other way? Still, since this was her fate, she tried to look upon it as her second chance. A chance to raise a child who was happy and healthy. Good. Sane. Whole. What other choice did she have? 'I have to believe it,' she said firmly. 'I do.'

CPSIA information can be obtained
at www.ICGtesting.com
Printed in the USA
JSHW081917221122
33599JS00002B/189